DOMAIN

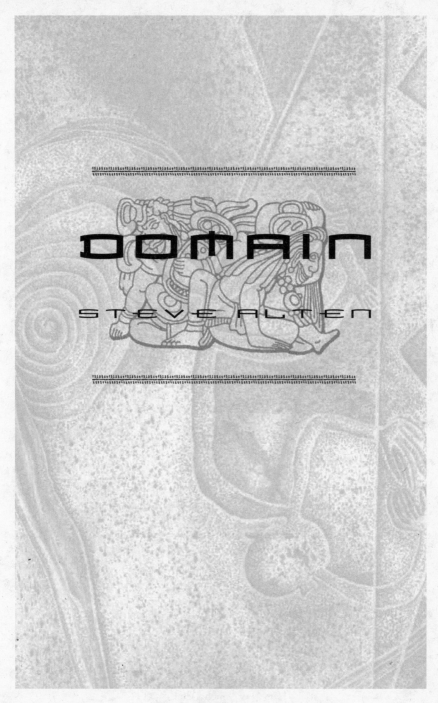

DOMAIN

STEVE ALTEN

TOR®

A Tom Doherty Associates Book
New York

DOMAIN

A Tor Book
Published by Tom Doherty Associates, LLC
175 Fifth Avenue
New York, NY 10010

www.tor-forge.com

Tor® is a registered trademark of Tom Doherty Associates, LLC.

Book design by Ellen Cipriano

The Library of Congress has catalogued this hardcover as follows:

Alten, Steve.
    Domain / Steve Alten.—1st ed.
        p. cm.
    "A Tom Doherty Associates book."
    ISBN 0-312-87476-6
    1. Life on other planets—Fiction. 2. Mayas—Antiquities—
Fiction. 3. End of the world—Fiction. 4. Archaeologists—
Fiction. I. Title.

PS3551.L764 D66 2001
813'.54—dc21
                                                00-048454

ISBN-13: 978-0-7653-2466-5 (trade pbk.)
ISBN-10: 0-7653-2466-0 (trade pbk.)

First Hardcover Edition: February 2001
First Trade Paperback Edition: May 2009

Printed in the United States of America

0 9 8 7 6 5 4 3 2 1

For Ken Atchity,
Manager, Mentor, Friend . . .

Acknowledgments

It is with great pride and appreciation that I acknowledge those who contributed to the completion of *Domain*.

First and foremost, to my literary manager, Ken Atchity, and his team at Atchity Editorial/Entertainment International for their hard work and perseverance. Kudos to editors Michael Wichman (AEI) for his vision and to Ed Stackler of Stackler Editorial for his excellent commentary.

Many thanks to Tom Doherty and the great people at TOR Books, editor Bob Gleason, and Brian Callaghan, as well as Matthew Snyder at Creative Arts Agency in Los Angeles, and Danny Baror of Baror International. Kudos to Bob and Sara Schwager for their great copyediting.

Thanks also to the following individuals whose own personal expertise contributed in some way to *Domain*: Gary Thompson, Dr. Robert Chitwood, and the terrific staff at the South Florida Evaluation and Treatment Center, Rabbi Richard Agler, Barbara Esmedina, Jeffrey Moe, Lou McKellan, Jim Kimball, Shawn Coyne, and Dr. Bruce Wishnov. And to authors Graham Hancock, John Major Jenkins, and Erich Von Daniken, whose work certainly influenced the story.

Very special thanks to Bill and Lori McDonald of Argonaut-Grey Wolf Productions/Web site: www.AlienUFOart.com, who contributed to the editing and are responsible for the incredible artwork found in this novel, and to Matt Herrmann of VILLAINDESIGN for his graphic input and photographic contributions.

I am also deeply indebted to Donna and Justin Lahey, whose dedication, creativity, and know-how have helped launch my novels via the Internet.

Last—to my readers: Thank you for your correspondence. Your comments are always a welcome treat, your input means so much.

—STEVE ALTEN

For more information about Steve Alten's novels or to contact the author personally, click on www.STEVEALTEN.com.

8

... and in these ancient lands encased and lettered as a tomb
and scored with prints of perished hands, and chronicled with dates of doom ...
I trace the lives such scenes enshrine and their experience count as mine.

—THOMAS HARDY

The most beautiful experience we can have is the mysterious. It is the
fundamental emotion that stands at the cradle of true art and true science.

—ALBERT EINSTEIN

Fear and religion. Religion and fear. The two are
historically entwined. The catalysts for most of the
atrocities committed by man. Fear of evil
fuels religion, religion fuels hatred, hatred
fuels evil, and evil fuels fear among the
masses. It is a diabolical cycle, and we
have played into the Devil's hand.

—JULIUS GABRIEL

DOMAIN

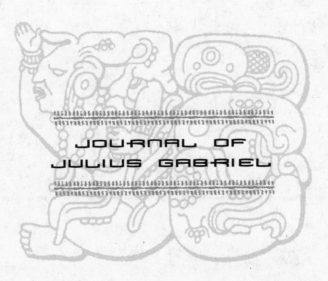

JOURNAL OF JULIUS GABRIEL

I stand before the vast canvas, sharing the feeling of loneliness
its creator must have surely felt thousands of years ago. Before
me lie the answers to riddles—riddles that may ultimately determine whether our species is to live or die. The future of the human
race—is there anything more important? Yet I stand here alone,
my quest condemning me to this purgatory of rock and sand as
I seek communion with the past in order to comprehend the peril
that lies ahead.

The years have taken their toll. What a wretched creature
I've become. Once a renowned archaeologist, now a laughingstock
to my peers. A husband, a lover—these are but distant memories.
A father? Scarcely. More a tortured mentor, a miserable beast of
burden left to my son to lead about. Each step across the stone-
laden desert causes my bones to ache, while thoughts forever
shackled in my mind repeat the maddening mantra of doom over
and over in my brain. What higher power has chosen my family
among all others to torture? Why have we been blessed with eyes
that can see the signposts of death while others stumble along as
if blind?

Am I mad? The thought never leaves my mind. With each

new dawn, I must force myself to reread the highlights of my chronicles, if only to remind myself that I am, first and foremost, a scientist, nay, not just a scientist, but an archaeologist—a seeker of man's past, a seeker of truth.

But what good is truth if it cannot be accepted? To my peers, I no doubt resemble the village idiot, screaming warning cries of icebergs to passengers boarding the <u>Titanic</u> as the unsinkable vessel leaves port.

Is it my destiny to save humanity, or simply to die the fool? Is it possible that I have spent a lifetime misinterpreting the signs?

The scraping of footsteps on silica and stone gives pause to this fool's entry.

It is my son. Named for an archangel fifteen years ago by my beloved wife, Michael nods at me, momentarily warming his father's shriveled pit of a heart. Michael is the reason I persevere, the reason I do not end my miserable existence. The madness of my quest has robbed him of his childhood, but far worse was my own heinous deed, committed years earlier. It is to his future that I recommit myself, it is his destiny that I wish to change.

God, let this feeble heart last long enough to allow me to succeed.

Michael points ahead, reminding me the next piece of the puzzle beckons us. Stepping carefully so as not to disturb the pampa, we stand at what I believe is the beginning of the 3,000-year-old message. Centered upon the Nazca plateau, laid sacred from the mysterious lines and colossal zoomorphs is this—a perfect circle, carved deeply between the black-patina-coated stones. Extending out from this mysterious centerpiece like sunbeams from a child's painting are 23 equidistant lines, all but one running some 600 feet. One line is aligned with the solstice, another with the equinox, variables consistent with the other ancient sites I've spent a lifetime exploring.

It is the 23rd line that is most intriguing—a bold carving within the pampa, extending over rock and hill for some 23 miles!

Michael shouts, his metal detector erupting as we approach the center of the figure. Something has been buried beneath the topsoil! With renewed vigor, we dig through the gypsum and stone, exposing the yellow dirt below. It is a heinous act, especially for an archaeologist, but I convince myself that the end shall ultimately justify the means.

And there it is, glistening beneath the broiling Sun. Smooth and white, a hollow cylinder of metal, a half meter long, that has no more right being on the Nazca desert than I have. A three-pronged candelabra-like design adorns one end of the object. My feeble heart flutters, for I know the symbol as I know the back of my weathered hand. The Trident of Paracas—the signature icon of our cosmic teacher. A similar glyph, 600 feet long, 200 feet across, adorns an entire mountainside not far from here.

Michael steadies his camera as I open the canister. Trembling, I remove what appears to be a length of parched canvas, my fingers registering its disintegration as it begins to unravel.

It is an ancient chart of the world, similar to the very one referenced 500 years ago by the Turkish admiral, Piri Re'is. (This mysterious map was believed to have been the inspiration for Columbus's daring expedition in 1492.) To this day, the 14th-century Piri Re'is map remains an enigma, for upon it appeared not just the undiscovered landmass of Antarctica, but the continent's geology, drawn as if the terrain possessed no ice. Satellite radar scans have since confirmed the incredible accuracy of the map, further baffling scientists as to how anyone could have drawn the charts without the aid of an airplane.

Perhaps the same way these very Nazca figures were drawn.

Like the Piri Re'is map, the parchment I now balance in my hand was laid out using an advanced knowledge of spherical trigonometry. Was the mysterious cartographer our ancient teacher? Of this I have no doubt. The real question is—why has he chosen to leave us this particular map?

Michael snaps a hurried Polaroid as the ancient document singes, then crumbles to dust within my hands. Moments later we are left to stare at the photograph, noting that an object, obviously of great importance, had clearly been highlighted. It is a small circle, drawn in the waters of the Gulf of Mexico, situated just to the northwest of the Yucatán Peninsula.

The location of the mark startles me. This is not one of the ancient sites, this is something else entirely. A cold sweat breaks out over my skin, a familiar numbness rising up my arm.

Michael senses death approaching. He searches my pockets and quickly locates a pill, placing it beneath my tongue.

My pulse eases, the numbness retreating. I touch his cheek, then coax my son to return to his work. With pride I watch as he examines the metallic container—his black eyes, portals to an incredibly disciplined mind. Nothing escapes my son's eyes. Nothing.

Within moments, he makes another discovery, one that may explain the location highlighted in the Gulf of Mexico. The metal detector's spectral analyzer has determined the molecular breakdown of the dense, white metal—its very composite, a story unto itself.

The ancient cylinder is composed of iridium.
Pure iridium.

—Excerpt from the Journal of Professor Julius Gabriel,
    June 14, 1990

16

PROLOGUE

65 MILLION YEARS AGO

MILKY WAY GALAXY

A spiral galaxy—one of 100 billion islands of stars moving through the dark matter of the universe. Rotating like some luminescent cosmic pinwheel in the vastness of space, the galaxy hauls more than 200 billion stars and countless other bodies within its titanic vortex.

Let us examine this galactic hub. Observing the formation within our three-dimensional limits, our gaze is first drawn to the galactic bulge, composed of billions of red and orange stars, swirling within clouds of galactic dust some 15,000 light-years across (a light-year being approximately 6 trillion miles). Revolving around this lens-shaped region is the flatter, circular disk of the galaxy, 2,000 light-years thick, 120,000 light-years across, containing most of the galactic mass. Whipping around this disk are the galaxy's spiral arms, home to bright stars and luminescent clouds of gas and dust—cosmic incubators birthing new stars. Extending above and beyond these spiral arms is the galactic halo, a sparsely populated region containing globular star clusters that support the more senior members of the galactic family.

From there, we move to the very heart of the galaxy—a complex region surrounded by swirling clouds of gas and dust. Hidden within this nucleus is the true power train of the celestial formation—a monstrous black hole—a dense, swirling vortex of gravitational energy, three million times heavier than the sun. This ravenous cosmic machine inhales everything within its unfathomable grasp—stars, planets, matter, even light, as it churns the heavenly bodies of the spiral galaxy.

Now let us look at the spiral galaxy from a higher dimension—a fourth dimension of time and space. Branching out through the galactic body like arteries and veins and capillaries are unseen conduits of energy, some so vast they could transport a star, others delicate, microscopic strings. All are powered by the unimaginable gravitational forces of the black hole, located at Galactic Central. Access a porthole into one of these conduits and you have accessed a fourth-dimensional highway crossing the boundaries of time and space—assuming, of course, your transportation vessel could survive the trip.

As the galaxy revolves around its behemoth center point, so too these snakelike streams of energy move, always circling, continuing their timeless trek across the galactic plain like some bizarre spokes on a forever-rotating cosmic wheel.

Like a grain of sand caught in the mighty current of a gravitational stream, the asteroid-size projectile races through the fourth-dimensional conduit, a porthole of time and space presently located in the Orion arm of the spiral galaxy. The ovoid mass, nearly seven miles in diameter, is protected from the cylinder's crushing embrace by an emerald green antigravitational force field.

The celestial traveler is not alone.

Concealed within the spherical object's charged magnetic wake, bathed within the protective tail of the force field is another vessel—smaller, sleek, its flattened, dagger-shaped hull composed of shimmering gold solar panels.

Navigating through the dimension of space and time, the cosmic highway deposits its travelers in a region of the galaxy located along the inner edge of Orion's arm. Looming ahead—a solar system containing nine planetary bodies, governed by a single yellow-white star.

Sailing by way of the star's gravitational field, the immense iridium vessel closes quickly on its intended target—Venus—the second planet from the Sun, a world of intense heat, enshrouded in a canopy of dense acidic clouds and carbon dioxide.

The smaller vessel closes from behind, revealing its presence to its enemy.

Immediately, the iridium transport alters its course, increasing its velocity by tapping into the gravitational pull of the system's third planet, a watery, blue world containing a toxic atmosphere of oxygen.

With a brilliant flash, the smaller ship expels a white-hot burst of energy from an extended finlike antenna rising from behind its bow. The charge streaks through the ion stream of the sphere's electromagnetic tail like a bolt of lightning coursing along a metal cable.

The charge ignites upon the iridium hull like an aurora, the electrical blast short-circuiting the vessel's propulsion system, knocking the behemoth violently off course. Within moments, the damaged mass is seized within the lethal embrace of the blue world's gravitational field.

The asteroid-size projectile hurtles toward Earth, out of control.

With a sonic boom, the iridium sphere violates the hostile atmosphere. The mirrorlike outer hull cracks and pits, then blazes briefly into a blinding fireball before plunging into a shallow, tropical sea. Barely slowed by thousands of feet of water, it strikes bottom in a fraction of a second—causing, for one surreal moment, a cylinder of ocean to empty to the seafloor.

A nanosecond later, the celestial impact detonates in a brilliant white flash, unleashing 100 million megatons of energy.

The thunderous explosion rocks the entire planet, generating temperatures that exceed 32,000 degrees Fahrenheit, hotter than the surface of the Sun. Two gaseous fireballs ignite at once. The first, a dust cloud of hot, powdered rock and iridium coming from the disintegrated outer hull of the vessel, followed by billowing clouds of highly pressurized steam and carbon dioxide, the gases released as the sea and its limestone bed are vaporized.

The rubble and superheated gases rise into the devastated atmosphere, drawn upward through the vacuum of air created by the object's descent. Enormous shock waves ripple across the sea, giving rise to monstrous tsunamis that crest to heights of three hundred feet or more as they hit shallow water and race for land.

Southern Coastline of North America

In deadly silence, the pack of Velociraptors closes around its prey, a thirty-one-foot-long female *Corythosaurus*. Sensing danger, the duck-billed reptile raises her magnificent fan-shaped crest and snorts the humid air, detecting the scent of the pack. Trumpeting a warning cry to the rest of the herd, she crashes through the forest, galloping toward the sea.

Without warning, a brilliant *flash* stuns the fleeing duckbill. The reptile staggers, shaking its great head, attempting to regain its sight. As its vision clears, two raptors leap from the foliage and screech at the larger beast, blocking her escape as the rest of the pack pounces upon the Corythosaur's back, gouging her flesh with their deadly, sickle-clawed feet. One of the first hunters finds the duckbill's throat, biting into the animal's esophagus as it digs its feet and sickle claws into the soft flesh below the sternum. The wounded reptile chokes out a cry, gagging on its own blood, as another raptor bites down upon its flat snout, plunging its front claws into the Corythosaur's eyes, bringing its heavier foe whimpering to the ground.

In moments, it is over. The predators snarl, snapping at each other as they tear mouthfuls of flesh from their still-quivering prey. Occupied with the kill, the Velociraptors ignore the trembling ground beneath their feet and the approaching thunder.

A dark shadow passes overhead. The birdlike dinosaurs look up as one, blood dripping from their jowls as they growl at the mountainous wall of water.

The twenty-two-story wave crests—then falls—pummeling the startled hunters, liquefying their bones into the sand with a thunderous *clap*. The wave sweeps north, its kinetic energy obliterating everything in its path.

The tsunami inundates the terrain, sweeping vegetation, sediment, and land creatures within its roaring swell as it submerges the tropical coastline for hundreds of miles in all directions. What little forest remains outside the wash path ignites as searing blast waves turn the air into a veritable furnace. A pair of *Pteranodons* attempt to escape the holocaust. Rising above the trees, their reptilian wings catch fire, incinerating in the thermal wind.

High above, chunks of iridium and rock that were launched skyward begin reentering the atmosphere as incandescent meteors. Within hours, the entire planet is shrouded in a dense cloud of dust, smoke, and ash.

The forests will burn for months. For nearly a year, no sunlight will penetrate the blackened sky to reach the surface of the once-tropical world. The temporary cessation of photosynthesis will obliterate thousands of species of plants and animals on land and in the sea, as the Sun's eventual return is followed by years of nuclear winter.

In one cataclysmic moment, the 140-million-year domain of the dinosaurs has come to an abrupt end.

For days, the sleek gold vessel remains in orbit high above the devastated world, its sensors continuously scanning the impact site. The fourth-dimensional highway home is long gone, the rotation of the galaxy having already moved the conduit's access point several light-years away.

On the seventh day, an emerald green light begins to glow from beneath the fractured seafloor. Seconds later, a powerful subspace radio signal ignites, the distress call directed into the outer reaches of the galaxy.

The life-forms within the orbiting vessel jam the signal—too late.

Evil has taken root in yet another celestial garden. It is just a matter of time before it is awakened.

The golden starship moves into a geosynchronous orbit directly above its enemy. A solar-powered automated hyperwave radio signal is engaged, jamming all outgoing or incoming transmissions. Then the vessel shuts down, its power cells diverted to its life-support pods.

For the starship's inhabitants, time now stands still.

For the planet Earth, the clock has begun ticking. . . .

The South Florida Evaluation and Treatment Center is a seven-story white-concrete building with evergreen trim, located in a run-down ethnic neighborhood just west of the city of Miami. Like most businesses in the area, the rooftops are rimmed in coils of barbed-wire fencing. Unlike other establishments, the barbed wire is not meant to keep the public out, but its residents in.

Thirty-one-year-old Dominique Vazquez weaves through rush-hour traffic, cursing aloud as she races south on Route 441. The first day of her internship, and she is already late. Swerving around a teenager riding the wrong way on motorized skates, she pulls into the visitors parking lot, parks, then hastily twists her waist-length, jet-black hair into a tight bun as she jogs toward the entrance.

Magnetic doors part, allowing her access into an air-conditioned lobby.

A Hispanic woman in her late forties sits behind the information desk, reading the morning news from a clipboard-sized, wafer-thin computer monitor. Without looking up, she asks, "Can I help you?"

"Yes. I have an appointment with Margaret Reinike."

"Not today you don't. Dr. Reinike no longer works here." The woman fingers the page-down button, advancing the news monitor to another article.

"I don't understand. I spoke with Dr. Reinike two weeks ago."

The receptionist finally looks up. "And you are?"

"Vazquez, Dominique Vazquez. I'm here on a one-year postgraduate internship from FSU. Dr. Reinike's supposed to be my sponsor." She watches the woman pick up the phone and press an extension.

"Dr. Foletta, a young woman by the name of Domino Vass—"

"Vazquez. Dominique Vazquez."

"Sorry. Dominique Vazquez. No, sir, she's down here in the lobby, claiming to be Dr. Reinike's intern. Yes, sir." The receptionist hangs up. "You can have a seat over there. Dr. Foletta will be down to speak with you in a few minutes." The woman swivels her back to Dominique, returning to her news monitor.

Ten minutes pass before a large man in his late fifties makes his way down a corridor.

Anthony Foletta looks like he belongs on a football field coaching defensive linemen, not walking the halls of a state facility housing the criminally insane. A mane of thick gray hair rolls back over an enormous head, which appears to be attached directly to the shoulders. Blue eyes twinkle between sleepy lids and puffy cheeks. Though overweight, the upper body is firm, the stomach protruding slightly from the open white lab coat.

A forced smile, and a thick hand is extended.

"Anthony Foletta, new Chief of Psychiatry." The voice is deep and grainy, like an old lawn mower.

"What happened to Dr. Reinike?"

"Personal situation. Rumor has it her husband was diagnosed with terminal cancer. Guess she decided to take an early retirement. Reinike told me to expect you. Unless you have any objections, I'll be supervising your internship."

"No objections."

"Good." He turns and heads back down the hall, Dominique hustling to keep pace.

"Dr. Foletta, how long have you been with the facility?"

"Ten days. I transferred down here from the state facility in Massachusetts."

They approach a guard at the first security checkpoint. "Give the guard your driver's license."

Dominique searches her purse, then hands the man the laminated card, swapping it for the visitor's pass. "Use this for now," Foletta says. "Turn it in when you leave at the end of the day. We'll get you an encoded intern's badge before the week's out."

She clips the pass to her blouse, then follows him into the elevator.

Foletta holds three fingers up to a camera mounted above his head. The doors close. "Have you been here before? Are you familiar with the layout?"

"No. Dr. Reinike and I only spoke by phone."

"There are seven floors. Administration and central security's on the first floor. The main station controls both the staff and resident elevators. Level 2 houses a small medical unit for the elderly and terminally ill. Level 3 is where you'll find our dining area and rec rooms. It also accesses the mezzanine, yard, and therapy rooms. Levels 4, 5, 6, and 7 house residents." Foletta chuckles. "Dr. Blackwell refers to them as 'customers.' An interesting euphemism, don't you think, considering we haul them in here wearing handcuffs."

They exit the elevator, passing a security station identical to the one on the first floor. Foletta waves, then follows a short corridor to his office. Cardboard boxes are piled everywhere, stuffed with files, framed diplomas, and personal items.

"Excuse the mess, I'm still getting situated." Foletta removes a computer printer from a chair, motioning for Dominique to sit, then squeezes uncomfortably behind his own desk, leaning back in his leather chair to afford his belly room.

He opens her personnel file. "Hmm. Completing your doctorate at Florida State, I see. Get out to many football games?"

"Not really." *Use the opening.* "You look like you've played a little football before."

It is a good parlay, causing Foletta's cherub face to light up. "Fighting Blue Hens of Delaware, class of '79. Starting nose tackle. Would have been a lower-round NFL draft pick if I hadn't torn my knee up against Lehigh."

"What made you get into forensic psychiatry?"

"Had an older brother who suffered from a pathological obsession. Always in trouble with the law. His psychiatrist was a Delaware alumnus and a big football fan. Used to bring him down to the locker room after games. When I injured my knee, he pulled a few strings to get me into grad school." Foletta leans forward, placing her file flat on the desk. "Let's talk about you. I'm curious. There are several other facilities closer to FSU than ours. What brings you down here?"

Dominique clears her throat. "My parents live over in Sanibel. It's only a two-hour ride from Miami. I don't get home very often."

Foletta guides a thick index finger across her personnel file. "Says here you're originally from Guatemala."

"Yes."

"How'd you end up in Florida?"

"My parents—my real parents died when I was six. I was sent to live with a cousin in Tampa."

"But that didn't last?"

"Is this important?"

Foletta looks up. The eyes are no longer sleepy. "I'm not much for surprises, Intern Vazquez. Before assigning residents, I like to know my own staff's psyche. Most residents don't give us much of a problem, but it's important to remember that we're still dealing with some violent individuals. Safety's a priority with me. What happened in Tampa? How was it that you ended up in a foster home?"

"Suffice it to say that things didn't work out with my cousin."

"Did he rape you?"

Dominique is taken back by his directness. "If you must know—yes. I was only ten at the time."

"You were under the care of a psychiatrist?"

She stares back at him. *Stay cool, he's testing you.* "Yes, until I was seventeen."

"Does it bother you to talk about it?"

"It happened. It's over. I'm sure it influenced my choice of career, if that's where this is leading."

"Your interests, too. Says here you have a second-degree black belt in tae kwon do. Ever use it?"

"Only in tournaments."

The lids open wide, the blue eyes baiting her with their intensity. "Tell me, Intern Vazquez, do you imagine your cousin's face when you kick your opponents?"

"Sometimes." She pushes a strand of hair from her eyes. "Who did you pretend to hit when you played football for those Fighting Blue Hens?"

"Touché." The eyes return to the file. "Date much?"

"My social life concerns you as well?"

Foletta sits back in his chair. "Traumatic sexual experiences like yours often lead to sexual disorders. Again, I just want to know who I'm working with."

"I have no aversions to sex, if that's what you're asking. I *do* have a healthy mistrust toward prying men."

"This isn't a halfway house, Intern Vazquez. You'll need thicker skin than that if you expect to handle forensic residents. Men like these have made names for themselves feasting on pretty college women like you. Coming from FSU, I'd think you could appreciate that."

Dominique takes a deep breath, relaxing her coiled muscles. *Dammit, tuck your ego away and pay attention.* "You're right, Doctor. My apologies."

Foletta closes the file. "Truth is, I have you in mind for a special assignment, but I need to be absolutely certain that you're up to the task."

Dominique reenergizes. "Try me."

Foletta removes a thick brown file from his top desk drawer. "As you know, this facility believes in a multidisciplinary-team approach. Each resident is assigned a psychiatrist, a clinical psychologist, social worker, psychiatric nurse, and a rehab therapist. My initial reaction when I first got here was that it's a bit overkill, but I can't argue with the results, especially when dealing with substance-abuse patients and preparing individuals to participate in their forthcoming trials."

"But not in this case?"

"No. The resident I want you to oversee is a patient of mine, an inmate from the asylum where I served as psychological services director."

"I don't understand. You brought him with you?"

"Our facility lost funding about six months ago. He's certainly not fit for society, and he had to be transferred somewhere. Since I'm more familiar with his history than anyone else, I thought it would be less traumatic for all concerned if he remained under my care."

"Who is he?"

"Ever hear of Professor Julius Gabriel?"

"Gabriel?" The name sounded familiar. "Wait a second, wasn't he the archaeologist who dropped dead during a Harvard lecture several years ago?"

"Over ten years ago." Foletta grins. "After three decades of research grants, Julius Gabriel returned to the States and stood before an assembly of his peers, claiming that the ancient Egyptians and Mayans had built their pyramids with the help of extraterrestrials—all to save humanity from destruction. Can you imagine? The audience laughed him right offstage. He probably died of humiliation." Foletta's cheeks quiver as he chuckles. "Julius Gabriel was a real poster child for paranoid schizophrenia."

"So who's the patient?"

"His son." Foletta opens the file. "Michael Gabriel, age thirty-four. Prefers to be called Mick. Spent the first twenty-plus years of his life working side by side with his parents in archaeological digs, probably enough to turn any kid psychotic."

"Why was he incarcerated?"

"Mick lost it during his father's lecture. The court diagnosed him paranoid schizophrenic and sentenced him to the Massachusetts State Mental Facility where I served as his clinical psychiatrist, remaining so even after my promotion to director in 2006."

"Same kind of delusions as his father?"

"Of course. Father and son were both convinced that some terrible calamity is going to wipe mankind off the face of the planet. Mick also suffers from the usual paranoid delusions of persecution, most of it brought about by his father's death and his own incarceration. Claims that a government conspiracy has kept him locked up all these years. In Mick Gabriel's mind, he's the ultimate victim, an innocent man attempting to save the world, caught up in the immoral ambitions of a self-centered politician."

"I'm sorry, you lost me on that last bit."

Foletta leafs through the file, removing a series of Polaroids from a manila envelope. "This is the man he attacked. Take a good look at the picture, Intern. Make sure you don't let your defenses down."

It is a close-up of a man's face, brutally battered. The right eye socket is covered in blood.

"Mick tore the microphone from the podium and beat the victim senseless with it. Poor man ended up losing his eye. I think you'll recognize the victim's name. Pierre Borgia."

"Borgia? You're kidding? The Secretary of State?"

"This was nearly eleven years ago, before Borgia was appointed UN representative. He was running for senator at the time. Some say the attack probably helped get him elected. Before the Borgia political machine pushed him into politics, Pierre was apparently quite the scholar. He and Julius Gabriel were in the same doctoral program at Cambridge. Believe it or not, the two of them actually worked together as colleagues after graduation, exploring ancient ruins for a good five or six years before having a major fallout. Borgia's family finally convinced him to return to the States and enter politics, but the bad blood never went away.

"Turns out it was Borgia who actually introduced Julius as the keynote speaker. Pierre probably said a few things he shouldn't have said, which helped incite the crowd. Julius Gabriel had a bad heart. After he dropped dead backstage, Mick retaliated. Took six cops to pull him off. It's all in the file."

"Sounds more like an isolated emotional outburst, brought on by—"

"That kind of rage takes years to build up, Intern. Michael Gabriel was a volcano, waiting to erupt. Here we have an only child, raised by two prominent archaeologists in some of the most desolate areas of the world. He never attended school or had the opportunity to socialize with other children, all of which contributed to an extreme case of antisocial-personality disorder. Hell, Mick has probably never gone out on a date. Everything he ever learned was taught to him by his only companions, his parents, at least one of which was certifiable."

Foletta hands her the file.

"What happened to his mother?"

"Died of pancreatic cancer while the family was living in Peru. For some reason, her death still haunts him. Once or twice a month he'll wake up screaming. Vicious night terrors."

"How old was Mick when she died?"

"Twelve."

"Any idea why her death still creates such trauma?"

"No. Mick refuses to speak about it." Foletta adjusts himself, unable to get comfortable in the small chair. "The truth, Intern Vazquez, is that Michael Gabriel doesn't like me very much."

"Transference neurosis?"

"No. Mick and I never had that kind of doctor-patient relationship. I've become his jailer, part of his paranoia. Some of that no doubt stems from his first years of residence. Mick had a hard time adjusting to confinement. One week before his six-month evaluation, he flipped out on one of our guards, breaking both the man's arms and kicking him repeatedly in the scrotum. Caused so much damage that both testicles had to be surgically removed. There's a picture somewhere in the file if you care—"

"No thanks."

"As punishment for the attack, Mick spent most of the last ten years in solitary confinement."

"That's a bit severe, isn't it?"

"Not where I come from. Mick's a lot more clever than the men whom we hire to guard him. It's best for all concerned to keep him isolated."

"Will he be allowed to participate in group activities?"

"They have strict rules about mainstreaming residents down here, but for now, the answer's no."

Dominique stares at the Polaroids again. "How concerned do I need to be about this guy attacking me?"

"In our business, Intern, you always have to be concerned. Is Mick Gabriel a threat to attack? Always. Do I think he will? Doubtful. The last ten years haven't been easy on him."

"Will he ever be permitted to reenter society?"

Foletta shakes his head. "Never. In the road of life, this is Mick Gabriel's last stop. He'd never be able to handle the rigors of society. Mick's scared."

"Scared of what?"

"His own schizophrenia. Mick claims he can sense the presence of evil growing stronger, feeding off society's hatred and violence. His phobia reaches a breaking point every time another angry kid grabs his father's gun and shoots up a high school. This kind of stuff really gets to him."

"It gets to me, too."

"Not like this. Mick becomes a tiger."

"Is he being medicated?"

"We keep him on zyprexa—twice a day. Knocks most of the fight out of him."

"So what do you want me to do with him?"

"State law requires that he receive therapy. Use the opportunity to gain some valuable experience."

He's hiding something. "I appreciate the opportunity, Doctor. But why me?"

Foletta pushes up from the desk and stands, the furniture creaking beneath his weight. "As director of this facility, it might be construed as a conflict of interest if I were the only one treating him."

"But why not assign a full team to—"

"No." Foletta's patience is wearing thin. "Michael Gabriel is still my patient, and I'll determine what avenue of therapy is best suited for him, not some board of trustees. What you'll soon find out for yourself is that Mick's a bit of a con artist—quite clever, very articulate, and very intelligent. His IQ's close to 160."

"That's rather unusual for a schizophrenic, isn't it?"

"Unusual, but not unheard of. My point is—he'd only toy with a social worker or rehab specialist. It takes someone with your training to see through his bullshit."

"So when do I meet him?"

"Right now. He's being brought to a seclusion room so I can observe your first encounter. I told him all about you this morning. He's looking forward to speaking with you. Just be careful."

The top four floors of the facility, referred to as units by the SFETC staff, each house forty-eight residents. Units are divided into north and south wings, each wing containing three pods. A pod consists of a small rec room with sofas and a television, centered around eight private dorm rooms. Each floor has its own security and nurses' station. There are no windows.

Foletta and Dominique ride the staff elevator to the seventh floor. An African-American security guard is speaking to one of the nurses at the central station. The seclusion room is to his left.

The director acknowledges the guard, then introduces him to the new intern. Marvis Jones is in his late forties, with kind, brown eyes that exude confidence gained through experience. Dominique notices that the guard is unarmed. Foletta explains that no weapons are permitted on residential floors at any time.

Marvis leads them through the central station to a one-way security glass looking in on the seclusion room.

Michael Gabriel is sitting on the floor, leaning back against the far wall facing the window. He is wearing a white tee shirt and matching slacks, his physique appearing surprisingly fit, the upper body well-defined. He is tall, nearly six-four, 220 pounds. The hair is dark brown, a bit on the long side, curling at the fringes. The face is handsome and cleanly shaven. A three-inch scar stretches across the right side of the jawline, close to the ear. His eyes remain fixed on the floor.

"He's cute."

"So was Ted Bundy," Foletta says. "I'll be watching you from here. I'm sure Mick will be quite charming, wanting to impress you. When I think you've had enough, I'll have the nurse come in and give him his medication."

"Okay." Her voice quavers. *Relax, God dammit.*

Foletta smiles. "Are you nervous?"

"No, just a little excited."

She exits the station, motioning to Marvis to unlock the seclusion room. The door swings open, stimulating butterflies to take wing in her stomach. Pausing long enough to allow her pulse to slow, she enters, shuddering as the double *click* seals the door behind her.

The seclusion room is ten by twelve feet long. An iron bed is bolted to the floor and wall directly in front of her, a thin pad serving as a mattress. A solitary chair faces the bed, also bolted to the floor. A smoked panel of glass on the wall to her right is the undisguised viewing window. The room smells of antiseptic.

Mick Gabriel is standing now, his head slightly bowed so she cannot see his eyes.

Dominique extends a hand, forcing a smile. "Dominique Vazquez."

Mick looks up, revealing animal eyes so intensely black that it is impossible to determine where the pupils end and the irises begin.

"Dominique Vazquez. Dominique Vazquez." The resident pronounces each syllable carefully, as if locking it into his memory. "It's so very nice to . . ."

The smile suddenly disappears, the pasted expression going blank.

Dominique's heart pounds in her ears. *Stay calm. Don't move.*

Mick closes his eyes. Something unexpected is happening to him. Dominique sees his jawline rise slightly, revealing the scar. The nostrils flare like an animal tracking its prey.

"May I come closer, please?" The words are spoken softly, almost whispered. She senses an emotional dam cracking behind the voice.

Dominique fights the urge to turn toward the smoked glass.

The eyes reopen. "I swear on my mother's soul that I won't harm you."

Watch his hands. Drive the knee home if he lunges. "You can come closer, but no sudden movements, okay? Dr. Foletta's watching."

Mick takes two steps forward, remaining half an arm's length away. He leans his face forward, closing his eyes, inhaling—as if her face is an exquisite bottle of wine.

The man's presence is causing the hairs on the back of her arms to stand on end. She watches his facial muscles relax as his mind leaves the room. Water wells behind the closed eyelids. Several tears escape, flowing freely down his cheeks.

For a brief moment, maternal instincts cause her defenses to drop. *Is this an act?* Her muscles recoil.

Mick opens his eyes, now black pools. The animal intensity has vanished.

"Thank you. I think my mother must have worn the same perfume."

She takes a step back. "It's Calvin Klein. Does it bring back happy memories?"

"Some bad ones as well."

The spell is broken. Mick moves to the cot. "Would you prefer the chair or the bed."

"The chair's fine." He waits for her to sit first, then positions himself on the edge of the cot so that he can lean back against the wall. Mick moves like an athlete.

"You look like you've managed to stay in shape."

"Living in solitary can do that if one's mind is disciplined enough. I do a thousand push-ups and sit-ups every day." She feels his eyes absorb her figure. "You look like you work out as well."

"I try."

"Vazquez. Is that with an s or a z?"

"Z."

"Puerto Rico?"

"Yes. My . . . my biological father grew up in Arecibo."

"Site of the largest radio telescope in the world. But the accent sounds Guatemalan."

"I was raised there." *He's controlling the conversation.* "I take it you've been to Central America?"

"I've been to many places." Mick tucks his heels into a lotus position. "So you were raised in Guatemala. How did you find your way to this great land of opportunity?"

"My parents died when I was young. I was sent to live in with a cousin in Florida. Now let's talk about you."

"You said your biological father. You felt it important to distinguish him as such. Who's the man you consider your true father?"

"Isadore Axler. He and his wife adopted me. I spent some time in an orphanage after I left my cousins. Iz and Edith Axler are wonderful people. They're both marine biologists. They operate a SOSUS station on Sanibel Island."

"SOSUS?"

"It's a sound underwater surveillance system, a global network of undersea microphones. The Navy deployed SOSUS during the cold war to detect enemy subs. Biologists took over the system, using it to eavesdrop on marine life. It's actually sensitive enough to listen in on pods of whales hundreds of miles away as—"

The penetrating eyes cut her off. "Why did you leave your cousin? Something traumatic must have happened for you to have ended up in an orphanage."

He's worse than Foletta. "Mick, I'm here to talk about you."

"Yes, but perhaps I've also had a traumatic childhood. Perhaps your story could help me."

"I doubt it. Everything turned out fine. The Axlers gave me back my childhood, and I'm—"

"But not your innocence."

Dominique feels the blood rush from her face. "All right, now that we've established that you're a quick study, let's see if you can focus that amazing IQ of yours in on yourself."

"You mean, so you can help me?"

"So we can help each other."

"You haven't read my file yet, have you?"

"Not yet, no."

"Do you know why Director Foletta assigned you to me?"

"Why don't you tell me?"

Mick stares at his hands, contemplating a response. "There's a study, written by Rosenhan. Have you read it?"

"No."

"Would you mind reading it before we meet again? I'm sure Dr. Foletta must have a copy stashed in one of those cardboard boxes he calls a filing system."

She smiles. "If it's important to you, then I'll read it."

"Thank you." He leans forward. "I like you, Dominique. Do you know why I like you?"

"No." The fluorescent bulbs perform a moonlight dance in his eyes.

"I like you because your mind hasn't become institutionalized. You're still fresh, and that's important to me, because I really want to confide in you, but I can't, at least not in this room, not with Foletta watching. I also think you may be able to relate to some of the hardships I've gone through. So I'd like to talk to you about a lot of things, very important things. Do you think we could talk in private next time? Perhaps down in the yard?"

"I'll ask Dr. Foletta."

"Remind him of the facility's rules when you do. Would you also ask him to give you my father's journal. If you're to be my therapist, then I feel it's of vital importance that you read it. Would you mind doing that for me?"

"I'd be honored to read it."

"Thank you. Would you read it soon, perhaps over the weekend? I hate to give you homework, this being your first day and all, but it's vitally important that you read it right away."

The door swings open, the nurse entering. The guard waits outside, watching at the doorway. "Time for your medication, Mr. Gabriel." She hands him the paper cup of water, then the white tablet.

"Mick, I have to go. It was nice meeting you. I'll do my best to have my homework done by Monday, okay?" She stands, turning to leave.

Mick is staring at the pill. "Dominique, the relatives on your mother's side. They're Quiche Maya, aren't they?"

"Mayan? I—I don't know." *He knows you're lying.* "I mean it's possible. My parents died when I was very—"

The eyes look up suddenly, the effect disarming. "Four *Ahau*, three *Kankin*. You know what day that is, don't you, Dominique?"

Oh, shit . . . "I—I'll see you soon." Dominique pushes past the guard, exiting the room.

Michael Gabriel places the pill carefully in his mouth. He drains the cup of water, then crumples it in the palm of his left hand. He opens his mouth, allowing the nurse to probe with her tongue depressor and pencil-thin flashlight, verifying that he has swallowed the medication.

"Thank you, Mr. Gabriel. The guard will escort you back to your room in a few minutes."

Mick remains on the cot until the nurse has closed the door. He stands, returning to the far wall, his back to the window, the index finger of his left hand casually sliding the white pill out of the empty cup and into his palm. Resuming his lotus position on the floor, he tosses the crumpled cup onto the bed while slipping the white tablet into his shoe.

The zyprexa will be properly disposed of in the toilet when he returns to his private cell.

2

Secretary of State Pierre Robert Borgia stares at his reflection in the washroom mirror. He adjusts the patch over his right eye socket, then pats down the short graying tufts of hair along both sides of his otherwise balding head. The black suit and matching tie are immaculate as usual.

Borgia exits the executive washroom and turns right, nodding to staff members as he makes his way down the corridor to the Oval Office.

Patsy Goodman looks up from her keyboard. "Go on in. He's waiting."

Borgia nods, then enters.

Mark Maller's gaunt, pale face shows the wear of having served as president for nearly four years. The jet-black hair has grayed around the temples, the eyes, piercing blue, are now more wrinkled around the edges. The fifty-two-year-old physique, noticeably thinner, is still taut.

Borgia tells him he looks like he's lost weight.

Maller grimaces. "It's called the Viktor Grozny stress diet. Have you read this morning's CIA briefing?"

"Not yet. What's Russia's newest president done now?"

"He's called for a summit between military leaders from China, North Korea, Iran, and India."

"For what purpose?"

"To conduct a joint nuclear deterrent exercise, in response to our latest tests involving the Missile Defense Shield."

"Grozny's grandstanding again. He's still fuming about the IMF canceling that twenty-billion-dollar loan package."

"Whatever his motive, he's succeeding in stirring up nuclear paranoia in Asia."

"Marko, the Security Council meeting's this afternoon, so I know you didn't bring me in just to discuss foreign affairs."

Maller nods, then drains his third cup of coffee. "Jeb's decided to step down as vice president. Don't ask. Call it personal reasons."

Borgia's heart skips a beat. "Christ, the election's in less than two months—"

"I've already held an unofficial meeting with the powers that be. It's between you and Ennis Chaney."

Jesus . . . "Have you spoken with him yet?"

"No. Thought I owed it to you to brief you first."

Borgia shrugs, smiling nervously. "Senator Chaney is a good man, but he can't hold a candle to me when it comes to foreign affairs. And my family still wields plenty of influence—"

"Not as much as you think, and the polls show that most Americans aren't interested in China's military buildup. They perceive the Missile Defense Shield as being the see-all, end-all of nuclear war."

"Then let me be blunt, sir. Does the Republican National Committee really think the country's ready for an African-American VP?"

"The election's going to be tight. Look what Lieberman did for Gore. Chaney would give us a much-needed toehold in both Pennsylvania and the South. Relax, Pierre. No decision's going to be made for at least another thirty to forty-five days."

"That's smart. Gives the press less time to pick us apart."

"Any skeletons in your closet we need to be concerned with?"

"I'm sure your people are already looking into that as we speak. Mark, level with me, does Chaney have the inside track?"

"Opinion polls show Chaney's popularity stretches across both party and racial lines. He's down-to-earth. The public trusts him even more than Colin Powell."

"Don't confuse trust with qualifications." Borgia stands, then paces. "The polls also show Americans are concerned about Russia's collapsed economy and how it will affect the European market."

"Pierre, take it easy. A lot can happen in forty-five days."

Borgia exhales. "I'm sorry, Mr. President. It's a great honor just to be considered. Listen, I'd better get going, I have to meet with General Fecondo before this afternoon briefing."

Borgia shakes his friend's hand, then starts for the camouflaged panel door. He turns before leaving. "Marko, any advice?"

The president sighs. "I don't know. Heidi did mention something at breakfast. Ever thought about replacing that patch with a glass eye?"

Dominique exits the treatment facility's lobby, the south Florida summer heat blasting her in the face. A distant bolt of lightning streaks across an ominous afternoon sky. Shifting the leather-bound journal from her right hand to her left, she presses her thumb to the keyless entry, unlocking the driver's side door of the brand-new, black Pronto Spyder convertible, an early graduation gift from Edie and Iz. She places the journal on the passenger seat, buckles her seat belt, then presses her thumb to the ignition pad, registering the annoying microscopic pinprick.

The dashboard computer jumps to life, flashing its message:

Activating Ignition Sequence.
Identification Verified. Antitheft System Deactivated.

She feels the now-familiar double *clunk* as the axle locks disengage.

Checking Blood-Alcohol Level. Please Stand By . . .

Dominique lays her head back against the leather seat, watching the first heavy drops of rain pelt the polyethylene terephthalate plastic hood of her roadster. Patience is a requirement of the new safety ignition features, but she knows it is well worth the extra three minutes. Drunk driving has become the leading cause of death in the United States. By the fall of next year, all vehicles will be required to have the blood-alcohol devices installed.

The ignition activates.

Blood Alcohol At Acceptable Levels. Please Drive Safely.

Dominique adjusts the air conditioner, then presses the power button of the Digital DJ CD player. The built-in computer processor reacts either to voice inflection or touch to interpret the driver's mood, selecting the appropriate music from among hundreds of preprogrammed selections.

The heavy bass of the Rolling Stones' latest album, *Past Our Prime*, begins pumping out of the surround-sound speakers. She backs out of the visitors lot and begins the forty-minute drive home.

It had not been easy convincing Dr. Foletta to relinquish Julius Gabriel's journal. His initial objection was that the late archaeologist's work had been sponsored by both Harvard and Cambridge University and that, legally, it would be necessary first to receive written permission from both grant departments before releasing any sort of research documents to her. Dominique countered that she needed access to the journal, not only to do her job properly but to gain Michael Gabriel's trust. An afternoon of phone calls to department heads at both Harvard and Cambridge confirmed that the journal was more a memoir than a scientific document and that she was free to use it, provided she did not go public with any information. Foletta had finally conceded, producing the two-inch-thick binder by day's end, releasing it only after she had signed a four-page nondisclosure agreement.

The rain has let up by the time Dominique pulls into the dark parking garage of the Hollywood Beach high-rise. She deactivates the car's engine, staring at a ghostly image appearing on the heads-up display of the windshield. The picture provided by the infrared camera mounted on the front of the roadster's radiator confirms the garage to be empty.

Dominique smiles at her own paranoia. She takes the antiquated elevator up to the fifth floor, holding the door open so Mrs. Jenkins and her white miniature poodle can enter.

The one-bedroom condominium owned by her adoptive parents is down the hallway, the last apartment on the right. As she enters the security code, the door at her back opens.

"Dominique—so how was your first day at work?"

Rabbi Richard Steinberg embraces her with a warm smile from behind a graying auburn beard. Steinberg and his wife, Mindy, are close friends of her parents. Dominique has known the couple since she was adopted nearly twenty years ago.

"Mentally exhausting. Think I'll skip dinner and climb into a hot bath."

"Listen, Mindy and I want you to come over for dinner next week. Tuesday sound okay?"

"Should be. Thanks."

"Good, good. Hey, I spoke to Iz yesterday. Did you know he and your mother are planning to drive over for the High Holy Days."

"No, I didn't—"

"Okay, I gotta run, I can't be late for Shabbat. We'll call you next week."

She waves, watching him hurry down the hallway. Dominique likes Steinberg and his wife, finds them both to be warm and genuine. She knows Iz has asked them to keep a parental eye on her.

Dominique enters the apartment and opens the balcony doors, allowing the ocean breeze to fill the musty room with a gust of salty air. The afternoon shower has chased off most of the beachgoers, the last rays of sun peeking out from the clouds, casting a crimson glow along the water.

It is her favorite time of day, a time for solitude. She contemplates a leisurely walk along the beach, then changes her mind. Pouring herself a glass of wine from an open bottle in the fridge, she kicks off her shoes and returns to the balcony. Placing the glass on a plastic table with the leather-bound journal, she lies down on the lounge chair, stretching as her body sinks into the soft cushion.

The pounding mantra of surf quickly works its magic. She sips the wine, closing her eyes, her thoughts again returning to her earlier encounter with Michael Gabriel.

Four Ahau, *three* Kankin. Dominique has not heard the words spoken since her early childhood.

Thoughts slip into a dream. She is back in the highlands of Guatemala, six years old, her maternal grandmother by her side. They are on their knees, toiling in the afternoon sun, working the onion crops. A cool breeze, the *xocomil*, blows in off Lake Atitlán. The child listens intently as the old woman's voice rasps at her. "*The calendar was handed down to us from our Olmec ancestors, its wisdom coming from our teacher, the great Kukulcán. Long before the Spanish invaded our land, the great teacher left us warnings of disastrous days ahead. Four Ahau, three Kankin, the last day of the Mayan calendar. Be wary of this day, my child. When the time comes, you must make the journey home, for the* Popol Vuh *says that it is only here that we can be restored to life.*"

Dominique opens her eyes, staring at the black ocean. Alabaster crests of foam roll in beneath the partially obscured moonlight.

Four *Ahau,* three *Kankin*—December 21, 2012.

Humanity's prophesied day of doom.

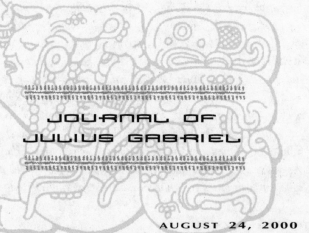

AUGUST 24, 2000

*M*y name is Professor Julius Gabriel.

I am an archaeologist, a scientist who studies relics of the past to understand ancient cultures. I use evidence left to us from our ancestors to frame hypotheses and formulate theories. I sift through thousands of years of myths to find single veins of truth.

Throughout the ages, scientists like myself have learned the hard way that man's fear often suppresses truth. Labeled heresy, its very breath is suffocated until Church and State, judge and jury are able to put aside their fears and accept what is real.

I am a scientist. I am not a politician. I am not interested in presenting years of evidence-backed theories to a lecture hall of self-appointed scholars so they can vote on what an acceptable truth about mankind's fate may or may not be. The nature of truth has nothing to do with the democratic process. Like an investigative reporter, I am only interested in what really happened, and what may indeed happen. And if the truth turns out to be so unbelievable that I am labeled a heretic, then so be it.

After all, I am in good company: Darwin was a heretic; and Galileo before him; 400 years ago, Giordano Bruno was burned at the stake because he insisted that other worlds besides our own existed.

Like Bruno, I will be dead long before humanity's bitter end arrives. _Here lies Julius Gabriel, the victim of a diseased heart._ My physician urges me to his care, warning me the organ is but a ticking time bomb set to detonate at any moment. Let it explode, I say. The worthless organ has only given me grief since it broke eleven years ago after the departure of my dearly beloved.

These are my memoirs, an accounting of a journey that began some 32 years ago. My purpose in summarizing this information is twofold. First, the nature of the research is so controversial and its ramifications so terrifying that I realize now that the scientific community will do everything in its power to suffocate, stifle, and deny the truth about man's destiny. Last, I know there are individuals among the populace who, like my own son, would prefer to fight rather than sit idly by as the end approaches. To you, my "_warriors of salvation_," I leave this journal, thereby passing the baton of hope. Decades of toil and misery are hidden within these pages—this slice of man's history, extracted from eons of limestone. The fate of our species now rests in my son's hands— and perhaps yours. At the very least, you'll no longer be part of the majority Michael calls the "innocent ignorant." Pray that men like my son can resolve the ancient Mayan riddle.

Then pray for yourselves.

It is said that fear of death is worse than death itself. I believe that witnessing the death of a loved one is worse still. To have experienced my soul mate's life slip away before my eyes, to have felt her body turn cold in my arms—this is too much despair for one heart to handle. At times, I am actually grateful to be dying, for I cannot begin to imagine the anguish of witnessing an entire population suffer amidst the planetary holocaust to come.

For those of you who scoff at my words, be forewarned: The day of reckoning is fast approaching, and ignorance of the event will do nothing to change the outcome.

Today, I sit backstage at Harvard, organizing these excerpts as I await my turn at the dais. So much rides on my speech, so many lives. My greatest concern is that the egos of my colleagues may be too large to allow them to listen to my findings with an open mind. If given a chance to present the facts, I know that I can appeal to them as scientists. If ridiculed, then I fear all is lost.

Fear. I have no doubt as to the motivational effect the emotion has on me now, yet it was not fear that started me on my journey on that fateful day in May of 1969, but the desire to seek fame and fortune. I was young and immortal back then, still full of piss and vinegar, having just received my doctorate degree with honors from Cambridge University. While the rest of my peers were busy protesting the war in Vietnam, making love, and fighting for equality, I set out with my father's inheritance, accompanied by two fellow archaeologists and companions, my (former) best friend,

Pierre Borgia, and the ravishing Maria Rosen. Our goal—to unravel the great mystery surrounding the Mayan calendar and its 2,500-year-old prophecy of doom.

Never heard of the Mayan calendar's prophecy? I'm not surprised. These days, who has time to concern themselves with an oracle of death originating from some ancient Central American civilization?

Eleven years from now, when you and your loved ones are writhing on the ground, gasping for your last breath, your lives flashing before your eyes—you may well wish you had made the time.

I'll even give you the date of your death: December 21, of the year 2012.

There—you've been officially warned. Now you can act, or shove your heads in the sands of ignorance like the rest of my learned colleagues.

Of course, it's easy for rational human beings to dismiss the Mayan calendar's doomsday prophecy as mere superstitious nonsense. I can still recall my own professor's reaction when he learned of my intended area of focus: You're wasting your time, Julius. The Maya were heathens, a bunch of jungle-dwelling savages who believed in human sacrifice. For God's sake, they hadn't even mastered the wheel . . .

My professor was both right and wrong, and this is the paradox, for while it is true the ancient Maya could barely grasp the significance of the wheel, they had, in fact, managed to acquire an advanced knowledge of astronomy, architecture, and mathematics that, in many ways, rivals and even exceeds our own. In laymen's terms, the Maya were the equivalent of a four-year-old child mastering Beethoven's Moonlight Sonata on the piano while remaining unable to pound out "Chopsticks."

I'm sure you find it hard to believe, most self-proclaimed "educated" individuals do. But the evidence is overwhelming. And this is what compelled me to embark on my journey, for simply to ignore the calendar's wealth of knowledge because of its unimaginable doomsday prophecy would have been as much a crime as to dismiss summarily the theory of relativity because Einstein was once employed as a junior clerk.

So what _is_ the Mayan calendar?

A brief explanation:

If I asked you to describe the function of a calendar, your initial response would probably be to describe the device as a means of keeping your weekly or monthly appointments. Moving beyond this somewhat limited scope, let us see the calendar for what it really is—a tool, designed to determine (as accurately as possible) the Earth's annual orbit around the Sun.

Our modern Western calendar was first introduced in Europe in 1582. It was based upon the Gregorian calendar, which calculated Earth's orbit around the Sun to take 365.25 days. This incorporated a very small plus-error of 0.0003 of a day per year, quite impressive for scientists of the 16th century.

The Maya derived their calendar from their predecessors, the Olmec, a mysterious people whose origins can be traced back some 3,000 years. Imagine for a moment, that you are living thousands of years ago. There are no televisions or radios, telephones, or watches, and it is your job is to chart the stars to determine the passage of time equating to one planetary orbit. Somehow the Olmec, without precision instruments, calculated the solar year to be 365.2420 days, incorporating an even smaller minus error of 0.0002 of a day.

Let me restate this so you can grasp the implications: The 3,000-year-old Mayan calendar is a 10,000th of a day more accurate than the calendar the world uses today!

There's more. The Mayan solar calendar is but one part of a three-calendar system. A second calendar, the "ceremonial calendar" operates concurrently, consisting of 20 months of 13 days. The third part, the "Venus calendar" or "Long Count," was based on the orbit of the planet Venus. By combining these three calendars into one, the Maya were able to forecast celestial events over great expanses of time, not just thousands but millions of years. (On one particular Mesoamerican monument, an inscription refers to a time period dating back 400 million years.)

Impressed yet?

The Maya believed in Great Cycles, periods of time that registered the recorded creations and destructions of the world. The calendar recorded the five Great Cycles or Suns of the Earth. The current and last cycle began on 4 Ahau 8 Cumku, a date corresponding to August 13, 3114 BC, considered by the Maya to be the birth date of the planet Venus. This last Great Cycle is predicted to end with the destruction of humanity on 4 Ahau 3 Kankin, a date determined as December 21, in the year 2012— the day of the winter solstice.

The Day of the Dead.

How convinced were the Maya that their prophecy was true? After the departure of their great teacher, Kukulcán, the Maya began practicing barbaric rituals involving human sacrifice, cutting out the hearts of tens of thousands of men, women, and children.

The ultimate sacrifice—all to forestall the end of humanity.

I'm not asking you to seek such outlandish remedies, just to open your mind. What you don't know can affect you, what you refuse to see can kill you. There are mysteries that surround us whose origins we cannot fathom—yet must! The pyramids of Giza and Teotihuacán, the Temples of Angkor in Cambodia, Stonehenge, the incredible message inscribed upon the Nazca desert, and most of all, the Kukulcán pyramid in Chichén Itzá. All these ancient sites, all these magnificent, unexplainable wonders were not intended as tourist attractions but are pieces to a single perplexing jigsaw puzzle that can prevent the annihilation of our species.

My journey through life is nearly over. I leave these memoirs, highlights of the overwhelming evidence I've accumulated over three decades, to my son, Michael, and to all those who would carry on my work ad finem—to the end. While presenting the clues in the manner in which I stumbled across them, I will also endeavor to paint for you an historical accounting of the events along the time line in which they actually occurred throughout man's history.

For the record, I take no satisfaction in being right. For the record, I pray to God that I'm wrong.

I'm not wrong. . . .

—Excerpt from the Journal of Professor Julius Gabriel,
   Ref. J G Catalogue 1969–70   pages 12–28

43

Michael Gabriel is dreaming.

Once more, he is lying on the backstage floor of an auditorium, his father's head resting against his chest as they await the ambulance. Julius beckons his son's ear so that he might whisper a secret he has kept to himself since his wife's death eleven years earlier.

"*Michael . . . the center stone.*"

"*Don't try to talk, Pop. The ambulance is on the way.*"

"*Listen to me, Michael! The center stone, the ball court marker—I replaced it.*"

"*I don't understand. What stone?*"

"*Chichén Itzá.*"

The weathered eyes glaze over, the weight of his father's body slumping against his chest.

"*Pop . . . POP!*"

Mick awakens, his body bathed in sweat.

Dominique gives the receptionist a half wave, then proceeds directly to the main security station. A heavily muscled security guard smiles as she approaches, the man's strawberry blond mustache lifting and spreading across his upper lip, revealing yellowed teeth.

"Well, good morning, Sunshine. I'm Raymond, and I bet you're our new intern."

"Dominique Vazquez." She shakes his callused hand, noticing beads of perspiration across the thick, freckled forearm.

"Sorry, just came from the gym." Raymond wipes his arms down with a hand towel, overexaggerating the movement to flex his pump. "I'm competing in the Mr. Florida Regional in November. Think I've got a chance?"

"Uh, sure." *God, please don't let him start posing. . . .*

"Maybe you could come down and watch me compete, you know, root me on?" The pale hazel eyes widen behind short amber eyelashes.

Be gentle. "Are a lot of the staff going?"

"A few, but I'll make sure you get a seat close to the stage. Come on back, Sunshine, I need to make you a security card and record a thermal image of your face." Raymond unlocks the steel security gate and holds it open for her by flexing his triceps. Dominique feels his eyes running over her as she passes through.

"Have a seat over there, we'll take care of the security card first. I'll need your driver's license."

She hands it to him, then sits in an upright chair positioned before a black machine the size of a refrigerator. Raymond loads a square disk into a slot on one side, then types in her information on the computer.

"Smile." The flash explodes in her eyes, leaving an annoying spot. "I'll have the card ready by the time you leave tonight." He hands back her driver's license. "Okay, come over here and have a seat in front of this infrared camera. Ever have your face mapped?"

Ever have your back shaved? "Uh, not that I know of."

"The infrared camera creates a unique image of your face by registering the heat emitted by the blood vessels beneath your skin. Even identical twins look different under infrared, and facial patterns never changes. The computer records nineteen hundred different thermal points. Pupil scans use 266 measurable characteristics, while fingerprints only have forty—"

"Ray, this is fascinating—really—but is it necessary? I haven't seen anyone use an infrared scan."

"That's because you haven't been here at night. The magnetic strip on your identification card is all you'll need to enter or exit the facility during the day. But after seven-thirty, you'll need to enter your password, then allow the infrared scanner to identify you. The machine will compare your thermal facial features with the ones we're about to place on your permanent file. No one gets in or out of this facility at night without being scanned, and nothing fools the machine. Smile."

Dominique stares sullenly at the sphere-shaped camera behind the plate-glass window, feeling foolish.

"Okay, turn to your left. Good. Now right, now look down. Done. Hey, Sunshine, do you like Italian?"

Here we go. "Sometimes."

"There's a great place not far from here. What time you get off?"

"Tonight's not really a good—"

"When is good?"

"Ray, I have to be honest, I usually make it a rule not to date anyone on staff."

"Who said anything about a date? I said dinner."

"If it's just dinner, then yes, I'd love to go sometime, but tonight's really not good. Give me a few weeks to get situated." *And to work on another excuse.* She smiles sweetly, hoping to ease the pain of rejection. "Besides, you can't go out for a big Italian meal if you're in training."

"Okay, Sunshine, but I'm going to hold you to that." The big redhead smiles. "Now listen, if you need anything, don't hesitate to ask."

"I won't. I really should be going, Dr. Foletta's waiting—"

"Foletta won't be in until later this afternoon. Monthly board meeting. Hey, I hear he assigned you that patient of his. What's his name?"

"Michael Gabriel. What do you know about him?"

"Not much. Transferred down from Massachusetts with Foletta. I know the board and medical staff were pretty pissed off when he arrived. Foletta must have pulled quite a few strings."

"What do you mean?"

Raymond looks away, avoiding her eyes. "Ah, never mind."

"Come on. Tell me."

"Nah. I gotta learn to keep my big yap shut. Foletta's your boss. I wouldn't want to say anything that might give you a bad impression."

"I'll keep it between the two of us."

Two more guards enter, waving at Raymond.

"Okay, I'll tell you, but not here. Too many ears with big mouths. We'll talk over dinner. I punch out at six." The yellow teeth flash a triumphant smile.

Raymond holds the gate open for her. Dominique exits the security station and waits for the staff elevator, grimacing. *Way to go, Sunshine. You should have seen that one coming a mile away.*

* * *

Marvis Jones watches her exit the elevator from his security monitor. "Morning, Intern. If you're here to see resident Gabriel, he's confined to his room."

"Can I see him?"

The guard looks up from his paperwork. "Maybe you should wait until the director returns."

"No. I want to speak with him now. And not in the seclusion room."

Marvis appears annoyed. "I highly advise against that. This man has a history of violence and—"

"I'm not sure I'd label one instance in eleven years a history."

They make eye contact. Marvis sees that Dominique will not back down. "Okay, miss, have it your way. Jason, escort Intern Vazquez to room 714. Give her your security transponder, then lock her in."

Dominique follows the guard through a short hall, entering the middle pod of three located in the northern wing. The lounge area is empty.

The guard stops at room 714 and speaks into the hall intercom. "Resident, remain on your bed where I can see you." He unlocks the door, then hands her what appears to be a thick pen. "If you need me, just double-click this pen." He demonstrates, causing the beeper on his belt to vibrate. "Just be careful. Don't allow him to get too close."

"Thank you." She enters the room.

The cell is ten by twelve feet long. Daylight streams in from a three-inch sliver of plastic running vertically along one wall. There are no windows. The bed is iron, fastened to the floor. A desk and set of cubbies are fastened next to it. A sink and steel toilet are anchored by the wall to her right, angled to give its occupant some privacy from the hall.

The bed is made, the room immaculate. Michael Gabriel is sitting on the edge of a magazine-thin mattress. He stands, greeting her with a warm smile. "Good morning, Dominique. I see Dr. Foletta hasn't arrived yet. How fortunate."

"How do you know?"

"Because we're speaking in my cell instead of the interview room. Please, sit on the bed, I'll take the floor. Unless you prefer the toilet?"

She returns his smile, sitting on the edge of the mattress.

Mick leans back against the wall to her left. His black eyes twinkle beneath the fluorescent light.

He wastes no time interrogating her. "So, how was your weekend? Did you read my father's journal?"

"I'm sorry. I only managed to make it through the first ten pages. I did manage to finish Rosenhan's study."

"On being sane in an insane place. Your thoughts, please?"

"I found it interesting, maybe even a bit surprising. His staff had quite the time sorting subjects from patients. Why did you have me read it?"

"Why do you think?" The ebony eyes glitter at her, exuding their animal-like intelligence.

"Obviously you want me to consider the possibility that you're not insane."

"Obviously." He sits up, pulling his heels into a lotus position. "Let's play a game, shall we? Let's imagine it's eleven years ago and you're me, Michael Gabriel, son of the soon-to-be-infamous and quite dead archaeologist, Julius Gabriel. You're standing backstage at Harvard University before a capacity crowd, listening to your father share a lifetime of information with some of the greatest minds in the scientific community. Your heart is pounding with adrenaline because you've worked side by side with your father from the day you were born, and you know how important this lecture is, not just to him but to the future of mankind. Ten minutes into his lecture, you see Julius's longtime nemesis stroll across the stage to another podium. Pierre Borgia, the prodigal son of a political family dynasty, decides he's going to challenge my father's research right there, onstage. Turns out the whole lecture was just one big setup, arranged personally by Borgia to engage my father in a verbal assault designed to destroy his credibility. At least a dozen members of the audience were in on the joke. After ten minutes, Julius couldn't even be heard over his colleagues' laughter."

Mick pauses, momentarily lost in the memory. "My father was a selfless, brilliant man who dedicated his life to the pursuit of truth. Halfway through the most important speaking engagement of his life, he had his entire existence pulled out from under him, his pride destroyed, his life's work—thirty-two years of sacrifice—desecrated in the blink of an eye. Can you imagine the humiliation he must have felt?"

"What happened next?"

"He staggered backstage and fell into my arms, clutching his chest. Julius had a bad heart. With his last ounce of strength, he whispered some instructions to me, then died in my arms."

"And that's when you went after Borgia?"

"The bastard was still onstage, spewing hatred. Despite what I'm sure you've been told, I'm not a violent man"—the dark eyes widen—"but at that moment, I wanted to shove that microphone down his throat. I remember stalking the podium, the world around me moving in slow motion. All I could hear was my own breathing, all I could see was Borgia, but it seemed like I was looking at him through a tunnel. The next thing I know, he's lying on the floor, and I'm bashing his skull in with the mike."

Dominique crosses her legs, disguising the shudder.

"My father's body ended up in the county morgue, cremated without a ceremony. Borgia spent the next three weeks in a private hospital room where his family ran his senatorial campaign, engineering what the press referred to as 'an unprecedented come-from-behind victory.' I sat rotting in a jail cell, no friends or family to bail me out, waiting to face what I assumed were assault charges. Borgia had other ideas. Using his family's political influence, he manipulated the system, striking a deal with the DA and my state-appointed attorney. The next thing I know, I'm being proclaimed a nutcase, the judge shipping me off to some run-down asylum in Massachusetts, a place where Borgia could keep an eye on me, no pun intended."

"You say Borgia manipulated the legal system. How?"

"The same way he manipulates Foletta, my state-appointed keeper. Pierre Borgia rewards loyalty, but God help you if you make his shit list. The judge who sentenced me was promoted to the state supreme court within three months of finding me criminally insane. A short time later our good doctor was made facility director, somehow managing to hopscotch over a dozen more qualified applicants."

The black eyes read her thoughts. "Say what you're really thinking, Dominique. You think I'm a delusional, paranoid schizophrenic."

"I didn't say that. What about the other incident? Are you denying that you brutally attacked a guard?"

Mick stares up at her, the look in his eyes unnerving. "Robert Griggs was more sadist than homosexual, a guard whose acts you'd probably diagnose as being anger-excitation rape. Foletta purposely assigned him to the night shift in my ward a month before my first evaluation was scheduled. Ol' Griggsy used to make his rounds about two in the morning."

Dominique feels her heart pounding.

"Thirty residents per ward, all of us sleeping with one wrist and one ankle shackled to the center posts of our beds. One night Griggs came in drunk, looking for me. I guess he decided I'd make a nice addition to his harem. First thing he did was lubricate me up a bit by shoving a broomstick—"

"Stop! Where were the other guards?"

"Griggs was it. Since there was nothing I could do to stop him, I sweet-talked him, trying to convince him that he'd enjoy things a bit more if both my legs were free. Dumb son of a bitch unlocked my leg shackle. I won't bore you with the details about what happened next—"

"I heard. You scrambled his eggs, so to speak."

"I could have killed him, but I didn't. I'm not a murderer."

"And for that you spent the rest of your days in solitary?"

Mick nods. "Eleven years in the concrete mother. Cold and hard, but she's always there. Now you tell. How old were you when your cousin sodomized you?"

"You'll excuse me, I don't feel comfortable discussing it with you."

"Because you're the psychotherapist and I'm the psycho?"

"No, I mean yes—because I'm the doctor and you're my patient."

"Are we really so different, you and I? Do you think Rosenhan's staff could determine which one of us belongs in this cell?" He leans back against the wall. "May I call you Dom?"

"Yes."

"Dom, solitary confinement can wear on a man. I'm probably suffering from sensory deprivation, and I might even scare you a bit, but I'm just as sane as you or Foletta or that guard posted by the door. What can I do to convince you of that?"

"It's not me you have to convince, it's Dr. Foletta."

"I told you, Foletta works for Borgia, and Borgia will never allow me out."

"I can talk to him. Push him into giving you the same rights and privileges as the other residents. In time, I could—"

"Christ, I can already hear Foletta now. 'Wake up, Intern Vazquez. You're falling for Gabriel's famous conspiracy theory.' He's probably got you convinced that I'm another Ted Bundy."

"Not at all. Mick, I became a psychiatrist to help people like—"

"People like me. Lunatics?"

"Let me finish. You're not a lunatic, but I think you need help. The first step is to convince Foletta to assign an evaluation team to you—"

"No. Foletta won't allow it, and even if he did, there's no time."

"Why isn't there time?"

"My annual evaluation and hearing is coming up in six days. Haven't you figured out why Foletta assigned you to me? You're a student, easily manipulated. 'The patient shows some encouraging signs of improvement, Intern Vazquez, but he's still unfit to rejoin society.' You'll concur with his diagnosis, which is all the evaluation board needs to hear."

Foletta's right, he's good. Maybe he's not as good when he isn't controlling the conversation. "Mick, let's talk a moment about your father's work? On Friday, you mentioned four *Ahau*, three *Kankin*—"

"Humanity's day of doom. I knew you recognized the date."

"It's just a Mayan legend."

"There's truth in many legends."

"Then you do believe we're all going to die in less than four months?"

Mick stares at the floor, shaking his head.

"A simple yes or no will suffice."

"Don't play head games, Dominique."

"How am I playing head games?"

"You know damn well the question as stated reeks of paranoid schizophrenia and delusions of—"

"Mick, it's a simple question." *He's getting upset. Good.*

"You're engaging me in a battle of wits to find weaknesses. Don't. It's not very effective, and you'll lose, which means we'll all lose."

"You're asking me to evaluate your ability to reenter society. How can I do that without asking questions?"

"Ask your questions, but don't set me up for failure. I'll be glad to discuss my father's theories with you, but only if you're really interested. If your goal is to see how far you can push me, then just give me the goddam Rorschach or Thematic Apperception Test and be done with it."

"How am I setting you up for failure?"

Mick is on his feet, moving toward her. Dominique's heart races. She reaches for the pen.

"The very nature of your question condemns me. It's like asking a reverend if his wife knows he masturbates. Either way, he looks bad. If I answer no about the doomsday prediction, then I'll have to justify why I suddenly changed my opinion after eleven years. Foletta will interpret that as a ruse designed to fool the evaluation committee. If I say yes, then you'll concur that I'm just another psycho who believes the sky is falling."

"Then how do you propose I evaluate your sanity? I can't just skirt the issue."

"No, but you can at least examine the evidence with an open mind before you rush to judgment. Some of the greatest minds in history were labeled mad, until the truth came out."

Mick sits down on the opposite end of the bed. Dominique's skin tingles. She is unsure if she is excited or frightened, or perhaps both. She shifts her weight, uncrossing her legs, the pen held nonchalantly in her hand. *He's close enough to strangle me, but if we were in a bar, I'd probably be flirting. . . .*

"Dominique, it's very important, very very important that we trust each other. I need your help, and you need mine, you just don't know it yet. On the soul of my mother I swear I'll never lie to you, but you have to promise to listen with an open mind."

"All right, I'll listen objectively. But the question still stands. Do you believe mankind will end on December 21?"

Mick leans forward, elbows on knees. He stares at the floor, pinching the bridge of his nose between both index fingers. "I assume you're Catholic?"

"I was born Catholic, but raised in a Jewish household since I was thirteen. What about you?"

"My own mother was Jewish, my father, Episcopalian. Do you consider yourself a religious person?"

"Not really."

"Do you believe in God?"

"Yes."

"Do you believe in evil?"

"Evil?" The question startles her. "That's a bit broad. Can you clarify that for me?"

"I'm not talking about men committing heinous acts of murder. I'm referring to evil as an entity unto itself, part of the very fabric of existence." Mick looks up, his eyes focusing on her. "For instance, Judeo-Christian belief is that evil first personified itself by entering the Garden of Eden disguised as a serpent, tempting Eve to bite the apple."

"As a psychiatrist, I don't believe any of us are born evil, or good, for that matter. I believe we have the capacity for both. Free will allows us to choose."

"And what if . . . what if something was influencing your free will without you knowing it?"

"What do you mean?"

"Some people believe there's a malevolent force out there, part of Nature. An intelligence unto itself that has existed on this planet throughout man's history."

"You lost me. What does any of this have to do with the doomsday prophesy?"

"As a rational person, you ask me if I believe humanity is about to end. As a rational person, I ask you to explain to me why every successful ancient civilization predicted the end of humanity. As a rational person, I ask you to tell me why every major religion foretells of an apocalypse and waits for a Messiah to return to rid our world of evil."

"I can't answer that. Like most people, I just don't know."

"Neither did my father. But being a rational man of science, he wanted to find out. And so he dedicated his life and sacrificed his family's happiness in pursuit of the truth. He spent decades investigating ancient ruins in search of clues. And in the end, what he found was so unfathomable that it literally pushed him to the brink of madness."

"What did he find?"

Mick closes his eyes, his voice inflection softening. "Evidence. Evidence deliberately and painstakingly left for us. Evidence that points to the existence of a presence, a presence so malevolent that its ascension will signal the end of humanity."

"Again, I don't understand."

"I can't explain it, all I know is that—somehow—I can feel its presence growing stronger."

He's struggling to remain rational. Keep him talking. "You say this presence is malevolent. How do you know?"

"I just know."

"You're not giving me a whole lot to go on. And the Mayan calendar's not what I'd call evidence—"

"The calendar's only the tip of the iceberg. There are extraordinary, unexplainable landmarks scattered across the face of this planet, astronomically aligned wonders, yet all pieces of a single, giant puzzle. Even the world's greatest skeptics can't refute their existence. The pyramids of Giza and Chichén Itzá. The temples of Angkor Wat and Teotihuacán, Stonehenge, the Piri Re'is maps, and the drawings along the Nazca desert. It took decades of intense labor to erect these ancient marvels, the methodology of which is still a mystery to us. My father discovered a united intelligence behind all of this, the same intelligence responsible for the creation of the Mayan calendar. Of greater importance is the fact that each of these landmarks is linked to a common purpose, the meaning of which has been lost over the millennium."

"And their purpose is?"

"The salvation of humanity."

Foletta's right. He really believes this. "Let me get this straight. Your father believed that each of these ancient sites was designed to save mankind. How can a pyramid or a bunch of desert drawings save us? And save us from what? This malevolent presence?"

The dark eyes stare into her soul. "Yes, but something infinitely worse—something that will arrive to destroy humanity on the December solstice. My father and I were close to resolving the mystery before he died, but there are still vital pieces of the puzzle remaining. If only the Mayan codices hadn't been destroyed."

"Who destroyed them?"

Mick shakes his head as if disappointed. "Don't you even know the history of your own ancestors? The creator of the doomsday calendar, the great teacher, Kukulcán, left behind critical information in the ancient Mayan codices. Four hundred years after his departure, Spain invaded the Yucatán. Cortez was a bearded white man. The Maya mistook him for Kukulcán, the Aztecs for Quetzalcoatl. Both civilizations basically lay down and allowed themselves to be conquered, thinking their Caucasian Messiah had returned to save humanity. The Catholic priests took possession of the codices. They must have been pretty frightened by what they read because the fools burned everything, essentially condemning us to death."

He's getting worked up. "I don't know, Mick. The instructions for the salvation of mankind seem way too important to leave to a bunch of Central American Indians. If Kukulcán was so wise, why didn't he leave the information somewhere else?"

"Thank you."

"For what?"

"For thinking. For using the logical hemisphere of your brain. The information *was* too important to leave to a vulnerable culture like the Maya, or any other ancient culture, for that matter. On the Nazca desert in Peru lies a visual, symbolic message, carved into the pampa in precise, four-hundred-foot glyphs. My father and I were close to interpreting the meaning of the message when he died."

She glances innocently at her watch.

Mick jumps to his feet like a cat, startling her as he grips her shoulders. "Stop treating this as part of your graduation requirements and listen to what I'm saying. Time is a commodity we don't have—"

She stares into his eyes as he rambles, their faces only inches apart. "Mick, let me go—" She fingers the pen.

"Listen to me—you asked me if I believe humanity will come to an end in four months. My answer is yes—unless I can complete my father's work. If not, then we're all going to die."

Dominique double-clicks the pen over and over, her heart racing, her mind full of fear.

"Dominique, please—I need you to get me out of this asylum before the fall equinox."

"Why?" *Keep him talking . . .*

"The equinox is only two weeks away. Its arrival will be announced at every site I mentioned. The Kukulcán pyramid in Chichén Itzá will mark the event along its northern balustrade with the descent of the serpent's shadow. At that moment, Earth will move into an extremely rare galactic alignment. A portal will begin to open at the center of the dark rift of the Milky Way, and the beginning of the end will be upon us."

He's raving . . . Recalling the photo of one-eyed Borgia, she shifts her weight, readying her knee.

"Dominique, I'm not a lunatic. I need you to take me seriously—"

"You're hurting me—"

"I'm sorry, I'm sorry—" He releases his grip. "Listen to me, this is vital. My father believed the evil can still be prevented from rising. I need your help—I need you to get me out of here before the equinox—"

Mick turns as Marvis thrusts his fist in front of his face, the pepper spray blinding him.

"No! No, no, no—"

Too flustered to speak, Dominique pushes the guard aside and runs from the room. She stops at the lounge, her pulse racing.

Marvis locks room 714, then ushers her out of the pod.

Mick continues pounding on the door, crying out to her like a wounded animal.

THE JOURNAL OF JULIUS GABRIEL

And it came to pass, when men began to multiply on the face of the earth, and daughters were born unto them, that the sons of God saw the daughters of men that they were fair; and they took them wives, whomsoever they chose . . . The NEPHILIM were in the earth in those days, and also after that, when the sons of God came in unto the daughters of men, and they bore children to them; the same were the MIGHTY men that were of OLD, the MEN of RENOWN."

—GENESIS 6: 1-2, 4

*T*he Bible. The sacred book of the Jewish and Christian religions. For the archaeologist in search of truth, this document of antiquity can offer vital clues to help fill in the missing gaps in the evolution of man.

Genesis 6 may be the least understood passage in all the Bible, yet it may turn out to be its most revealing. Occurring just before God instructed Noah, it refers to the <u>sons of God</u> and the

Nephilim, a name that literally translates into "the fallen ones," or "they who fell from the sky with fire."

Who were these "fallen ones," these "men of renown"? An important clue may be found in the Genesis Apocryphon, one of the ancient texts uncovered among the Dead Sea Scrolls. In a key passage, Lamech, Noah's father, questions his wife because he thinks his son's conception was the result of her having had intercourse with either an Angel or one of their offspring, a Nephilim.

Did extraterrestrial blood flow through Noah's body? The concept of "fallen" Angels, or "men of renown" interbreeding with human women may seem far-fetched, but there must be some element of truth to it, since the tale, like the story of Noah and the Great Flood, is repeated among different cultures and religions around the world.

As mentioned, I have spent a lifetime investigating mysterious wonders—magnificent structures left upon the face of this planet that have survived the ravages of time. I believe these structures were created by these "men of old, men of renown" for a single purpose—to save our species from annihilation.

We may never know who the Nephilim were, but geological evidence now allows us to reference the time frame in which they first appeared. The fact is—there was a great flood. Earth's last ice age was the culprit, the event dating back some 115,000 years. At the time, massive glaciers covered most of the northern and southern hemispheres, advancing and retreating, eventually peaking some 17,000 years ago. Most of Europe was buried under an ice cap two miles thick. Glaciers in North America pushed as far south as the Mississippi Valley and down to the 37th parallel.

It was the time of Homo sapiens neanderthalensis, Neanderthal Man. It was also around this time in our ancestor's history that the mysterious "fallen ones" arrived.

Perhaps the clans of early Homo sapiens did little to impress these men of renown. Perhaps the Nephilim felt it best that early man return to the evolutionary drawing board. Whatever their response, all we know is that miraculously, and quite suddenly, the world started melting.

It happened fast, triggered by some unknown, cataclysmic development. Millions of cubic miles of ice that had taken more than 40,000 years to advance suddenly melted in less than two millennia. The sea rose 300 to 400 feet, engulfing the land. Sections of Earth, once weighed down by billions of tons of ice, began rising, causing terrible earthquakes. Volcanoes erupted, spewing enormous amounts of carbon dioxide into the atmosphere, increasing global warming. Great tidal waves uprooted jungles, wiping out animals and devastating the land.

The planet became a very hostile place.

By 13,000 BC to 11,000 BC, most of the ice had melted, the climate stabilizing. And emerging from this muck and mire was a new subspecies, Homo sapiens sapiens— modern man.

Evolution or the Bible's story of creation—wherein lies the truth of modern man's rise? As a scientist, I am compelled to believe in Darwinism, but as an archaeologist,

I also recognize that truth is often concealed within myths passed down over millennia. The prophecy foretold by the Mayan calendar falls into the same category. As mentioned earlier, the calendar is a precise scientific instrument that utilizes advanced principles of astronomy and mathematics to derive its calculations. At the same time, the calendar's origins are centered around the most important legend in Mayan history—the *Popol Vuh*—the Mayan book of creation.

The *Popol Vuh* is the Bible of the Mesoamerican Indians. According to the *Popol Vuh*, written hundreds of years after Kukulcán's passing, the world was divided into an Overworld (heaven) a Middleworld (Earth), and an Underworld, a haven of evil known as *Xibalba* (pronounced She-bal-ba). As the ancient Maya looked to the night sky, they saw the dark rift of the Milky Way and interpreted it as being a dark serpent or Black Road (*Xibalba Be*) which led to the Underworld. Appearing in close proximity to the dark rift were the three belt stars of Orion. To the Maya, these stars were said to be the three stones of creation.

As mentioned earlier, the Mayan calendar is divided into five Great Cycles, the first of which began some 25,800 years ago. This is no arbitrary period of time, but the actual length in years that it takes Earth to complete one cycle of precession, the slow wobble of our planet on its axis. (More on this later.)

The creation story retold in the *Popol Vuh* begins some 25,800 years ago when ice still covered much of the Earth. The hero of the tale is a primitive man known as Hun (One) Hunahpu, later revered by the Maya as "First-Father." Hun Hunahpu's great passion in life was to play the ancient ball game known as *Tlachtli*. One day, the Lords of the Underworld, speaking through *Xibalba Be* (the Black Road), challenged Hun Hunahpu and his brother to a game. Hun Hunahpu accepted and entered the portal to the Black Road, which was represented in Mayan legends as the mouth of a great serpent.

But the Underworld lords had no intention of playing the game. Using trickery and deceit, they defeated the brothers and decapitated them, hanging Hun Hunahpu's head in the crook of a calabash tree. The Evil Lords then set the tree aside, forbidding anyone to visit it.

After a great many years, a brave young woman named Blood Moon ventured down the Black Road to see if the legend was true. Approaching the tree to pick some fruits, she was startled to find Hun Hunahpu's head, which spit into her palm, magically impregnating her. The woman fled, the Under Lords unable to destroy her before she could escape.

Blood Moon (also known as First-Mother) would give birth to twin sons. As the years passed, the boys grew into strong, capable warriors. Upon reaching adulthood, their genetic calling would push them to make the journey down the Black Road to *Xibalba* to challenge the evil ones and avenge their father's death. Once more, the Lords of the Underworld would use deceit, but this time, the Hero Twins would triumph, banishing evil while resurrecting their long-lost father.

What can we garner from the creation myth? The name, Hun or One Hunahpu, equates to the calendric name *One Ahau*, a day-sign meaning *first sun*. The first sun of the new year is the December solstice sun. The prophesied date of doom ends on the winter solstice in the year 2012—exactly one 25,800 year processional cycle from the very first day of the Mayan calendar!

Using a computer program that allows one to forecast the cosmos at any date in history, I have calculated the night sky as it will appear in 2012. Beginning at the time of the autumnal equinox, an extremely rare astronomical alignment will occur between the galactic and solar planes. The dark rift of the Milky Way will appear to sit on the Earth's horizon, and the Sun will begin to move into alignment at its center point. This stellar shift will culminate on the day of the winter solstice, a day considered by most ancient cultures to be the Day of the Dead. On this date, for the first time in 25,800 years, the Sun will move in conjunction with the crossing point of the Milky Way and the ecliptic in Sagittarius, marking the alignment of the Galactic Equator, the exact center of the galaxy.

Somehow, the Mayan calendar accurately predicted this celestial event more than 3,000 years ago. Interpreting the creation myth, the galactic alignment will climax with the opening of a cosmic portal that bridges the gap between our planet and the Mayan Underworld, Xibalba.

Call it fiction, call it fact, but somehow this intergalactic alignment will culminate in the deaths of every man, woman, and child on the face of our planet.

—Excerpt from the Journal of Professor Julius Gabriel,

Ref. Catalogue 1978–79   pages 43–52
    Catalogue 1998–99   pages 11–75

Wake up, Intern Vazquez. You're falling for Gabriel's famous conspiracy theory."

"I disagree." Dominique returns Dr. Foletta's cold stare from the opposite side of his desk. "There's no reason that Mick Gabriel shouldn't be assigned a full support team."

Foletta leans back in the swivel chair, his weight threatening the coiled springs. "Now let's just calm down for a moment. Look at you—you've spoken with the resident twice, and already you're making diagnoses. In my opinion, you're becoming emotionally involved, something we spoke about on Friday. This is exactly why I recommended to the board not to bring in a team at this time."

"Sir, I assure you, I'm not emotionally involved. It just seems to me that people have rushed to judgment in this case. Yes, I agree he's suffering from delusions, but they could easily be attributed to having spent the last eleven years in solitary. And as far as violence, there's nothing that I've seen in Mick's file which points to anything but a onetime case of simple assault."

"What about the attack on the guard?"

"Mick told me the guard tried to rape him."

Foletta pinches the bridge of his nose with two stubby fingers, grinning sheepishly as he shakes his great head back and forth. "He set you up, Intern Vazquez. I told you he's clever."

Dominique's stomach flutters. "You're saying it was all a lie?"

"Of course. He's preying on your maternal instincts, and he hit a grand slam."

Dominique stares at her lap, dumbfounded. Was Mick lying? Was she really that gullible? *Idiot! You wanted to believe him. You set yourself up.*

"Intern, you're not going to get very far with your patients if you believe everything they tell you. Next thing, he'll have you convinced the world is coming to an end."

Dominique sits back in her chair, feeling foolish.

Foletta sees the expression on her face and laughs out loud, causing his plump cheeks to turn red and dimple. He takes a breath, wiping tears from his eyes as he reaches into a cardboard box at the foot of the desk. He removes a bottle of scotch and two coffee mugs, pouring them each a shot.

Dominique drains the cup, feeling the liquid sear its way through her stomach lining.

"Feeling better?" The words, whispered and grainy, are spoken in a fatherly manner.

She nods.

"Despite what he tells you, Intern, I happen to like Mick. I don't want to see him in solitary confinement any more than you do."

The phone rings. Foletta answers it, eyeing her. "It's one of the security guards. Says he's waiting for you downstairs."

Shit. "Could you tell him I'm tied up in an important meeting? Tell him I can't make it tonight."

Foletta relays the message, then hangs up.

"Doctor, what about Mick's annual evaluation. Was that also a lie?"

"No, that was the truth; in fact it's on my list of things to discuss with you. I know it's a bit unusual, but I'll need you to sign off on that."

"What are you recommending?"

"That depends on you. If you can remain objective, then I'll recommend that you stay on as his clinical psychiatrist during your stay here."

"Mick's suffering from sensory deprivation. I'd want him to have access to the yard, as well as the rest of our rehab facilities."

"He just attacked you—"

"No he didn't. He just got a little excited, and I panicked."

Foletta leans back and stares at the ceiling as if weighing a great decision. "All right, Intern, here's the deal. Sign off on my annual evaluation, and I'll restore full privileges. If he improves, I'll assign a full rehab team to Mick in January. Fair enough?"

Dominique smiles. "Fair enough."

The yard at the South Florida Evaluation and Treatment Center is a rectangular stretch of lawn surrounded on all four sides. The L-shape of the main building encloses the perimeter to the east and south, the north and western borders walled off by a twenty-foot stark white concrete barrier topped with coils of barbed wire.

There are no doors in the yard. To exit the grass-covered atrium, one must ascend three flights of cement steps which lead to an open walkway running the length of the southern side of the facility. This mezzanine accesses the third-floor gymnasium, group-therapy rooms, an arts and crafts center, computer room, and a movie area.

Dominique takes cover beneath the aluminum roof extending out from the third-floor walkway as the lead gray clouds roll in from the east. Two dozen residents evacuate the yard as the first drops of afternoon rain splatter against the overhang.

A solitary figure remains behind.

Mick Gabriel continues walking along the perimeter of the yard, hands shoved deep in his pockets. He feels the humid air turn cool as the clouds open up overhead. Within seconds he is immersed in the downpour, his white uniform soaked, clinging to his wiry, muscular frame.

He continues walking, his soaked canvas tennis shoes sinking in the soft grass, the rainwater squishing between his toes and socks. With each step, he recites the name of another year of the Mayan calendar, a mental exercise that he uses to keep his mind sharp. *Three* Ix, *four* Cauac, *five* Kan, *six* Muluc . . .

The dark eyes focus on the concrete wall, seeking its flaws, his mind searching for options.

Dominique watches him through a veil of rain, feeling remorse. *You blew it. He trusted you. Now he thinks you betrayed him.*

Foletta approaches. He exchanges waves with several abnormally exuberant residents, then joins her.

"Is he still refusing to speak with you?"

Dominique nods. "It's been almost two weeks. Every day, the same routine. He eats breakfast, then meets with me and stares at the floor for a full hour. Once he gets to the yard, he paces back and forth until dinner. He never mingles with other residents and never says a word. He just paces."

"You'd think he'd be grateful; after all, you *are* the one responsible for his newfound freedom."

"This isn't freedom."

"No, but it's a big step up from eleven years in solitary."

"I think he really believed I could have gotten him out."

Foletta's expression gives him away.

"What, Doctor? Was he right? Could I have—"

"Whoa, slow down, Intern. Mick Gabriel's not going anywhere, at least not right now. As you've seen for yourself, he's still quite unstable, posing a danger not only to himself but to others. Keep working with him, encourage him to participate in his own therapy. Anything can happen."

"You *are* still planning to assign a rehab team."

"We agreed on January, provided he behaves himself. You should tell him about it."

"I've tried." She watches as Mick strides past the flight of stairs directly below them. "He no longer trusts me."

Foletta pats her on the back. "Get over it."

"I'm not doing him any good. Maybe he needs someone with more experience."

"Nonsense. I'll instruct his orderlies that he's no longer permitted to leave his room unless he actively participates in his therapy sessions."

"Forcing him to talk won't help."

"This isn't a country club, Intern. We have rules. If a resident refuses to cooperate, he forfeits his privileges. I've seen cases like this before. If you don't act now, Mick will crawl inside his own head, and you'll lose him forever."

Foletta signals to an orderly. "Joseph, escort Mr. Gabriel out of the rain. We can't have our residents getting sick on us."

"No, wait, he's my patient, I'll get him." Dominique pulls her hair into a tight bun, removes her shoes, then descends the two flights of stairs to the yard. She is drenched by the time she catches up with Mick.

"Hey, stranger, mind if I join you?"

He ignores her.

Dominique keeps pace, the rain pelting her face. "Come on, Mick, talk to me. I've been apologizing all week. What did you expect me to do? I had to sign off on Foletta's report."

She gets a hard look.

The rain comes down heavier, forcing her to shout. "Mick, slow down."

He continues walking.

She dashes ahead of him, then takes a fighting stance, fists up, blocking his way. "Okay, buddy, don't force me to kick your ass."

Mick stops. He looks up, the rain streaming down his angular face. "You let me down."

"I'm sorry," she whispers, dropping her fists. "Why did you lie to me about the guard attacking you?"

A pained expression. "So truth is no longer to be judged by your heart, but by your ambition, is that it? I thought we were friends."

She feels a lump growing in her throat. "I want to be your friend, but I'm also your psychiatrist. I did what I thought was best."

"Dominique, I gave you my word that I'd never lie to you." He lifts his head, pointing to the three-inch scar along his jawline. "Before Griggs tried to rape me, he threatened to cut my throat."

Goddam you, Foletta. "Mick, Jesus, I'm sorry. At our last meeting, when you flipped out on me—"

"My fault. I got excited. I've been locked up for so long—sometimes, well sometimes it's just hard to stay calm. I don't socialize well, but I swear, I never would have hurt you."

She sees tears in his eyes. "I believe you."

"You know, being outside has helped. It's caused me to think about a lot of different things . . . selfish things, really. My childhood, the lifestyle I was raised in . . . how I ended up in here, whether I'll ever get out. There are so many things that I've never done . . . so many things I would change if I could. I loved my parents, but, for the first time, I realize that I really hate what they did. I hate the fact that they never gave me a choice—"

"We can't choose our parents, Mick. What's important is that you not blame yourself. None of us have any control over the deck or the hand we've been dealt. What we do have is total responsibility as to how we play the hand. I think I can help you regain control of that."

He moves closer, the rain pouring down both sides of his face. "May I ask you a personal question?"

"Yes."

"Do you believe in destiny?"

"Destiny?"

"Do you think our lives, our futures have been . . . never mind, forget it—"

"Do I think what happens to us is prearranged?"

"Yes."

"I think we have choices. I think it's up to us to choose the right destiny to pursue."

"Have you ever been in love?"

She stares helplessly into the glistening puppy-dog eyes. "I've been close a few times. It never seemed to work out." She smiles. "Guess they weren't meant to be part of my destiny."

"If I wasn't . . . incarcerated. If we had met under different circumstances. Do you think you could have loved me?"

Oh, shit . . . She swallows hard, her pulse causing the base of her throat to twitch. "Mick, let's get out of the rain. Come on—"

"There's something about you. It's not just a physical attraction, it's like I've known you, or knew you in another life."

"Mick—"

"Sometimes I get these premonitions. I felt one the moment I first saw you."

"You said it was the perfume."

"It was something more. I can't explain it. All I know is that I care about you, and the emotions are confusing."

"Mick, I'm flattered, really I am, but I think you're right. Your emotions are confused, and—"

He smiles sadly, ignoring her words. "You're so beautiful." Leaning forward, he touches her cheek, then reaches out and loosens the knot of jet-black hair.

64

She closes her eyes, feeling the length of hair unravel down her back, becoming heavy with the rain. *Stop this! He's your patient, a mental patient, for God's sake.* "Mick, please. Foletta's watching. Could you just come inside? Let's talk inside—"

He stares at her, the ebony eyes despondent, revealing a soul tortured by forbidden beauty. " 'She doth teach the torches to burn bright. It seems she hangs upon the cheek of night, as a rich jewel in an Ethiop's ear—' "

"What did you say?" Dominique's heart is pounding.

"*Romeo and Juliet.* I used to read it to my mother at her bedside." He lifts her hand, bringing it to his lips. " 'And, touching hers, make blessed my rude hand. Did my heart love till now? Foreswear it, sight, for I never saw true beauty till this night.' "

The rain subsides. She sees the two orderlies approach. "Mick, listen to me. I forced Foletta to sign off on assigning you to a rehab team. You could be out of here within six months."

Mick shakes his head. "We'll never see the day, my love. Tomorrow's the autumnal equinox—" He turns, becoming anxious as he spots the men in white. "Read my father's journal. The fate of this world is about to cross another threshold, vaulting the human race to the top of the endangered species list—"

The two orderlies each grab an arm.

"Hey, go easy on him!"

Mick turns to face her as he is led away, the humidity rising off his body like steam. " 'How silver-sweet sound lovers' tongues by night, like softest music to attending ears.' You're in my heart, Dominique. Destiny has brought us together. I can feel it. I can feel it . . ."

JOURNAL OF JULIUS GABRIEL

*B*efore we continue on our journey through man's history, allow me to introduce you to a term unfamiliar to most of the public: forbidden archaeology. It seems that when it comes to the subject of human origins and antiquity, the scientific community is not always open-minded to evidence that may contradict the already established models of evolution. In other words, sometimes it's easier just to refute the facts than attempt to come up with a feasible explanation of what can't be explained.

Good thing Columbus used a Piri Re'is map instead of the accepted European version, or he'd have sailed right off the edge of the world.

When man thinks he knows everything, he ceases to learn. This unfortunate reality has led to the suppression of much important research. Because one cannot get published without the approval of a major university, it becomes nearly impossible to challenge the dominant views of the day. I have seen learned colleagues try, only to be ostracized, their reputations destroyed and their careers ruined, even though the evidence supporting their controversial viewpoints appeared insurmountable.

Egyptian Egyptologists are the worst of the lot, hating it

when scientists seek to challenge the accepted history of their ancient sites, becoming especially nasty when foreigners question the age and origin of their monolithic structures.

This brings us to methods of dating, the most controversial aspect of archaeology. The use of carbon-14 dating on bones and coal residue is both easy and accurate, but the technique cannot be applied to stone. As a result, archaeologists will often date an ancient site according to other more datable relics found within the vicinity of the dig, or, when none are found, merely by conjecture, leading to a wide range of human error.

Having stated this, let us return to our journey through history and time.

It was sometime after the Great Flood that the first civilizations began cropping up across the world. What we now accept as truth is that recorded history began in Mesopotamia in the Tigris-Euphrates river valley, sometime around 4000 BC, with some of the earliest urban remains found in Jericho dating back as far as 7000 BC. But new evidence now indicates that another civilization, a superior civilization, had flourished even earlier along the banks of the Nile, and it is <u>this</u> more ancient culture and its wise leader who left us the first of the mysterious wonders that may ultimately be responsible for saving our species from annihilation.

There are many temples, pyramids, and monuments spread across the Egyptian landscape, but none compare to the magnificent marvels erected in Giza. It is here, on the west bank of the Nile, that an incredible site plan was laid out, consisting of the Sphinx, its two temples, and the three great pyramids of Egypt.

Why am I speaking of the great pyramids of Giza? How could these ancient monoliths possibly be related to the Mayan calendar and the Mesoamerican culture, halfway across the world?

After three decades of research, I finally realized that, in order to resolve the riddle of the doomsday prophecy, one must put aside the preconceived notions of time, distance, cultures, and surface impressions when analyzing the ancient clues surrounding humanity's great mystery.

Allow me a moment to elaborate.

The largest and most unexplainable structures ever erected by man are the pyramids of Giza, the Temples of Angkor, located in the jungles of Cambodia, the pyramids in the ancient Mesoamerican city of Teotihuacán (also known as the "place of the gods"), Stonehenge, the Nazca drawings, the ruins of Tiahuanaco, and the Kukulcán pyramid in Chichén Itzá. Each and every one of these ancient marvels, built by different cultures in different parts of the world at vastly different periods in man's prehistory, are nevertheless related to humanity's impending doom referenced in the Mayan calendar. The architects and engineers who erected these cities all possessed a vast knowledge of astronomy and mathematics that easily exceeded the knowledge base of their day. Furthermore, the location for each of the ancient structures had been painstakingly set in accordance with the equinox and solstice, and, incredible as it seems, to each other, for if one wished to divide the surface of our planet using distinct landmarks, then these structures would easily complete the task.

But it is what we cannot see that forever links these monolithic structures to one another, for at the heart of their design lies a common mathematical equation that demonstrates an advanced knowledge—a knowledge of precession.

Again, a brief explanation:

As our planet floats through space on its yearly journey around the Sun, it rotates on its axis once every 24 hours. As the Earth spins, the gravitational pull of the moon causes it to tilt approximately 23.5 degrees to the vertical. Add the Sun's gravitational pull on our planet's equatorial bulge and you have a wobble at the Earth's axis, similar to that of a spinning top. This wobble is called precession. Once every 25,800 years, the moving axis traces a circular pattern in the sky, relocating the position of the celestial poles and equinoxes. This gradual westward drift also causes the signs of the zodiac no longer to correspond to their respective constellations.

The Greek astronomer and mathematician, Hipparchus, is credited with having discovered precession in 127 BC. Today we know the Egyptians, Mayans, and Hindu understood precession hundreds, if not thousands of years earlier.

In the early 1990s, archaeoastronomer Jane Sellers discovered that the Osiris myth of ancient Egypt had been encoded with key numbers that the Egyptians had used to calculate the Earth's varying degrees of precession. Of these, a particular set of digits stood out among the rest: 4320.

More than a thousand years before the birth of Hipparchus, both the Egyptians and Mayans had somehow managed to calculate the value of pi, the ratio of the diameter of a circle, sphere, or hemisphere, to its circumference. At 481.3949 feet, the Great Pyramid's height, multiplied by 2pi, precisely equals its base (3,023.16 feet). Incredible as it seems, the perimeter of the pyramid comes within 20 feet of equaling the diameter of the Earth, when our planet's dimensions are scaled down to a ratio equaling 1:43,200, numbers representing our mathematical code of precession. Using the same ratio, the Earth's polar radius is equal to the pyramid's height.

It turns out that the Great Pyramid is a geodetic marker lying almost exactly on the 30th parallel. If its measurements were projected onto a flat surface (with its apex representing the North Pole and its perimeter the equator), the monolith's dimensions would equal the Northern Hemisphere, scaled down to, again—1:43,200.

We know it takes 4,320 years for the equinoctial Sun to complete a precessional shift of two zodiacal constellations or 60 degrees. Multiply this number by 100 and you have 43,200, the number of days noted in the Mayan Long Count calendar equaling 6 Katuns, one of the key numerical values the ancient Maya used when they calculated precession. A complete cycle of precession takes 25,800 years. If you add up all the years of the Popol Vuh's five cycles, the time period equates exactly to one precessional cycle.

Hidden within the dense Kampuchea jungle in Cambodia are the magnificent Hindu Temples of Angkor. The bas-reliefs and statues proliferating on the complex include precessional symbols, the most popular being a gigantic serpent (Naga), its midsection coiled around a sacred mountain in the milky ocean, or Milky Way. The two ends of the serpent are being used as a rope in a cosmic contest of tug-of-war featuring two teams: one representing light and good, the other, darkness and evil. This movement, combined with the churning of the Milky Way, represents the Hindu interpretation of precession. The Puranas, the sacred scriptures of the Hindu, refers to the four ages of the Earth as Yugas. Our present day Yuga, the Kali Yuga, has a duration of 432,000 mortal years. At the end of this epoch, the scriptures claim the human race shall face destruction.

The ancient Egyptians, Maya, and Hindu—three distinct cultures located in different thirds of the world, each existing at different intervals in our past. Three cultures who shared a common, advanced knowledge of science, cosmology, and mathematics and used their wisdom to create mysterious architectural wonders, each structure constructed for a single, hidden purpose.

The oldest of these structures are the great pyramids in Giza and their timeless guardian, the Sphinx. Lying to the northwest of the temple known as the House of Osiris, the magnificent limestone figure of the human-headed lion is the largest sculpture in the world, towering six stories high and extending 240 feet in length. The creature itself is a cosmic marker, its gaze oriented precisely due east, as if waiting for the Sun to rise.

How old is the Giza complex? Egyptologists swear by the date of 2475 BC (a period that just happens to fit Egyptian folklore). For a long time it was difficult to argue, as neither the Great Pyramid nor Sphinx left behind any determining markings.

Or so we thought.

Enter the American scholar, John Anthony West. West discovered that the 25-foot-deep trench surrounding the Sphinx exhibited unmistakable signs of erosion. Upon further investigation, a team of geologists determined that the damage had not been caused by wind or sand, but purely from rainfall.

The last time the Nile Valley saw this type of weather was some 13,000 years ago, the resulting effects of the Great Flood, which occurred at the end of the last ice age. In the year 10,450 BC, Giza was not only fertile and green, its eastern sky also faced the very figure the Sphinx was modeled after, the constellation of Leo.

While all this was happening, Robert Bauval, a Belgian construction engineer, realized the three pyramids of Giza (when viewed from above) had been plotted precisely to the three belt stars of Orion.

Using a sophisticated computer program designed to account for all precessional movements from any view of the night sky at any geographical location, Bauval discovered that, while the Giza pyramids and the stars of Orion's belt had been somewhat aligned in 2475 BC, an infinitely more accurate alignment had occurred in 10,450 BC. During this latter date, the dark rift of the Milky Way had not only appeared over Giza, but would have mirrored the meridional course of the River Nile.

As mentioned earlier, the ancient Maya considered the Milky Way a cosmic snake, its dark rift referred to as <u>Xibalba Be</u> the Black Road to the Underworld. Both the Mayan calendar and the <u>Popol Vuh</u> reference the concepts of creation and death as originating from this cosmic birth canal.

Why were the three pyramids of Giza aligned to Orion's belt? What is the significance of the precessional number, 4320? What was the real motivation that drove our ancestors to erect the monuments of Giza, the pyramids of Teotihuacán, and the Temples of Angkor?

How are these three sites linked to the Mayan prophecy of doom?

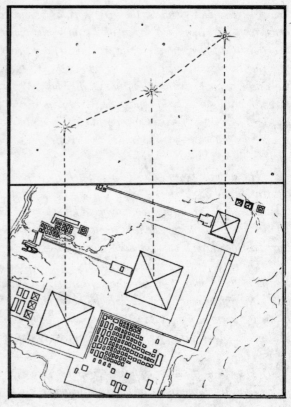

—Excerpt from the Journal of Professor Julius Gabriel,

Ref. Catalogue 1993–94   pages 3–108
Floppy Disk 4: File name: ORION-12

SEPTEMBER 23, 2012
MIAMI, FLORIDA

3:30 A.M.

Michael Gabriel's dream unravels into a night terror. Worse than any nightmare, it is a violent, recurring dream that creeps into his subconscious—a whisper in his brain that takes him back to a pivotal moment in his past.

He is back in Peru, a young boy again, not yet twelve. Staring out his bedroom window at the sleepy village of Ingenio, he listens to the muffled voices coming from the next room. He hears his father speaking to the physician in Spanish. He hears his father sobbing.

The adjoining door opens. "Michael, come in please."

Mick can smell the disease. It is a rancid odor, an odor of sweaty bedsheets and intravenous bags, of vomit and pain and human anguish.

His mother is lying in bed, her face jaundiced. She looks up at him through sunken eyes and squeezes his hand weakly.

"Michael, the doctor is going to teach you how to administer your mother's drugs. It's very important that you pay close attention and do it correctly."

The silver-haired physician looks him over. *"He's a bit young, Señor—"*

"Show him."

The physician pulls back the sheet, revealing a porticath tube protruding from his mother's bandaged right shoulder.

Mick sees the tube and is frightened. *"Pop, please, can't the nurse—"*

"We can't afford the nurse anymore, and I need to complete my work in Nazca. We talked about this, son. You can do this. I'll be home every evening. Now concentrate, focus your mind on what the doctor's going to show you."

Mick stands by the bed, watching the physician closely as he fills the syringe with morphine. He memorizes the dosage, then feels his stomach turn as the needle is injected into the porticath, his mother's eyes rolling upward . . .

"No! No! No!"

Michael Gabriel's screams wake every resident in the pod.

Deep Space

The lightweight probe Pluto-Kuiper Express soars through space, eight years, ten months, and thirteen days from home, a mere fifty-eight days and eleven hours from its destination, the planet Pluto and its moon, Charon. Resembling a high-tech satellite dish, the science craft continues broadcasting its uncoded signal back to Earth by way of its 1.5-meter high-gain antenna.

Without warning, an immense ocean of radio energy blasts through space at the speed of light, the low end of a hyperwave pulse bathing the satellite in its high-decibel transmission. In a nanosecond, the probe's telecommunication subsystem and monolithic microwave integrated circuits (MMICs) are fried beyond recognition.

NASA:
Deep Space Network Facility

2:06 P.M.

Jonathan Lunine, head of the Pluto Express science team, leans against a row of mission-control consoles, half-listening to Dr. Jeremy Armentrout as the engineer addresses the new members of their ground team.

"—the PKE's high-gain antenna continuously transmits one of three possible tones. These essentially translate to: Everything's okay, data ready to downlink, or there's a serious problem that needs immediate attention. Over the last eight years, these signals have been monitored by—"

Lunine stifles a yawn. Three consecutive eighteen-hour shifts have taken their toll, and he is beyond ready to start the weekend. *Another hour in the briefing room, then it's home to an afternoon nap. Redskins play the Eagles tomorrow, should be a good game . . .*

"Jon, can I see you please!" A technician is standing by his control console, signaling urgently. Lunine notices beads of sweat across the man's forehead. The operators on either side appear to be working feverishly.

"What's the situation?"

"We've lost contact with the PKE."

"Solar wind?"

"Not this time. My board's showing a massive power overload affecting the entire SDST communications system and both flight computers. Sensors, electronics, motive effectors—everything's down. I've ordered a complete systems analysis, but God only knows what effect this is having on the PKE's trajectory."

Lunine signals for Dr. Armentrout to join them. "Flight control has lost contact with the PKE."

"Backup systems?"

"Everything's down."

"Damn." Armentrout rubs his temple. "First priority, of course, is to reestablish contact. It's also imperative that we relocate and continue to track the probe before too much time elapses and we lose the PKE in deep space."

"You have a suggestion?"

"Remember back in the summer of '98 when we lost contact with SOHO for about a month? Before regaining contact, we were able to locate her by beaming radio signals from Arecibo's big dish off the satellite, then picking up the bounce using NASA's dish in California."

"I'll get Arecibo on the line."

National Astronomy and Ionosphere Center
Arecibo, Puerto Rico

"Understood, Jon." Robert Pasquale, director of operations at Arecibo, hangs up the phone, then blows his nose for the umpteenth time before paging his assistant. "Arthur, come in here, please."

Astrophysicist Arthur Krawitz enters his director's office. "Christ, Bob, you look awful."

"It's my goddam sinuses. First day of fall, and my head's already pounding. Have those Russian astronomers finished with the big dish yet?"

"About ten minutes ago. What's up?"

"I just received an emergency call from NASA. Seems they've lost contact with Pluto-Kuiper and want us to help relocate it. They're downloading the probe's last-known coordinates to your computer as we speak and are asking that we use the big dish to beam a radio beacon into space. If we get lucky, we'll bounce a signal that NASA will be able to detect using their big dish in Goldstone."

"I'm on it. Oh, what about SETI? You know Kenny Wong's going to want to listen in using SERENDIP's receivers? Is it a problem if—"

"Christ, Arthur, I don't care. If the kid wants to waste his life waiting for E.T. to come calling, it's no skin off my aching nose. If you need me, I'll be in my room, overdosing on Sudafed."

When Cornell's College of Engineering first conceived of the idea of building the world's most powerful radio telescope, they searched for years for a site that offered a natural geological depression possessing the approximate dimensions of a giant reflector bowl. The site had to be under US jurisdiction, and, since the dish would not move, the location also had be as close as possible to the equator so the moon and planets would appear almost directly overhead. Their search led them to the limestone karst mountain range of northern Puerto Rico, a lush, isolated terrain featuring deep valleys surrounded by towering hills that would shield the telescope from outside radio interference.

Completed in 1963, with upgrades in 1974, 1997, and 2010, the Arecibo telescope appears to first-time visitors as an enormous alien structure of concrete and steel. The 1,000-foot-diameter dish, made of almost 40,000 perforated aluminum panels, hangs concave side up, filling up the entire crater-shaped karst sinkhole like a giant, 167-foot-deep salad bowl. Dangling 426 feet above the center of the dish is the telescope's azimuth arm, Gregorian dome, and secondary and tertiary dishes. This 600-ton spiderweb of steel is held aloft by twelve cables attached to three immense obelisk-shaped support towers and numerous anchor blocks located around the perimeter of the valley.

Constructed within the mountainous limestone hillside overlooking the telescope stands Arecibo's lab, a multistoried concrete structure housing the computers and technical equipment used to run the facility. Adjacent to the lab is a four-story dormitory containing a dining room and library, as well as a heated pool and tennis court.

Arecibo's behemoth telescope was designed to be used by scientists in four separate fields. Radio astronomers use the dish to analyze the natural radio energy emitted by galaxies, pulsars, and other celestial bodies as far as ten million light-years away. Radar astronomers come to Arecibo to bounce powerful beams of radio energy off objects within our solar system, then record and study the echoes. Atmospheric scientists and astronomers use the telescope to study the Earth's ionosphere, analyzing the atmosphere and its dynamic relationship with our planet.

The last field of study involves the SETI program, or Search for Extraterrestrial Intelligence. SETI's goal of locating intelligent life within the cosmos uses a twofold approach. The first is to send radio transmissions into deep space in the hopes that, someday, an intelligent species will receive our message of peace. SETI's second approach uses the Gregorian dome and its two smaller dishes to receive incoming radio waves from deep space in an attempt to discern an intelligible pattern, proving that we are not alone in the universe.

Astronomers refer to the task of hunting for radio signals in the vastness of space as searching for a needle in the cosmic haystack. To simplify the search, Professor Frank Drake and his colleagues in Project Ozma, the founders of SETI, concluded that any intelligent life existing within the cosmos would (logically) have to be associated with water. With all of the radio frequencies to choose from, astronomers hypothesized that an extraterrestrial intelligence would broadcast its radio signals at 1.42 gigahertz, the point on the electromagnetic spectrum at which energy is released from hydrogen. Drake dubbed the region the waterhole, and since then, it has been the exclusive hunting ground for all interstellar radio signals.

An adjunct of the SETI project is SERENDIP, or the Search for Extraterrestrial Radio Emissions from Nearby Developed Intelligent Populations. With telescope time expensive and difficult to come by, SERENDIP simply piggybacks its receivers to the big dish during all observations. The major limitation for these SETI scientists is that they have no say in what they are listening to, their targets being chosen for them by their host.

Kenny Wong stands on the concrete-and-steel overlook situated just outside of the lab's huge bay windows. The disgruntled Princeton graduate student leans against the protective railing and stares at the tangle of metal and cable suspended over the heart of the big dish.

Fucking NASA. It's not enough that they cut our funding, now they have to hog telescope time to locate their damn probe . . .

"Hey, Kenny—"

Piggybacking is a goddam waste of time if we're not even tuned into the waterhole. I might as well hit the beach, for all the fucking good I'm doing here—

"Kenny, get the hell in here, your equipment's giving me a headache!"

"Huh?"

The grad student rushes into the lab, his pulse racing as he hears a sound he has never heard before.

"That damn computer of yours has been beeping like that for five minutes." Arthur Krawitz removes his bifocals and shoots him a nasty look. "Disconnect the goddam thing, will you, it's driving me crazy."

Kenny pushes past him, hurriedly typing in commands to activate the computer's search and identification program. The SERENDIP-IV program can simultaneously examine 168 million frequency channels every 1.7 seconds.

Within seconds, a response flashes on his monitor, taking his breath away.

Candidate Signal: Detected

"Oh my fucking God . . ."

Kenny races for the spectra analyzer, his heart pounding in his ears. He verifies that the analog signal is being recorded and digitally formatted.

Candidate Signal: Nonrandom

"Jesus Christ—it's a real fucking signal! Oh, shit, Arthur, I gotta call someone, I've got to verify before we lose it!"

Arthur is laughing hysterically. "Kenny, it's just the Pluto probe. NASA must have gotten it back on-line."

"What? Oh, shit." Kenny collapses in a chair, out of breath. "God, for a second there—"

"For a second there, you looked like Curly from the Three Stooges. Just sit there and calm down while I contact NASA and verify, okay?"

"Okay."

The physicist strikes a preset key on his video communicator, placing them directly on-line with NASA. Dr. Armentrout's face appears on his monitor. "Arthur, good to see you. Hey, thanks for helping us out."

"Thanks for what? I see you're already back on-line with the PKE."

"Negative, we're still dead as a doornail. What made you think that?"

Kenny rushes over. "NASA, this is Kenny Wong with SETI. We're picking up a deep-space radio transmission. We thought it was the PKE."

"It's not coming from us, but keep in mind the Pluto probe uses an uncoded carrier. Plenty of pranksters out there, SETI. What's the frequency of the signal?"

"Stand by." Kenny returns to his computer and types in a series of commands. "Oh, geez, we're at 4,320 MHz. God dammit, Arthur, that microwave band's way too high for any Earth-based telecommunications or even a geosynchronous satellite. Wait, I'll feed the signal through a speaker so we can listen."

"Kenny, wait—"

A piercing high-pitched tone screeches from the speakers, the searing blast of sound shattering Arthur's bifocals while causing the bay windows to rattle in their frames.

Kenny pulls the plug, rubbing his ringing ears.

Arthur is staring at the fragments of glass in his hands. "Unbelievable. How strong is the signal? Where's it coming from?"

"Still calculating the source, but the strength is off my puny scale. We're looking at a radio brilliance about a thousand times stronger than anything we could transmit from Arecibo." A chill runs down Kenny's spine. "God dammit, Arthur, this is it—this is the real thing!"

"Just calm down a second. Before we end up looking like the Stooges of the new millennium, get on-line and start confirming the signal. Start with the VLA in New Mexico. I'll contact Ohio State—"

"Arthur—"

Krawitz turns to face the video com. "Go ahead, Jeremy."

A half dozen technicians have crowded around a pale-faced Dr. Armentrout. "Arthur, we just confirmed the signal."

"You confirmed—" Krawitz feels light-headed, like he is living in a dreamworld. "Have you targeted a source?"

"Still working on that. We're running into a lot of interference because of the—"

"Arthur, I've got a preliminary trajectory!" Kenny is on his feet, very excited. "The signal's originating from the constellation of Orion, somewhere in the vicinity of Orion's belt."

Chichén Itzá
Yucatán Peninsula

4:00 P.M.

The ancient Mayan city of Chichén Itzá, located in the lowlands of the Yucatán Peninsula, is one of the great archaeological wonders of the world. Several hundred buildings occupy this twelve-hundred-year-old jungle-enclosed site, including some of the most intricately carved temples and shrines in all of Mesoamerica.

The actual origins of the city known as Chichén date back to A.D. 435. After a period of abandonment, the city was rediscovered by the Itzaes, a Maya-speaking tribe who occupied the region until the late eighth century, when the Toltecs migrated east from Teotihuacán. Under the tutelage and leadership of the great teacher, Kukulcán, the two cultures merged, the city flourishing to dominate the region as a religious, ceremonial, and cultural center. Kukulcán's departure in the eleventh century would lead to the city's fall, its people lost, their depravity leading them to diabolical forms of human sacrifice. By the sixteenth century, what little remained of the culture had quickly fallen under Spanish rule.

Dominating Chichén Itzá is arguably the most magnificent structure in all of Mesoamerica, the Kukulcán pyramid. Nicknamed *El Castillo* by the Spanish, this towering, nine-terraced ziggurat rises nearly a hundred feet above an open expanse of short-cropped lawn.

The Kukulcán is far more than just a pyramid—it is a calendar in stone. Each of its four sides possesses ninety-one steps. With the platform, the total equals 365—as in the days of the year.

To archaeologists and scientists, the bloodred pyramid remains an enigma, for its design exhibits a knowledge of astronomy and mathematics rivaling that of modern man. The structure has been geologically aligned in such a manner so that twice each year, on the spring and fall equinoxes, strange shadows begin undulating along its northern balustrade. As the late afternoon sun sinks, the enormous shadow of a serpent's body begins slithering down the steps until it meets up with its sculpted head, which rests at the base of the structure. (In the spring, the serpent descends the balustrade, in the fall, the illusion is reversed.)

Sitting atop the pyramid is a four-sided temple, originally used for worship, and only later, upon Kukulcán's departure, for human sacrifices. Believed to have been erected in A.D. 830, the Kukulcán was originally constructed on top of a much-older structure, the remains of which can only be accessed by way of a gated entry located along the northern base. A claustrophobic passage leads to a narrow stairwell, the limestone steps of which are slick from the humidity. Ascending the staircase, one finds two cramped inner chambers. The first contains the reclining figure of a Chac Mool, a Mayan statue supporting a ceremonial plate designed to hold the hearts of its sacrificial victims. Behind the security fencing of the second chamber sits the throne of a red jaguar, its jade eyes blazing green.

Brent Nakamura hits the steady-cam switch, then pans across the sea of sweltering bodies with his SONY video recorder. *Christ, there must be a hundred thousand people here. I'll be stuck in traffic for hours.*

The San Francisco native aims the camera back toward the northern balustrade, zooming in on the shadow of the serpent's tail as it continues its 202-minute journey up the limestone facing of the twelve-hundred-year-old pyramid.

The pungent scent of human sweat hangs heavy in the humid afternoon air. Nakamura records a Canadian couple arguing with two park officials, then shuts the camcorder off as a German tourist and his family jostle their way past him.

Glancing at his watch, Nakamura decides it best to take some footage of the sacred cenote before he loses the light. After stepping over a myriad of picnickers, he makes his way north down the ancient *sacbe,* an elevated dirt path lying in close proximity to the northern face of the Kukulcán. The *sacbe* is the only means of cutting through the dense jungle to reach the second-most-sacred site in Chichén Itzá—a freshwater sinkhole known as the cenote, or Mayan well of sacrifice.

A five-minute walk brings him to the mouth of the 190-foot-wide pit, a spot where thousands of maidens were once sacrificed to death. He looks down. Sixty feet below, the dark, algae-infested waters reek of stagnation.

The distant sound of thunder draws his attention skyward.

That's weird—not a cloud in the sky. Maybe it was a jet?

The sound grows louder. Several hundred tourists look at each other, uneasy. A woman screams.

Nakamura feels his body trembling. He looks down into the pit. Rings are spreading out across the once-tranquil surface.

Son of a bitch, it's an earthquake!

Grinning with excitement, Nakamura aims his camcorder down the mouth of the cenote. After surviving the big quake of 2005, it will take a lot more than a few tremors to upset this San Francisco native's psyche.

The crowd moves back as the tremor increases. Many rush back down the *sacbe* toward the park exit. Others scream as the ground beneath their feet bounces like a trampoline.

Nakamura stops smiling. *What the hell?*

The water within the pit is swirling like an eddy.

And then, as abruptly as they had started, the tremors cease.

Hollywood Beach, Florida

The synagogue is filled beyond capacity on this Yom Kippur, the holiest day of the Jewish calendar.

Dominique is seated between her adopted parents, Edie and Iz Axler. Rabbi Steinberg is standing at his pulpit, listening to the angelic voice of his cantor as she sings a haunting prayer to his congregation.

Dominique is hungry, having fasted nearly twenty-four hours since the Day of Atonement began. She is also premenstrual. Perhaps that is why she seems so emotional, unable to focus. Perhaps that is why her thoughts keep drifting back to Michael Gabriel.

The rabbi begins reading again:

"On Rosh Hashanah, we reflect. On Yom Kippur we consider. Who shall live for the sake of others? Who, dying, shall leave a heritage of life? Who shall burn with the fires of greed? Who shall drown in the waters of despair? Whose hunger shall be for the good? Who shall thirst for justice and right? Who shall be plagued by fear of the world? Who shall strangle for lack of friends? Who shall rest at the end of the day? Who lie sleepless on a bed of pain?"

Her emotions stir as she imagines Mick lying in his cell. *Stop it* . . .

"Whose tongue shall be a thrusting sword? Whose words shall make for peace? Who shall go forth in the quest for truth? Who shall be locked in a prison of self?"

In her mind's eye, she can see Mick pacing the yard as the equinox sun begins to set behind the concrete wall.

". . . the angels, gripped by fear and trembling, declare in awe: This is the Day of Judgment! For even the hosts of heaven are judged, as all who dwell on earth stand arrayed before You."

The emotional dam bursts, the hot tears streaking eyeliner down her face. Confused, she squeezes past Iz and hurries up the aisle and out of the temple.

Ennis Chaney is weary.

It has been two years since the Republican senator from Pennsylvania buried his mother, and he still misses her dearly. He misses visiting her in the nursing home where he used to bring her his specialty pork dish, and he misses her smile. He also misses his sister, who died eleven months after their mother, and his younger brother, whom cancer stole from him only last month.

He clenches his hands tightly, his youngest daughter rubbing his back. Four long days have passed since he received the call in the middle of the night. Four days since his best friend, Jim, died of a massive heart attack.

He sees the limo and security car pull up the driveway from the dining-room window and sighs. *No rest for the weary, no rest for the grieving.* He embraces his wife and his three daughters, hugs Jim's widow once more, then leaves the house, escorted by the two bodyguards. He pinches a tear from his deeply set eyes, the dark pigment surrounding the sockets creating the shadow of a raccoon's mask. Chaney's eyes are mirrors to his soul.

They reveal his passion as a man, his wisdom as a leader. Cross him, and the eyes become unblinking daggers.

Of late, Chaney's eyes have grown red from too much crying.

Reluctantly, the senator climbs into the back of the awaiting limousine, the two bodyguards getting into the other vehicle.

Chaney hates limos; in fact, he hates anything that calls attention to himself or reeks of the kind of preferential treatment associated with executive privilege. He stares out the window and thinks about his life, wondering if he is about to make a big mistake.

Ennis Chaney was born sixty-seven years ago in the poorest black neighborhood in Jacksonville, Florida. He was raised by his mother, who supported their family by cleaning white folks' homes, and by his aunt, whom he often referred to as Mama. He has never known his real father, a man who left home a few months after he was born. When he was two, his mother remarried, his new stepfather moving the family to New Jersey. It was there that young Ennis would grow up. It was there that he would hone his skills as a leader.

The playing field was the one place where Chaney felt at home, the one place where color didn't matter. Smaller than his peers, he nevertheless refused to be intimidated by anyone. After school, he would push himself through thousands of hours of drills, channeling his aggression to develop his athletic skills, learning discipline and self-control along the way. As a high-school senior, he would earn second-team, all-city honors at quarterback and first-team, all-state in basketball. Few defenders ever challenged the scrappy little point guard who would sooner break your ankle than allow you to steal the ball; but off the court, you couldn't find a warmer, more affectionate young man.

His basketball career would end after he tore his patellar tendon during his junior year of college. Though more interested in pursuing a coaching career, he allowed his mother, a woman who had grown up during the days of Jim Crow, to convince him to toss his hat into the political ring. Having lived through enough of his own experiences with racism, Ennis knew politics was the primary arena where change needed to be made.

His stepfather had connections with the Republican Party in Philadelphia. A fierce Democrat, Chaney nevertheless believed he could effect more change as a Republican candidate. Applying the same work ethic, passion, and intensity that allowed him to excel on the playing field, Ennis quickly rose through the ranks of the blue-collar city's politicians, never afraid to speak his mind, always looking to go out on a limb to help the underdog.

Despising laziness and lack of self-control among his peers, he became a breath of fresh air and something of a folk hero in Philadelphia. Deputy Mayor Chaney soon became Mayor Chaney. Years later, he would run for senator from Pennsylvania and win in a rout.

Now, less than two months from the November 2012 election, the president of the United States had come calling, urging him to join the ticket as his running mate. Ennis Chaney—the dirt-poor kid from Jacksonville, Florida—a veritable heartbeat away from the most powerful office in the world.

He stares out the window as the limo turns onto the Capital Beltway. Death frightens Ennis Chaney. There is no hiding from it and no reasoning with it. It provides no answers, only questions and confusion, tears and eulogies—far too many eulogies. How can one sum up a loved one's life in twenty minutes? How can anyone expect him to translate a lifetime of caring into mere words?

Vice president. Chaney shakes his head, allowing his mind to wrestle with his future.

It is not *his* future that concerns him as much as the burden his candidacy would place on his wife and family. Becoming a senator was one thing, accepting the Republican nomination as the first African-American vice president was an entirely different matter. The last and only Black who held a legitimate chance of being elected to the White House was Colin Powell, and the general had eventually backed off, citing family concerns. If Maller won reelection, Chaney would be the favorite to run in 2016. Like Powell, he knew his popularity crossed political and racial lines, but there was always a small segment of the population that, like death, couldn't be reasoned with.

And he had already put his family through so much.

Chaney also knows Pierre Borgia is hot for the ticket, and wonders how far the Secretary of State will go to get what he wants. Borgia is everything Chaney is not; brash, self-serving, politically motivated, egotistical, a bachelor, a military hawk—and white.

Chaney's thoughts return to his best friend and his family. He weeps openly, not caring one bit if the driver happens to notice.

Ennis Chaney wears his emotions on his sleeve, something he learned long ago from his mother. Inner strength and the tenacity to lead are no good unless one also allows himself to feel, and Chaney feels everything. Pierre Borgia feels nothing. Raised among the rich, the Secretary of State looks at life with blinders on, never pausing to consider what the other side may be feeling. This last fact weighs heavily upon the senator. The world is becoming a more complicated and dangerous place every day. Nuclear paranoia in Asia is rising. Borgia is the last person he wants to see running the country during a crisis situation.

"You all right back there, Senator?"

"Hell, no. What the hell kind of dumb-ass question is that?" Chaney's voice is a deep rasp, unless he's yelling, something he does quite often.

"Sorry, sir."

"Shut up and drive the damn car."

The driver smiles. Dean Disangro has been working for Senator Chaney for sixteen years and loves the man like a father.

"Deano, what the hell is so goddam important NASA'd want me at Goddard on a Sunday?"

"No idea. You're the senator, I'm just a lowly paid employee—"

"Shut up. You know more about what's going on than most of the dummies in Congress."

"You're NASA's liaison, Senator. Obviously, something important's happened for them to have the balls to summon you over the weekend."

"Thanks, Sherlock. You have a news monitor up there?"

The driver passes him the clipboard-sized device, already set to the *Washington Post.* Chaney glances at the headlines concerning preparations for nuclear deterrent exercises in Asia. *Grozny scheduled the event the week before Christmas. That was clever. No doubt hoping to dampen the holiday spirit.*

Chaney tosses the monitor aside. "How's your wife? She's due soon, isn't she?"

"Two weeks."

"Wonderful." Chaney smiles, pinching another tear from his bloodshot eyes.

NASA: Goddard Space Flight Center
Greenbelt, Maryland

Senator Chaney feels the anxious eyes of NASA, SETI, Arecibo, and God only knows who else upon him. He finishes scanning the twenty-page brief, then clears his throat, quieting the conference room. "Are you absolutely certain the radio signal originated from deep space?"

"Yes, Senator." Brian Dodds, NASA's executive director, looks almost apologetic.

"But you haven't been able to pinpoint the precise origin of the signal?"

"No, sir, not yet. We're pretty certain the source is located within Orion's arm, our own spiral arm of the galaxy. The signal passed through the Orion Nebula, a source of massive interference, making it difficult to determine exactly how far the signal may have traveled. Assuming it did come from a planet within the Orion belt, we're looking at a minimum distance of fifteen hundred to eighteen hundred light-years from Earth."

"And this signal lasted for three hours?"

"Three hours and twenty-two minutes, to be precise, Senator," Kenny Wong blurts out, standing at attention.

Chaney motions for him to sit. "And there have been no other signals, Mr. Dodds?"

"No, sir, but we'll continue to monitor the frequency and direction of the signal around the clock."

"All right, assuming the signal was real, what are the implications here?"

"Well, sir, the most obvious and exciting implication is that we now have evidence that we're not alone, that at least one more intelligent life-form does exist somewhere within our galaxy. Our next step is to determine if specific patterns or algorithms are hidden within the signal itself."

"You think the signal may contain some sort of communication?"

"We think it's very possible. Senator, this wasn't just some random signal transmitted across the galaxy. This beam was purposely directed at our solar system. There's another intelligence out there that knows we exist. By directing their beacon at Earth, they were letting us know they exist, too."

"Sort of a neighborly, 'how do you do,' is that it?"

The NASA director smiles. "Yes, sir."

"And when will your people finish their analysis?"

"Difficult to say. If an alien algorithm does exist, I'm confident our computers and team of mathematicians and cryptic code breakers will find it. Still, it could take months, years—or maybe never. How does one go about thinking like an extraterrestrial? This is exciting, but it's all very new to us."

"That's not exactly true, is it, Mr. Dodds?" The raccoon eyes stare down the director. "You and I both know that SETI has been using Arecibo's big dish to transmit messages into deep space for quite some time."

"Just as networks have been broadcasting television signals into space at the speed of light ever since *I Love Lucy* first aired."

"Don't play games, Mr. Dodds. I'm no astronomer, but I've read enough to know that television signals are far too weak to have reached Orion. When this discovery is announced, there are going to be a lot of very angry, very frightened people out there who will insist that SETI brought this unknown terror upon us."

Dodds hushes the objections from his assistants. "You're right, Senator. SETI transmissions are stronger, but television signals are infinitely more vast, spreading out into space in all directions. Of the two, television signals are far more likely to have reached a random receiver than a narrow beacon from Arecibo. Keep in mind that the strength of the radio signal we detected was produced by an alien transmitter far and away superior to our own. We'd have to assume that the intelligence behind the signal also has radio receivers capable of detecting our weaker signals."

"Regardless, Mr. Dodds, the reality of this situation is that millions of ignorant people are going to wake up tomorrow, frightened to death, waiting for little green men to break into their homes, rape their wives, and steal their babies. This situation has to be handled with finesse, or it'll blow up in all of our faces."

The NASA director nods. "That's why we called you in, Senator."

The deeply set eyes lose a bit of their harshness. "Okay, let's talk about this new telescope you're proposing." Chaney thumbs through his copy of the briefing. "It says here that the dish would be thirty miles in diameter and would be built on the dark side of the moon. That's gonna cost some chunk of change. Why the hell do you need to build it on the moon?"

"For the same reasons we launched the Hubble Space Telescope. There's too much radio interference escaping from Earth. The farside of the moon always faces away from Earth, offering us a natural radio-free zone. The idea is to construct a dish in the bottom of a massive crater, similar in design to Arecibo's big dish, only several thousand times larger. We've already selected a site—Saha Crater—only three degrees on the dark side of the moon, close to the lunar equator. A lunar telescope would give us the capability to communicate with the intelligence that contacted us."

"And why would we want to do that?" Chaney's voice booms across the conference room, losing its rasp as it rises. "Mr. Dodds, this radio signal may be the most important discovery in the history of mankind, but what NASA is proposing is going to frighten the masses. What if the American people say no? What if they don't want to spend a few billion dollars to contact E.T.? This is a pretty big financial pill you're asking Congress to swallow."

Brian Dodds knows Ennis Chaney, knows the man is testing his fortitude. "Senator, you're right. This discovery is going to frighten a lot of people. But let me tell you what frightens a lot of us even more. It frightens us when we pick up our daily news monitor and read stories about nuclear weapons in Iran. It frightens us when we read about the growing hunger problems in Russia, or about the strategic arms buildup in China, another country capable of destroying the world. It seems like every nation suffering political and economic unrest is armed to the teeth, Senator Chaney, and *that* reality is a lot more frightening than any radio signal coming from eighteen hundred light-years away."

Dodds stands. At just over six feet and a solid 220 pounds, he looks more a wrestler than scientist. "What the public needs to understand is that we're dealing with an intelligent species far superior to our own that has succeeded in making first contact. Whatever they are, wherever they are, they're too far away to be dropping by for a visit. By building this radio telescope, we enable ourselves to communicate with another species. Eventually, we may be able to learn from them, share our technologies, and gain a better understanding of the universe, and maybe even our own origins. This discovery could unite mankind—this project could be the catalyst that leads humanity away from nuclear annihilation."

Dodds looks Chaney square in the eye. "Senator, E.T. has called, and it's vitally important to the future of humanity that we call him back."

There are five residents gathered in the pod known as 7-C. Two are seated on the floor playing what they think is chess, another is asleep on the sofa. A fourth stands by the door, waiting for a member of his rehab team to arrive to escort him to his morning therapy session.

The remaining resident of 7-C stands motionless before a television set suspended above his head. He listens to President Maller extol the tremendous work of the men and women of NASA and SETI. He hears the president speak excitedly about world peace and cooperation, about the international space program and its impact on the future of humanity. The dawn of a new age is upon us, he announces. We are no longer alone.

Unlike the billions of other viewers watching the live news conference from around the world, Michael Gabriel is not surprised by what he is hearing, only saddened. The ebony eyes never blink, the body, held rigid, never moves. The blank expression never changes, even when Pierre Borgia's face appears on screen over the president's left shoulder. It is hard to tell if Mick is even breathing.

Dominique enters the pod. She pauses, taking a moment to observe her patient watching the special news broadcast while she verifies that the tape recorder fastened beneath her tee shirt is obscured by the white lab coat.

She moves beside him, the two now shoulder to shoulder in front of the television, her right hand by his left.

Their fingers entwine.

"Mick, do you want to watch the rest of this, or can we talk?"

"My room." He leads her across the hall, entering room 714.

Mick paces the cell like a caged animal, his cluttered mind attempting to sort through a thousand details at once.

Dominique sits on the edge of the bed, watching him. "You knew this was going to happen, didn't you? How? How did you know? Mick—"

"I didn't know *what* was going to happen, only that something *would* happen."

"But you knew it would be a celestial event, something to do with the equinox. Mick, can you stop pacing, it's hard to carry on a conversation like this. Come here. Sit down next to me."

He hesitates, then sits beside her. She can see his hands shaking.

"Talk to me."

"I can feel it, Dom."

"What can you feel?"

"I don't know . . . I can't describe it. Something's out there, a presence. It's still in the distance, but it's getting closer. I've felt it before, but never like this."

She touches the hair flowing down his neck, fingering a thick, brown curl. "Try to relax. Let's talk about this deep-space radio transmission. I want you to tell me how you knew the biggest event in humanity's history was about to happen."

He looks up at her, fear in his eyes. "This is nothing. This is only the beginning of the final act. The biggest event will happen on December 21, when billions of people die."

"And how do you know that? I know what the Mayan calendar says, but you're too intelligent to simply accept some three-thousand-year-old prophecy without the scientific evidence to support it. Explain the facts to me, Mick. No Mayan folklore, just the supporting evidence."

He shakes his head. "This is why I asked you to read my father's journal."

"I started to, but I'd rather you explain it to me in person. The last time we spoke, you warned me about some kind of rare galactic alignment orienting itself to Earth beginning on the fall equinox. Explain that to me."

Mick closes his eyes, drawing slow breaths as he forces his adrenaline-racked muscles to calm.

Dominique can hear the whirring of the tape recorder. She clears her throat, covering the noise.

He reopens his eyes, his gaze softer now. "Are you familiar with the *Popol Vuh?*"

"I know it's the Mayan book of creation, their equivalent of our Bible."

He nods. "The Maya believed in five suns or five Great Cycles of creation, the fifth and last of which is set to end on December 21, the day of this year's winter solstice. According to the *Popol Vuh*, the universe was organized into an Overworld, a Middleworld, and an Underworld. The Overworld represented the celestial heavens, the Middleworld—Earth. The Maya referred to the Underworld as *Xibalba,* a dark, evil place said to be ruled by Hurakan, the death god. Mayan legend claims the great teacher, Kukulcán, was engaged in a long, cosmic battle with Hurakan, pitting the forces of good and light against darkness and evil. It's written that the fourth cycle came to an abrupt end when Hurakan caused a great flood to engulf the world. The English word, 'hurricane,' comes from the Mayan word, 'Hurakan.' The Maya believed the demonic entity existed within a violent maelstrom. The Aztecs believed in the same legend, only their name for the great teacher was Quetzalcoatl, the underworld deity known as Tezcatilpoca, a name which translates to 'smoking mirror.' "

"Mick, wait—just stop a moment, okay. Forget about the Mayan myth. What I need you to stay focused on is the facts surrounding the calendar and how it relates to that deep-space transmission."

The dark eyes blaze at her like onyx lasers, the look causing her to shrink. "I can't discuss the science supporting the doomsday prophecy without explaining the creation myth. It's all related. There's a paradox surrounding the Maya. Most people think the Maya were just a bunch of jungle-dwelling savages that built some neat pyramids. The truth is, the Maya were incredible astronomers and mathematicians who possessed an unfathomable understanding of our planet's existence within the galaxy. And it was this knowledge that allowed them to predict the celestial alignment that led to yesterday's radio signal."

"I don't understand—"

Mick fidgets, then begins pacing again. "We have evidence that shows the Maya and their predecessors, the Olmec, used the Milky Way galaxy as their celestial background marker to calculate the Mayan calendar. The Milky Way is a spiral galaxy, about 100,000 light-years in diameter, made up of approximately 200 billion stars. Our own sun is located in one of the spiral arms—the Orion arm—about 35,000 light-years from the galactic center, which astronomers now believe to be a gigantic black hole, running straight through Sagittarius. The galactic center functions as a kind of celestial magnet, pulling the Milky Way in a powerful vortex. As we speak, our solar system is whipping around the galactic center point at a velocity of 135 miles per second. Despite that speed, it still takes Earth a good 226 million years to complete one revolutionary cycle around the Milky Way."

You're running out of tape. "Mick, the signal—"

"Be patient. As our solar system moves through the galaxy, it follows a fourteen-degree-wide path called the ecliptic. The ecliptic crosses the Milky Way in such a manner that it periodically moves into alignment with the central bulge of the galaxy. As the Maya looked to the night sky, they saw a dark rift, or dark elongated band of dense interstellar clouds, beginning where the ecliptic crosses the Milky Way in the constellation of Sagittarius. The *Popol Vuh*'s myth of creation refers to this dark rift as the Black Road, or *Xibalba Be*—a nexus shaped like a giant serpent, connecting life and death, the Earth and the Underworld."

"Again, this is all fascinating, but how does it relate to the deep-space radio signal?"

Mick stops pacing. "Dominique, this radio signal—it wasn't just some random transmission beamed across the universe; it was purposely directed toward our solar system. From a technological standpoint, you can't just transmit a radio beacon halfway across the galaxy and hope it somehow manages to reach a specific planetary speck of dust like Earth. The farther the beacon has to travel, the more the signal breaks up and loses its strength. The radio transmission SETI detected was a very powerful, precise, narrow beacon, indicating to me, at least, that whoever, or whatever sent it required a particular galactic alignment, a sort of celestial corridor that aimed the transmission from its point of origin to Earth. In essence, the signal traveled through a sort of cosmic corridor. I can't explain why, I can't explain how, but I *felt* the portal of this corridor as it began opening."

Dominique sees the fear in his eyes. "You felt it open? What did it feel like?"

"It was a sickening feeling, like icy fingers moving inside my intestines."

"And you believe this cosmic corridor must have opened up just enough to allow the radio signal through?"

"Yes, and the portal's widening a little bit more each day. By the December solstice, it will open completely."

"The December solstice—the Mayan doomsday?"

"That's right. Astronomers have known for years that our sun will move into alignment along the exact point of galactic center on December 21, 2012—the last day of the calendar's fifth cycle. At the same time, the dark rift of the Milky Way will move into alignment along our eastern horizon, appearing directly over the Mayan city of Chichén Itzá by solstice midnight. This combination of galactic events occurs only once every 25,800 years, and yet, somehow, the Maya were able to forecast the alignment."

"The deep-space transmission—what was its purpose?"

"I don't know, but it portends death."

Justify his schizophrenia. Blame the parents. "Mick, it seems to me that, aside from one isolated incident of violence, your continued incarceration has more to do with your fanatical belief in the apocalypse, a belief shared by tens of millions of people. When you say humanity's coming to an end, what I'm hearing is a belief system that was probably spoon-fed to you from birth. Isn't it possible that your parents—"

"My parents were not religious fanatics or millennialists. They didn't spend their time constructing subterranean bunkers. They didn't arm themselves with assault weapons and food supplies in preparation for Judgment Day. They didn't believe in the Second Coming of Jesus, or the Messiah, for that matter, and they didn't accuse every autocratic world leader with a bad mustache of being the Antichrist. They were archaeologists, Dominique—scientists, who were intelligent enough not to ignore the signposts that point to a disaster that will wipe out our entire species. Call it Armageddon, call it the Apocalypse, the Mayan prophecy—whatever makes you happy—just get me the hell out of here so I can do something about it!"

"Mick, stay calm. I know you're frustrated, and I'm trying to help you, more than you know. But, in order to gain your release, I have to appeal for another psychiatric evaluation."

"How long will that take?"

"I don't know."

"Christ—" He paces faster.

"Let's say you were released tomorrow. What would you do? Where would you go?"

"Chichén Itzá. The only chance we have of saving ourselves is to find a way inside the Kukulcán pyramid."

"What's inside the pyramid?"

"I don't know. No one knows. The entrance has never been found."

"Then how—"

"Because I can sense something's there. Don't ask me how, I just do. It's like when you walk down a street and can just sense someone's following you."

"These board members are going to want something more solid than a feeling."

Mick stops pacing to give her an exasperated look. "This is why I asked you to read my father's journal. There are two structures in Chichén Itzá that are linked to our salvation. The first is the great ball court, which has been aligned precisely to mirror *Xibalba Be*, the dark rift of the Milky Way, as it will appear on 4 *Ahau*, 3 *Kankin*. The second is the Kukulcán pyramid, the keystone structure of the entire doomsday prophecy. Every equinox, a serpent's shadow appears on the northern balustrade of the pyramid. My father believed the celestial effect was a warning left to us by Kukulcán, representing the ascent of evil upon mankind. The shadow lasts exactly three hours and twenty-two minutes—the same interval of time shared by the deep-space transmission."

"Are you certain about this?" *Make certain you verify these facts in your report.*

"As sure as I'm standing here, rotting in this cell." He starts pacing again.

She registers the click of the recorder as it runs out of tape and switches itself off.

"Dom, there was another story on CNN—I only caught the last blurb. Something about an earthquake hitting the Yucatán basin. I need to find out what happened. I need to know if the earthquake originated in Chichén Itzá, or in the Gulf of Mexico."

"Why the Gulf?"

"You haven't even read the journal entry concerning the Piri Re'is maps?"

"Sorry. I've been kind of busy."

"Jesus, Dom, if you were my intern, I'd have flunked you by now. Piri Re'is was a famous Turkish admiral who, back in the late fourteenth century, somehow came upon a series of mysterious charts of the world. Using these charts as a reference, the admiral constructed a set of maps that historians now believe were used by Columbus to navigate his way across the Atlantic."

92

"Wait, these charts were real?"

"Of course they're real. And these charts reveal topographical details that could only have been acquired using sophisticated seismic soundings. For instance, Antarctica's coastline appears as if there's no ice cap even present."

"What's so significant about that?"

"Dom, the map is over five hundred years old. Antarctica wasn't even discovered until 1818."

She stares at him, not sure of what to believe.

"If you doubt me, contact the United States Navy. It was their analysis that confirmed the accuracy of the cartography."

"So what does this map have to do with the Gulf, or the doomsday prophecy?"

"Fifteen years ago, my father and I located a similar map, only this one was an original, thousands of years old, like the one Piri Re'is found. It was sealed in an iridium container, buried in a precise location on the Nazca plateau. I managed to snap off a Polaroid just before the parchment deteriorated. You'll find the photo in the back of my father's journal. When you look at it, you'll see an area circled in red, located in the Gulf of Mexico, just north of the Yucatán Peninsula."

"What's the mark represent?"

"I don't know."

Wrap this up. "Mick, I don't doubt anything you're telling me, but what if . . . well, what if this deep-space transmission has nothing at all to do with the Mayan prophecy? NASA says the radio signal originated from some distant point more than eighteen hundred light-years away. That should give you some measure of comfort, right? I mean, come on"—she smiles—"it's a bit unlikely that we'll be seeing any extraterrestrials arriving from Orion's belt within the next sixty days."

Mick's eyes widen into dark saucers. He steps back, grabbing his temples with both hands.

Oh, shit, he's losing it. You pushed him too far. "Mick, what is it? Are you okay?"

He holds up a finger, motioning her to stay back, to remain silent.

Dominique watches him kneel on the floor, his eyes—dark windows to a mind whirling a thousand miles an hour. *Maybe you're wrong about him. Maybe he really is certifiable.*

The long moment passes. Mick looks up, the intensity of his glare positively frightening.

"You're right, Dominique, you're absolutely right," he whispers. "Whatever's been predestined to eradicate humanity won't be arriving from deep space.

"It's in the Gulf. It's already here."

93

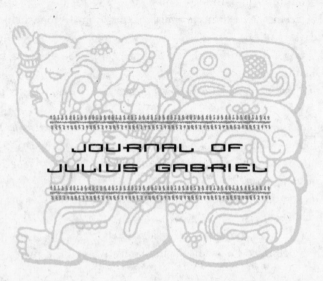

JOURNAL OF
JULIUS GABRIEL

In order better to understand and ultimately resolve the mysteries surrounding the Mayan calendar and its doomsday prophecy, one must explore the origins of the cultures that first rose to prominence in the Yucatán.

The first Mesoamericans were seminomadic, appearing in Central America around 4000 BC. Eventually they became farmers, developing corn, a hybrid of wild grass, as well as avocado, tomatoes, and squash.

Then, sometime around 2500 BC, He arrived.

He was a long-faced Caucasian with flowing white beard and hair, a wise man who, according to legend, arrived by sea along the Gulf of Mexico's tropical lowlands to educate and impart great wisdom unto the natives of the region.

We now refer to these educated natives as the Olmec (meaning: dwellers in the land of rubber) and they eventually became the "Mother Culture" of all Mesoamerica, the first complex society of the Americas. Under the influence of the "bearded one," the Olmec would unify the Gulf region, their achievements in astronomy, mathematics, and architecture influencing the Zapotec, Ma-

yan, Toltec, and Aztec—cultures which eventually rose to power over the next several thousand years.

Almost overnight, these simple jungle-dwelling farmers were suddenly establishing complex structures and extensive ceremonial centers. Advanced techniques of engineering were incorporated into the designs of architecture and public works of art. It was the Olmec who originated the ancient ball game, as well as the first method of recording events. They also fashioned great monolithic heads out of basalt, ten feet tall, many weighing up to 30 tons each. How these enormous Olmec heads were transported still remains a mystery.

Of greater importance, the Olmec was the first culture in Mesoamerica to erect pyramids using an advanced knowledge of astronomy and mathematics. It was these structures, aligned with the constellations, that reveal the Olmec's understanding of precession, a discovery that gave rise to the creation myth recorded in the Popol Vuh.

And so it was the Olmec, and not the Maya, who used their unexplainable knowledge of astronomy to create the Long Count Calendar and its prophecy of doom.

At the heart of the doomsday calendar is the creation myth, an historical account of an ongoing battle of light and good against darkness and evil. The hero of the story, One Hunahpu, is a warrior who is able to access the Black Road (Xibalba Be). To the Mesoamerican Indians, Xibalba Be equated to the dark rift of the Milky Way galaxy. The portal to Xibalba Be was represented in both Olmec and Mayan artwork as the mouth of a great serpent.

One can imagine the primitive Olmec, looking up at the night sky, pointing to the dark rift of the galaxy as a cosmic snake.

Around 100 BC, for reasons still unknown, the Olmec chose to abandon their cities and split into two camps, diversifying over two distinct regions. Those moving farther west into central Mexico became known as the Toltecs. Those venturing east would dwell in the jungles of the Yucatán, Belize, and Guatemala, and would call themselves the Maya. It would not be until AD 900 that the two civilizations would reunite under the influence of the great teacher, Kukulcán, in his majestic city of Chichén Itzá.

But I get ahead of myself.

Cambridge: 1969. It was from there that my two colleagues and I set out to unravel the mysteries of the Mayan prophecy. Unanimously, we decided our first stop should be the Olmec site of La Venta, for it was there, 20 years earlier, that the American archaeologist Matthew Stirling had unearthed his most startling discovery, an enormous Olmec fortification, consisting of a wall of 600 columns, each weighing in excess of two tons. Adjacent to this structure, the explorer had located a magnificent rock, covered with intricate Olmec carvings. After two days of intense labor, Stirling and his men were able to unearth the mammoth sculpture, which stood 14 feet high, seven feet wide, and nearly three feet thick. Although some of the carvings had been damaged from erosion, the image of one magnificent figure still remained: a large Caucasian male with a long head, high-bridged nose, and flowing white beard.

Imagine my fellow archaeologists' shock at finding a 2,000-year-old relief clearly depicting a Caucasian, the artifact created 1500 years _before_ the first European had even set foot in the Americas! Just as perplexing was the depiction of a bearded figure among the Olmec, for it is a genetic fact that full-blooded Amer-Indians _cannot_ grow beards. Since all forms of artistic expression must have roots somewhere, the identity of the bearded white man remained yet another enigma to be solved.

As for myself, I immediately theorized the Caucasian to be an earlier ancestor of the great Mayan teacher, Kukulcán.

We don't know much about Kukulcán, or his ancestors, although every Mesoamerican group appears to have worshiped a male deity who fits the same physical description. To the Maya, he was Kukulcán, to the Aztecs, Quetzalcoatl—a legendary bearded wise man who brought peace, prosperity, and great wisdom to the people. Records indicate that, sometime around AD 1000, Kukulcán/Quetzalcoatl was forced to abandon Chichén Itzá. Legend tells that, before leaving, the mysterious wise man promised his people that he would eventually return to rid the world of evil.

Upon Kukulcán's departure, a demonic influence quickly spread throughout the land. Both the Maya and Aztecs turned to human sacrifice, savagely killing tens of thousands of men, women, and children, all in an effort to usher in the return of their beloved god-king and forestall the prophesied end of humanity.

It was in the year 1519 that the Spanish Conquistador, Hernan Cortez, would arrive from Europe to invade the Yucatán. Though they easily outnumbered their enemy, the Mesoamerican Indians mistook Cortez (a bearded white man) as the Second Coming of Kukulcán/Quetzalcoatl and laid down their weapons. Having conquered the savages, Cortez sent for the Spanish priests, who, upon their arrival, were horrified to learn of the human sacrifices, as well as one other shocking ritual: Mayan mothers were strapping wooden boards to their infant's heads in an attempt to deform their newborn child's developing skull. By elongating the skull, the Mayan would appear more godlike, a belief no doubt inspired by evidence indicating the great teacher, Kukulcán, had possessed a similar elongated cranium.

Quickly proclaiming the Maya practice to be an influence of the Devil, the Spanish priests ordered the shamans burned alive and the rest of the Indians converted to Christianity—under penalty of death. The superstitious fools then proceeded to torch every important Mayan codex in existence. Thousands of volumes of text were destroyed—text that no doubt referenced the doomsday prophecy, and may have contained vital instructions, left to us by Kukulcán, to save our species from annihilation.

And so it came to pass that the Church, attempting to save our souls from the Devil, most likely condemned our species to ignorance some 500 years ago.

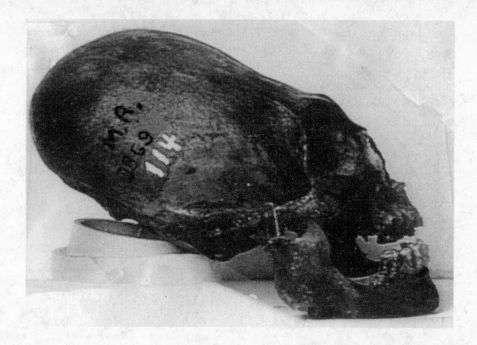

Artifact #114 elongated skull—discovered by Maria Rosen, La Venta 1969

* * *

While Borgia and I argued over the identity of the bearded one depicted on the Olmec relief, our colleague, the beautiful Maria Rosen, came upon a find that would redirect our efforts away from Central America and onto the next leg of our journey.

While excavating an Olmec dig in La Venta, Maria discovered an ancient royal burial site, and unearthed the remains of an elongated skull. Although this bizarre, inhuman-looking cranium was not the first such skull ever located in Mesoamerica, it would turn out to be the only one found in the Olmec homeland referred to as the Serpent Sanctuary.

Maria decided to donate the skull to the Museum of Anthropology in Merida. Upon speaking to their curator, we learned, quite to our surprise, that similar skulls had recently been unearthed in burial grounds located on the Nazca plateau in Peru.

Was there a link between the Maya and Inca civilizations?

The three of us found ourselves at an archaeological crossroad. Should we continue on to Chichén Itzá, an ancient Mayan city central to the doomsday prophecy, or leave Mexico and pursue our lead to Peru?

Maria's instinct was to travel to South America, believing that the Mayan calendar was but an important piece to the doomsday puzzle. And so the three of us boarded a plane bound for Nazca, unaware of where our journey was leading us.

As we flew across the Atlantic, I found myself perplexed by something the physician in Merida had shared with me. Upon examination of the elongated cranium, the medical examiner, a man of good reputation, had stated, quite emphatically, that the massive bone deformity of this particular skull could not have been caused by any known elongation technique. To back up his claim, he arranged for a dentist to examine the dental remains, the results of which yielded something even more startling.

It is a fact that human adults possess 14 teeth in the lower jaw.

The elongated skull Maria had found only possessed 10.

—Excerpt from the Journal of Professor Julius Gabriel,

Ref. Catalogue 1969–73   pages 13–347
Photo Journal Floppy Disk 4: File name: OLMEC-1-7

OCTOBER 9, 2012
WASHINGTON, DC

President Mark Maller enters the Oval Office from his private study and takes his place behind his desk. Seated before him are members of the White House staff.

"All right people, let's get started. We'll begin with the issue of nominating a new vice presidential running mate. Kathie?"

Chief of Staff Katherine Gleason reads from her laptop. "These are the results of a public opinion poll taken last Thursday. When asked who they preferred to see share the party ticket, registered voters selected Senator Ennis Chaney to Pierre Borgia by a fifty-three percent to thirty-nine percent margin. The issue of trust appears to be their key motivating factor. However, when asked to identify what they felt was the central issue going into the November election, eighty-nine percent of the public named the escalation of the strategic arms buildup in Russia and China as being their primary concern, with only thirty-four percent of registered voters interested in pursuing the construction of a radio telescope on the moon. Loosely translated: Chaney gets the ticket, we focus our campaign on stabilizing relations with Russia and China, and you remain noncommittal on the radio telescope, at least until after you're reelected."

"Agreed. Any new developments at NASA?"

"Yes, sir." Sam Blumner is the president's chief economic advisor. "I've reviewed NASA's preliminary budget for building this contraption on the moon."

"How bad?"

"Let's me put it to you this way, Mr. President. You've got two chances of pushing this through Congress—slim and none—and slim just left town with your former vice president."

"I thought NASA was linking the project with the moon base proposal that already passed through Appropriations?"

"They tried. Unfortunately, *that* moon base was designed to be built on the near side of the moon, close to the polar region where NASA located ice formations, and not on the dark side. You'll excuse the pun, but in fiscal terms, we're looking at the difference between night and day, as in solar panels are no longer an option when the Sun's not shining."

Kathie Gleason shakes her head in disagreement. "Sam, one of the reasons the American public is so opposed to this venture is that they perceive it as being an international project. The radio signal wasn't broadcast to the United States, it was received by our entire planet."

"And in the end, America's still the one who's going foot most of the bill."

Cal Calixte, the president's press secretary, raises his hand. "Mr. President, in my opinion, the radio telescope provides us with a means of pumping funds into Russia's economy, especially in light of the recent cutbacks by the IMF. Perhaps you could even link it to the new START-V treaty."

"The same thing was said about the International Space Station," interrupts Blumner. "That giant Tinker Toy cost America a cool $20 billion, plus the billions we lent the Russians so they could afford to participate. Meanwhile, it's the Russians who keep delaying the completion of the project."

"Sam, stop looking at everything from a financial standpoint," Kathie says. "This is as much a political issue as a space program. Protecting the Russian democracy is worth more than the telescope itself."

"Democracy? What democracy?" Blumner loosens his tie. "Here's a quick civics lesson for you, Kathie. What we've created is an economy of extortion, where the Russian rich get richer, the poor starve to death, and nobody seems to give a shit as long as we call it a democracy. The United States and the IMF have given the Russians billions of dollars. Where'd all the money go? From a fiscal standpoint, my three-year-old daughter is more fiscally accountable than Yeltsin or Viktor Grozny ever was."

Blumner turns to the president, his plump face red. "Before we start appropriating billions, let's keep in mind that this deep-space radio signal could just be a fluke. From what I understand, NASA still hasn't found an underlying pattern that would indicate the transmission was a genuine attempt at communication. And why haven't we heard a trace of a second signal?"

Cal shakes his head. "You miss the point. Grozny's people are starving. Civil unrest is reaching dangerous proportions. We can't just turn our backs on a desperate nation with a nuclear arsenal capable of destroying the world a dozen times over."

"In my book, it's still extortion," Blumner says. "We're creating a bogus project as a means of paying a faltering superpower and its corrupt leaders billions of dollars so they won't engage us in a nuclear war they could never hope to win anyway."

The president holds up his hand to interject. "I think Cal's point still has merit. The IMF has already made it clear that they won't give another dime to Russia unless the money is invested in technologies that can help jump-start their economy. Even if this radio signal turns out to be bogus, the telescope would still provide scientists with a real window to explore deep space."

"It'd help the Russian people more if we opened up a few thousand McDonald's and let 'em eat for free."

Maller ignores Blumner's remark. "The G-9 meeting's in two weeks. I want you and Joyce to prepare a preliminary proposal that uses the radio telescope as a vehicle to channel funds into Russia. At the very worst, maybe we can diffuse some of the paranoia surrounding Asia's upcoming joint nuclear deterrent exercises."

The president stands. "Cal, what time is tonight's press conference scheduled?"

"Nine o'clock."

"Good. I'll meet with our new vice president in an hour, then I want you to brief him about the reelection. And tell him to pack a bag. I want Chaney hitting the campaign trail, starting tonight."

Florida State University

Dominique is seated in the corridor outside her doctoral advisor's office, squirming uncomfortably on a cushionless wooden bench. She debates whether to chance another trip to the bathroom when the office door opens.

Dr. Marjorie Owen, portable phone pressed to one ear, ushers her inside with a quick gesture. Dominique enters the sanctuary of the department head's cluttered office and takes a seat, waiting for her professor to finish her phone conversation.

Marjorie Owen has been teaching clinical psychiatry for twenty-seven years. She is unmarried and unattached, her thin, wiry fifty-seven-year-old physique kept in reasonable shape by mountain climbing. A woman of few words, she is well respected, somewhat feared by her nontenured staff, and has a reputation for being strict with her graduate students.

The last thing Dominique wants is to get on her shit list.

Dr. Owen hangs up the phone, retucking her short-cropped gray hair back behind her ear. "Okay, young lady, I've listened to your tape and read your report on Michael Gabriel."

"And?"

"And what? He's exactly what Dr. Foletta says he is, a paranoid schizophrenic possessing an unusually high IQ," she smiles, "making for some delightful delusions, I might add."

"But does that warrant keeping him locked up? He's already served eleven hard years, and I've seen no evidence of criminal behavior."

"According to the file you showed me, Dr. Foletta just completed his annual evaluation, an evaluation you signed off on. If you had any objections, you should have spoken up then."

"I realize that now. Is there anything you could recommend, anything I can do to challenge Foletta's recommendations?"

"You want to challenge your sponsor's evaluation? Based on what?"

Here we go . . . "Based on my personal belief that—well, that the patient's claims might merit investigation."

Dr. Owen shoots Dominique her infamous "befuddled look," a look that has shattered many a grad student's hopes for graduating. "Young lady, are you telling me that Mr. Gabriel actually has you convinced the world is coming to an end?"

Christ, I'm toast. . . . "No, ma'am, but he did seem to know about that deep-space radio signal and—"

"No, as a matter of fact, according to the tape, he had no idea *what* was going to happen, only that something would happen on the equinox."

The silent stare resumes, causing beads of sweat to break out beneath Dominique's armpits.

"Dr. Owen, my only concern is to ensure my patient is receiving the best care possible. At the same time, I'm also concerned that, well, that he may not have been justly evaluated in the first place."

"I see. So, let me get this straight—having worked with your very first patient for nearly a month—" Owen checks her notes. "No, wait, my mistake, it's actually been over a month. Five weeks, to be exact." Dr. Owen walks to her office door and closes it with authority. "Five full weeks on the job, and you're not only questioning the last eleven years of the patient's treatment, but you're ready to challenge the director of the facility, hoping to release Mr. Gabriel back into society."

"I realize that I'm just an intern, but if I see something's not right, don't I have a moral and professional obligation to report it?"

"Okay, so based on your infinite experience in the field, you feel that Dr. Anthony Foletta, a well-respected clinical psychiatrist, is unable to evaluate his own patient properly. Is that it?"

Don't answer. Bite your tongue.

"Don't just sit there and bite your tongue. Answer me."

"Yes, ma'am."

Owen sits on the edge of her desk, purposely positioning herself to tower over her graduate student. "Let me tell you what I think, young lady. I think you've lost your perspective. I think you've made the mistake of becoming emotionally involved with your patient."

"No, ma'am, I—"

"He's certainly a clever man. By telling his young, new, *female* psychiatrist that he had been sexually abused in prison, he hoped to hit a soft spot, and boy did he ever. Wake up, Dominique. Can't you see what's happening? You're reaching out emotionally to your patient, based on your own childhood trauma. But Mr. Gabriel wasn't sodomized by his cousin for three years, was he? He wasn't beaten to within an inch of his life—"

Shut up, just shut the fuck up—

"Many women who've gone through similar experiences like yours often deal with post-traumatic symptoms by joining women's movements, or taking up self-defense, just as you have. Pursuing clinical psychiatry as your chosen profession was a mistake if you're planning on using it as an alternative means of therapy. How can you possibly hope to help your patients if you allow yourself to become emotionally involved?"

"I know what you're saying, but—"

"—but nothing." Owen shakes her head. "In my opinion, you've already lost your objectivity. For God's sake, Dominique, this lunatic actually has you convinced that everyone in the world is going to die in ten weeks."

Dominique wipes tears from her eyes and chokes back a laugh. It was true. Mick had her so emotionally wound up that she was no longer just humoring him as part of his therapy, she was allowing herself to be coerced by his doomsday delusions. "I feel embarrassed."

"And so you should. By feeling sorry for Mr. Gabriel, you've ruined the dynamics of the doctor-patient relationship. This forces me to contact Dr. Foletta and intervene on behalf of Mr. Gabriel."

Oh, shit. "What are you going to do?"

"I'm going to request that Foletta place you with another resident. Immediately."

Mick Gabriel has been walking the yard for six hours.

Pacing on automatic pilot, he maneuvers around the mentally inept and criminally insane as his mind focuses on reshaping the pieces of the doomsday puzzle floating in his brain.

The radio signal and the descent of the plumed serpent. The dark rift and Xibalba. Don't make the mistake of lumping everything together. Separate cause from action, death from salvation, evil from good. There are two factions at work here, two separate entities involved in the Mayan prophecy. Good and evil, evil and good. What's good? Warnings are good. The Mayan calendar is a warning, as are the Nazca drawings and the serpent's equinoctial shadow on the Kukulcán pyramid. Each warning, left to us by a bearded, Caucasian wise man, all portending the arrival of evil. But the evil is already here, it's been here. I've felt it before, but never like this. Could that deep-space transmission have triggered it? Somehow strengthened it? If so, where is it?

He pauses, allowing the late-afternoon sun to warm his face.

Xibalba—the Underworld. I can feel the Black Road leading to the Underworld growing stronger. The Popol Vuh *claims the Lords of the Underworld influenced evil on Earth. How's that possible . . . unless the malevolent presence on Earth hasn't always been here?*

Mick opens his eyes.

What if it wasn't always here? What if it arrived long ago, before the evolution of man? What if it's been lying dormant, waiting for this radio transmission to awaken it?

The loudspeaker's five o'clock *buzz* announcing dinner jars a distant memory. Mick imagines himself back on the Nazca desert, patrolling the flat plateau with his metal detector. The electric *buzz* of the metal detector has sent him digging in the soft yellow sand, his ailing father by his side.

In his mind's eye, he unearths the iridium canister, removing the ancient map. Focusing on the red circle . . . marking the mysterious location in the Gulf of Mexico.

The Gulf of Mexico . . . the canister—made of iridium! His eyes widen in disbelief. "God dammit, Gabriel, how could you be so fucking blind!"

Mick races up the two flights of concrete steps to the third-floor mezzanine and therapy annex. He pushes past several residents and enters the computer room.

A middle-aged woman greets him. "Well, hello. My name's Dorothy, and I'm—"

"I need to use one of your computers!"

She moves to her laptop. "And your name is?"

"Gabriel. Michael Gabriel. Look under Foletta." Mick spots an open terminal. Without waiting, he takes a seat, then notices the voice-activation system is not working. Using the mouse, he activates the Internet connection.

"Now just wait one minute, Mr. Gabriel. We have rules here. You just can't jump onto a computer. You have to have permission from your—"

Access Denied. Please Enter Password.

"I need a password, Dorothy. I'll only be a minute. Could you give me your password, please—"

"No, Mr. Gabriel, no password. There are three residents ahead of you, and I'll need to speak with your therapist. Then I can—"

Mick focuses on her identification badge: DOROTHY HIGGINS, #G45927. He begins typing in passwords.

"—schedule you for a future appointment. Are you listening to me, Mr. Gabriel? What are you doing? Hey, stop that—"

A dozen passwords fail. He focuses again on her name tag. "Dorothy, what a pretty name. Did your parents like the *Wizard of Oz,* Dorothy?"

Her stunned expression gives her away. Mick types in OZG45927.

Invalid Password.

"Stop this nonsense right now, Mr. Gabriel, or I'll call for security."

"The Wicked Witch, the Tin Man, Scarecrow . . . how about we ask the wizard." He types in WIZG45927.

Connecting To Internet . . .

"That's it, I'm calling security!"

Mick ignores her as he searches the web, typing in CHICXULUB CRATER, as he recalls the words he had spoken to Dominique. *The biggest event in history will happen on December 21, when humanity perishes.* Not entirely true, he realizes now. The biggest event in history, at least up until now, had occurred sixty-five million years ago, and it had taken place in the Gulf of Mexico.

The first file appears on screen. Without bothering to read it, he presses PRINT ALL.

He hears security approaching from the adjacent hall. *Come on, come on . . .*

Mick grabs the three sheets of printouts and shoves them into his pants pocket as several security guards enter the computer room.

"I've asked him three times to leave. He even managed to steal my password."

"We'll handle it, ma'am." The muscular redhead nods to his two guards, who grab Mick by the arms.

Mick offers no resistance as the redhead struts forward, getting up in his face. "Resident, you were asked to vacate this room. Is that a problem?"

Mick sees Dr. Foletta enter the room out of the corner of his eye. He glances at the guard's identification badge and offers the redhead a smile. "You know, Raymond, all the muscles in the world won't get you laid if your breath reeks of garlic—"

Foletta approaches. "Raymond, don't—"

The uppercut strikes Mick squarely on the solar plexus, driving the air from his lungs. He falls forward, doubled up in pain, his body still supported on either side by the two guards.

"God dammit, Raymond, I said to wait—"

"Sorry, sir, I thought you—"

Mick regains his feet and, in one motion, arches his back, raising his knees to his chest before kicking outward, the heels of his tennis shoes smashing hard into the redhead's face, shattering the man's nose and upper lip in a spray of blood.

Raymond drops to the floor in a heap.

Foletta bends over the semiconscious guard, staring at the man's face. "That was uncalled-for, Mick."

"An eye for an eye, eh, Doctor."

Two more orderlies enter, brandishing stun guns. Foletta shakes his head. "Escort Mr. Gabriel to his room, then get a physician down here to take care of this idiot."

It is late by the time Dominique pulls the black Pronto Spyder into the facility's parking lot. She enters the lobby, then swipes her magnetic identification card to pass through the first-floor security checkpoint.

"Won't work, Sunshine."

The voice is weak and a bit muffled. "Raymond, is that you?" Dominique can barely see the big redhead through the security gate.

"Use the facial scan."

She enters her code, then presses her face to the rubber housing, the infrared beam scanning her features.

The security door unlocks.

Raymond is leaning back in his chair. A heavy gauze bandage is wrapped around his head, covering his nose. Both eyes are black.

"Jesus, Ray, what the hell happened to you?"

"Your goddam patient flipped out in the computer room and kicked me in the face. Motherfucker broke my nose and loosened two teeth."

"Mick did this? Why?"

"Who the fuck knows? Guy's a fucking psycho. Look at me, Dominique. How am I supposed to compete in the Mr. Florida contest looking like this? I swear to God, I'm gonna get that son of a bitch if it's the last thing I do—"

"No you won't. You're not going to do a thing to him. And if anything should happen, I won't hesitate to bring criminal charges against you."

Raymond leans forward menacingly. "Is that the way it's gonna be between us? First you blow me off, then you're gonna have me arrested?"

"Hey, I didn't blow you off, I got tied up in a meeting with Foletta. You're the one who got himself switched to the night shift. As for Michael Gabriel, he's my patient, and I'll be damned if—"

"Not anymore. Foletta received a call this afternoon from your advisor. Looks like your patient load around here is about to change."

Damn you, Owen, do you always have to be so goddam efficient. "Is Foletta still here?"

"At this hour? You gotta be kidding."

"Ray, listen to me, I know you're mad at Mick, but I'll . . . I'll make you a deal. Stay away from him and—and I'll help you prepare for your body-building contest. I'll even apply makeup to those raccoon eyes of yours so you won't scare the judges."

Raymond folds his arms across his inflated chest. "Not good enough. You still owe me a night out." He flashes a yellowed smile. "Not just a quick Italian dinner, either. I want to have some fun, you know, do a little dancin', a little romancin'—"

"One date, that's it, and I'm not interested in any romance."

"Give me a chance, Sunshine. I tend to grow on people."

So does fungus. "One date, and you stay away from Gabriel."

"Agreed."

She passes through the security checkpoint and enters the elevator.

Raymond watches her leave, lust in his eyes as he focuses on the contours of her glutei maximi.

There is only one guard on duty on the seventh floor, and his attention is focused on the National League Championship Series.

"Hi, Marvis. Who's winning?"

Marvis Jones looks up from the television. "Cubs are up by two going into the bottom of the eighth. What are you doing here so late?"

"I came by to see my patient."

Marvis looks worried. "I don't know, Dom. It's kind of late—" A roar from the crowd forces him back to the screen. "Shit, the Phillies just tied it."

"Come on, Marvis."

Marvis checks the time. "Tell you what. I'll lock you in with him for fifteen minutes, as long as you leave when the nurse comes by to give him his medication."

"Deal."

The security guard escorts her to room 714, then hands her the transmitter pen linked to his beeper. "Better take this. He was violent earlier."

"No, I'll be okay."

"Take the pen, Dominique, or you don't go in."

She knows better than to argue with Marvis, who is as thorough as he is kind. She pockets the device.

Marvis activates the intercom. "Resident, you have a visitor. I'll allow her to enter once I see you fully clothed and seated on the edge of your bed." Marvis peeks through the spyhole. "Okay, he's ready. In you go." Marvis opens the door, then locks it behind her.

The lights in the room have been dimmed. She sees a dark figure sitting up on the bed. "Mick, it's Dom. Are you all right?"

Mick is leaning back against the wall. Dominique sees his face as she approaches, the left cheekbone badly bruised, the eye swollen shut.

Her heart races. "Oh, God, what did they do to you?" She grabs a hand towel, soaks it in cold water, then presses it to his face.

"Ow."

"Sorry. Here, keep this on your eye. What happened?"

"According to the official report, I slipped in the shower." He looks at her, his half smile causing pain. "I missed you. How was FSU?"

"Not good. My advisor doesn't think I'm handling my responsibilities in a professional manner."

"He thinks you're emotionally distracted by me, is that it?"

"She, and yes. As of tomorrow, I'll be assigned to a new resident. I'm sorry, Mick."

He squeezes her hand, then places it over his heart. "If it matters," he whispers, "you're the only one who's ever been able to reach me."

She swallows the lump in her throat. *Don't fall apart again.* "What happened while I was gone? I saw what you did to Raymond."

"He took the first shot."

"I heard you wouldn't leave the computer room."

"I needed to access the Internet." He releases her hand and removes several sheets of crumpled printouts from his pocket. "A major piece of the doomsday puzzle hit me today. It's so unbelievable that I had to verify the facts before I could accept it."

She takes the pages from him and begins reading.

In 1980, Nobel prize-winning physicist Luis Alvarez proposed that an extraterrestrial impact 65 million years ago was the cause of a mass extinction that ultimately ended the reign of the dinosaurs, forever changing the evolutionary pattern of life on Earth. This bold theory resulted from Alvarez's discovery of a centimeter-thick clay layer of sediment deposited across the planet's surface at the time of the asteroid cataclysm, between the Cretaceous (K) and Tertiary (T) geologic time periods. This K/T boundary clay was found to contain high concentrations of iridium, an extremely rare metal thought to exist deep within the Earth's core. Iridium is the only metal capable of surviving temperatures in excess of 4,000 degrees Fahrenheit and is practically insoluble, even to the strongest acids. The fact that high concentrations of iridium have been found in meteorites led Alvarez to propose his theory that the K/T sediment was the remains of a settled dust cloud created by the impact of a large (7-mile-wide) asteroid that struck Earth 65 million years ago. All Alvarez needed to prove his theory was to find the impact site.

In 1978, a helicopter pilot and geophysicist named Glenn Pennfield had been flying over the Gulf of Mexico completing aerial surveys designed to measure faint variations in the Earth's magnetic field, telltale signs indicating the presence of oil. Passing over an area of water just off the northwestern Yucatán Peninsula, Pennfield had detected a symmetrical ring of highly magnetic material one hundred miles across, buried one mile below the seafloor. Analysis of this immense donut-shaped configuration later confirmed that the area, covering both land and sea, was a crater—the impact site of a giant asteroid.

Named for the Yucatán town located between Progreso and Merida, the Chicxulub crater is the largest impact basin to form on our planet over the last billion years. The approximate center of the site is underwater, 21.4 degrees north latitude by 89.6 degrees west longitude, buried beneath 1,000 to 3,000 feet of limestone.

The crater is vast, 110 to 180 miles in diameter, spread out over the northwestern coast of the Yucatán Peninsula and the Gulf of Mexico. Surrounding the land-based section of the crater is a circular ring of sinkholes. These freshwater sources, called *cenotes* by the Mexican locals, are believed to have been formed in the Yucatán geography as a result of the extensive fracturing the limestone basin suffered during the asteroid's impact.

GULF OF MEXICO

Mérida

Yucatán Peninsula

BELIZE

110

Sixty-five million years ago, the Central American landmass was still underwater.

Dominique looks up, slightly irritated. "I don't get it. What's the big clue?"

"The Piri Re'is map, the one I located on the Nazca plateau. I found it sealed in an iridium canister. The map was marking the site of the Chicxulub crater. Chichén Itzá is located right along the outer rim of the impact ring. If you draw a line from the Kukulcán pyramid to the center point of the impact crater, the angle measures 23.5 degrees—the precise angle of the Earth's axis of rotation, a tilt responsible for providing us with the seasons of the year."

Here we go again. "Okay, so what does all this mean?"

"What does it mean?" Mick winces as he jumps to his feet. "It means the Kukulcán pyramid was deliberately and precisely positioned on the Yucatán Peninsula in relationship to the Chicxulub crater. There's no mistaking this, Dominique. There's no other ancient structure close to the impact site, and the angle of measurement is too precise to be happenstance."

"But how would the ancient Mayans have known about an asteroid impact 65 million years ago? Look how long it took modern man to figure it out."

"I don't know. Maybe they had the same technology the Piri Re'is map-maker used when he drew Antarctica's topography, even though it was covered by sheets of ice."

"So what's your theory—that humanity will be destroyed by an asteroid on December 21?"

Mick kneels on the floor by her feet, his swollen face in agony. "The threat to humanity isn't an asteroid. The likelihood of another asteroid impacting the same location is too astronomical even to consider. Besides, the Mayan prophesy points to the dark rift, not a celestial projectile."

He lays his aching head on her knee. Dominique smooths back his long brown hair, greasy with sweat and oil.

"Maybe you should get some rest?"

"I can't, my mind won't let me rest." He stands, pressing the compress to his swollen eye. "Something's always bothered me about the location of the Kukulcán pyramid. Unlike its counterparts in Egypt, Cambodia, and Teotihuacán, the structure always seemed displaced—like an exquisite thumb, geographically situated without rhyme or reason, while its sister fingers are dispersed at almost equal intervals across the face of the Earth. Now I think I understand."

"Understand what?"

"Good and evil, Dominique, good and evil. Somewhere within the Kukulcán pyramid lies good—the key to our salvation. Somewhere within the Chicxulub crater lies a malevolent force, growing stronger as the solstice approaches."

"How do you know—never mind, I forgot, you can feel it. Sorry."

"Dom, I need your help. You have to get me out of here."

"I tried—"

"Forget appeals, there's no time. I need out now!"

He's losing control.

Mick grabs her wrist. "Help me escape. I have to get to Chichén Itzá—"

"Let me go!" She reaches for the pen with her free hand.

"No—wait, don't call the guard—"

"Then back off, you're scaring me."

"I'm sorry, I'm sorry." He releases his grip. "Just hear me out, okay? I don't know how humanity is going to perish, but I think I know the purpose behind that deep-space radio transmission."

"Go on."

"The signal was an alarm clock, traveling down the Black Road, a celestial corridor that's aligning itself to whatever's buried in the Gulf."

Foletta was right. His delusions are getting worse. "Mick, take it easy. There's nothing down there—"

"You're wrong! I can feel it, just like I can feel the Black Road to *Xibalba* opening wider. The pathway's becoming more pronounced—"

He's rambling . . .

"I can feel it spreading, I don't know how, but I can, I swear it! And there's something else—"

She see tears of frustration leak from his eyes, or is it genuine fear?

"I can sense a presence looming on the other side of the Black Road. And it can sense me!"

The nurse enters, followed by three imposing orderlies.

"Good evening, Mr. Gabriel. It's time for your medication."

Mick spots the syringe. "That's not zyprexa!"

Two orderlies grab his arms, the third tackling him by the legs.

Dominique watches helplessly as he struggles. "Nurse, what's going on here?"

"Mr. Gabriel is to receive three shots of Thorazine a day."

"Three?"

"Foletta wants to turn me into a vegetable! Dom, don't let him—" Mick is thrashing wildly on the bed, the orderlies struggling to keep him down. "Don't let them do it. Dominique, please—"

"Nurse, I happen to be Mr. Gabriel's psychiatrist, and I—"

"Not anymore. Dr. Foletta's taken over. You can speak to him about it in the morning." The nurse swabs alcohol on Mick's arm. "Hold him steady—"

"We're trying. Just stick him—"

Mick raises his head, the blood vessels protruding from his neck. "Dom, you have to do something! The Chicxulub crater—the clock's ticking—the clock's—"

Dominique sees the dark eyes roll up, his head flopping back against the pillow.

"There, that's better," the nurse coos, retracting the syringe. "You can go now, Intern Vazquez. Mr. Gabriel won't be needing your services anymore."

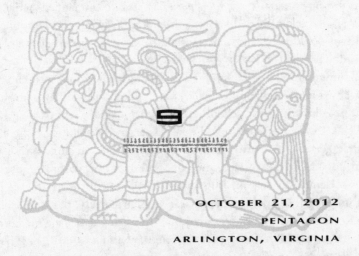

Pierre Borgia enters the briefing room and takes his seat at the oval conference table between Secretary of Defense Dick Przystas and US Army Chief of Staff General James Adams. Seated directly across from him is CIA Director Patrick Hurley, Air Force Chief of Staff, General Arne Cohen, and Chief of Naval Operations Jeffrey Gordon. The six-foot-six-inch Chief of Naval Operations acknowledges Borgia with a quick nod.

General "Big Mike" Costolo, Commandant of the Marine Corps, follows Borgia in, taking his place to Gordon's right.

At the head of the table is General Joseph Fecondo. The Chairman of the Joint Chiefs of Staff and veteran of the Vietnam and Persian Gulf Wars wipes the palm of a manicured hand across his tan, receding hairline and gazes at Borgia and Costolo with a look of annoyance. "Well, now that we're all finally here, I guess we can begin. Director Hurley?"

Patrick Hurley takes his place at the podium. Trim and fit, the fifty-two-year-old former all-American shooting guard from Notre Dame looks like he still plays competitive basketball.

Hurley activates a control switch at the podium. The lights dim, and a black-and-white satellite photo appears on the large screen to the CIA director's right.

Borgia recognizes the quality of the image. The digitalized photo comes from the C-8236 high-resolution thermal-imaging camera, mounted aboard the Air Force's top-secret aircraft, *Darkstar*. The stealth Unmanned Aerial Vehicle (UAV) is a flat, clam-shaped vessel with enormous wings. *Darkstar* operates at altitudes of 65,000 feet and can transmit close-up images in all weather conditions, day or night.

A computerized square appears in red. Hurley positions it, then enhances the image within. Details of a small school and children's playground enlarge and focus. Adjacent to the school is a well-enclosed concrete parking lot.

The CIA director clears his throat. "The series of photos you're about to see were taken above an area just northeast of Pyongyang along North Korea's western coast. On the surface, the site appears to be nothing more than a children's elementary school. But buried 1.3 kilometers beneath this parking lot is Kim Jong Il's underground nuclear-weapons facility, the same facility the North Koreans used when they first began test-firing two-stage medium-range missiles back in 1998. We suspect the site may also house the new TAEPODONG II missile, an ICBM with a range of twenty-two hundred miles, capable of carrying multiple nuclear warheads."

Hurley clicks to the next photo. "*Darkstar*'s been monitoring the facility for the last two weeks. The photos I'm going to show you were taken yesterday evening, between the hours of eleven o'clock and 1:00 A.M., Seoul." Hurley magnifies the image to reveal the figures of two men exiting a black Mercedes-Benz.

"The gentleman on the right is Iranian President Ali Shamkhani. The gentleman on the left is China's new Communist Party Leader and former military commander, General Li Xiliang. As Pierre will tell you, the general's hard-line Communist all the way."

Hurley clicks through several more photos, stopping at a man dressed in a long, black, leather coat, who seems to be staring up at the heavens as if he knows his picture is being taken.

"Christ," Borgia whispers, "it's Viktor Grozny."

"Almost looks like he's staring at our camera," General Cohen adds.

"The roll call's not quite over." The CIA director changes the image. "And our host for the evening—"

Borgia's heart races faster. "Kim Jong Il."

Hurley turns the lights back up and takes his place at the conference table. "Viktor Grozny's nuclear deterrent summit was held weeks ago. So why would the leaders of four nations representing thirty-eight percent of the nuclear weapons on this planet choose to meet in secrecy at this particular site?"

Secretary of Defense Dick Pryzstas leans back in his chair and brushes back his mop of white hair. "Admiral Gordon, would you share the information you and I spoke about earlier?"

The lanky admiral strikes a key on his laptop. "Our latest satellite surveillance indicates the Iranians have bolstered their military presence along the northern shores of the Persian Gulf. In addition to repositioning their Howitzers and mobile SAM sites, Iran recently purchased an additional forty-six Hudong-class patrol boats from China. Each of these vessels are equipped with C-802 antiship cruise missiles. The Iranians are also in the process of doubling their Chinese Silkworm missile sites along the coastline and, despite UN protests, have continued to fortify their surface-to-air and surface-to-surface missile batteries on Qeshm, Abu Musa, and the Sirri islands. In essence, Iran is preparing to effectuate a gauntlet at the narrowest section of the Strait of Hormuz, an area only fifty kilometers wide."

"The Iranians claim the military buildup is in preparation for Grozny's military exercise in December," Secretary of Defense Przystas states. "Of course, should hostilities break out in the Middle East, the Iranian gauntlet would prevent our fleet from accessing the Persian Gulf."

"Not to add to the paranoia, but what about nukes?" General Costolo pushes back from the table. "The Israelis claim Grozny sold the Iranians sickle missiles with nuclear warheads when he helped negotiate the 2007 Middle East Peace Accord."

Admiral Gordon turns to face Costolo. "Iran has the strength and geography to carve out a new domain for itself in the Middle East. If war broke out, Russia would be in a position to consolidate the Middle East as a hegemony."

"Grozny certainly looks like he's preparing for nuclear war," Borgia states.

"Pierre, Russia's been preparing for nuclear war for the last sixty years," General Fecondo interrupts. "Let's not forget that it was our own forging ahead to build a Missile Defense Shield that added to their own paranoia."

"There may be one other hidden variable to consider, General," the CIA director says. "NSA intercepted a communication between Russian Prime Minister Makashov and the Chinese Defense Minister. The conversation concerned some kind of new high-tech weapon."

"What sort of weapon?" Pryztas asks.

"Fusion was mentioned, nothing more."

Sanibel Island,
West Coast of Florida

Dominique slows the black Pronto Spyder convertible, keeping the roadster just under fifty as she passes through the Sanibel Island bridge toll booth. Electronic sensors record her vehicle's license plate and VIN, the information instantly fed to the Department of Transportation, which adds the amount of the toll to her monthly transit bill. She keeps the car under fifty for the next mile, knowing she is still in range of the automated system's radar gun.

Dominique maneuvers the Spyder across the bay bridge to Sanibel and Captiva Island, a residential and resort area nestled on a small island on the Gulf Coast of Florida. She drives north along the heavily shaded single-lane roadway, then winds her way west, passing several large hotels before entering a residential area.

Edith and Isadore Axler live in a two-story cube-shaped beach home situated on a half acre corner lot facing the Gulf of Mexico. At first glance, the exterior redwood slats enclosing the home give it the look of an enormous party lantern, especially at night. This protective layer of scrim protects the structure from hurricanes, creating, in effect, a house within a house.

The south wing of the Axler home has been renovated to accommodate a sophisticated acoustics lab, one of only three on the Gulf Coast interfaced with SOSUS, the United States Navy's Underwater Sound Surveillance System. The sixteen-billion-dollar network of undersea microphones, built by the federal government during the Cold War to spy on enemy submarines, is a global grid tied to Navy shore stations by some thirty thousand miles of undersea cables.

As the military's need for SOSUS began to dwindle in the early 1990s, scientists, universities, and private businesses successfully petitioned the Navy for access to the acoustics network. For oceanographers, SOSUS became the Hubble Telescope of undersea exploration. Scientists could now hear the super-low-frequency vibrations made by ice floes cracking, seabeds quaking, and underwater volcanoes erupting, sounds normally lying far below the range of human hearing.

For marine biologists like Isadore Axler, SOSUS provided a new way of studying the planet's most intelligent ocean-dwelling life-forms: the cetaceans. With the assistance of the National Fish and Wildlife Foundation, the Axler home had become a SOSUS acoustics station, focusing specifically on the cetacean inhabitants of the Gulf of Mexico. Using SOSUS, the Axlers could now record and analyze voiceprints of whales, identify species, count populations, even track single subjects across the northern hemisphere.

Dominique turns left down the cul-de-sac, then right into the last driveway, comforted by the familiar sound of pebbles crunching beneath the weight of her roadster.

Edith Axler greets her as the convertible top snaps shut into place. Edie is an astute, gray-haired woman in her early seventies, with brown eyes that exude a teacher's wisdom and a warm smile that projects a mother's love.

"Hi, doll. How was your drive?"

"Fine." Dominique hugs her adoptive mother, squeezing her tight.

"Something's wrong?" Edith pulls back, noticing the tears. "What is it?"

"Nothing. I'm just glad to be home."

"Don't play me for senile. It's that patient of yours, isn't it? What's his name—Mick?"

Dominique nods. "My former patient."

"Come on, we'll talk before Iz comes out." Edith leads her by the hand to the Gulf-access canal located on the south side of the property. Docked along the concrete seawall are two boats, the smaller of the two a thirty-five-foot fishing boat belonging to the Axlers.

They sit together, hand in hand, on a wooden park bench facing the water.

Dominique stares at a gray-and-white pelican basking on one of the wooden pilings. "I remember when I was young—whenever I had a bad day, you always used to sit with me out here."

Edie nods. "This has always been my favorite spot."

"You used to say, 'How bad can things be, if you can still enjoy such a beautiful view.'" She points to the rustic-looking forty-eight-foot trawler docked behind the Axler's fishing boat. "Whose boat is that?"

"It belongs to the Sanibel Treasure Hunters Club. You remember Rex and Dory Simpson. Iz rents the space out to them. See that canvas, there's a two-man minisub secured to the decking beneath it. Iz will take you out for a spin in it tomorrow if you'd like."

"In a minisub? That'd be fun."

Edie squeezes her daughter's hand. "Tell me about Mick. Why are you so upset?"

Dominique wipes away a tear. "Ever since fat-fucking Foletta switched my assignment, he's kept Mick on heavy doses of Thorazine. God, Ead, it's so cruel, I can't—I can't even bear to look at him anymore. He's so doped up—he just sits there, strapped in a wheelchair like some drooling vegetable. Foletta pushes him out to the yard every afternoon and just leaves him sitting in the arts and crafts area, like Mick's some kind of hopeless geriatric patient."

"Dom, I know you care a great deal about Mick, but you have to remember, you're only one person. You can't expect to save the world."

"What? What did you say?"

"I just meant that as a psychiatrist, you can't expect to help every institutionalized resident you come in contact with. You've worked with Mick for a month. Like it or not, this is out of your hands. You have to know when to walk away."

"You know me better than that. I can't just walk away, not when someone's being abused."

Edie squeezes her daughter's hand again. They remain silent, watching the pelican flap its wings as it maintains its precarious balance on the piling.

Not when someone is being abused. Hearing her own words, Edie thinks back to the first time she met the frightened little girl from Guatemala. She had been working part-time as a school nurse and counselor. The ten-year-old had been brought to her, complaining of stomach cramps. Edith had held the little girl's hand until the pain had subsided. This small act of motherly love would forever bind Dominique to the woman, whose own heart broke as she learned about the sexual abuse being inflicted upon the child by her older cousins. Edie had filed a report and arranged for foster care. She and Iz had adopted Dominique six months later.

"Okay, doll, tell me what we can do to help Mick."

"There's only one solution. We need to get him out of there."

"By out, I assume you mean to another asylum."

"No, I mean out, as in permanently out."

"A jailbreak?"

"Well, yes. Mick may be a bit confused, but he's not insane. He doesn't belong in a mental institution."

"Are you certain, because you don't sound too sure yourself. Didn't you tell me that Mick is convinced the world is coming to an end?"

"Not the world, humanity, and yes, he does believe that. He's just a little paranoid, but who wouldn't be after spending eleven years in solitary."

Edie watches Dominique fidget. "There's something else you're not telling me."

Dominique turns to face her. "This will sound crazy, but there seems to be truth in many of Mick's delusions. His whole doomsday theory is based on some three-thousand-year-old Mayan prophecy. I'm in the process of reading his father's journal, and some of the findings are mind-boggling. Mick practically predicted the arrival of that deep-space radio signal on the fall equinox. Ead, when I lived in Guatemala, my grandmother used to tell me stories about my maternal ancestors. The things she said were pretty frightening."

Edie smiles. "You're starting to scare me."

"Oh, I know it's just superstitious nonsense, but I feel like I owe it to Mick to at least check some of these things out. It might help alleviate some of his fears."

"What things?"

"Mick is convinced that whatever's going to destroy humanity is hidden in the Gulf of Mexico." Dominique reaches into her jeans pocket and removes several folded pages, handing them to Edie.

Edie glances at the printout. "The Chicxulub impact crater? How's a depression buried a mile beneath the seafloor going to kill humanity?"

"I don't know. Neither did Mick. But I was hoping—"

"—you were hoping that Iz could check it out using SOSUS."

Dominique smiles. "It would make *me* feel a lot better."

Edie gives her daughter a hug. "Come on. Iz is in the lab."

Professor Isadore Axler sits at the SOSUS station, headphones on, eyes closed. His face, speckled with liver spots, is serene as he listens to the haunting cetacean echoes.

Dominique taps him on the shoulder.

Iz opens his eyes, his thinning gray goatee spreading into a tight smile as he removes the headphones from his ears. "Humpbacks."

"Is that how you say hello? Humpbacks."

Iz stands and gives her a hug. "You look tired, kiddo."

"I'm fine."

Edie steps forward. "Iz, Dominique has a favor to ask."

"What, another one?"

"When did I ask the last one?"

"When you were sixteen. You asked to borrow the car. Most traumatic night of my life." Iz pats her cheek. "Speak."

She hands him the information on the Chicxulub crater. "I need you to use SOSUS and tell me if you hear anything down there."

"And what am I supposed to be listening for?"

"I don't know. Anything unusual, I guess."

Iz gives her his famous "stop wasting my time," stare, his tangled gray eyebrows knitting together.

"Iz, stop staring at her and just do it," Edie commands.

The elderly biologist returns to his chair, muttering, "Anything unusual, huh. Maybe we'll hear a whale farting." He types the coordinates into the computer, repositioning the headphones.

Dominique hugs him from behind, kissing his cheek.

"All right, all right, enough with the bribes. Listen, kiddo, I don't know what you're looking to accomplish, but this crater's spread out over a vast area. What I'll do is estimate the center point, which looks to be somewhere near the Campeche shelf, just southwest of the Alacan Reef. I'll program the computer to begin a low-frequency search. We'll start at one to fifty hertz and gradually increase the cycles. Problem is, you're focusing in on an area that's loaded with oil and gas fields. The Gulf basin is all limestone and sandstone, containing porous geological traps. Oil and gas are constantly leaking out from fissures along the seafloor, and SOSUS is going to register every one of these leaks."

"So what do you suggest?"

"I suggest we eat lunch." Iz finishes programming the computer. "The system will automatically home in on any acoustical disturbances in the area."

"How long do you think it'll take SOSUS to find something?" The remark earns Dominique another stare.

"What am I, God? Hours, days, weeks, maybe never. What difference does it make? In the end, all we'll probably have is a bunch of worthless background noise."

Washington, DC

The maître d' switches on his smile as the fourth-most-powerful person in the United States enters the posh French restaurant. *"Bon soir, Monsieur Borgia."*

"Bon soir, Felipe. I believe I'm expected."

"Oui, certainement. Follow me, please." The maître d' leads him past candlelit tables to a private room next to the bar. He knocks twice on the outer double doors, then turns to Borgia. "Your party is waiting inside."

"Merci." Borgia slips the twenty into the gloved palm as the door swings open from the inside.

"Pierre, come in." Republican Party cochairman Charlie Myers shakes Borgia's hand and slaps him affectionately on the shoulder. "Late as usual. We're already two rounds ahead of you. Bloody Mary, right?"

"Yes, fine." The private meeting room is paneled in deep walnut like the rest of the restaurant. A half dozen white-clothed tables fill the soundproof room. Seated at the center table are two men. The older, white-haired gentleman is Joseph H. Randolph, Sr., a Texas billionaire who has been a surrogate father and friend to Borgia for more than twenty years. Borgia does not recognize the heavyset man seated across from him.

Randolph stands to embrace him. "Lucky Pierre, good to see you, son. Let's have a look at you. You put on a few pounds?"

Borgia blushes. "Maybe a few."

"Join the club." The heavyset man stands, extending a thick hand. "Pete Mabus, Mabus Tech Industries."

Borgia recognizes the defense contractor's name. "Nice to meet you."

"Pleasure's all mine. Sit down and take a load off."

Charlie Myers brings Borgia his drink. "Gentlemen, you'll excuse me, I need to use the little boys' room."

Randolph waits until Myers has left the room. "Pierre, I saw your folks last week up in Rehobeth. All of us are real upset 'bout you not getting the vice presidential nomination. Maller's doing a real disservice to the entire party."

Borgia nods. "The president's concerned about getting reelected. The polls tell him Chaney will give him the support the party needs in the South."

"Maller ain't thinking down the road." Mabus points a chubby finger. "What this country needs now is strong leadership, not another dove like Chaney as second-in-command."

"I couldn't agree more, but I have no say in the matter."

Randolph leans closer. "Maybe not now, son, but in four years you'll have a big say. I've already spoken to some of the powers that be, and there's a general consensus that you'll represent the party in 2016."

Borgia holds back a smile. "Joe, that's great to hear, but four years is still a long time away."

Mabus shakes his head. "You need to prepare now, son. Let me give you a for instance. My boy Lucien's a fucking genius. I ain't shittin' you, kid's only three, and he already knows how to surf the Internet. I'm raisin' him to take over Mabus Tech by the time he's sixteen. We play our political cards right, and he'll be a goddam trillionaire by the time he's your age. Point I'm trying to make is that all of us gotta be ready long before opportunity knocks, and for you, it's already knocking. Take this upcoming Russian-Chinese military exercise. A lot of registered voters are pissed off—making it just the sort of squabble that can make or break a presidential candidate."

"Pete's right, Pierre. The way the public perceives your command presence during the next few months could help determine the outcome of the next election. They need to see a take-charge kinda guy, a hawk who's not about to let the goddam Russkies or sand niggers dictate the way we run our country. Hell, we haven't had a strong presence in the White House since Bush left office."

Mabus is close enough now for Borgia to smell what the man had for lunch. "Pierre, this conflict gives us a great opportunity to show the public your strength of character."

Borgia leans back. "Understood."

"Good, good. Now, there's one last item on our agenda, something we feel needs to be cleaned up."

Mabus picks at a hangnail. "Sort of a skeleton in your closet."

Randolph nods as he lights a cigarette. "It's this Gabriel character, Pierre, the one you had committed after your accident. Once we announce your nomination, the press is gonna start digging. Won't be long before they find out about what you did to manipulate things in Massachusetts. Could be real messy."

Borgia's face turns red. "See this eye, Mr. Mabus. That crazy motherfucker did this to me. Now you want me to release him?"

"Pay attention, son. Pete didn't say nothing about you letting him go. Just tie off the goddam loose end before the campaign starts. Hell, all of us worth a shit got skeletons in the closet. All we want you to do is take 'em out and bury 'em—Mr. President."

Borgia takes a calming breath, then nods. "I understand what you're saying, gentlemen, and I appreciate your support. I think I know what has to be done."

Mabus offers his handshake. "And we appreciate you, Mr. Secretary. We also know that when the time comes, you won't forget who your friends are."

Borgia shakes Mabus's sweaty palm. "Tell me honestly, gentlemen, my family's political presence aside—when I was chosen, how heavily did it weigh that Senator Chaney just happens to be black?"

Randolph flashes a knowing smile. "Well, son, let's just say they don't call it the White House for nothing."

JOURNAL OF JULIUS GABRIEL

*T*he Nazca plateau in southern Peru is a barren desert, 40 miles long and six miles wide. It is a desolate, unforgiving flatland, a dead zone cradled by the Andes Mountains. It also happens to have extraordinarily unique geology in that Nazca's underlying soil contains high levels of gypsum, a natural adhesive. Remoistened each day by the morning dew, the gypsum literally keeps the indigenous iron and silica stones that proliferate in the desert glued to its surface. These dark pebbles retain the sun's heat, giving rise to a protective shield of warm air that virtually eliminates the effects of the wind. It also makes the plateau one of the driest places on Earth, receiving less than an inch of rain every decade.

For the artist wishing to express himself on the grandest of scales, the Nazca plateau becomes the perfect canvas, for what is drawn upon this plateau tends to stay there. Yet it was not until a pilot flew overhead in 1947 that modern man first discovered the mysterious drawings and geometric lines carved upon this Peruvian landscape thousands of years ago.

There are more than 13,000 lines crossing the Nazca desert.

A few of these markings extend for distances exceeding five miles, stretching over rough terrain while miraculously remaining perfectly straight. Although some would like to believe the lines represent prehistoric runways for ancient astronauts, we now know them to be astronomically aligned, marking the positions of the winter solstice, the equinox, the constellation Orion, and perhaps other heavenly bodies as yet unbeknownst to us.

More bizarre are the hundreds of icons illustrating animals. At ground level, these colossal zoomorphs appear only as random indentations made by the scraping away of tons of black volcanic pebbles to expose the yellow gypsum below. But when viewed from high in the air, the Nazca drawings come alive, representing a unified artistic vision and engineering achievement that has survived unscathed for thousands of years.

The artwork of the Nazca plateau was completed at two very distinct time intervals. Although it seems contrary to our notion of evolution, it is the earlier drawings that are by far the superior. These include the monkey, the spider, the pyramid, and the serpent. Not only are the likenesses incredibly accurate, but the figures themselves, most larger than a football field, were each drawn using one continuous, unbroken line.

Who were the mysterious artists who created these desert images? How were they able to accomplish such a magnificent feat on such a grand scale? More importantly— what was their motivation for carving the figures into the plateau in the first place?

It was in the summer of 1972 that Maria, Pierre, and I first arrived in this wretched South American desert. At the time we weren't at all interested in the drawings, our intent being simply to determine the relationship between the elongated skulls of Mesoamerica and those found in Nazca. I can still recall my first week working on the plateau—swearing at the vile Peruvian sun which tortured me on a daily basis, blistering my face and arms. If you had told me then that I would eventually return to this purgatory of sand and rock to live out the rest of my days, I'd have thought you insane.

Insane.

I struggle to even write the cursed word. By now, many of you may question whether you are reading the accounts of a scientist or madman. I must confess, not a day goes by that I don't debate the very issue myself. If I have lost my mind, then it was Nazca that did the deed, her incessant heat causing my brain to swell, her unforgiving surface pounding the arthritis into my bones for decades. Any chance of attaining inner peace fled the day I condemned my family to that desert. I pray Michael forgives me for raising him in that hellhole, and for the other childhood unjustness I brought to bear upon his tortured soul.

From the summer of '72 to the winter of '74, our little trio toiled in Nazca, unearthing hundreds of deformed skulls found in ceremonial burial grounds located close to the Andes Mountains. A thorough examination of each skull revealed that the deformations had been caused by the strapping of wooden boards across the child's head at an early age.

It was in January of '74 that we discovered a royal burial ground, situated close to the Andes Mountains. The walls of this incredible tomb were made of enormous columns of rock, each weighing between 10 and 20 tons. Within the subterranean chamber were 13 male mummies, each possessing an elongated skull. Our excitement reached new levels after extensive X-rays and other tests revealed that the deceased, like the La Venta skull Maria had found, had achieved the shape of their skull purely as a result of genetics!

Discovering a new race of men proved to be as controversial as startling. Upon hearing of our find, Peru's president ordered all of our artifacts placed in a basement vault of the Archaeological Museum in Ica, away from public viewing. (To this day, the skulls can only be seen by special invitation.)

Who was this mysterious race? What caused them to be born with skulls twice that of normal size?

We know the first people to arrive in the Andean region were hunters and fishermen who settled along the Peruvian coastline sometime around 10,000 BC. Then, around 400 BC, another group arrived on the Nazca plateau. We know little about these mysterious people, other than they referred to their leaders as the Viracochas, demigods who were said to have migrated to South America just after the Great Flood. The Viracochas were described as pale-skinned wise men with deep, ocean blue eyes and flowing white beards and hair. These ancient rulers apparently possessed superior intelligence and larger than normal craniums, their bizarre appearance no doubt influencing their followers to practice the art of skull deformation in an attempt to emulate their royal leaders.

The physical resemblance between the Viracochas and the great Mayan teacher, Kukulcán, is too incredible to ignore. The fact that a tall, bearded Caucasian also appears in the legends of numerous other ancient Andean cultures provides further clues of a link between Mesoamerican Indians and those of South America.

The most dominant Indian civilization to rise out of the mountainous jungles of South America were the Inca. Like the Maya, they too worshiped a great teacher, a wise man who advanced his people through the teachings of science, agriculture, and architecture. Although we now know that most feats credited to Inca ingenuity actually originated from earlier ethnic groups, written accounts tell us it was this bearded Caucasian who inspired the creation of the great Inca roadways as well as the famous agricultural terraces built along steep mountain slopes. The bearded one is also believed to have been the artist who created the older, more sophisticated drawings of Nazca. Although he is known by different names among various Andean cultures, the Inca worshiped him simply as Viracocha, meaning "foam from the sea."

Fortress of Sacsayhuaman—Nazca photo #109 Julius Gabriel 1972

Like Kukulcán among the Maya and Quetzalcoatl to the Aztecs, Viracocha is the most revered figure in Inca history. Were the Viracochas of 400 BC his ancestors? Could he be a distant relative of Kukulcán? If so, does his presence in ancient South America have anything to do with the Mayan calendar and its forecast of doom?

Seeking answers, we abandoned the Nazca desert and headed for the Andes Mountains, intent on exploring two ancient sites believed to have been created by the Inca deity. The first of these was the fortress of Sacsayhuaman, a monstrous structure erected just north of Cuzco. Like the royal tomb, the walls of this mind-boggling citadel are composed of giant irregularly shaped granite boulders which have miraculously been fitted so perfectly together that I could not wedge the edge of my pocketknife between the stones.

It strains the imagination to think how the Andean Indians were able to transport stones weighing 100 tons or more over ten miles of mountainous terrain from their distant quarry, then fit them perfectly into place along the fortification. (One 28-foot-high monster weighs in excess of 700,000 pounds.) Archaeologists, still struggling to explain away this unfathomable feat, have attempted to duplicate a small fraction of Viracocha's legacy by transporting one medium-sized boulder from a distant quarry using advanced engineering principles and a small army of volunteers. To this day, every undertaking has failed miserably.

We know the fortress of Sacsayhuaman was erected to protect its inhabitants from hostile forces. The true purpose behind the design of Viracocha's other structure, the ancient Andean city of Tiahuanaco, still remains a mystery.

Situated 12,500 feet above the Pacific in the Andean Mountains of Bolivia, the ruins of Tiahuanaco rest on the ancient shoreline of Lake Titicaca, the highest body of navigable water in the world. After examining the impossible engineering feats at Sacsayhuaman, I would have sworn that nothing henceforth would surprise me. Despite this, the site of Tiahuanaco was simply overwhelming. The ground plan of this ancient city consists of three limestone temples and four other structures, all set on a series of raised platforms and sunken rectangles. As in Sacsayhuaman, the majority of construction consists of impossibly large boulders fitted together perfectly.

But there is clearly more to Tiahuanaco than meets the eye. A hidden agenda is present here—an agenda that may relate to the very salvation of our species.

Dominating the city is the remains of the Akapana, a step pyramid whose four directionally oriented sides each measure 690 feet. The purpose of Akapana, alas, must remain a mystery as the invading Spanish used the structure as a quarry, robbing the temple of 90 percent of its facing.

The most wondrous structure in Tiahuanaco is the Gate of the Sun, a single, massive block of stone weighing 100 tons. This mammoth work of art stands in the northwest corner of the complex like some prehistoric Arc de Triomphe. Somehow, its creator managed to transport this enormous block of stone from a quarry miles away, carve out a perfect portal of a door using God knows what kind of tool, then vertically align the piece into place.

Giant pillars proliferate in the city. At the center of a sunken, rectangular open-air pit stands a seven-foot-tall red rock carving of Viracocha himself. The elongated skull is present, as well as the prominent forehead, thin straight nose, and the beard-covered jawline. The arms and hands are folded. A final feature worth mentioning: Rising along either side of the wise man's robe are two serpents, similar to those depicted throughout Mesoamerica.

The most controversial structure of Tiahuanaco is the Kalasasaya, a sunken temple located in the center of the city, surrounded by huge walls. Twelve-foot-high stone blocks have been erected within its confines. Although Pierre concluded that the Kalasasaya had to have been a fortress, Maria believed otherwise, recognizing the alignment of the erect, monolithic blocks as being similar to those found at Stonehenge.

As usual, Maria turned out to be correct. The Kalasasaya is not a fortress but a celestial observatory, perhaps the oldest in the world.

So what does all this mean?

Five years out of Cambridge, my fellow archaeologists and I had found overwhelming evidence indicating a superior race of Caucasians had influenced the development of both the Mesoamerican and South American Indians. These bearded men, possessing genetically deformed skulls, had somehow designed and overseen the construction of magnificent monuments, the purpose of which still baffled us.

Maria was convinced that the design of the Kalasasaya observatory was too close to that of Stonehenge to be a mere coincidence. She believed that it was imperative that we continue following the trail of this Caucasian race and their ancient wisdom east to see where it would lead.

Pierre Borgia was not happy about this. Two years at Nazca had been more than enough to satiate his appetite for archaeology, and he was being pressured by his well-to-do family to return to the States to pursue a political career. The problem was that he loved Maria, in fact, the two of them had planned to wed in the spring.

As much as she cared for Pierre, Maria was not ready to give up her quest to resolve the Mayan prophecy, insisting that we continue to follow the bearded ones' ancient trail to Stonehenge.

The thought of returning to England was all the enticement we needed, and so I booked us passage and we flew on to the next leg of our journey, one I knew was destined to break up our little triumvirate forever.

—Excerpt from the Journal of Professor Julius Gabriel,

Ref. Catalogue 1972–75   pages 6–412
Photo Journal Floppy Disk 2: File name: NAZCA, Photo 109

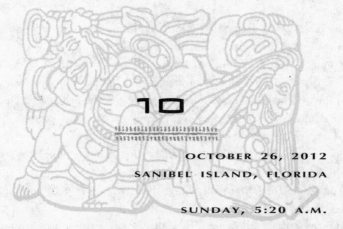

Doll, wake up!"

Dominique opens her eyes, yawning. "What's wrong?"

"Iz wants you down in the lab. SOSUS located something."

Adrenaline pumping, she kicks off the blanket and follows Edie down the back staircase to the acoustics lab.

Iz is seated at his SOSUS terminal, headphones on, his back to her. Dominique notices the sound system is recording data.

He swings around in his chair to face her. She sees he is dressed only in a bathrobe and slippers. Tufts of his thinning charcoal gray hair stand wildly on end around the headphones. The serious expression on his face stifles her laugh.

"I checked the system last night before I went to bed. The only unusual thing SOSUS had located was what we call a 'dead zone,' an area devoid of marine life. This in itself isn't that unusual. The Gulf experiences annual dead zones every summer when plankton blooms created by fertilizer runoff deprive the water of oxygen. But those dead zones usually occur off the coast of Texas and Louisiana, and never in water this deep. Anyway, I reprogrammed SOSUS to concentrate on this area and left the system on search mode all night. The alarm went off about fifteen minutes ago." Iz removes the headphones and hands them to her. "Listen to this."

She hears static, like the *zapping* sound a fluorescent tube makes before it shorts out. "Sounds like white noise."

"That's what I said. Keep listening." Iz changes the setting to a higher frequency.

The white noise disappears. Now Dominique hears an incessant, metallic *thumping* sound. "Wow. It sounds like hydraulics."

Iz nods. "Ask your mother, I said the same thing. In fact, I thought SOSUS had picked up a submarine resting on the bottom. Then I rechecked the location." Iz hands her a computer printout. "The acoustics aren't coming from the seafloor, they're coming from *below* the seafloor. Four thousand, six hundred and eighty feet below the seafloor, to be exact."

Dominique's heart is thumping like a kettledrum. "But how's that possible—"

"You tell me! What am I listening to, Dominique? Is this a joke, because if it is—"

"Iz, stop talking nonsense." Edie places a reassuring arm around Dominique's waist. "Dom had no idea what you'd find. The information was given to her by, well, by a friend."

"Who's this friend? I want to meet him."

Dominique rubs the sleep from her eyes. "You can't."

"Why not? Ead, what's going on here?"

Dominique glances at Edie, who nods. "He's—he's a former patient of mine."

Iz looks from Dominique to his wife, then back to Dominique. "Your friend's a mental patient? *Oy vey*—"

"Iz, what difference does it make? Something's out there, right? We need to investigate—"

"Slow down, kiddo. I can't just contact the National Oceanic and Atmospheric Administration and tell them that I located hydraulic sounds originating a mile below the Campeche shelf. The first thing they're going to want to know is *how* I discovered the acoustics in the first place. What am I supposed to tell them—that some looney-tune gave my daughter the coordinates from his cell in Miami."

"Would it make a difference if Stephen Hawking gave you the coordinates?"

"Yes, actually it would, it would make a huge difference." Iz rubs his forehead. "The old bull in a china shop routine doesn't work anymore, Dominique, at least not when it comes to SOSUS. About three years ago, I used the system to detect vibrations originating from beneath the Gulf floor that sounded exactly like a sea quake." Iz shakes his head at the memory. "You tell her, Ead."

Edie smiles. "Your father thought we were minutes away from getting hit by a major tsunami. He panicked and ordered the Coast Guard to evacuate all the beaches."

"Turns out I had the system set too high. What I thought were sea quakes was actually the phone company dredging cable sixty miles offshore. I felt like a goddam moron. I called in a lot of favors to get our station hooked up to SOSUS. I can't afford another screwup like the last one."

"So you're not going to investigate?"

"Now, I didn't say that. What I'll do is start a bible and continue to record and monitor the area closely, but I'm not going to contact any federal agency until I'm absolutely certain that this discovery of yours warrants it."

Miami, Florida

10:17 P.M.

Mick Gabriel is sitting on the edge of his bed, rocking silently. His black eyes are vacant, his lips slightly parted. A thin string of saliva drools from his unshaven chin.

131

Tony Barnes enters Mick's room. The male orderly has just returned from a three-week suspension. "Trick or treat, vegetable. Time for your nightly shot." He lifts Mick's limp right arm from his lap and inspects the series of purple contusions appearing along the anterior forearm.

"Ah, fuck it." The orderly jabs the needle into the arm, injecting the Thorazine into an already butchered vein.

Mick's eyes roll upward as his body falls forward, collapsing in a heap at the orderly's feet.

The orderly prods Mick's head with the toe of his sneaker. He glances over his shoulder to verify they are alone, then licks Mick's ear.

Barnes hears Marvis making his rounds. "Pleasant dreams, girlfriend." He hurries out.

The door double-clicks shut. The lights in the pod dim.

Mick's eyes open.

He staggers to the sink and washes his face and ear with cold water. Cursing under his breath, he presses a thumb to the bleeding, bruised vein. Then, feeling the haze closing in around him, he slumps painfully to his knees and takes up a push-up position.

For the next two hours, Mick forces his body through an agonizing ritual of calisthenics. Push-ups, sit-ups, jumping jacks, running in place—anything to keep his metabolism racing, anything to burn off the tranquilizer before it can overwhelm his central nervous system.

Of the three, the morning shots were always the worst. Foletta would administer the dose himself, monitoring his patient as he cooed softly in Mick's ear, taunting him. Once the drug took effect, he'd place Mick in a wheelchair and push him around from pod to pod on his morning rounds, sending a warning to the other residents that dissidence of any kind would not be tolerated.

The nightly exercises after the third shot of the day were a worthwhile struggle. By increasing his metabolism, Mick found he was able to burn off the effects of the drug faster, gradually giving him a toehold on sanity. By the fourth morning, he had regained enough of his mental equilibrium to focus on a plan.

From that moment forward he had acted the part of a mindless bag of bones. The seventh-floor orderlies would arrive each morning to find him lying on the floor of his cell in a deep stupor, totally incoherent. This angered the attendants, who were now forced to feed their incapacitated patient, and, to their utter disgust, even change his soiled clothing. After a week of this routine, Foletta was forced to cut Mick's dosage from three times a day to just an afternoon and an evening injection.

Over the last few weeks, Foletta's schedule had become inundated with other matters. He stopped checking in on Mick, trusting his care to the orderlies.

For the first time in his eleven years of captivity, the security surrounding Michael Gabriel had become lax.

NASA Goddard Space Flight Center
Greenbelt, Maryland

NASA Director Brian Dodds stares in disbelief at the immense computer printout scrolled out across his desk. "Explain it to me again, Swicky."

Dodds's assistant, Gary Swickle, points a thick index finger to the checkerboard pattern, consisting of thirteen square boxes across, running continuously over thousands of sheets of paper. "The radio signal is made up of thirteen different harmonics, represented here by these thirteen columns. Each harmonic can be played out over any one of twenty distinct, consecutive frequencies. This allows for a possible combination of 260 different sound bytes, or commands."

"But you say there's no repeating pattern?"

"Only at the very beginning." Swickle locates the first page of the printout. "When the signal first appears, the harmonics are kept very simple, several notes played out over just one frequency, yet repeated over and over again. Now look here. At the seventeen-minute mark, everything changes, all thirteen harmonics and twenty frequencies suddenly coming into play at once. From that point on, the signal never repeats itself. The remaining 185 minutes use all 260 combinations of sound bytes, indicating a highly structured communiqué."

"You're absolutely certain that no primer exists within the first seventeen minutes? No mathematical equations? Nothing that indicates translation instructions of any kind?"

"Nothing."

"Damn." Dodds rubs his blood shot eyes.

"What are you thinking, boss?"

"Do you remember back in the summer of '98 when we lost contact with SOHO? Before Arecibo relocated the satellite, we kept transmitting the same simple radio signal over and over again, attempting to reestablish contact with the satellite's main computer. That's what the first seventeen minutes of this signal reminds me of. No primer, no instructions or codex, just a deep-space carrier signal repeating itself like a ringing telephone, waiting for the other party to pick up so the information can be downloaded."

"I agree, but it makes no sense. The extraterrestrials that transmitted this signal couldn't possibly have expected our species to be able to translate all this information without a primer."

Swickle notices that his director's face looks pale. "What?"

"Just a crazy thought. Ignore me, I'm wiped out."

"Come on, boss."

"Well, I was thinking about SOHO. Our transmission obviously didn't require a primer because SOHO's computer was already programmed under our command. Maybe this signal contains no primer because it's not necessary."

"You mean, this radio signal wasn't intended to be translated?"

"No, Swick." Dodds shoots his assistant a worried look. "I mean, what if the signal wasn't intended for *us*?"

November 5, 2012
Sanibel Island, Florida

The chant of "*four more years—four more years*" stirs Edith Axler awake. She sits up and checks the time, then switches off the television and heads downstairs to the lab.

Isadore is still hunched over at the SOSUS station, listening.

"Iz, for God's sake, it's eleven-thirty—"

"*Shhh.*" He removes his headphones and switches on the exterior speaker. "Listen."

She hears a deep *humming* sound. "Sounds like a generator."

"That's nothing. Wait."

Moments pass, and then a high-pitched whine of what sounds like a hydraulic drill whistles at them through the speakers, followed immediately by a metallic *clanking* that continues for several minutes.

Iz smiles at his wife. "Is that incredible?"

"It sounds as if something's being pieced together. Probably an oil rig preparing to drill."

"Either that, or another one of those geological expeditions investigating the crater. Whatever it is, the degree of activity has intensified over the last thirty hours. I sent an e-mail to the NOAA to check on both possibilities but haven't heard a word. Who won the election?"

"President Maller."

"Good. Now that that's over with, maybe someone at the State Department will get back to me."

"And what if they don't?"

Iz looks up at his wife and shrugs. "No big deal. Like you said, it's probably just an oil rig. Carl and I are planning our annual fishing trip within the next two weeks. Maybe we'll take a quick detour out to the area and take a closer look, just to be sure."

Miami, Florida

Dominique watches in disgust as the big redhead shovels another forkful of eggplant into his mouth. *Maybe he'll choke.*

"So, Sunshine, you proud of me or what?"

A spittle of tomato sauce strikes her cheek. "God, Ray, didn't your mother teach you to swallow your food before talking?"

He smiles, revealing a piece of eggplant caught between his yellowed teeth. "Sorry. I've been dieting for six months. Feels good to eat again. So what do you think?"

"I told you, I think sixth place is terrific, especially for your first contest."

"What can I say? You inspired me."

"Now tell me about Foletta. What we first met, you said something about the board and medical staff being upset when he arrived from Massachusetts. What did you mean by that?"

"This stays between us, right?"

"Right."

Raymond washes another mouthful of food down with a swig of beer. "I have a good friend whose father sits on the state board. In fact, he was the one who helped me get the job at the treatment center. Anyway, the word is that Dr. Reinike, Foletta's predecessor, will be back sometime next month to run things again."

"Really? But I thought she retired. Foletta told me her husband had terminal cancer."

Ray shakes his head, inhaling another bite. "It was all bullshit. My buddy told me Reinike's been on paid leave since September. Turns out there's a brand-new asylum opening up in Tampa in three weeks, and Foletta's been promised the directorship."

"Wait, if Foletta's leaving in three weeks, then he must have known he was getting the Tampa job before coming to Miami. Why push Dr. Reinike out, just to take the Miami job for three months?"

Ray points his fork at her. "Because of your former patient. The asylum in Massachusetts was closing, and Tampa wasn't ready yet. Reinike's a stickler for detail. Apparently, somebody with a lot of pull wanted Foletta in charge so there'd be no risk of your boy Gabriel getting reshuffled in the system."

Or receiving a proper evaluation. God damn you, Foletta.

"What's the matter, Sunshine?"

"I made a deal with Foletta. He promised me that Mick would be placed in the care of one of our rehab teams no later than January."

The yellowed teeth smile at her. "Guess you got lied to, girl. In three weeks, Michael Gabriel will be long gone."

The sleek, cherry red Dodge Intrepid ESX2's electric motor whines as it kicks in, assisting the 1.5-liter three-cylinder diesel engine as it accelerates up the steep southbound ramp to I-95.

Dominique stares out the passenger window as Raymond whips the car in and out of traffic. She grits her teeth, angry at Foletta for deceiving her. *I should have known better. I should have trusted my heart.*

She closes her eyes, recalling one of her first conversations with Mick. *"Pierre Borgia manipulated the legal system. The DA made a deal with my state-appointed attorney and shipped me off to an asylum in Massachusetts. Foletta became my state-appointed keeper. Pierre Borgia rewards loyalty, but God help you if you make his shit list."*

She had been manipulated, and once more, Michael Gabriel was left to suffer the consequences.

"Ray, I'm really not up for dancing tonight. Would you mind taking me home."

"Home? We're halfway to South Beach."

"Please."

Raymond eyes the tan, sculpted legs protruding beneath the black skirt, imagining them wrapped around his thrusting, muscular torso. "Okay, Sunshine, home it is."

The Intrepid pulls into the parking lot of her high-rise twenty minutes later.

Dominique smiles. "Thank you for dinner. I'm sorry to put a damper on the evening, but I really don't feel well. Next time, I'll treat, okay?"

He shuts off the engine. "I'll walk you up."

"That's okay, I'll be fine. I'll see you at work." She opens the door and heads for the elevator.

Ray scurries after her.

Dammit. "Ray, I told you, it's really not necessary."

"Hey, it's no trouble, besides, I'd love to see your place." He waits for her to key-in to use the elevator.

"Ray, not tonight."

"That wasn't our deal." He slips a thick arm around her waist, pulling her closer.

"Don't—"

Before she can stop him, he has pushed her against the concrete wall, burying his tongue in her mouth, his right paw groping her breasts.

A wave of white-hot panic rushes over her as a dozen childhood memories race through her mind at once.

Fight back! She gags at the taste in her mouth, then bites down on the intruding tongue, drawing blood.

"Oww. God dammit—" Raymond slaps her across the face, then pins her against the wall with one hand as he tears at her skirt with the other.

"Let her go!"

Dominique looks up to see Rabbi Steinberg and his wife approaching.

Raymond maintains a grip on her arm. "Beat it, this ain't your concern."

"Let her go, or we'll alert the police." Mindy Steinberg holds up the portable alarm.

Raymond takes a threatening step toward the couple, dragging Dominique with him.

"Don't be foolish," Steinberg says, pointing to the security cameras.

"Hey, Ray—"

Raymond turns.

The point of Dominique's high heel slams hard on Raymond's big toe. He yelps in agony, releasing his grip. In one motion, the blade of her wrist strikes the bodybuilder square on the Adam's apple, silencing his scream.

Raymond clutches his windpipe, wheezing for air. As he drops to his knees, Dominique wheels around, preparing to drive the heel of her foot down upon the back of his exposed neck.

"Dominique, no—" Steinberg grabs her arm before she can execute the crescent kick. "Let the police handle it."

Mindy keys open the elevator and the three duck inside.

Raymond struggles to his feet. He turns to face Dominique, his eyes crazed, his mouth gasping to form sounds. As the elevator doors begin to close, he mouths the word, "Gabriel," and slides a finger across the base of his throat.

11

The group-therapy rooms at the South Florida Evaluation and Treatment Center are located on the third floor, situated opposite the gymnasium, between the movie hall and computer room.

Dominique is seated in the back of room 3-B, half-listening to Dr. Blackwell's afternoon group-therapy session when she notices an orderly wheel a semiconscious Michael Gabriel into the movie hall. She waits until the orderly leaves, then slips out of the classroom.

The movie area is dark, the only light coming from the large-screen television. Eight residents, spread out over the three dozen folding chairs, are watching the latest *Star Trek* movie.

The wheelchair is in the last row. Dominique takes a seat, sliding her chair close to Mick. He is leaning to one side, slumped forward. A single belt strapped across his chest is all that prevents him from falling on his face. The dark eyes, once intense beacons, are now lifeless black pools reflecting the television screen. Mick's long brown hair is pulled back. Dominique catches a whiff of scalp oil, then a vulgar scent coming from his rancid clothes. A heavy five o'clock shadow is thickening to a beard, covering all but the jagged scar along his jawline.

Damn you, Foletta. She removes a Kleenex from her coat and dabs at the spittle drooling from his lower lip. "Mick, I don't know if you can understand me, but I miss you, I really do. I hate what Foletta's done to you. You were absolutely right about him, and I feel terrible for not believing you." She places her hand over his. "I wish you could understand me."

To her surprise, Mick's left hand turns over, his fingers entwining in hers. "Oh my God," she whispers.

Mick winks.

She can barely contain her excitement. "Mick, there's so much I have to tell you—"

"Shhh." The eyes remain vacant.

She leans forward casually, feigning interest in the video. "Raymond, the guard who attacked you, tried to rape me. He's been suspended, but I hear he may be back to work as early as next week. Be careful, he's threatened to hurt you to get back at me." She returns his squeeze. "You remember me telling you about SOSUS? I convinced Iz to use the system to check out the Gulf coordinates you gave me. Mick, you were right. It turns out something is definitely down there, buried about a mile beneath the seafloor. Iz promises he'll investigate."

Mick squeezes her hand tighter. Without moving his lips, he whispers, "Too dangerous."

"Too dangerous? Why? What do you think is down there?" She releases his hand as Dr. Blackwell's therapy session ends. "Mick, Foletta lied about everything. I found out he's going to Tampa to be the director of a new maximum-security facility. You're being transferred next week."

"Help me escape."

"I can't—"

She stands as Dr. Blackwell approaches. "Intern, I didn't realize you were such a *Star Trek* fan. I take it this movie is more important than my therapy session?"

"No, sir. I was just—I was just checking on this patient. He nearly fell out of his wheelchair."

"That's why we have orderlies. Here, take these." He hands her a thick stack of patient files, then leads her away from Mick. "I want every chart updated and sent to billing within the hour. Be sure to note today's therapy session. When you're finished, you can join our team meeting in the conference room on the second floor."

"Yes, Doctor."

"And Intern, stay away from Dr. Foletta's resident."

Gulf of Mexico

The forty-eight-foot fishing craft, *Manatee*, plows its way southwest through two-to-three-foot seas, its bow bathed in golden light as the setting sun kisses the horizon.

Below deck, Iz Axler pours himself a mug of coffee while his best friend, Carl Reuben, cooks dinner in the small galley.

The retired dentist rubs a hand towel over his balding scalp, then wipes the steam from his thick bifocals. "God, it's hot down here. How close are we to this mysterious location of yours?"

"Three more miles. What's for dinner?"

"I already told you, grilled dolphin."

"We had that for lunch."

"Catch lobster, and you'll eat lobster. Tell me about this spot. You say it has no fish?"

"That's right. We call it a dead zone."

"Why's it dead?"

"Don't know. That's why I want to take a look."

"And how long are you planning to keep us in this dead zone?"

"How long until dinner?"

"Twenty minutes."

"Well, if there's an oil rig sitting over the area like I suspect there is, we'll be in and out of there by dessert."

Iz leaves the galley and heads up on deck, savoring the smell of the salt air seasoned by the scent of grilled fish. For him, Carl, and Rex Simpson, the annual five-day fishing trip is the highlight of their year. After a long hurricane season, the Gulf waters have calmed and the weather cooled, offering ideal conditions for boating. Two days have yielded a dozen dolphin fish, eight yellowtail, and one grouper. Facing the fading sun, Iz closes his eyes and inhales, allowing the warm gusts of wind to soothe his sunburned face.

A dull *thud* causes him to turn. Rex repositions the air tank, then finishes strapping it to the back of a buoyancy-control vest.

"You planning on doing some diving, Rex?"

The fifty-two-year-old owner of the Sanibel Treasure Hunters Club glances back over his shoulder. "Why not? Since we can't do any fishing in this secret spot of yours, I thought I'd get in some night diving."

"I'm not sure there'll be much to see." Iz resumes his place at the captain's chair. He grabs the binoculars and scans the empty horizon, then verifies their location on the Global Positioning System. "That's strange."

"What's strange?"

Iz deactivates the autopilot and cuts the *Manatee*'s engines. "We're here. This is it, the location I was telling you about."

"Nothing here but water." Rex twists his long gray hair into a ponytail. "I thought you said there'd be an oil rig."

"I guess I was wrong." Iz activates the ship-to-shore radio. "*Manatee* calling Alpha-Zulu-three-nine-six. Alpha-Zulu, come in. Ead, you there?"

"Go ahead, *Manatee*. How's the fishing?"

"Not bad. Mostly yellowtail and dolphin. Rex caught a grouper this morning. Ead, we just arrived at the site above the Chicxulub crater. There's nothing here."

"No oil rig?"

"Nothing. But the weather's perfect, and the seas are calm. I think we'll stay here for the night while I complete some tests."

"Just be careful."

"I will. Call you later."

The sun is now a molten ball of crimson setting spectacularly off the portside bow. Iz drains the mug of coffee, then activates the boat's sonar to check the depth of the seafloor.

Just over two thousand feet.

Rex watches Isadore root through a dry-storage compartment. "Hey, Iz, check out your compass, it's doing the mambo."

"I know. There's a massive crater buried beneath the seafloor, about a hundred kilometers across. We're close to the center point, which possesses a very strong magnetic field."

"What are you doing?"

Iz finishes attaching an underwater microphone to a large spool of fiberoptic cable. "I want to listen in on what's happening below. Here, take this microphone and lower it over the starboard bow. Feed the line slowly."

Iz takes the free end of the cable and connects it to an amplitude modulator. He boots the computer, then plugs in a set of headphones to the acoustics system and listens.

Jesus Christ . . .

Rex returns. "Microphone's lowered. What are you listening to? Sinatra?"

Iz passes him the headset.

Metallic churning sounds resembling high-pitched hydraulic pistons and gears cackle into Rex's ears. "What in the fuck is that?"

"I don't know. SOSUS detected the sounds a few weeks ago. They're originating about a mile below the seafloor. I just assumed it was an oil rig."

"Pretty bizarre. Have you told anyone about this?"

"I filed a report with the Navy and NOAA, but no one has gotten back to me yet."

"Too bad we didn't bring the *Barnacle*."

"I didn't know your sub could dive this deep?"

"Hell, yes. I've taken her to down to six thousand feet in the Bahamas."

Carl climbs topside, his face beet red. "Hey, are you guys eating, or what?"

A tapestry of stars covers the cloudless night sky.

Carl is leaning on the transom, organizing his tackle box for the third time that day. Rex is below, cleaning up dinner, while Iz listens to the undersea acoustics from the pilothouse:

"*Manatee*, come in."

"Go ahead, Ead."

"I've been listening on SOSUS. The noises are getting louder and faster."

"I know. Almost sounds like a runaway locomotive."

"Iz, I think you ought to leave the area. Iz?"

The sonic *screeech* torches his ear canal like a white-hot poker. Iz flings the headphones from his head in agony and drops to one knee, feeling disoriented, the ringing in his ears unbearable.

"Rex! Carl!" He hears only a muffled echo.

An unearthly green light causes him to look up. The interior of the pilothouse is aglow with an iridescent emerald shimmer radiating from the water.

Rex pulls Iz to his feet. "You okay?"

Iz nods, his ears still ringing slightly. The two men stumble over the scuba gear and join Carl in the stern, too focused on the brilliant light to notice the smoke coming from the amplitude modulator's sizzling electronics board.

God Almighty. Iz and his two friends stare dumbfounded at the sea, their faces glowing a ghostly green from the ethereal light.

The *Manatee* is bobbing along the surface of a circular swatch of luminescent sea, at least a mile in diameter. Iz leans overboard, stupefied by the surreal visibility created by the incandescent beacon originating somewhere along the seafloor, some two thousand feet beneath the boat.

"Iz, Rex, your hair!"

Carl points to their hair, which is standing on end. Rex fingers his ponytail, sticking up like an Indian feather. Iz rubs a palm across his hairy forearm, registering sparks of static electricity.

"What the hell's happening?" Carl whispers.

"I don't know, but we're moving out of here." Iz hurries back to the pilothouse and pushes the engine's POWER button.

Nothing.

He pushes three more times. He checks the radio, then the GPS navigational system.

"What's wrong?" Carl asks nervously.

"Everything's dead. Whatever's glowing down there has short-circuited all of our electronics." Iz turns to see Rex pulling on his wet suit. "What are you doing?"

"I want to see what's down there."

"It's too dangerous. There could be radiation."

"Then I'll probably be safer in my wet suit than you guys will on board." He fastens the straps of the vest holding his air tank, checks his regulator, then slips on his fins. "Carl, my underwater camera's by your feet."

Carl tosses it to him.

"Rex—"

"Iz, thrill-seeking's my hobby. I'll snap a few quick shots and be back on board in five minutes."

Iz and Carl watch helplessly as Rex slips over the side.

"Carl, grab an oar. We're moving the boat."

The sea is so visible that Rex feels like he is swimming toward the underwater lights of a deep swimming pool. He hovers six feet below the hull, feeling totally at peace, his body and escaping air bubbles immersed in the soft, emerald green glow.

Movement above his head causes him to look up. *My God* . . .

Rex blinks twice, staring incredulously at the grotesque creature that has attached itself lengthwise along the center of the *Manatee*'s keel. Thirty-five feet of willowy tentacles flow from a caterpillar-like girth of gelatinous goo. No less than one hundred bell-shaped stomachs traverse the creature's cream-colored, ropelike body, each digestive aperture containing its own hideous mouth and poisonous, fingerlike projections.

Incredible. Rex has never seen a live specimen before, but he knows the creature is an *Apolemia,* a species of siphonophore. These bizarre life-forms, which can grow upwards of eighty to one hundred feet in length, inhabit only the deepest waters and, as a result, are rarely seen by man.

The light must have chased it to the surface.

He snaps several pictures, remaining at what he hopes is a safe distance from the creature's poisonous stingers, then releases air from his BCD vest and descends.

The surreal lighting gives him the strangest sensation of falling in slow motion. Rex scissor kicks at sixty feet to slow his descent, the pressure building within his ears. He pinches his nose and equalizes, surprised to find the pain getting worse. Then, looking down, he notices something rising at him from the luminescent void.

Rex smiles and extends his arms as thousands of Volkswagen-size air bubbles ascend all around him.

Incredible.

The sinus-cavity pain forces him to refocus. A dull baritone roar fills his ears, causing his face mask to reverberate and tickle his nose.

Rex Simpson stops smiling as he registers a gut-wrenching feeling in the pit of his stomach, a feeling similar to being suspended at the summit of a towering roller coaster just as it begins its downward plunge. The roar gets louder.

It's an underwater earthquake!

Two thousand feet below, an enormous section of the limestone seafloor collapses in upon itself, revealing a gaping tunnel-like aperture. The sea begins swirling as it is sucked into the growing hole, the torrent drawing everything into its plunging vortex.

The emerald green light intensifies, nearly blinding him.

Iz and Carl have managed to paddle the *Manatee* to the perimeter of the brilliant patch of sea when an unseen force seems to grip the stern, dragging the fishing boat backward. The two men turn, horrified, the sea now churning in a great counterclockwise vortex.

"It's a whirlpool! Paddle faster!"

Within seconds, the *Manatee* is caught, moving backward along the outer edge of the maelstrom.

The powerful suction has clamped onto Rex's body with frightening strength, dragging him into deeper waters. He kicks harder, the pressure building in his ears as he struggles to release his weight belt with one hand and grab on to the flailing rubber hose behind his head with the other.

The belt slips off his waist, disappearing in the intense light. Rex fingers the buoyancy-control device and squeezes the handle, inflating his vest.

His descent slows but does not stop.

An unfathomably strong current suddenly wrenches him sideways as if he is being sucked out of a plane. He lurches sideways, the current threatening to rip the regulator and mask from his face. He bites down hard and grabs his precious mask, twisting futilely against the unrelenting turbulence.

The sea drops open beneath him. He stares one hundred stories below into the blazing green eye of the vortex, a hole in the sea whose centrifugal force now pins him against the inner wall of its widening, churning funnel.

Rex's heart pounds wildly in fear. The grip on his torso increases, tearing at the Velcro straps, all that prevents the air tank from being torn from his vest. He closes his eyes, sickened, as the whirlpool whips him along its interior wall at a dizzying velocity, all the while sucking him deeper into its mouth.

I'm going to die, oh, God, please help me—

His face mask cracks. A viselike pressure squeezes his face. Blood pours from his nostrils. He gags, then squeezes his eyes shut as tightly as he can, screaming into his regulator as his eyeballs are pulled away from their optic nerves, bulging out of their socket.

A final scream is obliterated as Rex Simpson's brain implodes.

The monstrous G forces created by the funnel of water have impaled the *Manatee*'s hull against the steep, swirling walls, tearing sections of the boat away with each revolution. Centrifugal force has pinned Carl Reuben's unconscious body against the back of Iz's legs, crushing the terrified biologist against the fiberglass transom.

Iz grips the guardrail in front of him with two hands. The whirlpool is roaring in his ears, its dizzying speed pushing him toward unconsciousness.

He wills his eyes open, focusing them on the source of the green light. Death is minutes away, the thought somehow both frightening and comforting.

The brilliant beacon suddenly dulls. Iz cranes his neck forward, leaning precariously over the transom. He sees a gurgling, tarlike ooze spew forth from an enormous hole within the seafloor. The black substance belches—Iz can smell its sulfurous, rotting stench—then finishes blanketing the emerald glow as it continues to rise within the funnel of water, darkening the still-churning sea.

Iz closes his eyes, forcing himself to think of Edie and Dominique as the maddening torrent pushes the *Manatee* down into its spiraling vortex.

God, let it be quick.

Carl reaches up. He squeezes Iz's hand as the black ooze rises to greet them.

The boat strikes the thick, tarlike substance and flips, bow over stern, tossing Iz and Carl headfirst into the mouth of the inky maelstrom.

12

Bill Godwin kisses his sleeping wife on the cheek, grabs his microdisc player, and slips out of the second-floor hotel room of the Holiday Inn.

Another perfect morning.

He descends the aluminum-and-concrete staircase to the pool deck, then exits the fenced-in area and crosses Route 27 to the beach, the morning light forcing him to squint. Stretched out before him are miles of unblemished, pristine white sands and crystal-clear azure coastal waters.

Beautiful . . .

Brilliant specks of gold are just peeking over a line of clouds on the eastern horizon by the time he reaches the water's edge. A Mexican girl in her teens zigzags along the serene Gulf waters on a purple-and-white waverunner. Bill admires her figure as he finishes stretching, then adjusts his headphones and sets out at a leisurely pace.

The forty-six-year-old senior marketing analyst at Waterford-Leeman has been jogging three times a week since recovering from his second heart attack six years ago. He figures the "morning mile," as his wife calls it, has probably added another ten years to his life while keeping his weight under control for the first time since his college days.

Bill passes another jogger and nods, momentarily picking up his pace. A week's vacation in the Yucatán has done wonders for his blood pressure, but the rich Mexican cuisine has not helped his waistline. He reaches the deserted lifeguard stand, but decides to go a little farther. Five minutes and a half mile later he stops, totally exhausted. Bending over, he removes his running shoes, stuffs the disc player inside one sneaker, then strides into the balmy waters of the Gulf for his morning dip.

Bill wades out until the incoming swells reach his chest. He closes his eyes and relaxes in the warm sea, mentally organizing his day.

"Son of a bitch . . ." Bill jerks sideways, clutching his arm, searching the water for the jellyfish that stung him. "What in the hell?"

A black, tarlike substance has adhered to his forearm, searing his flesh. "Goddam oil companies." He swishes his arm back and forth in the water, unable to wash the ooze away.

The scorching pain increases.

Swearing aloud, Bill turns and takes several strides inland. Blood is pouring from both nostrils by the time he staggers onto the beach. Purplish spots blind his vision. Feeling light-headed and confused, he drops to his knees in the sand.

"I need help! Can somebody help me?"

An older Mexican couple approaches and stops. *"¿Qué pasó, Señor?"*

"I'm sorry, I don't speak Spanish—*no hablo*. I need a doctor—*el doctor*."

The man looks at him. *"¿El doctor?"*

A stabbing pain inflames Bill's eyeballs. He cries out in agony and slams his fists into his eyes. "Oh, God, my head!"

The man looks at his wife. *"Por favor, llame a un médico."* The woman hurries off.

Bill Godwin's eyes feel like they are being skewered. He tears at his hair, then bends over and pukes a bloody, acidic black bile.

The older Mexican is leaning over, futilely attempting to assist the sick American when he pulls back suddenly and grabs his ankle. *"¡Hijo de la chingada!"*

Sizzling vomit has splattered on the man's foot—searing the flesh.

The White House
Washington, DC

Ennis Chaney feels the eyes of President Maller and Pierre Borgia upon him as he reads the two-page report.

"No clue about where this toxic crud came from?"

"It came from the Gulf, probably from one of PEMEX's well fields," Borgia states. "What's more important is that a dozen Americans and several hundred Mexicans have died. The currents have confined the black tide to the Yucatán coast, but it's important that we monitor the situation to make sure the ooze doesn't reach American shores. We also feel it important that we maintain a diplomatic presence in Mexico during this environmental crisis."

"Meaning?"

Chaney notices Maller's discomfort. "Pierre thinks it would be best if you headed the investigation. The drug-trafficking problem has strained our relationship with Mexico. We feel this situation might present us with an opportunity to mend a few fences. The press will be accompanying you—"

Chaney sighs. Although his official term as vice president was not to begin until January, Congress had confirmed his appointment him to the vacant seat earlier. The new post, combined with helping his senatorial staff adjust to his leaving the Senate, was wearing him thin. "Let me get this straight. We're preparing for a potential conflict in the Persian Gulf, but you want me to head a diplomatic mission to Mexico?" Chaney shakes his head. "What the hell am I supposed to do, other than offer my condolences? With all due respect, Mr. President, our ambassador to Mexico can handle this."

"This is more important than you realize, besides"—the President forces a tight smile—"who else has the stomach for it. Your work with the CDC during the dengue fever outbreak in Puerto Rico three years ago was a terrific public relations coup."

"My participation had nothing to do with public relations."

Borgia slams his briefcase shut. "The president of the United States just gave you an order, Mister Vice President. Are you planning on fulfilling your duties, or are you planning on resigning?"

The raccoon eyes open wide, shooting daggers at Borgia.

"Pierre, would you give us a few minutes."

The Secretary of State tries to stare Chaney down with his one good eye, but he is overmatched.

"Pierre, please."

Borgia leaves.

"Ennis—"

"Mr. President, if you're asking me to go, then of course, I'll go."

"Thank you."

"You don't have to thank me. Just inform cyclops that Ennis Chaney quits for no one. As far as I'm concerned, that boy just rose to the top of my shit list."

The vice president boards the Sikorsky MH-60 Pave Hawk two hours later. His newly promoted assistant, Dean Disangro, is already on board, along with two Secret Service agents and a half dozen members of the press.

Chaney is angry. Throughout his political career, he has never allowed himself to be used as a public-relations lackey. Party lines and political correctness mean nothing to him. Poverty and violence, education and equality among the races, these are the fights worth fighting. He often imagines himself a modern-day Don Quixote—fighting the windmills, he calls it. *That one-eyed Jack may think he can yank my strings, but he just got himself into a street fight with the king of all brawlers.*

Dean pours the vice president a cup of decaf. He knows Chaney hates flying, especially in helicopters. "You look nervous."

"Shut up. What's this I hear about us making a detour?"

"We're scheduled to stop at Fort Detrick to pick up personnel from USAMRIID before heading on to the Yucatán."

"Wonderful." Chaney closes his eyes, gripping the armrest as the Sikorsky leaps into the sky.

Thirteen minutes later, the chopper touches down at the United States Army Medical Research Institute of Infectious Diseases. From his window, Chaney sees two men supervise the loading of several large crates.

The two men climb aboard. A silver-haired officer introduces himself. "Mr. Vice President, Colonel Jim Ruetenik. I'm the military biohazard specialist assigned to your team. This is my associate, Dr. Marvin Teperman, an exobiologist on loan to us from Toronto."

Chaney looks over the short Canadian with the pencil-thin mustache and annoyingly warm smile. "What exactly is an exobiologist?"

"Exobiology concerns the study of life outside our planet. This sludge may contain a strain of infectious virus that we've never seen before. AMRIID thought I might be of some help."

"What's in the crates?"

"Racal suits," the colonel answers. "Portable, pressurized space suits we use in the field when dealing with potentially hot agents."

"I'm familiar with Racal suits, Colonel."

"That's right, you were in Puerto Rico during the dengue outbreak in 2009."

"This stuff is going to be a bit nastier, I'm afraid," Marvin says. "From what we've been told, physical contact with the substance is causing immediate crash and bleed outs—profuse hemorrhaging from all orifices of the body."

"I can handle it." Chaney grips the seat as the chopper takes off. "It's the damn chopper that gets me queasy."

The colonel smiles. "Once we land, our first concern will be to assist the Mexicans in establishing gray zones—intermediate areas between the contaminated sites and the rest of the population."

Chaney listens for a while longer, then eases his chair back and closes his eyes. *Racal suits. Crash and bleed outs. What the hell am I doing here?*

Four hours later, the Sikorsky slows to hover over a white beach blotted with a black, tarlike substance. Sections of the infected shoreline have been cordoned off with orange, wooden barriers.

The helicopter follows the deserted shoreline to the east, approaching a series of Red Cross Army tents that have been erected along a secured stretch of beach. A massive bonfire burns fifty yards from the site, its dark brown smoke leaving a thick trail, miles long, in the cloudless sky.

The Sikorsky slows, then touches down on a cordoned-off parking lot adjacent to the tented area.

"Mr. Vice President, this suit looks to be about your size." Colonel Ruetenik hands him an orange space suit.

Chaney sees Dean pulling on a suit. "Wrong. Sit your ass down, Papa, you're staying here. The press and security men, too."

"My job is to assist you—"

"Assist me by staying here."

Chaney emerges from the copter twenty minutes later, accompanied by Teperman and the colonel. All three are wearing the bulky orange Racal suits and air tanks.

A physician greets them outside the main tent. Chaney notices a green ooze dripping from the man's white environmental suit.

"I'm Dr. Juarez. Thank you for coming so quickly."

Colonel Ruetenik makes the introductions.

"Is that the toxic substance on your suit, Doctor?" Chaney asks, pointing to the green liquid.

"No, sir. That's envirochem, the good stuff. We use it as a disinfectant. Make sure you douse your suit in it before getting changed. If you'll follow me, I'll show you the bad stuff."

Chaney feels beads of sweat drip down the side of his face as he follows the others into the quarantined area.

Beneath the Red Cross tent are dozens of people lying on plastic cots. Most are in bathing suits. All are covered in black blotches of blood and bile.

Those who are conscious are moaning in agony. Workers dressed in plastic bodysuits and heavy rubber boots and gloves are removing body bags from the tent as fast as newcomers are being led inside.

Dr. Juarez shakes his head. "This place has turned into a real hot zone. Most of the damage occurred during the early-morning hours before anyone realized how contagious the sludge was. We had the beaches quarantined by noon, but the first wave of physicians and volunteers just kept getting contaminated, making things worse. We've resorted to identifying the victims, then burning the bodies just to slow the spread."

They enter an adjacent tent. A pretty Mexican nurse in an environmental suit is seated next to a cot, holding a middle-aged American man's hand in her gloved palm.

Dr. Juarez gives the nurse an affectionate pat on the shoulder. "Nurse, who do we have here?"

"This is Mr. Ellis, an artist from California."

"Mr. Ellis, can you hear me?"

Mr. Ellis is lying on his back, staring into space, his eyes wide-open.

Ennis Chaney shudders. The man's eyeballs are completely black.

The colonel pulls the doctor aside. "How does the infection appear to be spreading?"

"Physical contact with either the black tide or another infected subject's excretions. No evidence to suggest an airborne virus."

"Marvin, hand me the microcassette recorder please, then stand by with the hatbox." The colonel takes the miniature recorder from Teperman and begins speaking into it as he assists Dr. Juarez with his examination.

"Subject appears to have come in physical contact with the tarlike substance on thumb and second and third fingers of right hand. Flesh on all three digits has been seared clear to the bone. Eyeballs are fixed and hemorrhaging and have completely turned black. Subject appears to be in a stupor. Nurse, how long ago did Mr. Ellis come in contact with the black tide?"

"I don't know, sir. Maybe two hours."

Marvin leans close to Chaney. "This stuff works very fast."

The colonel overhears and nods. "Subject's skin is clammy, almost yellow, with black blotches appearing along both upper and lower extremities." Colonel Ruetenik gently manipulates pockets of blood beneath the skin of Ellis's arm. "Third spacing is evident along both upper extremities—"

Dr. Juarez sits next to his patient, who appears to be coming out of his stupor. "Try not to move, Mr. Ellis. You've come in contact with some kind of—"

"—my fucking head is killing me." Ellis sits up suddenly, black blood dripping from both nostrils. "Who the fuck are you people? Oh, God . . ." Without warning, a massive quantity of thick, black blood and tissue is forcibly expelled from Ellis's mouth. The sizzling bile pours down his chest, splattering Teperman and the nurse across the headpieces of their protective suits.

Chaney backs off several steps, the sight of the black bile causing a gag reflex. He swallows back the vomit rising in his throat and turns away, trying to regain his composure.

The nurse remains kneeling before her patient, holding both of Ellis's hands in her own, compassion preventing her from looking away from the dying man's horrified face.

Mr. Ellis stares at Dr. Juarez and the colonel through two dark holes, a zombielike expression plastered on his bloodied face, the victim sitting in a rigid, upright posture as if he is afraid to move. "My insides are melting," he moans.

Chaney sees the man's upper torso begin to quiver and convulse. With a sickening gurgle, the black bile is vomited again, this time pouring from the nostrils and eyes as well. It runs down Ellis's neck, followed by a stream of bright, crimson blood.

Dr. Juarez grabs the heaving body by its elbows as the victim's upper torso spasms violently in his grasp. Chaney closes his eyes and prays.

The doctor and nurse lay the lifeless bag of infected organs back onto the cot.

Colonel Ruetenik stands over the bleeding corpse and coldly continues his examination. "Subject appears to have suffered a massive crash and bleed out. Marvin, bring the hatbox over here. I want several vials of this black excrement as well as tissue and organ samples."

It is taking all of Ennis Chaney's willpower to keep himself from puking within his headpiece. His legs are shaking noticeably as he watches Marvin Teperman kneel next to the dead man and fill several small containers with contaminated blood. Each sample is placed carefully into the hatbox, a cylindrical biohazard container made of waxed cardboard.

Chaney is sweating profusely. He feels as if he is suffocating within the protective suit.

The four men leave the nurse to clean up.

The colonel pulls Chaney aside. "Sir, Marvin will fly back to Washington with you to complete an analysis of these samples. I'd prefer to stick around here a while longer. If you could arrange—"

"Diego!" The nurse stumbles out of the isolation tent, screaming in Spanish. Dr. Juarez grabs her by the wrists.

"¡Icarajo!" Juarez stares at the small tear along the left elbow of her protective suit. The skin along the exposed arm is sizzling, a blotch of black vomit the size of a quarter already burning through most of the flesh down to the bone.

Colonel Ruetenik douses her arm with the green disinfectant.

"Stay calm, Isabel, I think we caught it in time." Dr. Juarez looks back at the vice president, desperation on his face, tears in his eyes. "My wife—"

Chaney feels a lump growing in his throat as he stares into the terrified eyes of the condemned woman.

"Diego, cut off my arm!"

"Isa—"

"Diego, the baby will become infected!"

Chaney stays long enough to watch Juarez and Reutenik carry the shrieking woman into surgery. Then he runs from the tent, tearing at his headpiece as he stumbles across a sand dune. He falls to his knees, groping for the zipper along the neckline of his hood as the bile rises from his throat.

"NO!" Marvin grabs Chaney's wrist just as he is about to remove the headpiece. The exobiologist douses the vice president's orange suit with green disinfectant as Ennis vomits across the inside of his face plate.

Marvin waits until he is finished, then takes him by the arm and leads him to the chemical showers. The two men remain in their Racal suits beneath the spray of disinfectant, then move to a second shower of water where they strip off their suits.

Chaney tosses his soiled shirt in a plastic bag. He washes his face and neck, then sits down on a plastic bench, feeling weak and vulnerable.

"Are you all right?"

"Shit, I'm a far cry from being all right." He shakes his head. "I lost control back there."

"You did well. This is my fourth time in a hot zone; the colonel's been in at least a dozen."

"How do you guys do it?" he rasps, his hands still shaking.

"You do your best to depersonalize it while you're out there, then you hit the decon shower, remove your suit, and puke."

Depersonalize it. Goddam windmills. I'm getting too old to fight 'em anymore. "Let's go home, Marvin."

Chaney follows Teperman back to the chopper. As he boards, he turns to see two men toss another body onto the funeral pyre.

It is the nurse.

13

NOVEMBER 24, 2012
HOLLYWOOD BEACH, FLORIDA

The tears are flowing so hard from her eyes that Dominique can barely see Edie's image on the video-comm. Rabbi Steinberg squeezes her hand tighter, his wife rubbing her back.

"Ead, I don't understand. What happened? What was Iz doing out there?"

"He was investigating those sounds within the crater."

A wail rises from her throat. She covers her face in the rabbi's chest, sobbing uncontrollably.

"Dominique, look at me!" Edie commands.

"—it's my fault."

"Stop it. This has nothing to do with you. Iz was out there, doing his job. It was an accident. The Mexican Coast Guard is investigating—"

"What about the autopsy?"

Edie looks away, struggling to stifle her own grief.

Rabbi Steinberg turns to Dominique. "All three bodies were infected by the black tide. They had to be burned."

Dominique closes her eyes, her body shaking.

Edie's face appears back on-screen. "Doll, listen to me. We're going to have a memorial service in two days. I want you to come home."

"I'll be there. I'm going to come home for a while. Okay?"

"What about your internship?"

"It doesn't matter anymore." She wipes back tears. "Edie, I'm really sorry—"

"Just come home."

The gray afternoon sky is threatening by the time Dominique exits the ground-level entrance of the Hollywood Beach high-rise. She crosses A-1-A and unlocks the driver's side door of the Pronto Spyder, tossing her suitcase onto the passenger seat. She inhales deeply, smelling the sea and the incoming rain, then climbs in.

Dominique keys the ignition and presses the starter switch, laying her forehead on top of the steering wheel while she waits for the antitheft and safety system to complete its analysis.

Iz is dead. He's dead, and it's my fault. She squeezes her eyes shut, shaking her head. *It's all my goddam fault.*

The CD player activates.

The disc player is preset to Digital DJ. The Roadster's built-in computer processor registers the temperature of her touch on the steering wheel, interpreting her mood.

The *Best of the Doors* CD clicks into place.

Think this thing through. The weather was calm, and Iz was too experienced a sailor for the boat just to sink. Something terrible, something unforeseen must have happened out there.

The familiar sound of drumsticks dancing across a rod cymbal interlace with her thoughts. Haunting Eastern guitar licks reach out, feeding her sorrow, yet somehow soothing her. Memories of Iz flash across her mind's eye. A deep sadness refuels her spent emotions as the lyrics tear at her heart, pushing her once more over the edge. Hot tears blind her as Jim Morrison's melodic verse echoes in her ears.

> *This is the End . . . beautiful friend,*
> *This is the End . . . my only friend, the End.*

Mesmerized by the haunting epitaph, she lifts her head from the steering wheel as the first droplets of rain splatter across the windshield. She closes her eyes to the deluge as memories of Iz and Edie and Mick swirl uncontrollably across her mind's eye.

"You look tired, Kiddo . . ."
"Just come home . . ."

       Lost in a romance, wilderness of pain,

"If I wasn't locked up . . . do you think . . . do you think you could have loved me?"

       And all . . . the children . . . are insane,
       Waiting for the summer rain, yeahhh . . .

"Four Ahau, *three* Kankin. *You know what day that is, don't you, Dominique?"*
"Do you believe in God?"
"You look tired, Kiddo . . ."
"Do you believe in evil?"

       There's danger on the edge of town . . .

"You have to do something! The Chicxulub crater—the clock's ticking . . ."
"Doll, you're only one person. You can't expect to save the world . . ."
"The clock's ticking . . . and all of us are going to die!"
"You can't expect to save the world . . ."
"The clock's ticking . . .

       Father, I want to kill you . . .

Dominique slumps forward against the steering wheel, her sobs competing with Jim Morrison's rants of Oedipal lust.
Mellowing again, as the Eastern licks regain control.

       This is the End . . . beautiful friend,
       This is the End . . . my only friend, the End,

"None of us have any control over the deck or the cards we're dealt. What we do have is total responsibility as to how we play the hand."
The Spyder's engine jumps to life, startling her.

       This is the End . . .

She shuts off the sound system and wipes the tears from her eyes as the rain continues pelting the windshield. Glances up, staring at herself in the rearview mirror.

Play the hand that's dealt.

For several minutes, she continues staring straight ahead, determination replacing grief as her mind focuses on a plan. Then she activates the car phone and dials Rabbi Steinberg's number.

"It's me. No, I'm still downstairs. There's something important I have to do before I head over to Sanibel, but I need your help."

14

NOVEMBER 25, 2012
MIAMI, FLORIDA

9:54 P.M.

The black Pronto Spyder turns right onto Twenty-third Street, executes a U-turn, then parks next to a telephone pole by the curb, just adjacent to the twenty-foot-high, stark white concrete wall. The side street, which borders the asylum to the north, runs west another two blocks before dead-ending at an abandoned textile mill. The neighborhood is run-down, the street deserted, except for a Dodge minivan parked at the far end of the block.

Dominique exits the car, adrenaline pumping. She pops the trunk, verifies that no one is around, then removes a fifty-foot length of white, half-inch-thick nylon rope. Knots have been tied in the line at two-foot intervals. Bending down as if inspecting her right rear tire, she secures one end of the rope to the base of the telephone pole, then returns to the trunk.

She opens the large cardboard box and removes the thirty-two-inch radio-controlled model helicopter. A mechanical claw hangs from beneath the tiny landing gear.

Dominique positions the last knot at the free end of the nylon rope within the claw's grasp, then closes it.

Okay, don't fuck this up. Keep the rope clear of the barbed wire.

She starts the miniature copter's battery-powered engine, cringing at the loud, high-pitched whine of the rotors. The toy chopper lifts off, wobbling as it struggles to tow the nylon rope with it. Dominique maneuvers the model airship into a steep vertical climb high above the concrete security wall, taking up all the slack.

Okay, nice and easy . . .

Using the joystick, she guides the chopper past the wall and over the yard, then activates the claw, releasing the rope.

The freed knot drops to the yard, its length slipping between the coils of barbed wire to rest on top of the concrete barrier.

Perfect. Go! Dominique slams the joystick to the right. The model helicopter races toward the textile mill at the end of the street and disappears over the rooftop of the abandoned property. She powers the radio control OFF, hearing the telltale sound of plastic crashing in the distance.

Slamming the trunk closed, she climbs back in the roadster and guides the car into the staff parking lot.

Dominique checks her watch: 10:07. *Almost time.* She reaches into the glove compartment, removes the worn spark plug and ratchet, then turns off the car's engine and pops the hood of the Spyder.

She closes the hood three minutes later, using a wet rag to wipe the grease from her hands. After fixing her makeup, she takes a moment to adjust the tight-fitting halter top before covering her half-exposed cleavage with the pink cashmere sweater.

Okay Mick, now it's up to you.

She hurries to the entrance of the facility, praying that Mick had been lucid during their conversation earlier that afternoon.

10:14 P.M.

Michael Gabriel is seated on the edge of the wafer-thin mattress, his vacant black eyes staring at the floor. His mouth is open, saliva dripping from his lower lip. His bruised left forearm is turned palm side up and is resting on his thigh, an offering to the butcher. The right arm is tucked by his side, the fist slightly balled.

He hears the orderly approach. "Hey, Marvis, is it true? Is this the vegetable's last night?"

Mick takes a breath, trying to calm his racing pulse. The presence of the seventh-floor security guard complicates things. *You only have one shot. Take them both out if you have to.*

Marvis turns off the television in the pod and finishes wiping down the grape-juice stains on the coffee table. "Yeah. Foletta's taking him to Tampa tomorrow."

The door swings open. In his peripheral vision, Mick sees the sadist approach, the shadow of another man waiting by the door.

Not yet. Marvis will slam the door closed if you jump. Wait until it's clear. Let the animal stick you.

The orderly grabs Mick's left wrist, then jabs the syringe into the swollen vein, nearly breaking the tip of the needle off as he injects the Thorazine into the abused blood vessel.

Mick tightens his abdominal muscles in agony, forcing his upper body not to flinch.

"Hey, Barnes, go easy on him, or I'll write you up again."

"Fuck you, Marvis."

Marvis shakes his head, then walks away.

Mick's eyes roll up in his head. His body turns to Jell-O and he falls onto his left side, staring straight ahead on the bed like a zombie.

Barnes verifies that Marvis has left, then unzips his fly. "Hey, girlfriend, you wanna taste something?" He bends down and leans closer to Mick's face. "How about we open that pretty little mouth of yours and—"

The orderly never sees the fist, only the explosion of purple light as Mick's second and third knuckles slam into his exposed temple.

Barnes collapses to the floor, shaken but still conscious.

Mick pulls him up by the hair and looks into his eyes. "Trick or treat, motherfucker." He drives his knee into Barnes's face, careful not to get any blood on the orderly's uniform.

10:18 P.M.

Dominique enters her numerical password, then waits while the infrared camera scans her face. The red light flashes green, allowing her to enter the central security station.

Raymond turns to face her. "Well, look who it is? Come to pay your last respects to your psycho boyfriend?"

"You're not my boyfriend."

Raymond slams his fist against the steel cage. "We both know who I'm talking about. Little bit later, I'm gonna be paying him a nice visit." He flashes a yellow smile. "Yeah, Sunshine, me and your boy are gonna have a real good time."

"Do whatever you want." She heads for the elevator.

"What's that supposed to mean?"

"I'm through." Dominique pulls an envelope from her purse. "See this?

This is a letter of resignation. I'm dropping out of the internship program and quitting school. Is Foletta in his office?"

"You know he's not."

"Fine, then I'll leave this with Marvis. Buzz me up to the seventh floor, if you think you can handle it."

Raymond eyes her suspiciously. He activates the elevator, pressing the button on his console for the seventh floor, then watches her on the security-camera monitor.

Marvis is about to leave his desk to find Barnes when the elevator door opens. "Dominique? What are you doing here?"

She leads Marvis by the arm and walks him around the desk, turning him away from the elevator and the hallway leading to Mick's pod. "I wanted to talk to you, but I don't want that orderly Barnes to hear."

"Hear what?"

Dominique shows him the envelope. "I'm resigning."

"Why? Your semester's almost over."

Her eyes well with tears. "My—my father died in a boating accident."

"Damn. Hey, I'm sorry."

She gives a sob, then allows Marvis to comfort her. She lays her head on his shoulder, her eyes focused on the corridor leading to pod 7-C.

Mick staggers out of his room, dressed in Barnes's uniform and baseball cap. He slams the door shut and heads for the elevator.

Dominique places her hand on Marvis's neck as if hugging him, making sure he doesn't turn around. "Would you do me a favor and make sure Dr. Foletta gets this letter?"

"Yeah, sure. Hey, you wanna hang out, you know, talk or something?"

The elevator doors open. Mick staggers inside.

She pulls away. "No, I'm already late. I have to get on the road. The funeral ceremony's tomorrow morning. Barnes, hold the elevator, please—"

A white sleeve prevents the doors from closing.

Dominique kisses Marvis on the cheek. "Take care of yourself."

"Yeah, you too."

Dominique hustles for the elevator, stepping inside just as the doors close. Instead of looking at Mick, she stares directly up at the camera situated in the far corner of the elevator's ceiling.

Casually, she reaches into her purse. "What floor, Mr. Barnes?"

"Three."

She can hear the fatigue in his voice. She holds up three fingers to the camera, then one finger, continuing to stare at the lens as Mick takes the heavy pair of wire cutters from her other hand and pockets them.

The elevator stops at the third floor. The doors open.

Mick stumbles out, nearly falling on his face.

The doors close.

Mick find himself alone in the corridor. He staggers forward, the green-tiled hallway spinning in his head. The heavy dose of Thorazine is pulling him under, and there is nothing he can do now to fight back. He falls twice, then leans against the drywall and wills himself to the courtyard.

The night air momentarily revives him. He manages to reach the concrete steps and hugs the steel rail. Swirling in his vision are three steep flights of stairs. He blinks hard, unable to clear the fog from his vision. *Okay, you can do this. Step . . . now, push your foot down.* He stumbles down the first three steps, then catches himself. *Concentrate! One at a time. Don't lean . . . .*

He falls the last ten feet, landing painfully on his back.

For a dangerous moment, he allows his eyes to close, giving sleep an opportunity to gain a foothold. *No!* He rolls over, pushes himself to his feet, then staggers painfully toward the concrete monster spinning ahead of him.

Dominique unbuttons the cashmere sweater, takes a deep breath, and steps off the elevator. As she approaches the security station, she trains her eyes on the dozen security monitors at Raymond's back which continuously provide alternating images of the facility.

She spots the view of the courtyard. A uniform-clad figure is struggling to pull his way up the stark concrete wall.

Raymond looks up and stares at her cleavage.

Mick's arms are like rubber. Try as he may, he cannot seem to get his muscles to obey his commands.

He feels the nylon knot slip through his fingers and falls eight feet, nearly breaking both ankles on the hard sod.

Dominique sees Mick fall and stifles a cry. Before Raymond can react, she removes her sweater, revealing her cleavage. "God, why do you keep it so hot in here?"

Raymond's eyes are bulging. He is out of his chair, standing by the gate. "You like fucking with me, don't you?"

In her peripheral vision, she sees Mick stand. He begins climbing again. The image changes.

"Ray, let's face it, with all the steroids pumping through that body of yours, you couldn't keep it up long enough to please me."

Raymond opens the gate. "Pretty nasty talk for a girl who nearly crushed my windpipe three weeks ago."

"You don't get it, do you? No girl enjoys it when it's forced on her."

"You fucking tease—you're trying to get me to violate my probation, aren't you?"

"Maybe I'm just trying to apologize." *Come on, Mick, move your ass . . .*

The pain is keeping him conscious.

Mick grits his teeth harder, groaning as he pulls himself higher, walking the wall like a mountain climber. *Three more steps, just three more, asshole, come on. Now two—two more, work your arms, squeeze your fists tighter. Good, good. Stop, catch your breath. Okay, last one, come on—*

He reaches the top of the wall. Holding on for dear life, he quickly winds the rope a half dozen times around his left arm to keep from falling. The coil of barbed wire is inches from his forehead. Mick takes the wire cutters from his back pocket and lines the open blades along a section of coil just to the right of the rope.

He squeezes the clippers shut with all his might until the steel snaps in half. Repositioning the cutters, he struggles to focus on the next section of wire through the Thorazine haze, now closing fast on his peripheral vision.

Raymond leans against the wall and stares at the two perfect swells bulging beneath Dominique's top. "So here's the deal, Sunshine. You and me do the wild thing, and I promise I'll leave your boy alone."

She feigns an itch, catching a quick glimpse of the monitor through the security cage. Mick is still cutting through the barbed wire.

Stall the pig. "You want to do it here?"

His hand reaches higher along her arm. "You won't be the first." A wave of nausea washes over her as he rubs the outline of her nipple with the tip of his index finger.

Mick frees the section of barbed wire, then pulls himself on top of the wall, balancing precariously on his chest. He inches closer to the edge and looks down the other side at the twenty-foot drop. "Whoa . . ."

Grunting, he pulls the free end of the nylon rope toward him, then loops it several times around the remaining coils of wire, the barbs tearing holes in his flesh. Wrapping the free end of the rope around his wrists, he eases himself over the wall—and falls.

Mick drops twelve feet before the rope catches along the barbed wire, stopping his descent. Dangling by his wrists, he feels his weight pull the coils of wire away from the top of the cement wall as he drops onto the sidewalk below.

Seconds later, he is up on all fours, staring into the oncoming headlights like a disoriented deer.

"Wait, Ray, I said stop!" Dominique pushes his hand from her breast and pulls a small container of Mace from her purse.

"You fucking whore—you are fucking with me!"

She backs away. "No, I just decided that Mick's life isn't worth the price you're asking."

"You little bitch—"

She turns and presses her face to the thermal scan. *Come on*— She waits for the *buzz*, then wrenches the door open and slips out.

"All right, Sunshine, you made your choice. Now your boy's gonna have to live with it." Raymond opens his desk drawer. He removes a half-inch-thick length of rubber hose, then heads for the elevator.

Dominique reaches the parking lot, relieved to see the Dodge minivan pull out onto Route 441. She pops open the hood of her car, then dials the preset emergency roadside-service telephone number.

The elevator stops at the seventh floor. Raymond keys the power OFF and steps out.

Marvis looks up. "Something wrong?"

"Just watch your television, Marvis." Raymond walks through pod 7-C, stopping at room 714. He keys in.

The room is dimly lit. The rancid scent of disinfectant and soured clothing fills the air.

The resident is lying on the mattress, his back to Raymond, a sheet pulled up to his ear.

"Evening, asshole. Here's a little gift from your girlfriend."

Raymond swings the rubber hose down hard across the sleeping man's face. An agonized cry. The man attempts to get up. The hulking redhead kicks him back down, then beats him again and again across his back and shoulders until the testosterone rage is vented.

Raymond stands over the body, heaving from the effort. "Was that good for you, shithead? Hope so, cause it sure was good for me."

He pulls back the sheet. "Oh, fuck . . ."

Rabbi Steinberg pulls the Dodge minivan over to the side of the road, parking next to the trash bin behind the convenience store. He slides opens the side door, removes the length of nylon rope, and quickly tosses it into the garbage. Then he climbs in back and helps Mick off the floor and onto the seat. "Are you all right?"

Mick looks up through vacant eyes. "Thorazine."

"I know." The rabbi lifts his head and gives him a sip of bottled water, cringing at the bruises along the man's arms. "You're going to be all right. Just rest, we have a long ride."

Mick is unconscious before his head hits the car seat.

The tow truck is already pulling the Pronto Spyder onto its flatbed by the time the first Dade County police cars arrive.

Raymond runs out of the entrance to greet them, then spots Dominique. "It's her! Arrest her!"

Dominique feigns surprise. "What are you talking about?"

"Fuck you, you know what I'm talking about. Gabriel's escaped."

"Mick escaped! Oh my God, how?" She looks at the police officers. "You don't think I had anything to do with it. I've been stuck out here for twenty minutes."

The tow-truck driver nods. "It's true, Officer, I can vouch for that. And we haven't seen a damn thing."

A brown Lincoln Continental screeches to a halt in front of the main entrance. Anthony Foletta climbs out, dressed in a pale yellow jogging suit. "Raymond, what's . . . Dominique, what the hell are you doing here?"

"I stopped by to drop off my letter of resignation. My father was killed in a boating accident. I'm leaving the program." She glances over at Raymond. "Looks like your goon here screwed up pretty good."

Foletta looks at her, then pulls one of the officers aside. "Officer, my name's Dr. Foletta. I'm the director of this facility. This woman used to work with the resident that escaped. If they planned this together and she was his ride, then there's a good chance he's still inside."

The police officer instructs his men to enter the facility with the canine patrol, then he turns his attention to Dominique. "Young lady, get your things, you're coming with me."

JOURNAL OF JULIUS GABRIEL

*I*t was in the late fall of 1974 that my two colleagues and I arrived back in England, all of us quite happy to return to "civilization." I knew Pierre had lost his appetite for the work and wanted to return to the States, the pressure from his politically oriented family finally persuading him to run for office. What I feared most was that he'd insist on Maria joining him.

Yes, feared. Truth be known, I had fallen in love with my best friend's fiancée.

How does one allow such an act to occur? I pondered the question a thousand times. Affairs of the heart are difficult to justify, though, at first, I certainly tried. It was lust, I convinced myself, brought on by the very nature of our work. Archaeology tends to be a profession of isolation. Teams are often forced to live and labor, often in primitive conditions, forgoing the simplest pleasures of privacy and hygiene in order to complete the task at hand. Modesty takes a backseat to practicality. The evening bath in a freshwater stream, the daily ritual of dressing and undressing—the very act of cohabitation can become a feast for the senses. A seemingly innocent act can stir the loins and prime the heart's pump, easily deceiving the weakened mind.

In my heart, I knew these were all excuses, for Maria's dark beauty had intox-icated me from the moment Pierre had introduced us during our first year together at Cambridge. Those high cheekbones, the long black hair, those ebony eyes radiating an almost animal intelligence—Maria was a vision that had captured my soul, a thunderbolt that struck my being yet forbade me to act, lest I destroy my friendship with Borgia.

But I did not give in. Convincing myself that Maria must remain an exquisite bottle of wine I longed to taste but could never open, I locked up my emotions and threw away the devil's key—or so I thought.

As we journeyed from London to Salisbury on that fall day, I sensed that a fork in the road loomed ahead for our trio, and that one of us, most likely me, would be venturing down a path of isolation.

Stonehenge is undoubtedly one of the most mysterious places on Earth, a bizarre temple of upright megalithic stones, arranged in a perfect circle as if by giants. Because we had spent time at the ancient site as part of our degree requirements, none of us truly expected to find any new revelations awaiting us on those rolling green plains of southern England.

We were wrong. Another piece of the puzzle <u>was</u> there, staring us straight in the face.

Although not nearly as old as Tiahuanaco, Stonehenge incorporates the same seemingly impossible feats of engineering and astronomy we had seen earlier. The site itself is believed to have been a spiritual magnet for farmers who first appeared on the plains following the end of the last ice age. The hillside must certainly have been deemed holy, for within a two-mile circumference of the monument are no less than 300 burial sites, several of which would provide us with vital clues linking the area with artifacts found earlier in Central and South America.

Carbon dating tells us that Stonehenge was built approximately 5,000 years ago. Phase one of the construction began with a precise, circular outline of 56 wooden totemlike poles surrounded by a ditch and embankment. Small blue stones, transported from a mountain range nearly 100 miles away, would later replace these wooden markings.

They, in turn, would be replaced by megalithic stones, the remains of which are still present today.

The mammoth vertical rocks that make up Stonehenge are called sarsan stones. They are the hardest rocks in the region and are found in the town of Avery, some 20 miles to the north. Stonehenge's original design consisted of 30 such stones, each weighing an incredible 25 to 40 tons. Each of the great columns of rock had to be transported many miles over hilly terrain, then set upright to form a perfect circle, 100 feet across. Linking the top of these sarsans were nine-ton lintel stones, 30 in all. Each lintel had to be raised 20 feet off the ground, then set into place atop the sarsans. To ensure a proper fit, the ancient engineers carved rounded projections on

top of every sarsan column. These "plugs" fit into rounded-out hollow "sockets" formed along the underside of each lintel, allowing the pieces to fit together like giant Lego building blocks.

Once the monumental circle of stone was complete, the builders erected five pairs of trilithons, two upright sarsans connected by a single lintel. These trilithons, composed of the largest stones at the site, stand 25 feet off the ground, with another third of their mass buried underground. Five trilithons were set into place within the circle to form a horseshoe, the open end of which faces an altar stone aligned to the summer solstice. The center and largest of the trilithons has been set to the winter solstice, December 21, the day of the Mayan prophecy, a date considered by most ancient cultures to be associated with death.

How were the Stone Age villagers of ancient England able to haul sarsans weighing 80,000 pounds over 20 miles of rough, hilly terrain? How did they manage to lift 18,000-pound lintels 20 feet off the ground and set them perfectly into place? Moreover, what mission could possibly be so important as to motivate these prehistoric people to complete such an incredible endeavor?

There are no written records left behind to identify the builders of Stonehenge, but one popular (though absurd) legend points to Merlin, the magician of King Arthur's court, as being the brains behind the brawn. It is said the bearded wise man designed the temple to function as a cosmic observatory and celestial calendar, as well as a place of communion and worship, until it was mysteriously abandoned in 1500 BC.

While Pierre returned to London, Maria and I left Stonehenge to explore the large moundlike tombs surrounding the monument, hoping to find the remains of elongated skulls that would link the Central and South American sites to this ancient burial ground. The largest tomb in the area is a 340-foot-long subterranean burial mound, also constructed of sarsans. Within this tomb lie the skeletal remains of 47 individuals. For some reason, the bones have been anatomically segregated into different chambers.

What we found was not as startling as what we didn't find—at least a dozen skulls belonging to the largest individuals were missing!

We spent the next four months moving from tomb to tomb, always finding the same results. Eventually we arrived at what many archaeologists believed was the holiest of the sites, a fortification of stone located beneath a burial mound in Loughcrew, a remote area in central Ireland.

Carved within the sarsan walls of this tomb are magnificent hieroglyphs, the premier design being a series of spiraling concentric circles. I remember watching Maria's face in the lantern's light as her dark eyes focused upon the bizarre emblems. My heart leapt as her face lit with recognition. Dragging me from the tomb into daylight, she ran to our auto and began tearing open boxes containing hundreds of photos we had taken together in a hot-air balloon over the Nazca desert.

"Julius, look, it's here!" she had proclaimed, thrusting a black-and-white photo to my face.

The photo was of the Nazca pyramid, one of the older desert drawings we believed to be of extreme importance. Within its triangular borders were two figures: one, an inverted four-legged animal, the other, a series of concentric circles.

The circles were identical to the carvings found within the burial tomb.

Maria and I were excited by the discovery. Both of us had, for some time, shared the belief that the Nazca drawings represented an ancient message of salvation relating to the doomsday prophecy, intended only for modern man. (Why else would the mysterious artist draw the figures so large that they could be seen only from an aircraft?)

Our enthusiasm was quelled by the next logical question: Which pyramid did the Nazca drawing represent?

Maria insisted the structure had to be the Great Pyramid of Giza, the largest stone temple in the world. By her logic, Giza, Tiahuanaco, Sacsayhuaman, and Stonehenge all consisted of megalithic stones, their dates of construction were close (or so we believed) and the angle of the Nazca pyramid closely resembled the steep sides of the Egyptian pyramid.

I was not so easily convinced. It was my theory that many of the older etchings of Nazca were drawn as navigational markers, intended as references to point us in the right direction. Surrounding the Nazca pyramid were several clues which I believed had been left for us to identify the mysterious triangular figure.

The most important of these icons appears within the pyramid's own border, drawn below the concentric circles. It is an image of an inverted, four-legged animal, one I reasoned to be a jaguar, arguably the most revered beast in all of Mesoamerica.

The second clue is that of the Nazca monkey. This immense icon, drawn in one continuous line, features a tail that ends in a concentric spiraling circle, identical to the shape appearing within the pyramid figure.

The Maya glorified the monkey, treating it as another species of people. In the creation myth of the _Popol Vuh_, the fourth cycle of the world was said to have been destroyed by a great flood. The few people who survived were believed to have been turned into monkeys. The fact that monkeys do not exist in either Giza or the southern region of Peru indicated to me that the pyramid referenced on the Nazca pampa had to be in Mesoamerica.

Whales do not belong in the desert either, yet there are likenesses of three of these

majestic beasts present on the Nazca plateau. Theorizing the mysterious artist had used the whales to represent a three-sided boundary of water on the pampa, I attempted to convince Maria that the pyramid in question had to represent one of the Mayan temples located on the Yucatán Peninsula.

For his part, Pierre Borgia was not interested in either one of our theories. Chasing after Mayan ghosts no longer mattered to Maria's fiancé; what mattered was power. As mentioned earlier, I could see this development coming for some time. While Maria and I had been busy exploring the tombs, Pierre had been finalizing plans to run for Congress back in the States. Two days after we had made our discovery, he announced, with great pomp and circumstance, that it was high time he and the future Mrs. Borgia moved on to more important things.

I was heartbroken.

Wedding plans were quickly arranged. Pierre and Maria would be married at St. John's Cathedral, I to serve as best man.

What could I do? I felt desperate, believing with all my heart that Maria was destined to be my soul mate. Pierre treated her as a possession, not an equal. She was his trophy, his Jackie Onassis—arm-candy he deemed would serve well as first lady to his political ambitions. Did he love her? Perhaps, for what man could not? But did she truly love him?

This I had to know.

It was not till the eve of their wedding day that I managed the courage to confess my love to her aloud. Looking into those beautiful eyes, swimming in black pools of velvet, I could only imagine the gods smiling upon my wretched soul as Maria pulled my head to her bosom and sobbed.

She had been harboring the same feelings for me! Maria confessed that she had been praying for me to come forward and rescue her from a life with Pierre, whom she cared for but did not love.

In that blessed moment, I became her salvation and she mine. Like desperate lovers, we stole away that night, each leaving Pierre a note, apologizing for our unforgivable act and intentions, neither of us strong enough to face the man in person.

Twenty hours later we arrived in Egypt—Mr. and Mrs. Julius Gabriel.

—Excerpt from the Journal of Professor Julius Gabriel,

Ref. Catalogue 1974–75   pages 45–62
    Photo Journal Floppy Disk 2: File name: NAZCA, Photos 34 & 65
    Photo Journal Floppy Disk 3: File name: STONEHENGE, Drawing 6

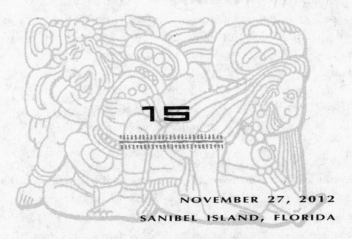

15

NOVEMBER 27, 2012
SANIBEL ISLAND, FLORIDA

The shrill caw of a seagull causes Mick to open his eyes.

He is lying in a double bed, his wrists bound along either side of the frame. His left forearm is heavily bandaged. An IV tube drips into his right.

He is in a bedroom. Slats of golden sunlight reflect along the far wall, seeping in through venetian blinds rattling above his head. He can smell the salt air. He can hear the ocean's surf from the open window above his head.

A gray-haired woman in her seventies enters the room. "So, you're awake." She removes the Velcro strap from his right wrist, then checks the IV bag.

"Are you Edie?"

"No, I'm Sue, Carl's wife."

"Who's Carl? What am I doing here?"

"We felt it was too dangerous to take you to Edie's. Dominique's there, and—"

"Dominique?" Mick struggles to sit up, the dizziness forcing him down again like a heavy, unseen hand.

"Just take it easy, fella. You'll see Dominique soon enough. Right now, the police are watching her, waiting for you to show up." She removes the IV tube and places a Band-Aid on his arm.

"Are you a doctor?"

"I was my husband's dental nurse for thirty-eight years." Methodically, she wraps up the IV bag and tube.

Mick notices the red-rimmed eyes.

"What was in the IV?"

"Vitamins mostly. You were in pretty bad shape when you arrived two nights ago. Mostly just malnourished, although your left arm was butchered pretty good. You've slept for almost two days. Last night, you had a nasty nightmare, screaming in your sleep. I had to secure your wrists so you wouldn't pull out the IV."

"Thank you. And thanks for getting me out of that asylum."

"Thank Dominique." Sue reaches into the pocket of her housecoat.

Mick is startled to see her remove a .44 Magnum. She points the gun at his groin.

"Whoa, hey, wait a second—"

"My husband drowned several days ago aboard Isadore's boat. Three men died while investigating that location in the Gulf you told Dominique about. What's down there?"

"I don't know." He stares at the gun, shaking within the elderly woman's hands. "Do you think you could aim that gun at a less vital organ?"

"Dominique's told us all about you, about why you were locked up, and about your screwball father and his doomsday stories. Personally, I couldn't give a goddam about whatever psychotic apocalyptic mumbo jumbo you believe in, the only thing I care about is finding out what happened to my Carl. In my book, you're a dangerous escaped felon. You so much as look at me the wrong way, and I'll put a bullet in you."

"I understand."

"No you don't. Dominique took a big risk in freeing you. So far, everything having to do with your escape points back to the orderly screwing up and not to her, but the police are still suspicious. They're watching her closely, which means all of us are at risk. Later tonight, we're going to smuggle you aboard Rex's boat. There's a minisub on board—"

"A minisub?"

"That's right. Rex used it to search sunken ships. You're going to use it to find out what's buried beneath the seafloor. Between now and then, you're going to stay in this bedroom and rest. If you try to escape, I'll shoot you and turn your body over to the cops to collect the reward money."

She lifts the sheet by his feet. His left ankle is shackled to the bedframe.

"Now you understand."

NASA: Goddard Space Flight Center
Greenbelt, Maryland

Ennis Chaney begrudgingly follows the NASA technician down the antiseptic, white-tiled corridor.

The vice president is not in a good mood. The United States is on the threshold of war, and his place is with the president and his Joint Chiefs of Staff, not racing to the beck and call of the director of NASA. *Goddam one-eyed Jack, no doubt sending me on another one of his goddam wild-goose chases . . .*

He is surprised to find a security guard posted by the conference-room door.

Spotting Chaney, the guard types in a security code and opens the door. "Go ahead in, sir, they're waiting."

NASA Director Brian Dodds is seated at the head of the conference table, flanked by Marvin Teperman and a woman in her late thirties wearing a white lab coat.

Chaney notices the dark circles under Dodds's eyes.

"Mr. Vice President, come in. Thank you for coming on such short notice. This is Dr. Debra Aldrich, one of NASA's top geophysicists, and I think you already know Dr. Teperman."

"Hello, Marvin. Dodds, this better be important—"

"It is. Sit down, sir—please." Dodds touches a switch on the keypad before him. The lights in the room dim as a holographic image of the Gulf of Mexico appears above the table.

"This image comes from NASA's SEASAT oceanographic observation satellite. At your request, we began scanning the Gulf in an attempt to isolate the origins of the black tide."

Chaney watches the image jump, refocusing on a stretch of sea framed by a superimposed dotted white circle.

"Using X-Band Synthetic Aperture Radar, we were able to trace the black tide back to these coordinates, an area located about thirty-five miles northwest of the Yucatán Peninsula. Now watch."

Dodds presses another switch. The holographic sea dissolves into bright blotches of greens and blues, at the center of which is a brilliant white circle of light, its outer borders fading to cooler shades of yellow, then red. "We're looking down on a thermal image of the targeted area. As you can see, something very large is down there, and it's radiating tremendous amounts of heat."

"At first, we thought we had located an underwater volcano," Dr. Aldrich adds, "but geological surveys completed by Mexico's National Oil Company confirm there are no volcanoes present in the area. We ran a few more tests and found the site to be radiating high amounts of electromagnetic energy. This in itself isn't particularly surprising. The site lies almost dead center of the Chicxulub impact crater, an area containing strong magnetic and gravitational fields—"

Chaney holds up his palm. "Excuse me for interrupting, Doctor. I'm sure this subject is fascinating to you people, but—"

Marvin grabs the VP's wrist. "They're trying to tell you that something is down there, Ennis. Something more important than your war. Brian, the vice president's a busy man. Why don't you skip the gravity gradiometric readings and pull up the acoustic tomography images."

Dodds changes the hologram. The blotches of color dissolve into a black-and-white image of the seafloor. A deep, well-defined tunnel-like aperture shows black on the fractured gray background of the bottom.

"Sir, acoustic tomography is a remote sensing technique which passes beams of acoustic radiation, in this case, ultrasonic pulse echoes, through the seafloor, allowing us to see objects buried below."

Chaney watches in amazement as a massive, three-dimensional ovoid object begins to define itself beneath the larger hole. Dodds manipulates the image, pulling the shape out and away from the seafloor so that it hovers freely above their heads.

"What in the hell is that?" Chaney rasps.

Marvin grins. "Only the most magnificent discovery in the history of mankind."

The ovoid-shaped mass hovers just above Chaney's head. "What are you yapping about, Marvin? What the hell is this thing?"

"Ennis, sixty-five million years ago, an object seven to eight miles in diameter, weighing about a trillion tons and traveling at a speed of thirty-five miles per second smashed into a shallow tropical sea of what is now the Gulf of Mexico. What we're looking at are the remains of the very object that struck our planet and killed off the dinosaurs."

"Come on, Marvin, this thing's huge. How could anything that large survive such an impact?"

"Most of it didn't. The mass you're looking at is only about a mile in diameter, about an eighth of its original size. Scientists have been debating for years whether the object that struck Earth was a comet or an asteroid. But what if it was neither?"

"Stop talking in riddles."

Marvin stares at the rotating holographic image as if mesmerized. "What we're looking at is a uniform structure, composed of iridium and God-knows-what other composite materials, resting over a mile beneath the seafloor. The outer casing is far too thick for our satellite sensors to penetrate—"

"Outer casing?" The raccoon eyes are bulging. "Are you saying this buried mass is a spaceship?"

"The remains of a spaceship, perhaps even a separate, internal pod, po-

174

sitioned within the vessel like a cork in a golf ball. Whatever it is, or was, it managed to survive while the rest of the craft disintegrated upon impact."

Dodds holds up his palm. "Wait a moment, Dr. Teperman. Mr. Vice President, this is all just supposition."

Chaney stares at Dodds. "Yes or no, Director Dodds—is this *thing* a spaceship?"

Dodds wipes the sweat from his brow. "At this point, we just don't know—"

"This hole in the seafloor—does it lead into this vessel?"

"We don't know."

"God dammit, Dodds, what the hell *do* you people know?"

Dodds takes a breath. "For one thing, we know it's imperative that we get our surface ships into the area before another nation stumbles upon this buried mass."

"You're dancing around the facts like a politician, Director Dodds, and you know that pisses me off. There's something you aren't telling me. What is it?"

"I'm sorry, you're right, there is more, a lot more. I guess I'm still a bit stunned myself. Some of us, including me, now believe the deep-space radio signal we received was never meant for us. It—it may have been intended to trigger something within this alien structure."

Chaney stares at Dodds, incredulous. "By trigger, you mean awaken?"

"No, sir. More like activate."

"Activate? Explain."

Debra Aldrich removes a six-page report from her file. "Sir, this is a copy of a SOSUS report sent to NOAA last month from a biologist in Florida. The report details unidentifiable sounds originating from beneath the seafloor within the Chicxulub impact crater. Unfortunately, the acting NOAA director was a little slow getting around to verifying the information, but we've now confirmed the high-pitched acoustics are originating from directly within this buried ovoid structure. There appears to be a high level of complex activity going on within this mass, most likely mechanical in nature."

The NASA director nods. "As a follow-up, we had the Navy's central receiving station in Dam Neck run a complete analysis of all high-decibel acoustics recorded within the Gulf area over the last six months. Although the sounds appear only as background static, data confirms the subterranean acoustics first began on September 23, at precisely the same time the deep-space radio signal first reached Earth."

Chaney closes his eyes and massages his temples, feeling overwhelmed.

"There's something else, Ennis."

"Oh, sweet Jesus, Marvin. Do you think you could give me a minute to swallow before you . . . never mind, just go ahead."

"Sorry, I know this is all a bit mind-boggling, eh?"

"Finish—"

"We completed our analysis of the black tide. Once the toxin comes in contact with organic tissue, it doesn't just cause the cellular walls to decompose, it actually alters its basic chemical composition at the molecular level, leading to a total loss of cell-wall integrity. The stuff works like acid, and the result, as we've seen, is a total bleed out. But here's what's interesting—the substance isn't a virus or even a living organism, but it does carry heavy traces of silicon and a bizarre DNA."

"DNA? Christ, Marvin, what are you saying?"

"It's just a theory—"

"No more games. What is it?"

"Zoological elimination. Fecal matter."

"Fecal matter? You mean it's shit?"

"Uh, yes, but more accurately, alien shit—very old alien shit. The sludge contains chemical traces of elements we believe originated from a living organism, a silicon-based life-form."

Chaney sits back in his chair, mentally fried. "Dodds, turn that damn hologram off, will you, it's giving me a headache. Marvin, are you saying that something could still be alive down there?"

"No, absolutely not, sir," interrupts Dodds.

"I'm asking Dr. Teperman."

Marvin smiles. "No, Mr. Vice President, I'm not implying anything of the sort. As I said, the fecal matter, if it is fecal matter, is very old. Even if an alien life-form did manage to survive the crash, it's certainly been dead for longer than our own species has inhabited the Earth. And a silicon-based life form like this probably couldn't exist in an oxygen environment."

"Then explain to me what the hell's going on."

"Okay, as incredible as it sounds, an alien vessel, obviously light-years ahead of our own technology, crash-landed on Earth sixty-five million years ago. This impact was a tremendous event in human history, eh, in that the cataclysm, by wiping out the dinosaurs, led to the eventual evolution of our own species. Whatever life-form was inside this vessel probably sent a distress signal to its homeworld, which we believe is located somewhere within the constellation of Orion. This would be standard operating procedure—our own astronauts would do the same thing if they found themselves marooned on Alpha Centauri or some other distant world light-years away. Of course, the distances involved make a rescue mission out of the question. Once our Extraterrestrial NASA Control counterparts in Orion received the deep-space distress call, their only course of action would be to attempt to reactivate the alien computers on board their space craft and collect whatever data they could."

Dr. Aldrich nods in agreement. "The black sludge was probably released automatically when the signal reactivated some kind of alien life-support system."

The NASA director can barely contain his excitement. "Forget about building a transmitter on the moon. If Marvin's correct, we could access this ship and potentially communicate directly with the alien intelligence using their own equipment."

"You're assuming this alien homeworld still exists," Marvin says. "The deep-space signal would have been transmitted millions of years ago. For all we know, the planet's sun could have gone supernova—"

"Yes, yes, of course you're right about that. My point is that we have an incredible opportunity to access advanced technologies which may have survived within this vessel. The potential wealth of knowledge down there could accelerate our civilization well into the next millennium."

The vice president can feel his hands shaking. "Who else knows about this?"

"Just the people in this room and a handful of NASA officials."

"What about that SOSUS biologist, the one in Florida?"

"The biologist is dead," Aldrich states. "The Mexican Coast Guard fished his body from the Gulf earlier this week, covered in the sludge."

Chaney swears under his breath. "All right, obviously I need to brief the president about this right away. Meanwhile, I want all public access to SOSUS shut down immediately. Information is to be kept on a need-to-know basis only. From now on, this operation remains covert, understood?"

"What about satellite photos?" Aldrich asks. "The mass may just represent a tiny pinprick in the Gulf, but it's still a bright pinprick. Eventually a GOES or SPOT satellite is going to run across the object. Once we send a Navy ship or even a science vessel into the area, we'll tip our hand to the rest of the world."

The NASA director nods in agreement. "Sir, Debra's right. However, I think I know a way we can keep this operation covert while still allowing our scientists unlimited access to whatever's down there."

Washington, D.C./Miami, Florida

Anthony Foletta locks the door to his office before sitting down at his desk to receive the long-distance communication.

Pierre Borgia's image appears on the telemonitor. "Do you have an update, Director?"

Foletta keeps his voice low. "No, sir, but the police are keeping a close surveillance on the girl. I'm certain he'll eventually contact her—"

"Eventually? Listen, Foletta, you make it absolutely clear that Gabriel's dangerous, do you understand? Instruct the police to shoot to kill. I want him dead, or you can kiss that Tampa directorship good-bye."

"Gabriel hasn't murdered anyone. We both know the police won't kill him—"

"Then hire someone who will."

Foletta looks down at his lap as if allowing the Secretary of State's words to sink in. In reality, he has been anticipating this directive ever since his resident first escaped. "I might know of someone who could handle it, but to do the job right will be expensive."

"How much?"

"Thirty. Plus expenses."

Borgia sneers. "You're a lousy poker player, Foletta. I'll send twenty, not a dime more. You'll have it within the hour."

The telemonitor flashes its dial tone.

Foletta switches off the system, then verifies that the conversation had been recorded. For a long moment, he contemplates his next move. Then he removes his cellular phone from his desk drawer and dials Raymond's pager.

Sanibel Island, Florida

178

The white Lincoln pulls into the gravel driveway. Thirty-one-year-old Karen Simpson, a deeply tanned, peroxide blonde wearing a bright aqua dress, steps out from the driver's seat and ceremoniously walks around to the passenger door to assist her mother, Dory, from the vehicle.

A half block down the road, a plainclothes police officer watches from a surveillance van as the two grieving women, arm in arm, slowly make their way around to the back of the Axler home to where *shivah*, the Jewish gathering of the bereaved, is taking place.

Tables of food have been set up for family and friends of the deceased. Three dozen guests mill about, talking, eating, telling stories—doing whatever they can to comfort each other.

Dominique and Edie sit alone together on a cushioned bench facing the Gulf, watching the sun as it begins to set along the horizon.

A half mile offshore, a fisherman aboard the fifty-two-foot *Hatteras* struggles to net his catch.

Edie nods. "Looks like they finally caught something."

"That's all they'll catch."

"Doll, promise me you'll be careful."

"I promise."

"And you're sure you know how to operate that minisub?"

"Yes, Iz showed me—" Her eyes tear up at the memory. "I'm sure."

"Sue thinks you should take her gun."

"I didn't go to all of the trouble of helping Mick escape just to shoot him."

"She doesn't think you should be so trusting."

"Sue's always been paranoid."

"And what if she's right? What if Mick really is a psycho? He could become violent and rape you. After all, he's been locked up for eleven years and—"

"He won't."

"At least take my stun gun. It's small, in fact it looks just like a cigarette lighter. It'll fit right in the palm of your hand."

"Fine, I'll take it, but I won't need it."

Edie turns to see Dory Simpson approach, her daughter Karen heading for the house.

Dominique stands and gives the woman a hug. "Would you like something to drink?"

Dory sits down next to Edie. "Yes, a diet soda would be nice. Unfortunately, we can't stay long."

Aboard the *Hatteras*, Detective Sheldon Saints watches Dominique head toward the house through high-powered binoculars set upon a tripod inside the boat's main cabin.

Another detective, dressed in jean shorts and a Tampa Bay Buccaneers tee shirt and baseball cap enters the cabin to join him. "Hey, Ted just caught a fish."

"It's about fucking time. We've only been sitting out here for eight goddam hours. Hand me the night glasses, it's getting too dark to see."

Saints fixes the ITT Night Mariner-260 binoculars to the tripod and peers through, adjusting the optic which turns the fading light to shades of green, allowing him to see. Five minutes later, he observes the beautiful female suspect with the long, black hair emerge from the house, carrying a can of soda in each hand. She approaches the bench, offering a soda to each woman, then sits down between them.

Twenty more minutes pass. Now the detective sees the tan blonde in the aqua dress emerge from the house to join the three women. She hugs the Axler woman, then helps her mother up from the bench, leading her around front.

Saints watches for a moment, then returns his focus to the bench, where the older woman and the dark-haired beauty remain, hand in hand.

Dory Simpson climbs into the front seat of the Lincoln as the girl starts the car. The blonde backs the car down the gravel driveway, then heads southwest toward the island's main road.

Dominique reaches beneath the wig to scratch her itching scalp. "I always wanted to be a blonde."

"Leave it on until we leave the dock." Dory hands her the small stun gun, which is the size of a butane lighter. "Edie said to keep this on you at all times. I promised her I'd make you do it. Now, are you sure you feel comfortable operating the minisub?"

"I'll be fine."

"Because I can come with you guys."

"No, I feel better knowing you and Karen are here to look after Edie for me."

It is late by the time they arrive at the private dock in Captiva. Dominique hugs the older woman good-bye, then walks across the wooden deck to the awaiting twenty-four-foot Grady-White motorboat.

Sue Reuben directs her to untie the stern line. Seconds later, they are racing across the Gulf.

Dominique removes the wig before it blows off, then pulls back the gray tarpaulin.

Mick is lying on his back, his right wrist handcuffed to the bottom of the passenger seat. He smiles up at her, then cringes as the bow bounces along the two-to-three-foot seas, smashing the back of his head painfully against the fiberglass deck.

"Sue, where's the key?"

"I think you ought to leave him right there until we get to the boat. No sense taking any chances—"

"At this rate, he'll be seasick by the time we get there. Give me the key." Dominique opens his shackle, then helps him onto the seat. "How are you feeling?"

"Better. Nurse Ratched here has done a fine job."

They arrive at the forty-eight-foot trawler. Sue cuts the engines, allowing the boat's wake to push them in close.

Mick climbs aboard.

Sue hugs Dominique. "You be careful now." She shoves the Magnum into the girl's hand.

"Sue—"

"Hush. Don't make a fuss. Blow his head off if he tries anything."

Dominique slips the gun into the pocket of her windbreaker, then climbs on board, waving as the motorboat races away.

Now everything is quiet, the trawler bobbing in a black sea beneath a starlit sky.

Dominique looks at Mick, unable to see his eyes in the dark. "I guess we ought to get going, huh?" *Relax, you sound nervous as hell.*

"Dom, there's something I need to say first."

"Forget it. You can thank me by helping me find out what happened to Iz."

"I will, but that's not what I wanted to tell you. I know you still have doubts about me. You need to know that you can trust me. I know I've asked a lot, but I swear on my mother's soul that I'd sooner hurt myself than allow any harm to come to you."

"I believe you."

"And I'm not crazy. I know I sound it at times, but I'm not."

Dominique looks away. "I know. Mick, I really think we should get going, the police were watching the house all day. The keys should be under the passenger cushion in the pilothouse. Would you mind?"

Mick heads for the cabin. She waits until he is out of sight before removing the gun from her jacket pocket. She stares at the weapon, recalling Foletta's words of warning. *I'm sure the resident will be quite charming, wanting to impress you.*

The engines sputter to life.

She stares at the weapon, hesitates, then tosses the gun overboard.

God, help me . . .

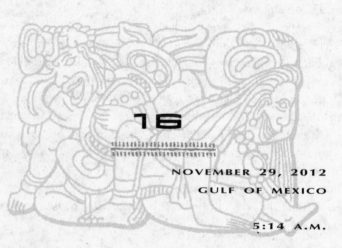

16

NOVEMBER 29, 2012
GULF OF MEXICO

5:14 A.M.

The forty-eight-foot trawler *Jolly Roger* continues its westward trek beneath a starry morning sky. Dominique is in the pilot's chair, struggling to stay awake, her eyelids getting heavy. Exhausted, she lays her head back on the vinyl seat and again forces her attention on the paperback. After rereading the same passage a fourth time, she decides to allow her bloodshot eyes a moment's reprieve.

Just a few seconds. Don't fall asleep . . .

The book drops from her hand, the noise startling her awake. She sucks in a cool breath of air and stares at the darkened passageway leading to the quarters below deck. Mick is somewhere inside, sleeping in the shadows. The thought both comforts and frightens her. Despite the fact that the boat is on autopilot, she has refused sleep. Alone in the pilothouse, her imagination has allowed her innermost fears to get the best of her.

This is ridiculous. He's not Ted Bundy. He'd never hurt you. . . .

She notices the horizon turning gray at her back. Fear has convinced her that sleeping during the day is her best option. She decides to wake Mick at dawn.

"*Jolly Roger*, come in. Alpha-Zulu-three-nine-six, calling *Jolly Roger*, come in please—"

Dominique grabs the radio transmitter. "*Jolly Roger*, go ahead Alpha-Zulu."

"How are you holding up, Doll?"

"Slow and steady. What's wrong? You sound upset."

"The Feds shut SOSUS down. They claim it's just a technical problem, but I don't believe a word of it."

"Damn. Why do you think—"

"*Ahhhhh—Ahhhhhhh—*" Mick's screams send Dominique's heart leaping from her chest. "Oh, Jesus, Ead, I'll call you back—"

"Was that screaming?"

"It's okay, I'll call you right back."

She clicks off the radio and runs down the shallow stairwell, flipping on light switches as she goes.

Mick is sitting up in the corner bunk like a frightened, confused animal, his black eyes wide and shimmering from the bare bulb swinging by his head.

"Mom?" The voice is throaty. *Terrified.*

"Mick, it's okay—"

"Mom? Who is that? I can't see you."

"Mick, it's Dominique." She turns on two more lights, then sits on the edge of the bed. Mick is bare-chested, his taut muscles drenched in a cold sweat. She sees his hands shaking.

He looks into her eyes, still confused. "Dominique?"

"Yes. Are you all right?"

He stares at her face, then looks around the cabin. "I gotta get out of here—" He pushes past her and stumbles up the wooden stairs, heading out on deck.

Dominique follows quickly, fearing he may jump.

She finds him standing in the bow, the cold wind blowing in his face. Dominique grabs a wool blanket and wraps it around his bare shoulders. She sees tears in his eyes.

"Are you okay?"

For a long moment he just stares at the dark horizon. "No. No, I don't think so. I used to think I was okay, now I think I'm pretty fucked up."

"Can you tell me about your dream?"

"No. Not now." He looks down at her. "Bet I scared the shit out of you."

"It's okay."

"The worst thing about being in solitary . . . the scariest part . . . was waking up screaming, only to find myself all alone. You can't imagine the emptiness."

She guides him down to the fiberglass decking. He leans back against the pilothouse windshield and unfurls the blanket from his left shoulder, beckoning her to join him.

Dominique lies down beside him, laying her head on his cold chest. Mick pulls the blanket over her shoulders.

Within minutes, they are both fast asleep.

4:50 P.M.

Dominique removes two cans of peach iced tea from the galley's refrigerator, rechecks their position on the GPS, then returns to the bow. The late-afternoon sun is still intense, its reflection off the fiberglass decking making her squint. She puts on her sunglasses and sits next to Mick.

"See anything?"

Mick lowers the binoculars. "Nothing yet. How far out are we?"

"About five miles." She hands him the can of iced tea. "Mick, I've been meaning to ask you something. Do you remember back in the asylum when you asked me if I believed in evil. What did you mean by that?"

"I also asked you if you believe in God."

"Are you asking me from a religious standpoint?"

Mick smiles. "Why is it psychiatrists can never answer a question without asking one?"

"I guess we like to be clear."

"I just wanted to know if you believed in a higher power."

"I believe someone watches over us, touching our souls on some higher plane of existence. I'm sure part of me believes that because I need to believe that, because it's comforting. What do you think?"

Mick turns, gazing at the horizon. "I believe we possess a spiritual energy, which exists on a different dimension. I believe a higher power exists on that level, which we can only access when we die."

"I don't think I ever heard heaven described quite like that. What about evil?"

"Every Yin has its Yang."

"Are you saying you believe in the Devil?"

"The Devil, Satan, Beelzebub, Lucifer, what's in a name? You said you believed in God. Would you say that God's presence in your life influences you to be a good person?"

"If I'm a good person, it's because I chose to be a good person. I believe human beings have been given the freedom to choose."

"And what influences those choices?"

"The usual suspects—family life, peer pressures, environment, life experiences. We all have certain predispositions, but in the end it's our ability to understand what's happening to us that allows our id to make decisions on a daily basis. If you want to segregate those decisions into good and evil—fine—but it's still free choice."

"Spoken like a true psychiatrist. But let me ask you something, Ms. Freud. What if this freedom to choose is not as free as we think? What if the world around us is exerting an influence on our behavior as a species that we can't see or understand?"

"What do you mean?"

"Take the moon. As a psychiatrist, I'm sure you're familiar with the moon's effect on psychosis."

"The effects of the moon are controversial. We can see the moon; therefore, its effect on the psyche could be self-induced."

"Can you feel the Earth moving?"

"What?"

"The Earth. As we speak, it's not only rotating, it's soaring through space at a velocity of forty-eight miles per second. Can you feel it?"

"What's your point?"

"There are things going on all around us that our senses can't perceive, yet they still exist. What if these things are exerting an influence on our ability to reason, our ability to choose between right and wrong? You think you have free will, but what makes you *really* decide to do something? When I asked if you believed in evil, I was referring to evil as an unseen entity whose presence can blind our judgment."

"I'm not sure I'm following you?"

"What influences a teenager to fire an Uzi into a crowded playground? Why does a desperate mother lock her young children in a car and push it into a lake? What causes a man to rape his stepchild, or . . . or to suffocate a loved one?"

She sees a tear form in the corner of his eye. "You think there's an evil force that influences our behavior? Mick?"

"Sometimes . . . sometimes I think I can actually feel something."

"What do you feel?"

"A presence. Sometimes I feel its icy fingers reaching out from a higher dimension. Whenever I get these feelings, terrible things seem to happen."

"Mick, you were locked in solitary confinement for eleven years. It would be unusual if you didn't hear voices—"

"Not voices, it's more like a sixth sense." He massages his eyes.

This trip may have been a big mistake. He needs help. He could be close to a nervous breakdown. Dominique suddenly feels very isolated.

"You think I'm a psycho—"

"I didn't say that."

"No, but you're thinking it." He turns and looks at her. "The ancient Maya believed in good and evil as a physical presence. They believed that the great teacher, Kukulcán, was banished by an evil force, an evil god the Aztecs called Tezcatilpoca, the smoking mirror. It was said that Tezcatilpoca could reach into the souls of man, deceiving him, causing him to commit great atrocities."

"Mick, that's all Mayan folklore. My grandmother used to tell me the same stories."

"They're not just stories. When Kukulcán died, the Mayans began butchering tens of thousands of their own people. Men, women, and children were sacrificed in bloody rituals. Many were taken to the temple summit atop the Kukulcán pyramid, where they had their hearts cut out from their chests. Virgins were led down the ancient causeway to the sacred cenote where they had their throats slit before they were tossed into the sinkhole to die. The temples in Chichén Itzá are decorated with the skulls of the dead. The Maya had lived in peace for a thousand years. Something must have influenced them suddenly to start butchering one another."

"According to your father's journal, the Maya were superstitious, believing the sacrifices would forestall the end of the world."

"Yes, but there was another influence, the cult of Tezcatilpoca, that was also said to have influenced the atrocities."

"Nothing you've told me so far proves the existence of evil. Man has been slaughtering his own kind since our ancestors dropped from the trees. The Spanish Inquisition butchered thousands, Hitler and the Nazis gassed and burned six million Jews. Violence erupts all the time in Africa. The Serbs slaughtered thousands in Kosovo—"

"Exactly my point. Man is weak, he allows his free will to be corrupted by outside influences. The evidence is everywhere."

"What evidence?"

"The corruption is spreading to our most innocent members of society. Children are using their freedom of choice to commit atrocities, their conscience unable to grasp the difference between right and wrong, reality and fantasy. I watched a CNN story a few nights ago where a ten-year-old took his father's automatic weapon to class and murdered two kids who were picking on him in school." Mick stares out to sea, his eyes brimming again. "A ten-year-old child, Dominique."

"It's a sick world—"

"Exactly. Our world *is* sick. The fabric of society is riddled with a malevolent influence, a sort of cancer, and we're looking for it in all the wrong places. Charles Baudelaire once said the devil's deepest wile is to persuade us he doesn't exist. Dominique, I can feel the influence gaining strength. I can feel it moving closer as the galactic portal opens and we near the winter solstice."

"And what if this evil presence of yours doesn't appear in three weeks? What are you going to do then?"

Mick looks puzzled. "What do you mean?"

"What, you've never considered the possibility that maybe you're wrong? Mick, your entire life has been devoted to resolving the Mayan prophecy and saving humanity. Your conscience, your very identity, has been influenced by the beliefs instilled in you by your parents—enhanced, I suspect, by whatever trauma you experienced that keeps haunting you in your dreams. It doesn't take a Sigmund Freud to tell you that the presence you feel is inside of you."

Mick's eyes widen as her words sink in.

"What happens when the winter solstice comes and goes and all of us are still around? What are you going to do with your life then?"

"I . . . I don't know. I've thought about it, I just never allowed myself to dwell upon it. I was afraid that if I did, if I thought about living a normal life, then I'd eventually lose sight of what's really important."

"What's really important is that you live your life to its fullest." She takes his hand in hers. "Mick, use that brilliant mind of yours to see inside yourself. You've been brainwashed since birth. Your parents condemned you to save the world, but the person who really needs to be saved is Michael Gabriel. You've spent your entire existence chasing white rabbits, Alice. Now, we have to convince you that Wonderland doesn't exist."

Mick lies back, staring at the late-afternoon sky, Dominique's words echoing in his ears.

"Mick, tell me about your mother."

He swallows, clearing his throat. "She was my best friend. She was my teacher and companion, my whole childhood. While Julius was spending weeks on end analyzing the Nazca desert, Mom was giving me her warmth and love. When she died . . ."

"How did she die?"

"Pancreatic cancer. She was diagnosed when I was eleven. Toward the end, I became her nurse. She became so weak . . . the cancer just eating her alive. I used to read to her to keep her mind off the pain."

"Shakespeare?"

"Yes." He sits up. "Her favorite was *Romeo and Juliet*. 'Death, that hath sucked the honey of thy breath, hath had no power yet upon thy beauty.' "

"Where was your father during all this?"

"Where else? Out on the Nazca desert."

"Were your parents close?"

"Very close. They always referred to each other as soul mates. When she died, she took his heart with her to the grave. Part of mine, too."

"If he loved her so much, how could your father have left her when she was dying?"

"Mom and Julius told me their quest was more important, more noble than sitting around, watching death invade her body. I was taught at an early age about destiny."

"What about it?"

"Mom believed that certain people have been blessed with special gifts that determine their paths in life. These gifts come with great responsibilities, staying on the path requiring great sacrifices."

"And she believed you were blessed?"

"Yes. She said I inherited a unique insight and intelligence that was passed down from her maternal ancestors. She explained to me that those without the gift would never understand."

Christ, Mick's parents really screwed him up good. It'll take decades of therapy to right his compass. Dominique shakes her head sadly.

"What?"

"Nothing. I was just thinking about Julius, leaving his eleven-year-old boy to handle the burden of taking care of his dying mother."

"It wasn't a burden, it was my way of thanking her for all she'd given me. In retrospect, I'm not sure I'd have it any other way."

"Was he there when she passed?" Her words cause Mick to wince.

"Yeah, he was there all right." He looks up at the horizon, his eyes growing harsh at the memory—then suddenly focusing like a hawk. He grabs the binoculars.

An object has become visible, towering above the western horizon.

Mick points. "There's an oil platform out there, a big one. I thought you said Iz reported seeing nothing in the vicinity?"

"He did."

Mick refocuses the glasses. "It's not a PEMEX rig, it's bearing an American flag. Something's not right."

"Mick—" Dominique points.

He sees the incoming boat, focusing on it with the glasses. "Damn, it's the Coast Guard. Cut the engines. How fast can we get that sub of yours into the water?"

Dominique hurries to the pilothouse. "Five minutes. You want to dive now?"

"It's now or never." Mick races to the stern, pulling the gray tarp off the capsule-shaped submersible. He starts the winch. "The Coast Guard will ID us. We'll be arrested on the spot. Hey, grab some supplies."

Dominique tosses cans of food and jugs of bottled water into a knapsack, then climbs down into the minisub as—

—the cutter closes to a hundred yards, its commander blaring a warning across the water.

"Mick—come on!"

"Start the engines, I'll be right there!" Mick ducks into the cabin, searching for his father's journal.

"THIS IS THE UNITED STATES COAST GUARD. YOU HAVE ENTERED RESTRICTED WATERS. CEASE ALL ACTIVITY AND PREPARE TO BE BOARDED."

Mick grabs the journal as the Coast Guard cutter reaches the *Jolly Roger*'s bow. He hurries back to the stern, releases the winch's cable—

"Freeze!"

Ignoring the command, he jumps down into the protective internal sphere of the eighteen-foot-long minisub, balancing precariously on an iron ladder as he reaches up and seals the hatch. "Take us down, fast!"

Dominique is buckled in the pilot's seat, trying to recall everything Iz had shown her. She pushes down on the wheel, the minisub submerging—as the keel of the Coast Guard cutter collides with the top of the submersible's sail.

"Hold on—"

The sub descends at a steep forty-five-degree angle, the titanium alloy plates groaning in Mick's ear. He leans down and grabs a diver's air tank as it rolls precariously toward the bow. "Hey, Captain, you sure you know what you're doing?"

"Don't be a backseat driver." She eases the descent. "Okay, now what are we supposed to do?"

Mick squeezes past the ladder to join her up front. "We find out what's going on down here, then head for the Yucatán coastline." Mick bends down to take a peek through one of the eight-inch-diameter, four-inch-thick viewports.

The deep blue environment is obscured by a myriad of tiny bubbles rising up along the outer hull. "I can't see a thing. I hope this tub has sonar."

"Right in front of me."

Mick leans over her shoulder to glance at the luminescent orange console. He notices the depth gauge: 344 feet. "How deep can this thing go?"

"This thing is called the *Barnacle*. I'm told it's a very expensive French sub, a smaller version of the *Nautile*. It's been rated for depths of eleven thousand feet."

"You sure you know how to pilot it?"

"Iz and the owner took me out one weekend and gave me a crash course."

"Crash, that's what I was afraid of." Mick looks around. The interior of the *Barnacle* is a ten-foot-diameter reinforced sphere situated within the rectangular hull of the vessel. Data-processing equipment lines the tight compartment like three-dimensional wallpaper. The control station for a mechanical arm and retractable isothermic sampling basket protrudes from one wall, high-tech underwater monitors and acoustic transponders from another.

"Mick, make yourself useful and activate the thermal imager. It's that monitor above your head."

He reaches up, powering up the device. The monitor switches on, revealing a tapestry of greens and blues. Mick pulls back on a stub-nosed joystick, aiming the exterior sensor at the seafloor.

"Whoa, what have we here?" The monitor reveals a brilliant white light appearing at the top of the screen.

"What is it?"

"I don't know. How deep are we?"

"Eleven hundred feet. What should I do?"

"Keep us moving west. Something massive is up ahead."

Gulf of Mexico
1.1 miles due west of the *Barnacle*

The Exxon oil rig, *Scylla,* is a free-floating, fifth-generation Bingo 8000-series semisubmersible oil drilling unit. Unlike platform rigs, the superstructure floats four stories above the surface (and three stories below) on eighty-two-foot-high vertical columns attached to two enormous 390-foot-long pontoons. Twelve mooring lines anchor the structure to the seafloor.

Three continuous decks sit upon the *Scylla*'s base. The open upper deck, as long and wide as a football field, supports a seventy-two-foot-high derrick that contains the drill string, made up of lengths of thirty-three-foot steel pipe. Two immense cranes are positioned along the northern and southern sides, with an elevated octagonal helo-deck covering the west deck. The control and engineering rooms as well as the galley and two-person cabins are located on the middle or main deck. The lower or machinery deck houses the rig's three 3080-hp engines as well as the equipment necessary to handle a hundred thousand barrels of crude oil per day.

Although the superstructure is filled to its 110-person capacity, not a drop of oil flows through its drill string. The *Scylla*'s lower deck has been hastily gutted to accommodate myriads of NASA's high-tech multispectral sensors, computers, and imaging systems. Support equipment, tether cables, and operator control boards for three ROVs (Remotely Operated Vehicles) sit next to bundles of steel pipe stockpiled along the semienclosed lower deck.

Positioned at the very center of the concrete and steel decking is a twelve-foot-diameter circular hole, designed to accommodate the drill string. A soft emerald radiance rises from the sea, filtering through the gap to bathe the ceiling and surrounding work area in an unearthly green light. Technicians overcome by curiosity pause every so often to sneak peeks at the artificially illuminated seafloor, located 2,154 feet below the floating superstructure. The *Scylla* is positioned directly above a massive, tunnel-like aperture located along the bottom. Somewhere within this mysterious five-thousand-foot pit lies the source of the brilliant, incandescent green light.

Naval Commander Chuck McKana and NASA Director Brian Dodds huddle over the two technicians operating the *Sea Owl*, a six-and-a-half-foot ROV, attached to the *Scylla*'s winch by a seven-thousand-foot tether cable umbilical cord. They stare at the ROV's monitor as the small submersible reaches the fractured seafloor to begin its descent into the glowing vortex.

"Electromagnetic energy's increasing," the ROV's virtual pilot reports. "I'm losing maneuverability—"

"Sensors are failing—"

Dodds squints at the bright light glaring from the sub's minicam monitor. "How deep is the ROV?"

"Less than a hundred feet into the hole—God dammit, there goes the *Sea Owl*'s electrical system."

The monitor goes blank.

Commander McKana runs his stubby fingers through his graying crew cut. "That's the third ROV we've lost in the last twenty-four hours, Director Dodds."

"I can count, Commander—"

"I'd say you need to focus on finding an alternative way in."

"We're already working on it." Dodds motions to where a dozen workers are busy rigging lengths of steel pipe to the derrick above. "We're going to lower the drill string right into the hole. Sensors will be hooked up within the first length of pipe."

Rig Captain Andy Furman joins them. "We've got a situation, gentlemen. The Coast Guard reports two people aboard a trawler just launched a minisub two miles east of the *Scylla*. Sonar shows them heading for the object."

Dodds looks alarmed. "Spies?"

"More like civilians. The trawler's registered to an American salvage company licensed out of Sanibel Island."

McKana appears unconcerned. "Let them look. When they surface, have the Coast Guard arrest them."

Aboard the *Barnacle*

Mick and Dominique press their faces to the viewports' reinforced LEXAN glass as the minisub approaches the eerie beacon of light, the beam blasting upward from the seafloor like a 168-foot-wide spotlight.

"What the hell could be down there?" Dominique asks. "Mick, you okay?"

Mick's eyes are closed, his breathing erratic.

"Mick?"

"I can feel the presence. Dom, we shouldn't be here."

"I didn't come all this way just to turn back." A red light flashes above her head. "The sub's sensors are going crazy. There's massive amounts of electromagnetic energy rising out of the hole. Maybe that's what you're feeling?"

"Don't pass through that beacon or you'll short-circuit every system on board."

"Okay, maybe there's another way in. I'll circle the area while you complete a sensor sweep."

Mick opens his eyes, scanning the stacks of computer consoles lining the cabin. "What do you want me to do?"

She points. "Activate the gradiometer, it's an electromechanical gravity sensor rigged beneath the *Barnacle*. Rex used it to detect gravity gradients beneath the seafloor."

Mick boots the system's monitor, which reveals a tapestry of orange and reds, the brighter colors indicating high levels of electromagnetic energy. The hole itself blazes a brilliant, almost blinding white. Mick pulls back on the gradiometer's joystick, widening the field to examine the rest of the seafloor's topography.

The intense glow shrinks to a white dot. Hues of green and blue create a circular border around the reds and orange. "Wait a second—I think I found something."

Encircling the crater-shaped area are a series of dark spots set in a precise, equidistant circular pattern along the mile-diameter perimeter.

Mick counts the holes. He feels his gut tightening, a cold sweat breaking out across his body. He grabs his father's journal, leafing through the parched pages until he locates the June 14, 1997, entry.

He stares at the photograph of the nine-foot circular icon, located at the center point of the Nazca plateau. Within its circular boundaries Mick had found the original Piri Re'is map, sealed within an iridium container. He counts twenty-three lines extending outward from the Nazca figure like a sunburst, the last one, seemingly endless.

Twenty-three dark spots surround the monstrous hole in the seafloor.

"Mick, what is it? Are you okay?" Dominique sets the minisub on autopilot to glance at the monitor. "What are they?"

"I don't know, but an identical pattern was drawn on the Nazca plateau thousands of years ago."

Dominique glances at the entry. "It's not really identical. You're comparing lines carved in the desert with a bunch of dark holes in the seafloor—"

"Twenty-three holes. Twenty-three lines. You think that's just a coincidence?"

She pats his cheek. "Take it easy, gifted one. I'll head for the nearest hole, and we'll take a closer look."

The *Barnacle* slows to hover above a dark burrow, twenty feet across, the orifice spewing a steady profusion of bubbles. Dominique directs one of the sub's external lights down into its steep gullet. The beacon reveals a vast tunnel, descending through the seafloor at a forty-five-degree angle.

"What do you think?"

Mick stares at the burrow, the familiar feeling of dread growing in his gut. "I don't know."

"I say we investigate."

"You want to enter that hellhole?"

"That's why we're here, isn't it? I thought you wanted to resolve the Mayan doomsday prophecy?"

"Not like this. It's more important that we get to Chichén Itźa."

"Why?" *He's frightened.*

"Salvation lies in the Kukulcán pyramid. The only thing waiting down this hole is death."

"Yeah, well I didn't toss seven years of college in the toilet and risk being thrown in prison just so you could chase some bullshit Mayan prophecy. We're here because my family and I need a sense of closure, we need to find out what really happened to Iz and his friends. I'm not blaming you for my father's death, but since you're the one who started us on this little adventure, you're the one who's going to see it through."

Dominique pushes down on the wheel, driving the capsule-shaped minisub straight into the heart of the tunnel.

Mick grabs for a ladder rung, holding on as the *Barnacle* accelerates through the pitch-dark shaft.

A *squishing* sound echoes within the sub.

Dominique stares out her viewport. "The sound's coming from the walls of this passage. The internal lining seems to be acting like some kind of giant sponge. Mick, to your left, there's a sensor marked spectrophotometer—"

"I see it." He activates the system. "If I'm reading this thing right, the gas being filtered out of this hole is pure oxygen."

A baritone thrumming reverberates throughout the cabin, growing louder as they descend deeper. Mick is about to say something when the *Barnacle* suddenly lurches forward, accelerating down the shaft.

"Hey, slow down—"

"It's not me. We're caught in some kind of current." He can hear the panic in her voice. "External temperature's rising. Mick, I think we're being sucked into a lava tube!"

He grips the ladder tighter as the deep pulsating sounds cause the glass instrument panels in front of him to resonate.

The minisub plunges, spinning blindly down the hole like a beetle being flushed down a drainage pipe.

"Mick!" Dominique screams as she loses control of the *Barnacle*. She squeezes her eyes shut and grips the seat's shoulder harness as the power fails and they are blanketed in darkness.

She feels herself hyperventilating, waiting for the jolt that will cause the sub to lose integrity to the suffocating sea. *Oh, Jesus, God, I'm going to die, help me, please—*

Mick has locked his arms and legs around the ladder, his palms clenching the steel bars in a viselike grip. *Don't fight it, let it come. Let the madness end . . .*

Intense vertigo as the minisub spins round and around as if caught in a giant washing machine.

A sonic boom—a bone-jarring jolt: Mick is sent flying blindly through the pitch, the *Barnacle* driven bow-first into an immovable, unseen force, the air exploding from his lungs as his face and chest slam blindly into a stack of computer consoles.

The incessant pounding in his head forces Mick to open his eyes.

Silence.

He is lying on his back, his legs propped in the air, his upper body entangled in a sizzling array of broken equipment. The cabin is humid and pitch-dark, save for the dull glow of an orange console flickering somewhere in the distance. Up is down, left is right, and a warm liquid is dripping down his throat, gagging him.

He rolls over painfully, spitting out a mouthful of blood, his head still spinning. Tracing the blood to his dripping nostrils, he pinches off the flow.

For a long moment he just sits there, balancing un- steadily on sharp fragments of shattered computer mon- itors and navigational equipment as he tries to remember his name and where he is.

The minisub. The burrow . . . Dominique!

"Dom?" He spits out more blood as he climbs over a pile of equipment blocking his path to the pilot's chair. "Dom, can you hear me?"

He finds her unconscious, still strapped within the pilot's chair, her chin on her chest. His heart pounds with fear as he carefully reclines the chair all the way back, supporting her bleeding head in his hand before allowing it to rest on the back of the seat. He checks her airway, detecting shallow breaths. He loosens the harness, then tends to the deep, bleeding gash on her forehead.

Mick removes his tee shirt, tearing the sweaty fabric into long strips. He ties a makeshift bandage across the wound, then searches the battered cabin for the first-aid kit.

Dominique moans. She sits up painfully, turns her head, and retches.

Mick locates the first-aid kit and a bottle of water. Returning to her side, he dresses the wound, then removes a cold pack.

"Mick?"

"Right here." He squeezes the cold pack, puncturing its internal contents, then presses it to her head, securing it with the remains of his tee shirt. "You've got a nasty head wound. Most of the bleeding's stopped, but you probably suffered a concussion."

"I think I cracked a rib, I'm having a hard time breathing." She opens her eyes and looks up at Mick in pain. "You're bleeding."

"I broke my nose." He hands her the container of bottled water.

She closes her eyes and takes a sip. "Where are we? What happened?"

"We descended through the burrow and hit something. The minisub's dead. Life-support systems are barely functioning."

"Are we still in the hole?"

"I don't know." Mick moves to the forward viewport and peers out.

The *Barnacle*'s emergency exterior lighting reveals a dark, tight chamber, devoid of seawater. The minisub's bow appears to be wedged in between two dark, vertical barriers. The spacing between the two walls narrows sharply before dead-ending at a curved, metallic sheath.

"Jesus, where in the hell are we?"

"What is it?"

"I don't know—some kind of subterranean chamber. The sub's wedged in between two walls, but there's no water outside."

"Can we get of here?"

"I don't know. I'm not even sure where *here* is. Have you noticed those deep vibrations have stopped?"

"You're right." She hears him rummaging through the debris. "What are you doing?"

"I'm looking for the scuba gear." He locates the wet suit, mask, and air tank.

Dominique groans as she sits up, then lays her head back again, the pain and vertigo overwhelming. "What are you going to do?"

"Wherever we are, we're stuck. I'm going to see if I can find a way to free us."

"Mick, wait. We must be a mile down. The pressure will crush us the moment you open the hatch."

"There's no water in the chamber, which means it must be depressurized. I think we have to take the chance. If we just sit here, we'll die anyway." He pulls off his sneakers and climbs into the tight, neoprene wet suit.

"You were right. We never should have entered the burrow. It was stupid. I should have listened to you."

He stops dressing to lean over her. "If it wasn't for you, I'd still be Foletta's vegetable. Just sit here and try not to move while I get us out of here."

She blinks back tears. "Mick, don't leave me. Please, I don't want to die alone—"

"You're not going to die—"

"The air, how much air's left?"

He searches the control console, checking the gauge. "Almost three hours. Try to stay calm—"

"Wait, don't go yet." She grips his hand. "Just hold me a minute. Please."

He kneels down, placing his right cheek gently against hers, feeling her muscles quivering as he hugs her and inhales her scent. He whispers in her ear, "I'll get us out of here, I promise."

She squeezes him tighter. "If you can't—if there's no way out—promise me you'll come back."

He swallows the lump in his throat. "I promise."

They hold on to each other for several more minutes until the constriction of Mick's wet suit becomes unbearable.

"Mick, wait. Reach under my seat. There should be a small kit filled with emergency supplies."

He pulls out the tin suitcase and opens it, removing a knife, a handful of flares, and a butane lighter.

"There's a small air tank beneath the seat as well. Pure oxygen. Take it."

He removes the tank, which is attached to a plastic mask. "It's a lot of equipment to carry. I should leave this for you."

"No, you take it. If you run out of air, then we're both dead."

He slips his sneakers back on, secures the knife to his ankle with adhesive tape, then opens the valve of the larger air tank to verify that the regulator is working. He hoists the BCD vest and tank onto his back, then secures the smaller tank of oxygen around his waist by its Velcro strap. He shoves the flares and lighter into the vest, then, feeling like a pack mule, pulls himself up the ladder of the minisub, which is now listing at a thirty-degree angle.

Mick unbolts the hatch, takes a deep breath, then tries to push it open. Nothing.

If I'm wrong about the pressure, we'll both die right here. He pauses, weighing his options, then tries again, this time wedging his shoulder beneath the titanium lid. With a *hiss*, the hatch frees itself from its rubber housing and opens.

Mick pushes his way out of the minisub, climbing out on top of the hull, allowing the hatch to slam shut as he stands—

Whack! He bites into the regulator as the top of his head smacks painfully against a rock-hard ceiling.

Hunched over, balancing atop the minisub, he rubs the knot on his head as he looks around. From his vantage atop the *Barnacle*, he sees they are in a giant torus, a donut-shaped chamber, illuminated by the sub's emergency lights, the ship's bow wedged tightly between two curved, seven-foot-high vanelike blades. The beam of his flashlight reveals the upper portion of at least a dozen more of the partition-like objects, all splaying out from a curved centerpiece like multiple fans on a horizontal windmill.

Mick stares at the structure, analyzing his surroundings, the regulator wheezing in his ears as he breathes. *I know what this is—it's a turbine, a giant turbine. We must have been sucked down an inlet shaft. The thrumming sound's gone. The minisub's blocking the rotation of the blades, jamming the turbine, clogging the inlet.*

Mick climbs down from the *Barnacle* and steps onto a slick, antiquated metallic surface. *What happened to the seawater?*

And then he is falling backward, his bare feet slipping out from under him, his right elbow and hip slamming against the hard, slimy surface with a hollow *thud*. Mick groans in pain, then looks up.

The flashlight's beam reveals a porous, black, spongelike substance coating the entire central section of the ceiling. Droplets of seawater drip on his head.

Mick crawls to his feet and reaches up, surprised to find the porous material extremely brittle, like Styrofoam, only harder. He removes the knife and hacks at the substance, carving out several chunks of crumbling, chalky rock, drenched in seawater.

Mick pauses. The sound of air racing down a shaft echoes somewhere to his right. He reaches up and grabs on to the top of the metallic partition on his right, shining the flashlight's beacon along the metallic ceiling.

The sound is coming from a four-foot-wide hollow shaft, situated in the ceiling above the next rotor blade over. Rising at a near-vertical angle, the dark passage appears to lead up through the roof like a bizarre laundry chute.

Mick climbs over the steel wall, then stands beneath the aperture, feeling hot gusts strike his face.

An outlet shaft?

Moving to the next turbine blade, he pulls himself up the barrier and straddles the two-inch-wide ledge, feeling for the edge of the shaft, his hands probing a steep but manageable incline.

Carefully, Mick gropes the ceiling and stands, balancing precariously along the top of the blade as he pulls himself upward into the dark cavity, crawling into the shaft on his belly. Rolling onto his side, he extends his legs out to the opposite side of the four-foot-wide cylinder, his air tank and elbows pressed against the wall to his back. He looks up, the hot wind in his face, his light revealing a vast conduit, rising into the darkness above at a steep, seventy-degree angle.

This is going to be tough . . .

Keeping his back and feet pressed firmly against the interior, he crab-walks his way up the wall of the shaft, inch by painful inch, like a mountain climber ascending a sheer, vertical crawl space. For every five feet he rises, he slips back a foot, falling and groaning until the sweat is wiped clear from his palms and his scorched flesh can reestablish a grip on the slippery, metallic surface.

It takes him twenty minutes to ascend eighty-five feet to the top. Awaiting him at the pitch-dark summit—a dead end.

Mick slams his head back against the wall and groans through his regulator in desperation. His leg muscles, weary from the climb, begin shaking, threatening to send him plunging from his perch. Feeling himself slip, he lunges outward with both hands, dropping the flashlight in the process.

Shit . . .

Surrounded by darkness, he listens to it clatter down the shaft, cracking open as it strikes the surface below.

You're next if you're not careful.

With excruciatingly slow movements, he removes the butane lighter and one of the flares tucked inside his wet suit. Dripping with sweat, he wastes the next five minutes futilely attempting to light the flare.

Mick stares at the butane lighter, which is full of fuel but refuses to ignite. *Dummy, you can't start a fire without oxygen.*

Taking a deep breath, he removes the regulator from his mouth and presses the purge button, releasing a gust of air toward the lighter. An orange flame ignites, allowing him to light the flare.

The sizzling pink light reveals what appears to be two small hoses connected to a hydraulic hinge. Using his knife, he severs both hoses, which leak a hot, dark blue fluid onto his wetsuit. He returns the regulator to his mouth, then presses the crown of his head against the lid.

The hatch yields a half inch.

Maneuvering as close to the lid as he dares, Mick pushes open the alien manhole a crack and shoves his fingers in the gap. In one motion he rolls, dangling in the darkness before managing to pull himself out of the shaft onto what appears to be a metallic grid. He collapses on all fours, his body shaking from exhaustion, as the searing heat from his new surroundings causes his face mask to fog up and blind him.

Mick removes the mask, but finds his mouth too dry to spit. He wipes the tears from his red-hot face and looks up.

Oh, sweet Jesus . . .

He sits up, bedazzled, his quivering limbs no longer his to control. His eyes widen, his mind racing so fast that he cannot form a single cohesive thought. Sweat pours off his face and body from the furnacelike heat, causing pools to form in his wet suit. His heart is pounding so hard that it feels like it is weighing him down, pressing him to the scorching metal grating beneath his wet suit.

I'm in hell . . .

He has entered a mammoth, darkened, ovoid chamber, its dimensions rivaling the New Orleans Superdome if the arena were gutted. Licking the surface of the surrounding walls is an inundating layer of searing-hot, crimson red flames which rise in ripples like an inverted waterfall along the sizzling perimeter, disappearing into an oblivion of darkness above.

But not darkness! Swirling hundreds of feet above his head, illuminating the very center of the gargantuan abyss is a brilliant, emerald green vortex of swirling energy—a miniature spiral galaxy rotating in a slow, omnipotent, counterclockwise sweeping motion like a cosmic ceiling fan, pulsating with power.

Mick stares at the galaxy's unearthly radiance, transfixed by its beauty, humbled by its magnificence, and absolutely terrified by its implications. He forces his eyelids to close over his burning pupils, trying desperately to clear his head.

Dominique . . .

Struggling to his feet, he reopens his eyes and takes in the rest of his ethereal surroundings.

He is standing on a perch, a metallic grating supporting the hatch that had sealed the cylindrical shaft. Four feet below, filling the entire chamber like a lake in a mountainous crater, is a billowing, silvery, mercury-like liquid, its glistening, mirror surface reflecting the dancing vermilion flames. Ebony whiffs of smoke drift above the undulating sea of molten metal like steam escaping from a boiling cauldron.

Mick turns to face the glowing wall of red-hot embers. Situated just below the flames is a grillelike facade that rings the entire interior of the chamber. Distortion reveals invisible gases gushing out from tiny pores along the facing like heat rising along a desert tarmac road.

The intake burrow . . . a ventilation shaft?

Mick stares at the surreal wall of flame, which neither burns nor consumes, but flows straight up the vertical enclosure like a raging river of blood. Feverish thoughts swirl through his mind. *Am I dead? Maybe I died in the minisub? Maybe I'm in hell?*

He collapses onto his buttocks, half-sitting, half-lying along the edge of the platform, too weak and dizzy to move. He manages to spit into his face mask and reposition it, then remembers the smaller tank. Unfastening it, he sucks in several breaths of pure oxygen, managing to clear his head.

That's when he notices the tear in his wetsuit. The skin of his right knee is exposed, the wound bleeding profusely. Baffled, he touches the hot blood, scrutinizing it as if it is some kind of alien broth.

His blood is bleeding blue.

Where am I? What's happening to me?

As if in response, a violet surge of energy ignites like a bolt of lightning from somewhere across the lake. He leans forward, struggling to see through his mask, which has fogged again despite the fresh coating of saliva.

And then another bizarre thing happens. As he removes the mask, a powerful wave of invisible energy rises like a gust of air from the surface of the lake and strikes his arm. The face mask is levitated straight into the air, where it remains hovering, three feet above his head.

Mick stands. As he reaches out to retrieve it, he registers an intense field of electromagnetic energy, which resonates through his brain like a reverberating tuning fork.

Disoriented, he reaches blindly for the oxygen tank as the cardinal fires dance in his blurry vision. Giving up, he falls backward against the metal and sucks in more oxygen, closing his eyes to the vertigo.

Michael . . .

Mick opens his eyes, stifling his breath.

Michael . . .

He stares out at the lake. *Am I hallucinating?*

Come to me, my son.

The oxygen mask falls from his mouth. "Who's out there?"

I've missed you.

"Who are you? Where am I? What is this place?"

We used to call Nazca our own private little purgatory, do you remember, Michael? Or has that brilliant mind of yours finally failed you after so many lonely years in the asylum?

Mick feels his heart flutter. Scorching tears stream down his beet red cheeks. "Pop? Pop, is that really you? Am I dead? Pop, where are you? I can't see you. How can you be here? Where *is* here?"

Come to me, Michael, and I'll show you.

In a dreamlike state, he steps off the grating and drops to the lake.

"Oh, shit, oh, God!"

Mick looks down, his mind overwhelmed by what his senses are reporting.

He is weightless, defying gravity, floating above the silvery surface on an emerald green cushion of energy that courses through every fiber of his being, intoxicating him. Exhilarating sensations rise up through his bones and exit his scalp, causing every strand of hair on his head to stand on end. Adrenaline and fear battle for control of his bladder. Feeling the air tank levitate away from his back, he hurriedly tightens the Velcro strap around his waist, then returns the regulator to his mouth.

Come to me, Michael.

A single step forward propels him along the energy field like an unbound Baryshnikov. Emboldened, he executes a half dozen more strides, then finds himself soaring across the lake's mirrorlike expanse, a wingless angel guided by an invisible force.

"Pop?"

A little farther . . .

"Pop, where are you?"

As he approaches the far side of the chamber he sees an immense, charred-black platform looming thirty feet above the glistening surface like a barge from hell. A ripple of terror grips his soul as he realizes that he cannot stop, that his momentum through this weightless world is guiding him to the object against his will.

I have you.

Panicking, Mick turns to flee, only to find his legs churning in place as he is drawn upward and away from the lake's surface. He dives onto his belly in midair, clawing helplessly at the energy field as his body is wrenched backward and onto the platform by an overpowering, icy-cold, malevolent presence.

Mick lands hard on his knees, falling forward as if thrust into worship. Hyperventilating, his mind gripped in fear, he looks up to gaze upon his keeper.

It is a pod, as high and wide as a locomotive, as long as a football field. A myriad of scorched tentaclelike conduits originating from beneath the platform feed into the enclosed, smoked-glass object like a thousand alien intravenous tubes.

Why do you fear me, Michael?

A violet surge of energy ignites within the interior of the cylinder, the flash momentarily exposing the shadowy presence of an immense being.

Mick is paralyzed, his face a frozen mask of terror, his limbs no longer able to support his weight.

Look at me, Michael. Gaze upon the face of your flesh and blood!

Mick's thoughts shatter as he is shoved headfirst against the glasslike surface by an invisible force. He can *feel* the presence within the smoke-filled chamber—a presence of pure evil that causes a sulfuric bile to rise from his throat and gag him. He squeezes his eyes shut, his mind unable to grasp what terror may lie before him.

A wave of energy jolts his eyelids open, pinning them back.

He sees a face appear through a yellow haze within the pod. Mick's heart pounds through his chest.

No—

It is Julius, his father's snow-white hair tousled about like Einstein's, the tan, wrinkled face appearing like worn leather. The soft, familiar brown eyes stare back at him.

Michael, how can you fear your own father?

You're not my father—

But of course I am. Think back, Michael. Don't you remember how your mother died? You were so angry at me. You hated me for what I had done. You looked into my eyes just as you do now—AND YOU CONDEMNED ME TO HELL!

The monstrous voice deepens as it echoes in his ears. Mick screams through the regulator, feeling his mind snap as Julius's face dissolves into a pair of bloodred, demonic headlight-sized reptilian eyes—the pupils—golden, diabolical slits that burn into his soul and scorch the very fabric of his sanity.

Mick lets out a bloodcurdling scream as his tormented mind is fondled by icy-cold fingers of death. In one adrenaline-enhanced motion, he leaps off the platform, only to be snatched in midair and held.

You are my flesh, you are my blood. I've been watching you, waiting for this day to come. I know you've felt my presence. We'll be together soon. United . . . father and son.

Through his delirium, he looks up to see the spiraling galaxy above his head rotating faster. As its speed increases, an immense, hollow cylinder of emerald energy forms from within the center of the molten lake, rising toward the ceiling like a luminescent green tornado. The funnel of energy merges with the vortex, the two whirling in unison, faster and faster.

Mick's mind is screaming, his eyes bulging from his head. Through the madness he sees a solitary ripple form at the center of the lake, the disturbance created by something rising just below the molten surface.

And now he can see it—rising up through the emerald funnel of energy—a being—black as night, a predatory life-form with a thirty-foot reptilelike wingspan. A pair of three-pronged talons dangle from below its torso. A faceless, anvil-shaped skull tapers back to a curved, hornlike protrusion, the beak-shaped tail half the size of the wings. An incandescent, amber-colored orb glows brightly along the neckline like a pupilless eye.

Mick watches, spellbound, as the ceiling above the spiraling galaxy of energy seems to disappear, revealing a vertical shaft of rock cut within the seafloor. The water within the shaft is also swirling, forming the base of a monstrous whirlpool.

Mick grasps the small tank of oxygen tightly to his chest. He tears away the mask, aiming the sealed valve away from his body.

With a resounding *whoosh*, the center of the ceiling retracts, causing a tremendous roar to fill the chamber. Mick feels his ears pop as the sea rushes in, the torrent of water channeled along either side of the cylindrical, vertical force field like Niagara Falls.

Desperate, Mick scans the perimeter of the chamber, his eyes focusing upon the twenty-three identical shafts, all but one of which pop open to inhale the rising tide.

The sound of rising thunder as the alien vessel's giant turbines begin reversing gears in order to expel the seawater.

Mick grips the butane lighter, then opens the valve on the smaller air tank, touching the flame to an invisible, combustible stream of pure oxygen. The pressurized gas ignites like a rocket, slamming the base of the tank into his gut as it propels him backward through the air and away from the pod.

Mick soars above the molten lake of metal, then plunges into the raging river of seawater draining atop the lake's molten metal surface.

Mick releases the emptied tank as he is inhaled by the torrent, fear and adrenaline driving his arms and legs as he directs his way toward the inoperable shaft from which he came. He grabs onto the grating and pulls himself up as the rising tide races in behind him.

Mick yanks open the hatch, staring down into the dark shaft. *Don't stop, don't think, just jump!*

He jumps, plunging feetfirst down the seventy-degree chute in total darkness, the air tank screeching at his back, the roar above his head momentarily receding. Pressing his forearms to the slick metallic surface, he tries desperately to slow his descent, using the neoprene wet suit as a brake pad.

Mick shoots out of the shaft opening, tumbling headfirst into the vertical facing of a rotor blade. Dazed, he struggles to his feet, registering powerful vibrations as the giant turbine growls to life beneath his feet.

Climb over—get back to the sub!

Mick pulls himself up and over the seven-foot-high blade as a river of seawater explodes out of the ceiling. He lands on his feet, panicking as turbine blades begin rotating, reversing, fighting to push the *Barnacle* free.

Don't let the minisub leave without you!

Mick stumbles through knee-deep water, sucking in a deep breath of air before releasing the cumbersome air tank from his back. Freed from the weight, he leaps onto the titanium hull as a raging wall of water slams into him from behind, nearly tossing him from the vessel.

The donut-shaped chamber is filling quickly with water, the pressure building, threatening to burst the sub free at any moment. Mick pulls himself to the top of the *Barnacle*, feeling the pressure in his head intensify as he wrenches open the hatch and stumbles down the opening, slamming the entry shut behind him, sealing it with a twist.

An explosion of water flips the minsub sideways.

Mick tumbles down the ladder, landing hard on shards of broken equipment as the *Barnacle* is freed.

A screeching, deafening whine as the giant turbine accelerates to a hundred revolutions per second, propelling the minisub back up and out of its intake shaft like a speeding bullet.

Aboard the *Scylla*

"It's a maelstrom!" Captain Furman is thrown over a control console, the floor twisting out from under him as twelve tons of steel drill pipe are hurled across the lower deck.

Sounds of screeching metal rend the air. With an agonized groan, the upper deck of the seven-story platform sways against the monstrous current, the *Scylla* listing at a sixty-degree angle as half a dozen submerged mooring lines attached to one pontoon refuse to yield to the growing vortex.

Technicians and equipment slide across the open decking, plunging helplessly into the raging emerald sea.

The remaining moor lines snap, releasing the rig from the seafloor. The buoyant superstructure rights itself—then spins, bobbing and pitching within the swirling mouth of the luminescent whirlpool.

Alarms howl against the night. Bewildered crewmen stagger from their cabins, only to be battered by flying debris. As their world gyrates around them in dizzying revolutions, they stumble down aluminum stairwells, moving to the lower deck, where a dozen lifeboats hang suspended from winches.

Brian Dodds clutches the lines of one lifeboat, his ears filled with the howling roar of the maelstrom. The craft is suspended six feet below, but the *Scylla* is now tossing so violently that climbing down to the lifeboat is no longer an option.

The oil rig lurches sideways, caught within the centrifugal force of the maelstrom, which pins the *Scylla* against the wall of the funnel. The NASA director opens his eyes, forcing himself to look upon the dazzling source of energy radiating upward from the center of the turbulent sea. Dodds holds on, sucking in a desperate breath as a forty-foot wave washes over him, crashing through the lower deck as it snags the last of the lifeboats in its fury.

Dodds's stomach lurches sickeningly, his eyes widening in disbelief as the center of the vortex suddenly drops to the seafloor, the rig spinning precariously atop the two-thousand-foot watery precipice. Within the blinding emerald madness he sees something—a black, winged creature, levitating steadily upward through the whirlpool's vortex like a demon rising from hell.

The winged beast soars past him, disappearing into the night—as the *Scylla* tumbles sideways, free-falling into the mouth of oblivion.

The lifeless being streaks along the surface of the Gulf at supersonic speed, gliding effortlessly on a dense cushion of antigravity. Moving southwest, it ascends to a higher altitude, its energy stream rattling the mountain peaks over Mexico as it races toward the Pacific.

Upon reaching the ocean, its preprogrammed sensory array alters its course to a more precise westerly route. The being slows, adjusting its speed so that it will remain on the darkened side of the planet during the entire length of its fateful journey.

JOURNAL OF JULIUS GABRIEL

*O*ur honeymoon in Cairo was bliss.

Maria was everything to me—my soul mate, my lover, my companion, my best friend. To say her presence consumed me is no exaggeration. Her beauty, her scent, her sexuality—everything about her was so intoxicating that I often felt myself drunk with love, ready, if not eager, to forsake my sworn oath to unravel the riddle of the Mayan calendar, just to return to the States with my young bride.

To start a family. To live out a normal life.

Maria had other plans. After a week's honeymoon, she insisted we continue our journey into man's past by searching the Great Pyramid for clues linking this magnificent Egyptian structure to the icon drawn upon the Nazca plateau.

Who can argue with an angel?

When it comes to Giza, the subject of <u>who</u> built the pyramids is just as important as <u>when</u>, <u>how</u>, and <u>why</u>. You see, the Giza structures are a paradox unto themselves, erected with unfathomable precision for a purpose that still remains a mystery thousands of years after their completion. Unlike the other ancient monuments of Egypt, the pyramids of Giza were not built as tombs; in fact, they lack any identifying hieroglyphics, internal inscriptions, sarcophagus, or any treasures to speak of.

As mentioned earlier, erosion at the base of the Sphinx would later prove that the structures of Giza had been erected in 10,450 BC, distinguishing them as the oldest in all of Egypt.

You'll notice that I do not refer to these wonders as the pyramids of Khufu, Khafre, and Menkaure. Egyptologists would have us believe it was these three pharaohs who commissioned the monoliths built. What utter nonsense! Khufu had about as much to do with the design and construction of the Great Pyramid as Arthur, a Christian king, did Stonehenge, which was abandoned 1500 years before Christ.

The fallacy dates back to 1837, when Colonel Howard Vyse was commissioned to excavate Giza. The archaeologist, having made no significant discoveries to speak of (and quite desperate for funds), conveniently managed to locate quarry marks bearing Khufu's name in a rather obscure tunnel he himself had haphazardly excavated within the pyramid. For some reason, no one seemed to question the fact that the identifying markings had been painted upside down (some even misspelled), and that no other inscriptions were found anywhere else inside the Great Pyramid.

The Egyptologists, of course, preach Vyse's discovery as the gospel.

Many years later, an inventory stela would be unearthed by the French archaeologist, Auguste Mariette. The text appearing on this stone, the ancient equivalent of an historical placard for tourists, clearly indicates the pyramids were built long before Khufu's reign, referring to the structures at Giza as the House of Osiris, Lord of Rostau.

Osiris—perhaps the most revered figure in all Egyptian history—a great teacher and wise man who abolished cannibalism and left a lasting legacy to his people.

Osiris . . . the bearded god-king.

Maria and I spent most of our time examining the Great Pyramid, although the entire Giza site plan lends itself to one mysterious, yet very distinct purpose.

The exterior of the Great Pyramid is as mind-boggling as its interior. Having previously discussed the temple's measurements in relationship to the value pi, precession, and the dimensions of the Earth, I'll proceed to the structure's four limestone-block sides. As incredible as it may seem, each side spans 755 feet, the pyramid coming within a mere eight inches of being a perfect square. Each side is also aligned to true north, east, south, and west, facts that make a greater impact when one realizes the Great Pyramid is constructed of 2,300,000 stone blocks, each weighing between 2.5 and 15 tons. (In the smallest of the three Giza pyramids lies a single stone weighing 320 tons. As I record these words in the year 2000, there are only three cranes in the entire world that could lift such a monumental weight off the ground.) Yet, as was the case in Tiahuanaco and Stonehenge, no machinery was used to move these incredible weights, which had to be transported from a distant quarry, then placed in position, oftentimes hundreds of feet off the ground.

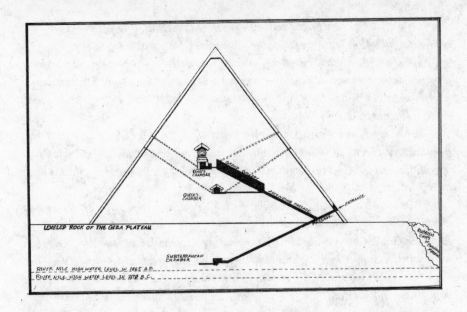

Most onlookers gazing upon the Great Pyramid do not realize that the structure's sides were originally finished with highly polished casing stones, each of these 144,000 blocks weighing 20,000 pounds. Only remnants of these casing stones remain today, the majority having been destroyed after a massive earthquake in AD 1301, yet we know the limestone blocks had been cut with such precision and skill that the blade of a knife could not be inserted between them. One can only imagine what the Great Pyramid must have looked like thousands of years ago—a six-million-ton structure covering 13 acres—shimmering under the Egyptian sun like glass.

While the exterior of the pyramid is a wondrous sight to behold, it is the interior of this mysterious structure that may conceal its true purpose.

The Great Pyramid contains several passageways leading to two barren rooms, innocuously named the King's Chamber and the Queen's Chamber. The true purpose of these rooms is still unknown. A concealed doorway along the northern face leads one down a narrow passage connecting to a corridor ascending straight into the heart of the pyramid. After a brief climb, one can either enter a claustrophobic, 130-foot-long horizontal tunnel leading to the Queen's Chamber, or continue ascending still farther by way of the Grand Gallery, an impressive vaultlike corridor that leads up to the King's Chamber.

The Queen's Chamber is a barren, 17-by-18-foot room, with a 20-foot-high gabled ceiling. Its only notable feature is a narrow ventilation shaft, the opening a mere eight-inch-by-nine-inch rectangle. This shaft, as well as the two found in the King's Chamber, had remained sealed until 1993, when the Egyptians, seeking to improve the pyramid's ventilation, hired the German engineer Rudolf Gantenbrink to use his miniature robot to excavate the blocked ventilation shafts. Images taken by the robot's miniature camera revealed the shafts

209

DOMAIN

were not blocked, but sealed from within by a sliding apparatus, a tiny door held in place with metal fittings. When unimpeded, the shaft would open directly to the sky.

Using a sophisticated clinometer, Gantenbrink was able to calculate the exact angles of projection to the night sky. At 39 degrees, 30 feet, the Queen's southern shaft had been directly targeted on the star Sirius. The King's shaft, at 45 degrees, on Al Nitak, the lowest star among the three situated on Orion's belt.

Astronomers soon thereafter discovered that the three pyramids of Giza had been painstakingly aligned to mirror the three belt stars of the constellation Orion as they appeared in 10,450 BC. (The legend of Osiris is also linked with Orion; his wife, Isis, with the star of Sirius.)

Was cosmic alignment the true purpose behind the excavation of the shafts, or were they designed to fulfill another function?

The Grand Gallery is an incredible engineering accomplishment unto itself. Less than seven feet wide at floor level, the walls of this corbeled shaft gradually narrow along either side as they rise to meet the 28-foot-high ceiling. Climbing at a 26-degree incline, the tight passageway runs upward more than 150 feet, an amazing architectural accomplishment considering that the Gallery's vaulted masonry supports the entire weight of the upper three-quarters of the pyramid.

At the summit of the Grand Gallery is a mysterious antechamber, its walls composed of red granite. Strange pairs of parallel grooves resembling tracks for an ancient set of partitions have been carved into the wall. From here, a small tunnel leads into the King's Chamber, the most impressive room in the pyramid. The chamber is a perfect rectangle, 17 feet, 2 inches wide, 34 feet, 4 inches long, its ceiling rising 19 feet, 1 inch off the floor. The entire chamber is composed of 100 blocks of red granite, each weighing in excess of 70 tons!

How could the ancient builders possibly have managed to lift these granite blocks into place, especially in such confined spaces?

Only one object is present within the King's Chamber, a solitary block of mud-colored granite, its interior sculpted out like a giant bathtub. Situated along the western wall, the piece is seven and a half feet long, its width and depth each measuring three and a half feet. The solid block of granite has been cut with unexplainable machinelike precision. Whatever technology was used to slice this object was superior to any tool possessed by modern man.

Though no mummy has ever been found, Egyptologists continue to identify this hollowed object to be a lidless sarcophagus.

I have a different theory.

The King's Chamber appears to function as an acoustical instrument, gathering and amplifying sounds. On several occasions, I have found myself alone in the room and used the opportunity actually to climb into the bathtub-shaped coffer. Upon lying down, I became overwhelmed by what felt like deep reverberations, as if I had climbed into the ear canal of a giant. I do not exaggerate when I state that my bones actually rattled from the overwhelming vibrations of sound and energy. Further discussions with electronic engineers reveal that the geometry of the apex of the Great Pyramid (at 377 ohms) makes it the perfect resonator, matching the impedance of free space.

As bizarre as it sounds, it is my theory that the Great Pyramid had been designed to function like some incredible, monolithic energy-channeling tuning fork, capable of resonating radio frequency-type currents, or perhaps some other as yet unknown energy fields.

More sobering facts: In addition to our own investigation of the Great Pyramid, Maria and I spent countless hours interviewing some of the top architects and engineers in the world. Upon calculating the tonnage, labor, and space requirements involved with building the structure, each of these professionals rendered the same startling conclusion—the Great Pyramid could not be duplicated—not even today.

Let me reiterate this: Even using our most sophisticated cranes, human beings of our own era could _never_ have erected the Great Pyramid.

And yet, the Great Pyramid _was_ constructed, some 13,000 years ago!

So then, who _did_ build the Great Pyramid?

How does one seek answers to define the impossible? What _is_ the impossible? Maria prescribed it as "a faulty conclusion drawn by an uninformed observer, whose own limited experience lacks the information base to comprehend accurately something that is simply not within their own acceptable parameters of reality."

What my beloved was trying to express was this—mysteries remain mysteries until the observer opens their mind to new possibilities. Or, to put it more succinctly—in order to find a solution to what is perceived as the impossible, seek impossible solutions.

And we did.

Logic dictates that, if human beings alone could not have built the Giza pyramids, then someone else had assisted them, in this case—another species—one obviously superior in intelligence.

This simple yet disturbing conclusion was not derived out of thin air, but from hard, empirical evidence.

The elongated skulls found in both Central and South America tell us the members of this mysterious species were humanoid in appearance. Various legends describe them as being tall Caucasian males, with ocean blue eyes, and flowing white beards and hair. Several of the most successful ancient cultures in history, including the Egyptian, Inca, Maya, and Aztec, had revered these beings as men of great wisdom and peace who had arrived to establish order from the chaos. All were great teachers, possessing an advanced knowledge of astronomy, mathematics, agriculture, medicine, and architecture that elevated our savage race to nations of ordered societies.

The physical evidence left to confirm their existence is undisputable.

This humanoid species also had a clear agenda—to preserve the future of humanity, their adopted children.

What a bizarre and frightening conclusion Maria and I had stumbled upon. Here we were, two modern-day thinkers, doctoral graduates from Cambridge, presenting each other with theories that would have made Erich von Däniken proud. Yet we were not proud. In fact, our initial reaction was one of shame. We were not some Swiss hotelier turned author. We were scientists, renowned archaeologists. How could we possibly approach our colleagues with such preposterous notions of alien intervention? And yet, for the first time, my young bride and I felt as if our eyes had finally, truly opened. We could sense a master plan at work, yet still felt frustrated that we could not decipher its hidden meaning. Our humanoid elders had left us instructions in the Mayan codices, painstakingly duplicating the message upon the Nazca plateau, but the codices had been burned by the Spanish priests, and the message of Nazca still eluded us.

Maria and I felt frightened and alone, the Mayan calendar's prophecy of doom hanging over our heads like the sword of Damocles.

I remember holding my wife, feeling like a lost child who, after learning about death, struggles to comprehend his parents' concept of heaven. The thought made me realize that, for all our exploits and accomplishments, our species, from an evolutionary standpoint, is really still in its infancy. Perhaps this is why we are so prone to violence, or why we remain such nourishing, emotional creatures, always wanting for love, always feeling alone. Like 30,000-year-old toddlers, we simply don't know any better. We're a planet of children, Earth—a massive orphanage, with no adult minds to guide us as to the ways of the universe. We've been forced to teach ourselves, learning the hard way as we go, living and dying like red blood cells circulating with reckless abandon throughout the body of humanity—so young, so inexperienced, and so naive. The dinosaurs had ruled the Earth for 200 million years, yet our first ancestors had only fallen from the trees less than two million years ago. In our incredible ignorance, we fancied ourselves superior.

The truth is, we are nothing but a species of children—curious, ignorant children.

The Nephilim, the "fallen ones" had been our elders. They had been here long ago, had taken <u>Homo sapien</u> women as their wives, providing our species with their DNA. They had taught us what they felt we could grasp, and had left us clear markers as to their presence. They had also tried to warn us of a calamity to come, but like most children, we had turned a deaf ear, refusing to heed our parents' warning.

"We're still infants," I remember telling Maria. "We're fragile, naive infants, thinking we know everything, obliviously rocking in our cradle while the serpent crawls in through the open nursery window to slaughter us."

Maria agreed. "You realize, of course, that the scientific community will scorn us."

"Then we mustn't tell them, at least not yet," I said. "Humanity's prophecy may be written in stone, but the future is still ours to determine. The Nephilim would not have gone to all this trouble to warn us of 4 <u>Ahau</u>, 3 <u>Kankin</u> without also leaving behind some weapon, some means of saving ourselves from annihilation. We must find the means to our salvation—then, and only then, will the rest of the world listen with an open mind."

Maria hugged me, agreeing with my logic. "We won't find the answers here, Julius. You were right all along. While the Great Pyramid is part of the prophecy's puzzle, the temple appearing on the Nazca plateau is in Mesoamerica."

—Excerpt from the Journal of Professor Julius Gabriel,

Ref. Catalogue 1975–77   pages 12–72
    Photo Journal Floppy Disk 4: File name: GIZA, Blueprint 17

18

The Nullarbor plain, the largest flat expanse of land on the planet, is a desolate region of limestone that stretches out over ninety-five thousand square miles along Australia's barren southern Pacific coastline. It is an uninhabitable area, devoid of vegetation and wildlife.

But for part-time naturalist Saxon Lennon and his girlfriend, Reneè, the Nullarbor plain has always provided the perfect escape. No people, no noise, no project managers yelling—just the soothing sounds of the surf crashing against the sheer limestone cliffs one hundred feet below their campsite.

The sonic reverberation causes Saxon to stir from his sleeping bag. He opens his eyes, pushing back the tent flaps to gaze at a canopy of stars.

Reneè slips her arm around his waist, playfully fondling his genitals. "You're up early, luv."

"Stop for a second—did you hear something whiz by?"

"Like what?"

"Dunno—"

The tremendous *thud* causes the earth beneath their tent to shake, sending Saxon scurrying out of his girlfriend's grasp.

"Come on!"

The young couple hurries from the tent half-naked, slipping on their hiking boots without bothering to lace them. They hop in their Jeep and head east, Saxon being sure to keep the vehicle a safe distance from the edge of the coastal cliffs running parallel on their right.

The dark horizon has turned gray by the time they arrive.

"Goddam, Sax, what the bloody hell is it?"

"I—I dunno."

The object is enormous, as tall as a two-story house, with reptilian wings that expand a good sixty feet from tip to tip. The creature is black as night, perched on a pair of three-pronged talons that seem to grip the barren limestone surface. An enormous, reflective, fan-shaped tail remains motionless, several feet above the ground, while a series of tentacles jut out from the abdomen. The faceless, horn-shaped head seems to be pointed at the heavens. The statuesque being appears lifeless, save for the luminescent amber-gold glow of a disk-shaped organ located on one side of its torso.

"Could be one of them remote aerial vehicles the Air Force is always flying about?"

"Maybe we ought to call someone?"

"You go ahead. I'm going to take some photos." Saxon aims his camera, snapping several shots while his girlfriend tries the car phone.

"Phone's dead, nothing but static. You sure you paid the bill?"

"Positive. Here, take a photo with me in the picture, you know, so I can show how big this thing is."

"Not too close, okay, luv."

Saxon hands Reneè the camera, then moves to within fifteen feet of the being. "I don't think this thing's even alive. It's just perched here, like a char-broiled condor."

A golden hue appears on the horizon. "Perfect timing. Wait for the sun, it'll make for a better photo."

The first rays of dawn peek out over the Pacific, the solar light kissing the surface of the creature's reflective tail.

Saxon jumps back as the tail rises with an hydraulic *hiss*.

"Son of a bitch, the thing's activating."

"Sax—look—its eye's starting to blink."

Saxon stares at the amber disk, which is flashing off and on faster and faster, its color darkening to a crimson hue.

"Come on—" He grabs Reneè's wrist and runs back to the Jeep. Slamming the vehicle into gear, he accelerates north across the wide-open expanse of flatland.

The orb deepens to bloodred, then stops blinking. A spark ignites along the outstretched wings, bursting into a brilliant, white-hot, silvery flame.

With a blinding flash, the creature detonates, unleashing an unfathomable amount of combustible energy that expands outward across the entire Nullarbor plateau at the speed of sound. Shock waves from the nuclear explosion seep through the porous limestone rock.

Vaporizing everything in its path.

Saxon registers the searing-hot, sixteen thousand-degree blast wave a nanosecond before his body, his girlfriend, the Jeep, and the terrain evaporate into a sizzling, toxic gas which is swept upward into the atmosphere in a hellish vacuum of microcosmic dust and flame.

Gulf of Mexico

The Oliver Hazard Perry-class guided-missile frigate USS *Boone* (FFG-28) floats silently on an ominous lead gray sea beneath a threatening, afternoon sky. Surrounding the warship, scattered along the surface over a two-mile radius are all that remains of the semisubmersible oil rig, *Scylla*. A dozen motorized rubber rafts maneuver carefully through the debris field as emotionally drained sailors pull the bloated remains of the dead from the water.

Ensign Zak Wishnov seals another body bag as Sublieutenant Bill Blackmon weaves the motorboat slowly through the flotsam.

"Zak, there's another one, starboard bow."

"God, I hate this." Wishnov leans out over the bow and hooks the corpse with a reach-pole. "Oh, geez, this one's missing an arm."

"Shark?"

"No, it's been severed cleanly. You know, now that you mention it, I haven't seen one shark since we've been out here."

"Neither have I."

"Makes no sense. There's blood everywhere, and these are shark-infested waters." Zak rolls the mangled corpse into the boat, shoving it quickly into a body bag. "It's that thing down there, isn't it, Lieutenant? The source of that green glow. That's why the sharks are staying away."

The lieutenant nods. "The sharks know something we don't. The sooner the skipper takes us out of here, the better."

Captain Edmund O. Loos III stands motionless on his bridge, his hazel eyes staring out at the foreboding horizon, his lower jaw clenched in anger. The thirteenth officer to command the *Boone* and her crew of 42 officers and 550 enlisted men is seething inside, has been ever since he received the orders from his CO to divert his warship away from his Persian Gulf-bound battle group and report to the Gulf of Mexico.

A goddam salvage operation in the middle of what could turn out to be the biggest conflict we've had in twenty years. We'll be the laughingstock of the whole fucking Navy.

Commander Curtis Broad, the ship's Executive Officer and second-in-command, approaches. "Excuse me, skipper. One of the LAMPS has located a submersible, floating 1.7 kilometers due west. Two survivors on board. One claims to know what destroyed the *Scylla*."

"Have him brought to the briefing room. What's the VP's ETA?"

"Thirty-five minutes."

A bolt of lightning flashes silently in the distance, followed seconds later by the growl of thunder.

"Recall all boats, Commander. I'll be in the briefing room. Inform me when the vice president arrives."

"Aye, sir."

The Kaman SH-2G Seasprite antisubmarine helicopter, also known as the Light Airborne Multi-Purpose System, or LAMPS, bounces twice before coming to rest on the missile cruiser's helo-pad.

Mick Gabriel grabs one end of Dominique's stretcher, a crewman the other. As the chopper's bay door slides open, they are joined by the ship's physician and his medical team.

The medical officer leans over the unconscious Hispanic beauty. He verifies that she is breathing, checks her pulse, then flashes a light in her eyes. "This one has a bad concussion, possible internal injuries. We need to get her to sick bay."

A corpsman pushes Mick aside, relieving him of the stretcher. He is too weak to protest.

The physician looks him over. "Son, you look like you've been through hell. Any injuries, other than the cuts and bruises?"

"I don't think so."

"When's the last time you slept?"

"I don't know. Two days? My friend, will she be all right?"

"Should be. What's your name?"

"Mick."

"Come with me, Mick. We'll dress those wounds, get some grub in you, then clean you up a bit. You need to get some rest—"

"Negative," interrupts the lieutenant. "Captain wants him in the briefing room in fifteen minutes."

It is raining by the time Ennis Chaney's chopper touches down on the aft deck of the *Boone*. The vice president leans over and nudges the sleeping man to his right. "Wake up, Marvin, we're here. How you can sleep through all this rickety-rack is beyond me."

Marvin Teperman flashes a tight grin as he wipes the sleep from his eyes. "The traveling wears me out."

An ensign slides open the bay door, salutes, then leads the two men into the superstructure. "Sir, Captain Loos is waiting for you in his briefing room—"

"Not yet. First, I want to see the bodies."

"Right now, sir?"

"Right now."

The ensign leads him inside a large hangar. Lying in rows along the concrete floor are body bags.

Chaney moves slowly from bag to bag, pausing at each to read the identification tag. "Oh, Lord . . ." The vice president kneels next to a bag and pulls back the zipper, his hands shaking. He stares at the pale, lifeless face of Brian Dodds. With a fatherly touch, he reaches out and smooths back the auburn hair from the forehead, the emotion welling in his eyes.

"How did this happen?" Chaney's voice is a whispered rasp.

"Uncertain, sir. The one man who may know is in the captain's briefing room, waiting to speak with you."

Chaney reseals the bag and struggles to his feet. "Take us there."

Mick shoves the last bite of turkey-and-cheese sandwich into his mouth, draining it with a swig of ginger ale.

"Feeling better?"

He nods to the captain. Although exhausted, the food, hot shower, and change of clothing have improved his spirits.

"Now, you say your name is Michael Rosen, and you're a marine biologist working out of a facility in Tampa, is that correct?"

"Yes, sir. You can call me Mick."

"And you discovered the object below us—how?"

"SOSUS. It's an underwater sound observation—"

"I'm familiar with SOSUS, thank you. Now, your companion—"

A knock interrupts the question. Mick looks up to see Vice President Ennis Chaney enter, followed by a shorter, older gentleman with a pencil-thin mustache and warm smile.

"Welcome aboard, sir. I'm sorry you couldn't visit us under more auspicious circumstances."

"Captain, this is Dr. Marvin Teperman, an exobiologist on loan to us from Canada. And who is this gentleman?"

Mick extends his hand. "Dr. Michael Rosen."

"Dr. Rosen claims to have entered the object below us in his minisub."

Chaney sits down at the conference table. "Update us."

Captain Loos refers to his notes. "Dr. Rosen has described a layout that resembles something out of Dante's *Inferno*. He says the emerald glow is being emitted from a powerful energy field, originating from within this subterranean chamber."

Chaney stares at Mick through intense, raccoon eyes. "What happened to the *Scylla*?"

"The oil rig," Loos clarifies. "It was a sensory observational post positioned above the hole."

"The energy field created a powerful vortex. The whirlpool must have destroyed the rig."

Loos's eyes grow wide. He strikes the switch of an intercom. "Bridge."

"Aye, sir, Commander Richards here—"

"Release sensor buoys, Commander, then move the ship one kilometer due east of our present position."

"One kilometer due east, aye sir."

"Double-time that order, Commander."

"Understood, sir."

Mick looks from Captain Loos to the vice president. "Moving your ship's not good enough, Captain. We're in terrible danger. There's a life-form down there—"

"A life-form!" Marvin practically leaps across the table. "Something's still alive down there? How can that be? What did it look like?"

"I don't know."

"Didn't you see it?"

"It remained concealed within an enormous pod."

"Then how do you know it was alive? Did it move?"

"It communicated with me—telepathically. It has the ability to access our thoughts, even our most subconscious memories."

Teperman is on his feet, unable to contain his excitement. "This is incredible. What thoughts did it communicate?"

Mick hesitates. "It accessed a memory of my deceased father. It—it wasn't a very good memory."

Chaney leans forward. "You said we're in terrible danger. Why? Is this life-form a threat to us?"

"It's more than a threat. Unless we destroy the being and its vessel, every man, woman, and child on this planet will be dead by 4 *Ahau* . . . uh, by December 21."

Marvin stops smiling. Chaney and the captain look at each other, then back at Mick, who can almost feel the tension behind the vice president's eyes as they bear down on him.

"How do you know this? Did the being communicate the threat?"

"Did you see a weapon of some kind?" the captain asks.

"I'm not sure. Something was released. I don't know what it was. It looked like an enormous, deformed bat, only it didn't flap its wings, it just sort of rose out of this pool of liquid silver energy—"

"Was it alive?" Marvin asks.

"I don't know. It seemed more mechanical than organic—sort of like a drone. The energy field churned, the whirlpool formed, then the ceiling of the chamber was partially vented to the sea, and the thing just rose straight up and out of the funnel."

"Straight up through the funnel?" Chaney shakes his head in disbelief. "This is some pretty wild stuff, Dr. Rosen."

"I realize that, but I assure you, it's all true."

"Captain, have you examined this man's submersible?"

"Yes, sir. The electronics are totaled, and the hull's badly battered."

"How did you access the alien craft?" Marvin asks.

Mick looks at the exobiologist. "That's the first time you referred to it as an *alien* craft. It's the remains of the object that struck Earth sixty-five million years ago, isn't it, Doctor?"

Marvin's eyebrows raise in surprise.

"And the deep-space radio signal—it must have activated the vessel's life-support system."

Teperman looks impressed. "How do you know all this?"

"Is this true?" Captain Loos asks, incredulous.

"It's very possible, Captain, although, based on what Dr. Rosen has just told us, it seems more likely that the alien's life-support system never completely shut down. This pod Dr. Rosen refers to must have continued to function, keeping the being alive in some kind of protective stasis."

"Until the deep-space signal activated it," Mick finishes.

Chaney eyeballs him suspiciously. "How is it that you know so much about this alien being?"

A loud knock, and Commander Broad enters. "Sorry to interrupt, skipper, but I need to see you in private."

Captain Loos follows him out.

"Dr. Rosen, you say this being will destroy humanity on December 21? How do you know that?"

"Like I said, Dr. Teperman, it communicated with me. Its intentions may not have been verbal, but they were quite clear."

"It conveyed the twenty-first to you?"

"No." Mick reaches for the captain's notes. He glances over them, nonchalantly removing the paper clip from the stack. "I've spent a lifetime studying the Mayan prophecies, as well as a half dozen ancient sites located around the globe which link this malevolent presence to the end of the world. The twenty-first is the date referenced in the Mayan calendar, the date humanity will perish from the face of the Earth. Before you scoff, you should know that the calendar is a precise instrument of astronomy—"

Chaney rubs his eyes, losing patience. "You don't sound like a biologist to me, Doctor, and this Mayan prophecy of yours doesn't amuse me in the least. A lot of people died on board that rig, and I want to know what killed them."

"I told you." Mick slips the paper clip into his waistband.

"And how were you able to access the alien craft?"

"There are twenty-three burrows situated in a perfect circle in the seafloor about a mile from the central hole. My companion and I directed our minisub down one of these burrows. We became caught in an enormous turbine, which sucked our submersible into—"

"A turbine!" Teperman's eyebrows raise again. "Incredible. What's the turbine's function?"

"I suspect ventilation. The minisub jammed the rotary blades during its intake phase. When the rotors reversed to drain the chamber, we were flushed back out to sea."

Captain Loos reenters the briefing room, a smug look on his face. "We have a situation, Vice President Chaney, one that may explain a lot. It seems Dr. Rosen isn't quite who he says he is. His real name is Michael Gabriel, and he escaped last week from a mental facility in Miami."

Chaney and Marvin give Mick a cynical look.

Mick looks the VP squarely in the eye. "I'm not mentally deranged. I lied about my identity because the police are after me, but I'm not insane."

Captain Loos reads from a fax. "Says here you've been incarcerated for the last eleven years after an incident involving Pierre Borgia."

Chaney's eyes grow wide. "Secretary of State Borgia?"

"Borgia verbally assaulted my father, humiliating him in front of an assembly of his peers. I lost control. Borgia manipulated the justice system. Instead of serving time for simple assault, he had me committed to an institution."

Captain Loos hands Chaney the fax. "Mick's father was Julius Gabriel."

Marvin looks surprised. "Julius Gabriel, the archaeologist?"

The captains sneers. "More like the quack that tried to convince the scientific community that humanity was on the brink of destruction. I remember reading about it. His death made the cover of *Time*."

Chaney looks up from reading the fax. "Like father, like son."

"Maybe he was right," Marvin mumbles.

The captain's face turns red. "Julius Gabriel was a lunatic, Dr. Teperman, and, in my opinion, the acorn hasn't fallen far from the tree. This man has wasted enough of our time."

Mick stands, his temper flaring. "Everything I just told you is true—"

"Why don't you drop the charade, Gabriel. We found your father's journal in the minisub. The entire purpose of your story is to convince us—and the rest of the world—that your father's ridiculous theories were true."

The captain opens the door.

Two armed security guards enter.

"Mr. Vice President, unless you have some further use for this man, I've been instructed to throw him in the brig."

"Instructed by whom?"

"Secretary Borgia, sir. He's en route, as we speak."

Sydney, Australia

The Dassault supersonic jet cruises over the South Pacific at twelve hundred miles per hour, its sleek design barely registering a ripple of turbulence. Although there are eight passenger seats within the three-engine, 104-foot double-delta winged plane, only three are occupied.

Ambassador to Australia Barbara Becker stretches as she awakens. She checks her watch as the jet begins its descent over Australia. *Los Angeles to Sydney in under seven and a half hours, not bad.* She stands, then moves across the aisle to her right to join the two scientists from the Institute for Energy and Environmental Research.

Steven Taber, a large man who reminds Barbara of Senator Jesse Ventura, is leaning against the window, snoring, while his colleague, Dr. Marty Martinez, types furiously on a laptop computer.

"Excuse me, Doctor, but we're going to be landing soon, and there's still a few more questions I wanted to ask you."

"Just a moment, please." Martinez continues typing.

Becker sits down next to him. "Maybe we should wake your friend—"

"I'm up." Taber lets out a bear-size yawn.

Martinez turns off the computer. "Ask your questions, Madam Ambassador."

"As you know, the Australian government is in an absolute uproar. They're claiming more than sixty-seven thousand square miles of geography was vaporized in the explosion. That's an ungodly amount of terrain simply to vanish into thin air. Based on your preliminary assessment of satellite photos, would you say this accident was caused by a natural phenomenon, like Mount St. Helens, or are we looking at a man-made explosion?"

Martinez shrugs. "I'd rather not say, at least not until we complete our tests."

"I understand. But—"

"Ambassador, Mr. Taber and I are here on behalf of the United Nations Security Council, not the United States. I understand that you're in the middle of a political maelstrom, but I'd rather not speculate—"

"Lighten up, Marty." Taber leans forward. "I'll answer your question, Madam Ambassador. First, you can forget about anything like a natural disaster. This was no earthquake or volcano. In my opinion, we're looking at a test explosion of new type of thermonuclear device, the likes of which, if you'll excuse the expression, frighten the absolute shit out of me."

Martinez shakes his head. "Steven, you cannot say this for certain—"

"Come on, Marty, let's cut the crap. You and I both suspect the same thing. It's all gonna come out in the wash anyway."

"What's going to come out? Speak to me, gentlemen. What is it you suspect?"

Martinez slams the top of his computer shut. "Nothing that project scientists at IEER haven't been protesting for the last decade, Ambassador. Fusion weapons, pure-fusion weapons."

"I'm sorry, I'm not a scientist. What do you mean by *pure* fusion?"

"I'm not surprised you haven't heard of the term," Taber says. "For some reason, this particular subject has always managed to avoid public scrutiny. There are three types of nuclear devices, the atomic bomb, the hydrogen or H-bomb, and the pure-fusion bomb. The atomic bomb uses fission, which is the process of splitting a heavy atomic nucleus into two or more fragments. Essentially, the A-bomb is a sphere filled with electronically timed explosives. Within the sphere is a grapefruit-size ball of plutonium, at the core of which is a device that releases a spray of neutrons. When the explosives detonate, the plutonium is crushed into a molten mass. Atoms are split into fragments, exciting a chain reaction which, in turn, releases mega amounts of energy. If I'm going too fast for you, just stop me."

"Go on."

"In a hydrogen bomb, uranium-235 absorbs a neutron. Fission occurs when the neutron breaks apart to produce two smaller nuclei, several neutrons, and lots of energy. This, in turn, produces the temperature and density necessary for the fusion of deuterium and tritium, which are two isotopes of hydrogen—"

"Whoa, slow down, you've lost me."

Martinez turns to face the ambassador. "The intricacies are not important. What you need to know is that fusion is different than fission. Fusion is a reaction that occurs when two atoms of hydrogen combine together, or fuse, to form an atom of helium. This process, the same process that powers the sun, releases much greater quantities of energy than fission, causing an even larger explosion."

Taber nods. "The key factor that ultimately determines the strength of a thermonuclear weapon is how the explosion is triggered. A pure-fusion bomb is much different than an atomic bomb or hydrogen bomb in that it doesn't require a fission trigger to cause fusion. This means that plutonium or enriched uranium is not required in the design. The good news here is that no plutonium means little to no radioactive fallout. The bad news is that the explosive power of a relatively small, pure-fusion device would be much greater than even our most modern hydrogen bomb."

"How much greater?"

"I'll give you an example," Martinez says. "The atomic bomb we dropped on Hiroshima generated an amount of energy equivalent to 15 kilotons or 15,000 tons of TNT. Temperatures at the explosion center reached 7,000 degrees, with a wind velocity estimated at 980 miles per hour. Most of the people within a half mile radius died.

"That was a 15-kiloton explosion. Our modern version of the H-bomb carries the equivalent of 20 to 50 megatons, or 50 million tons of TNT, the equivalent of two to three thousand Hiroshima-size bombs. A pure-fusion bomb carries an even greater damage volume. It would only take a small 2-kiloton pure-fusion bomb to equal the same impact created by a 30-megaton H-bomb. That's one ton of pure-fusion TNT to equal fifteen million tons of TNT generated by a hydrogen bomb. If you want to wipe out 67,000 square miles of geography, pure fusion is the way to go."

My God... Despite the heavy air-conditioning, Barbara feels herself sweating. "And you think it's possible that a foreign power was able to develop such a device?"

Martinez and Taber look at each other.

"What? Speak!"

Taber pinches the bridge of his nose. "The feasibility of developing a pure-fusion device hasn't officially been proven, Madam Ambassador, but the United States and France have been tinkering with it for more than a decade now."

Dr. Martinez looks her square in the eye. "As I said, none of this should be that shocking. IEER scientists have been protesting the morality and legality of this work for years. All of this is in direct violation of the Comprehensive Test Ban Treaty."

"Hold it a second, Marty," Taber says. "We both know the CTBT doesn't mention pure fusion."

"Why the hell not?" the ambassador asks.

"It's a legal loophole that hasn't been addressed, mostly because no nation has ever formally announced its intention of building a pure-fusion weapon."

"Do you think the French would have sold the technology to the Australians?"

"We're not politicians, Ambassador Becker," Taber states. "And anyway, who's to say it was the French? Could have been the Russians or even the good ol' U. S. of A., for all we know."

Martinez nods. "The United States has had the inside track. Field-testing this weapon in Australia keeps everybody guessing."

Barbara shakes her head. "Christ, I'm walking into a goddam hornets' nest. All five of the Security Council's permanent members are sending delegates. Everyone's going to be pointing fingers at one another."

Martinez lays his head back and closes his eyes. "You haven't really grasped the significance in all this, have you, Madam Ambassador? Pure fusion is the doomsday bomb. No country, including the United States, should have ever been permitted to conduct pure-fusion experiments of any kind in the first place. It doesn't matter which country developed it first, the weapon can destroy us all."

Barbara registers a dip in her stomach as the Dassault touches down. The jet taxis across the runway to an awaiting Sikorsky S-70B-2 Seahawk.

A tall gentleman wearing a black, neoprene body suit greets them on the tarmac. He approaches Barbara, extending his hand. "Madam Ambassador, Karl Brandt, Australian Geological Survey Organization, how'd you do? Excuse the outfit, but the lead suits we'll be wearing can become quite confining. I gather these gentlemen are from the IEER?"

Taber and Martinez introduce themselves.

"Very good. Look, I don't mean to rush you, but Nullarbor's still a good two hours away, at least what's left of it, and I don't want to lose the light."

"Where are the other members of the Security Council's delegation?"

"Already waiting in the chopper."

Gulf of Mexico

Mick kneels by the steel door of the eight-by-ten-foot cell, fighting to stay awake as he probes the keyhole with the metal wire. "God dammit!" He slumps back against the wall, staring at the end of the broken paper clip, now jammed in the lock.

This is no good—I can't stay focused. I've got to sleep, gotta get some rest. He closes his eyes, then opens them. "No! Stay awake—work the lock. Borgia will be here soon and—"

"Mick?"

The voice startles him.

"Mick Gabriel, are you in there?"

"Teperman?"

A key jiggles the lock and the door swings open.

Marvin enters, leaving the door ajar. "There you are. I've had one tough time finding you, eh, this boat is huge." He hands Mick the leather-bound journal. "Interesting reading. Then again, you're father's always been quite imaginative."

Mick eyes the door.

"Did you know that I met your father? It was in Cambridge, back in the late sixties. I was a third-year undergraduate. Julius was guest speaker in a lecture series entitled, 'Mysteries of Ancient Man.' I thought he was quite brilliant; in fact, it was his speech that pushed me toward a career in exobiology."

Marvin notices Mick eyeing the door. He turns and sees the paper clip protruding from the lock. "You won't get very far that way."

"Dr. Teperman, I've got to get out of here."

"I know. Here, take this." Marvin reaches into his jacket pocket, pulling out a wad of bills. "There's a little more than six hundred dollars there, some of it Canadian. It's not a lot, but it should get you where you need to go."

"You're freeing me?"

"Not me, I'm just the messenger. Your father was a big influence, but I wasn't *that* fond of him."

"I don't understand?"

"Your escape has been arranged by someone who despises Secretary Borgia about as much as you do."

Chaney? "Then, you're not releasing me because you believe my story?"

Marvin smiles, patting him affectionately on the cheek. "You're a nice kid, Mick, but like your old man, you're just a little *meshuga*. Now listen carefully. Turn left and follow this access corridor as far as you can go. You'll reach a stairwell that will lead you up three flights to the main deck. There's a hangar located in the stern. Inside, lying on the floor, are the bodies of the victims who died aboard the oil rig. Grab yourself an empty body bag, climb in, and wait. Within thirty minutes, an EVAC chopper is due to arrive to transport the dead to the airport in Merida. After that, you're on your own."

"Thanks—wait, what about Dominique?"

"Your girlfriend's doing better, but she's in no condition to travel. Do you want me to get her a message?"

"Please. Tell her that I'm going to see this thing through."

"Where will you go?"

"You really want to know that?"

"Probably not. Better get going, eh, before they lock us both up."

Southern Australia

Ambassador Becker stares out her window, listening intently to the conversation taking place in the back of the helicopter between the delegates from the Russian Federation, China, and France. Spencer Botchin, the representative from the United Kingdom, leans over to whisper into her ear. "Had to be the French. I just pray they weren't foolish enough to sell it to the Iranians."

She nods in agreement, whispering, "They wouldn't have tested the weapon without support from Russia and the Chinese."

It is late in the afternoon by the time the chopper arrives over southern Australia. Barbara Becker stares out her window, the sight below literally causing her skin to tingle.

The landscape is an enormous charred pit, a sizzling depression running as far and as wide as the eye can see.

Karl Brandt slides in next to her. "Three days ago, the elevation of the geography you're looking at was 133 feet above sea level. Now, in most places, it barely reaches higher than five feet."

"How the hell could something have vaporized so much rock?"

Steve Taber pauses from assisting Dr. Martinez into the lead body suit. "Judging by the crater we're looking at, I'd say the device had to have been a subsurface explosion of incredible magnitude."

Brandt slips into his radiation suit and zippers the hood. "The tanks on these suits will provide us with thirty minutes of air."

Dr. Martinez struggles to give him a thumbs-up in the heavy gloves. Taber hands his associate the Geiger counter. "Marty, are you sure you don't want me down there with you?"

"I can handle it."

The copilot joins them, assisting Brandt and Martinez into the two harnesses linked by cable to twin hydraulic winches. "Gentlemen, there's a two-way receiver in your headpieces. You'll be able to communicate with us and each other. We need you to release your harnesses once you touch down." He slides open the cargo-bay door, yelling over the deafening sound of the rotors. "Okay, fellas, out you go."

All five ambassadors gather round to watch. Martinez feels his heart leap into his throat as he stumbles out the door and dangles 155 feet above the ground. He closes his eyes, feeling himself spin as he drops.

"You okay, Doctor?"

"Yes, Mr. Brandt." He opens his eyes and checks the Geiger counter. "No radiation so far. Lots of heat."

"Don't worry, the suits should protect us."

"Should?" Martinez looks down. Steamy whiffs of white smoke are rising up at him, fogging his faceplate. Another ten feet—

"Wait! Stop—stop!" Martinez tucks his knees to his chest, struggling to keep away from the molten surface beneath him. "Raise us higher—higher!"

They stop descending, the two men dangling only inches above the boiling, 650-degree milky white geology.

"Raise us twenty feet," Brandt yells.

The winch lifts them higher.

"What's the problem?" Barbara's voice tears into their eardrums.

"The surface is boiling, it's a cauldron of melted rock and seawater," Martinez says in a nervous, high-pitched voice. "We'll do our tests right here. It'll only take a minute."

Taber's deep voice causes him to jump. "Any radiation?"

Martinez checks his sensors. "No. Wait a second, I'm detecting argon-41."

Brandt looks over. "That's not a plutonium by-product."

"No, it's a short-lived activation product of pure fusion. Whatever vaporized this landscape must have been some kind of hybrid pure-fusion weapon." Martinez hooks the Geiger counter to his belt, then analyzes the gases rising from below. "Wow. Carbon dioxide levels are off the scale."

"That's understandable," Brandt says. "This entire plain was composed of limestone, which, as I'm sure you know, is nature's storehouse for carbon dioxide. When the geology vaporized, it released a toxic cloud of CO_2. We're actually quite fortunate, the southerly winds blew it away from our cities and out to sea."

"I'm also detecting high levels of hydrochloric acid."

"Really? That is bizarre."

"Yes, Mr. Brandt, this whole thing's bizarre, and quite frightening. Take us up, I've seen all I need to see."

Merida Airport
Mexico

The transport helicopter lands with a bone-jarring jolt.

Mick opens his eyes, sucking in a deep breath to rouse his body from sleep. He lifts his head from the unzipped body bag and looks around.

Sixty-four plastic Army green body bags holding the remains of the *Scylla* crew line the interior. Mick hears the bay doors rattle. He lies back, zipping his bag.

The door opens. Mick recognizes the pilot's voice. "I'll be in the hangar. Tell your men to be very careful, *comprende, amigo?*"

A flurry of Spanish. Men begin moving body bags. Mick remains perfectly still.

Several minutes pass. He hears a truck's engine start, then fade in the distance.

He unzips the bag, then peers through the open cargo door, spotting the tram heading for an open hangar.

Mick climbs out of the bag, jumps down from the EVAC chopper, and jogs toward the main terminal.

JOURNAL OF JULIUS GABRIEL

*I*t was in the fall of 1977 that Maria and I returned to Mesoamerica, my wife now six months pregnant. Desperate for
funds, we decided to submit the body of our work to Cambridge
and Harvard, careful to omit any information pertaining to the
presence of an alien race of humans. Impressed with our research,
the powers that be awarded each of us a research grant to continue
our work.

After purchasing a used mobile trailer home, we set off to
explore the Mayan ruins, hoping to identify the Mesoamerican
pyramid the artist of Nazca had drawn upon the desert pampa,
as well as a means of saving humanity from the prophesied destruction to come.

Despite the morbidity of our mission, our years spent in
Mexico were happy ones. Our favorite moment—the birth of our
son, Michael, born at sunrise on Christmas morning, in the waiting room of a tiny medical clinic in Merida.

I must admit that I was quite concerned about raising a
child under such harsh conditions, worried that Michael's isolation
from other children his own age might impede the boy's social
development. At one point, I even suggested to my wife that we

send him to a private boarding school when he turned five. Maria would hear nothing of it. In the end, I acceded to her wishes, realizing that she needed the child's companionship as much as he needed hers.

Maria was more than Michael's mother, she was his mentor, guide, and best friend—and he, her prize pupil. Even at an early age, it was easy to see that the boy possessed his mother's keen mind, to go along with those dark, ebony eyes and their disarming focus.

For seven years, our family searched the dense jungles of present-day Mexico, Belize, Guatemala, Honduras, and El Salvador. While other fathers taught their sons how to play baseball, I taught my son how to excavate artifacts. While other students learned a foreign language, Michael learned how to translate Mayan hieroglyphics. Together, the three of us climbed the temples of Uxmal, Palenque, and Tikal, explored the fortifications of Labna, Churihuhu, and Kewik, and marveled at the castle in Tulum. We investigated the Zapotec capital of Monte Alban, and the religious centers in Kaminaljuyu, and Copán. We crawled through tombs and scuba dived into subterranean caves. We unearthed ancient platforms and interviewed Mayan elders. And in the end, we narrowed the identity of the Nazca pyramid drawing down to one of two ancient sites, both of which we believed were pieces of the Mayan calendar's doomsday puzzle.

The first site was Teotihuacán, a magnificent Toltec city situated on a 6,600-foot-high plateau in the Mexican highlands, located some 30 miles northeast of present-day Mexico City. Believed to have been founded during the time of Christ, Teotihuacán was the first great metropolis of the Western Hemisphere, and was believed to be one of the largest.

Like the structures in Giza, the origins of Teotihuacán remain a mystery. We have no clue as to which culture designed the city, how the feat was accomplished, or even the language spoken by its original occupants. As is the case with the Sphinx and the Giza pyramids, the date of Teotihuacán's construction is still widely debated. Even the name of the complex and its pyramids come to us from the Toltec civilization, which moved in centuries _after_ the city was abandoned.

It has been estimated that the labor involved in building the structures of Teotihuacán would have taken an army of 20,000 men more than 40 years to complete. Yet it is not the mystery of how this city was constructed that first caught our attention, but its design and the obvious similarities to the site plan in Giza.

As mentioned earlier, there are three principal pyramids in Giza, laid out in reference to the stars of Orion's belt, with the Nile intended as a reflection of the dark rift of the Milky Way. Teotihuacán also features three pyramids, situated in a surprisingly similar staggered formation, although the orientation differs by nearly 180 degrees. Connecting one end of the city to the other is the Avenue of the Dead, the major access route through the complex. The avenue, like the River Nile in Giza, was intended to represent the dark rift of the Milky Way.

To the ancient Mesoamerican Indians, the dark rift was known as Xibalba Be,

the Black Road that leads to <u>Xibalba</u>, the Underworld. New excavations in Teotihuacán have discovered large channels located beneath this roadway, which we now know were designed to gather rainwater. This would indicate that the Avenue of the Dead may not have been a roadway at all, but a magnificent cosmic reflecting pool.

The similarities between Giza and Teotihuacán do not stop there. The largest of the Mesoamerican city's three temples is called the Pyramid of the Sun, a precise, four-sided structure whose base, at 742.5 feet, is only twelve and a half feet shorter than its Egyptian counterpart, the Great Pyramid of Giza. This makes the Sun pyramid the largest man-made structure in the Western hemisphere, the Great Pyramid the largest in the east. Interesting enough, the Sun pyramid points west, the Great Pyramid east, a fact that caused Maria to think of these two immense structures as giant planetary bookends.

Precise measurements of both the Great Pyramid and Pyramid of the Sun clearly indicate the ancient architects at both sites possessed a firm grasp of advanced mathematics, geometry, and the value of <u>pi</u>. The perimeter of the Pyramid of the Sun equals its height multiplied by 2<u>pi</u>, the great pyramid twice its height at 4<u>pi</u>.

One clue as to who designed Teotihuacán may be found in the smallest of the three structures, the pyramid of Quetzalcoatl. The temple is located in an enormous squared enclosure, called the Ciudadela (Citadel), a plaza large enough to accommodate 100,000 people. The most elaborately adorned structure in all of Teotihuacán, the Pyramid of Quetzalcoatl contains a myriad of sculptures and three-dimensional facades that feature one distinct character—a menacing plumed serpent.

To the Toltecs and Aztecs, the plumed serpent symbolized the great Caucasian wise man, Quetzalcoatl.

Once more, the presence of a mysterious bearded teacher seemed to be directing our journey into the past.

Upon abandoning Teotihuacán, the Toltecs and their leader had migrated east, settling in the Mayan city of Chichén Itzá. It was here that the two cultures would again meld into one, creating the most magnificent and perplexing structure in all the ancient world—the Kukulcán pyramid.

I didn't know it at the time, but it would be in Chichén Itzá that we would come face-to-face with a discovery that would not only change my family's destiny, but condemn us to remain on our journey forever.

—Excerpt from the Journal of Professor Julius Gabriel,

Ref. Catalogue 1977–81   pages 12–349
    Photo Journal Floppy Disk 5. File name: MESO, Air Balloon Photo
    176

19

Secretary of State Pierre Borgia steps down from the helicopter, to be greeted by Captain Edmund Loos. "Morning, Mr. Secretary. How was your flight?"

"Lousy. Has the psychiatric director from Miami arrived yet?"

"About twenty minutes ago. He's waiting for you in my briefing room."

"What's the latest on Gabriel?"

"We're still not certain how he was able to escape from the brig. The lock shows some signs of tampering, but nothing significant. Our best guess is that someone freed him."

"Was it the girl?"

"No, sir. She suffered a concussion and was in sick bay, unconscious. We're still conducting a full investigation."

"And how did he manage to get off this ship?"

"Probably hitched a ride on an EVAC. They were coming and going all day."

Borgia gives the captain a cold stare. "I hope you don't run your ship like you guard your prisoners, Captain."

Loos returns the look. "I'm not running a baby-sitting service, Mr. Secretary. I seriously doubt one of my men would risk a future in prison to free your nutcase."

"Who else could have released him?"

"I don't know. We have teams of scientists on board, new ones arriving every day. Could have been one of them, or even someone from the vice president's party."

Borgia's eyebrows raise.

"As I said, we're still conducting a full investigation. We've also alerted the Mexican police about Gabriel's escape."

"They'll never find him. Gabriel has too many friends in the Yucatán. What about the girl? What does she know about the alien object?"

"She claims the only thing she can remember is her minisub being sucked down a tunnel. One of our geologists has her convinced that her vessel was caught in the currents of a lava tube, created by a dormant, subterranean volcano that's becoming active again." Loos smiles. "He explained the glow as being caused by a subterranean lava field that can be seen as it flows past the pit in the seafloor. Even showed her a few doctored infrared satellite shots of the whirlpool, claiming the vortex was caused by the collapse of subterranean pockets beneath the seafloor. She believes this is what sunk her father's boat, killing him and his two friends."

"Where is she now?"

"Sick bay."

"Give me a few minutes to speak with the psychiatric director alone, then bring the girl in. While we're speaking with her, have this sewn into the lining of her clothes." He hands Loos a tiny device the size of a watch battery.

"A tracking device?"

"A gift from the NSA. Oh, and Captain, when you bring the girl to see me, have her in handcuffs."

Two armed sailors lead a shackled and unnerved Dominique Vazquez through several tight corridors, then up three flights to a cabin labeled CAPTAIN'S BRIEFING ROOM. One of the guards knocks, then opens the door and leads her inside.

Dominique enters the small conference room. "Oh, God—"

Anthony Foletta looks up from the conference table and smiles. "Intern Vazquez, come in." The gravelly voice has a fatherly tone. "Mr. Secretary, are the handcuffs really necessary?"

The one-eyed man closes the door behind her, then takes his place at the table across from Foletta. "I'm afraid so, Dr. Foletta. Ms. Vazquez has aided and abetted a dangerous felon." He motions for her to sit. "You know who I am?"

"Pierre Borgia. I—I was told you were coming three days ago."

"Yes, well, we had a little situation in Australia that took precedence."

"Are you here to arrest me?"

"That depends entirely on you."

"It's not you we want, Dominique," Foletta says, "it's Mick. You know where he is, don't you?"

"How would I know that? He escaped while I was still unconscious."

"She's a pretty one, isn't she, Doctor?" Borgia's glare causes sweat to break out along her upper lip. "It's no wonder Mick took a fancy for you. Tell me, Ms. Vazquez, what motivated you to help him break out of the asylum?"

Foletta jumps in before she can answer. "She was confused, Mr. Secretary. You know how clever Gabriel can be. He used Dominique's childhood trauma to coerce her into helping him escape."

"That's not entirely true," she says, finding it difficult not to focus on Borgia's permanent eye patch. "Mick knew something was in the Gulf. And he knew about that deep-space radio transmission—"

Foletta places a sweaty palm across her forearm. "Intern, you need to face reality. Mick Gabriel used you. He was planning his escape from the moment he met you."

"No, I don't believe that—"

"Maybe you just don't want to believe it," Borgia says. "The fact is, your father would still be alive today if Mick hadn't coerced you into helping him."

Dominique's eyes cloud with tears.

Borgia removes a file from his brief, taking a moment to examine it. "Isadore Axler, a biologist residing in Sanibel Island. Certainly has a long list of credentials. He wasn't your real father, was he?"

"He was the only father I ever knew."

Borgia continues looking through the file. "Ah, here we are—Edith Axler. Did you know the two of us met? Fine woman."

Dominique feels her skin crawl beneath the Navy-issue sweats. "You met Edie?"

"Just long enough to place her under arrest."

The words send her springing to her feet. "Edie had no part in Mick's escape! It was all me. I arranged everything—"

"I'm not interested in a confession, Ms. Vazquez. What I want is Michael Gabriel. If I can't have him, I'll simply lock you and your mother up for a very long time. Of course, in Edith's case, that may not be too long a sentence. She's getting up there in age, and her husband's death has obviously taken its toll."

Dominique's heart races. "I told you, I don't know where he is."

"If you say so." Borgia stands and heads for the door.

"Wait, let me talk to her," Foletta says. "Give us five minutes."

Borgia looks at his watch. "Five minutes." He exits the cabin.

Dominique lays her head on the table, her insides quivering, her tears pooling on the steel tabletop. "Why is all this happening?"

"*Shh.*" Foletta strokes her hair, his voice a soothing whisper. "Dominique, Borgia doesn't want to lock you and your mother up. He's just scared."

She lifts her head. "Scared of what?"

"Of Mick. He knows Mick wants revenge, that he'll stop at nothing to kill him."

"Mick's not like that—"

"You're wrong. Borgia knows him a lot better than you or I. Their history goes back a long way. Did you know Borgia was engaged to Mick's mother? Julius Gabriel stole the bride-to-be on the eve of their wedding ceremony. There's a lot of bad blood between the families."

"Mick doesn't care about revenge. He's more concerned about this Mayan doomsday thing."

"Mick's clever. He's not going to tell you or anyone else about his true motive. My guess is that he's hiding out in the Yucatán. His family had a lot of friends there who could help him. He'll lie low for a while, then go after Borgia, probably during a public appearance. Think about it, Dominique, do you really believe the Secretary of State of the United States would travel all the way out here to see you if he wasn't frightened? In a few years he'll be running for president. The last thing he needs to worry about is some paranoid schizophrenic with a 160 IQ plotting his assassination."

Dominique wipes her eyes. *Is it true? Did Mick really use his family's apocalyptic research to set me up?* "Let's say I believe you. What do you think I should do?"

Foletta's eyes twinkle back at her. "Let me help you strike a deal with Borgia. Full immunity for you and your mother if you lead the authorities to Mick."

"The last time I struck a deal with you, you lied to me. You never had any intention of reevaluating Mick or getting him the treatment he needs. Why should I believe you now?"

"I didn't lie!" He stands, barking the words. "I hadn't been officially awarded the Tampa job, and anyone who says otherwise is a goddam liar!" He wipes the sweat from his forehead, then back through his mane of gray hair, his cherub face bright red. "Dominique, I'm here to help you. If you don't want my help, then I suggest you get yourself a good lawyer."

"I want your help, Doctor, I just don't know if I can trust you."

"The immunity would be arranged by Borgia, not me. What I'm offering is your old life back."

"What are you saying?"

"I've already spoken with your advisor at FSU. I'm offering you an internship in the new Tampa facility, close to your mother's home. Your job will be to head up Mick's treatment team, with a permanent position and full benefits waiting for you after you graduate."

The offer brings tears of relief. "Why are you doing this?"

"Because I feel bad. I should have never assigned Mick to you in the first place. You'll make a fine psychiatrist one day, but you weren't ready for a patient as manipulative as Michael Gabriel. Your father's death, the turmoil your family's gone through—all of this is my fault. I knew better, but I took a chance. I saw in you a strong woman who would be the perfect addition to my staff, but I rushed your development. I'm sorry, Dominique. Give me the chance to make it up to you."

He extends a thick palm.

Dominique stares at it for a long moment, then shakes the offered hand.

DECEMBER 6, 2012
WASHINGTON, D.C.

Vice President Ennis Chaney looks up from the report, acknowledging the president's National Security staff as they file into the White House war room and take their places around the oval conference table. A half dozen military and science advisors follow, filling the extra folding chairs lining the perimeter of the room.

Ennis closes the document as the president enters, the secretary of state in his wake. Borgia bypasses his own chair to address Chaney. "You and I need to talk."

"Mr. Secretary, if we can begin?"

"Yes, Mr. President." Borgia finds his place, giving Chaney a perturbed look.

President Maller rubs his bloodshot eyes, then reads from a fax. "This afternoon, the United Nations Security Council will issue a statement, deploring the testing of pure-fusion weapons as being contrary to the de facto moratorium on the testing of nuclear weapons and to global nuclear nonproliferation and nuclear-disarmament efforts. Further, the Council is seeking immediate ratification of a new resolution designed to close the loophole on pure-fusion technology."

Maller holds up a report labeled UMBRA, a code word used to classify files beyond TOP SECRET. "I'll assume everyone has reviewed this document. I've asked its author, Dr. Brae Roodhof, Director of the National Ignition Facility in Livermore, California, to join us this morning as I'm sure all of us have questions we want answered. Doctor?"

Dr. Roodhof is in his early fifties, a tall gray-haired man with a tan, weathered face and calming demeanor. "Mr. President, ladies and gentlemen, I want to start by stating emphatically that it was not the United States who detonated this pure-fusion weapon."

Ennis Chaney's insides have been churning since he finished reading the UMBRA file. His eyes blaze as he stares down the nuclear physicist. "Doctor, I'm going to ask you something, but I want you to know that I'm directing my question to every person in this room." The tone of the vice president's voice stifles all peripheral movements. "What I want to know is why, Doctor. Why is the United States of America even engaged in this type of goddam suicidal research?"

Dr. Roodhof's eyes dart around the table. "Sir, I . . . I'm only the project director. It's not my place to determine US policy. It was the federal government who funded nuclear-weapons laboratories to research pure fusion back in the 1990s, and it was the military that applied the pressure for the bombs to be designed and built—"

"Let's not reduce this issue to finger-pointing, Mr. Vice President," interrupts General Fecondo. "The reality of the situation is that other foreign powers were pursuing the technology, which obligated us to follow suit. The LMJ, the Laser Megajoule complex in Bordeaux, France, has been conducting pure-fusion experiments since early 1998. The British and Japanese have been working on nonexplosive magnetic-fusion research for years. Any or all of these countries could have bridged the feasibility gap in order to create thermonuclear nonfission ignitions."

Chaney turns to face the general. "Then why does the rest of the world, including scientists from our own country, seem to think that we're responsible for the detonation in Australia?"

"Because everyone in the scientific community believed our research was farthest along," Dr. Roodhof answers. "The IEER recently published a report stating that the United States was two years away from field-testing a pure-fusion device."

"Were they right?"

"Ennis—"

"No, I'm sorry, Mr. President, but I want to know."

"Mr. Vice President, this is not the time—"

Chaney ignores Maller, his eyes boring into Roodhof's. "How close are we, Doctor?"

Roodhof looks away. "Fourteen months."

The room erupts into a dozen side conversations. Borgia smiles to himself as the president's expression turns to anger. *That's it, Chaney, keep rocking the boat.*

Ennis Chaney sits back wearily in his chair. He is no longer fighting the windmills, he is fighting global madness.

President Maller bangs his palm against the tabletop, restoring order. "That's enough! Mr. Chaney, this is neither the time nor place to engage in a free-for-all debate over the policies of this presidency or those of my predecessors. The reality of the situation is that another government has detonated one of these weapons. I want to know who it was and whether the timing of the explosion has anything to do with Iran's military buildup along the Strait of Hormuz."

CIA Director Patrick Hurley is the first to respond. "Sir, it could be the Russians. The magnetized target fusion studies conducted at Los Alamos were joint US-Russian experiments."

Dr. Roodhof shakes his head. "No, I disagree. The Russians backed off when their economy collapsed. It had to be the French."

General Mike Costolo, Commandant of the Marine Corps, raises a thick palm. "Dr. Roodhof, from what I've read, these pure-fusion weapons contain very little radiation, is that correct?"

"Yes, sir."

"What's your point, General?" Dick Przystas asks.

Costolo turns to face the secretary of defense. "One of the reasons the DoD pushed for the development of these weapons in the first place was that we knew Russia and China were supplying Iran with nuclear weapons. If a nuclear war were to break out in the Persian Gulf, pure fusion would not only give its owner a tactical advantage, but the lack of radiation would allow the flow of oil to go on, unimpeded. In my opinion, it doesn't matter whether it was the French or Russians who achieved the technology first; the only thing that matters is whether the Iranians possess the weapon. If so, then the threat alone changes the balance of power in the Middle East. Should Iran detonate one of these weapons in the Persian Gulf, then Saudi Arabia, Kuwait, Bahrain, Egypt, and other moderate Arab regimes would be forced to turn away from Western support."

Borgia nods in agreement. "The Saudis are still hedging about allowing us access to our prepositioned supplies. They've lost confidence in our ability to keep the Strait of Hormuz open."

"Where are the carriers?" the president asks Jeffrey Gordon.

"In preparation for Asia's upcoming nuclear detention exercise, we've ordered the *Harry S Truman* and her fleet to the Red Sea. The *Ronald Reagan* battle group should arrive in the Gulf of Oman in three days. The *William J. Clinton* will remain on patrol in the Indian Ocean. We're sending a message to Iran, plain and simple, that we have no intention of allowing the Strait of Hormuz to be closed."

"For the record, Mr. President," Chaney states, "the French ambassador is vehemently denying any responsibility for this explosion."

"What did you expect?" Borgia responds. "Look beyond the denials. Iran still owes France billions of dollars, yet the French continue to support the Iranians, as do Russia and China. Let me also point out that Australia is one of the nations that has continued to give Iran subsidized interest rates, which they've used to build up their nuclear, chemical, and biological arsenal. Do you really think it's just a coincidence that the weapon happened to be tested in the Nullarbor region."

"Don't be so quick to point the finger at the Aussies," Sam Blumner interjects. "If you remember, it was the United States's massive credits to Iraq in the late 1980s that led to Saddam Hussein's invasion of Kuwait."

"I agree with Sam," the president says. "I've spoken at length with Australia's PM. The Liberal and Labor Parties are showing a united front, declaring the incident to be an act of war. I doubt very much they would have condoned such a test."

General Fecondo rubs both palms across his tan, receding hairline. "Mr. President, the fact that these pure-fusion weapons exist changes nothing. Testing a weapon and using it in battle are two different things. No nation is going to challenge the United States to a nuclear showdown."

Costolo looks at the Chairman of the Joint Chiefs. "Tell me, General, if we had a cruise missile that could wipe out every SAM site along the Iranian coast, would you use it?"

Dick Przystas raises his eyebrows.

"A tempting thought, isn't it? I wonder if the Iranians will be any less tempted to wipe out the *Ronald Reagan* and her fleet?"

"I'll tell you what I think," the lanky Chief of Naval Operations says. "I interpret this action as a sort of warning shot across our bow. The Russians are letting us know they possess pure-fusion weapons, hoping their little demonstration we'll persuade us to cancel the Missile Defense Shield."

"Which is something we cannot do," Przystas states. "The number of rogue states with access to nuclear and biological weapons has doubled in the last five years—"

"While we continue to spend more money on nuclear-weapons technology," Chaney interrupts, "sending a clear message to the rest of the world that the United States is more interested in maintaining a first-strike nuclear posture than continuing arms reductions. The world's heading straight down the path of nuclear confrontation. They know it, and we know it, but we're all too damn busy pointing fingers at one another to change course. We're all acting like a bunch of shitheads, and before we know what's happened, we're all gonna be stepping right in it."

*   *   *

Borgia is waiting for Ennis Chaney in the corridor when the meeting adjourns. "I need a minute."

"Speak."

"I spoke with the captain of the *Boone*."

"So?"

"Tell me, Chaney, why would the vice president of the United States aid and abet an escaped felon?"

"I don't know what you're talking about—"

"This sort of thing could ruin a politician's career."

The raccoon eyes bore into Borgia. "You want to accuse me of something—do it. In fact, how about you and I put everything in the wash and we'll see who comes out clean."

Borgia flashes a nervous grin. "Take it easy, Ennis. No one's calling for a grand jury. All I want is Gabriel back where he belongs, under the care of a psychiatric ward."

Chaney pushes past the secretary of state, choking back a laugh. "Tell you what, Pierre, I'll keep an eye out for him."

The incessant ringing rouses Edmund Loos from his sleep. He fumbles for the receiver, then clears his throat. "Captain here. Speak."

"Sorry to wake you, sir. We've detected activity along the seafloor."

"On my way."

The sea has begun churning by the time the captain enters the Combat Information Center. "Report, Commander."

The executive officer points to a light table where a real-time, cube-shaped holographic three-dimensional image of the sea and seafloor is being projected in midair. Positioned along the bottom of the ghostlike image, buried within the slate-shaded limestone topography is the ovoid alien object, color-coded luminescent orange. An emerald green circle of energy blazes atop the ovoid's dorsal surface, causing a shaft of light to rise up through a vertical burrow leading to the seafloor. The image of the *Boone* can be seen floating along the surface.

As the captain and his executive officer watch in amazement, the green beacon appears to widen as an eddy forms. Within seconds, the swirling torrent of water tightens into a powerful underwater funnel, stretching from the hole along the seafloor clear up to the surface. "Christ, it's like watching a tornado form," Loos whispers. "It's just as Gabriel said."

"Pardon me, sir?"

"Nothing. Commander, keep us clear of the maelstrom. Have communications patch me through to NORAD, then launch our LAMPS. If anything emerges from that whirlpool, I want to know about it."

"Aye, sir."

Lieutenant First-Class Johnathan Evans dashes across the aft deck, helmet in hand, his copilot and crew already on board the LAMPS antisub helicopter. Huffing and puffing, he climbs into the Seasprite's cockpit, then fastens himself in.

Evans glances over at his copilot as he struggles to catch his breath. "Damn cigarettes are killing me."

"Want some coffee?"

"Bless you, my son." Evans takes the Styrofoam cup. "Three minutes ago I'm lying in my bunk, dreaming of Michelle, the next thing I know, the XO's yelling at me, asking me why I'm not airborne yet."

"Welcome to the Navy adventure."

Evans pulls back on the joystick. The chopper lifts away from the helo-pad, turning south as it climbs to three hundred feet. The pilot hovers the LAMPS directly over the swirling emerald sea.

"Hol-lee shit—" Evans and his crew stare at the growing maelstrom, mesmerized by its beauty, frightened by its intensity. The vortex is a monster, a spiraling eddy straight out of Homer's *Odyssey*, its walls oscillating with the force of Niagara Falls. Looking down upon the otherwise dark waters, the whirlpool's glowing emerald eye resembles a luminescent green galaxy, its cluster of stars brightening as the mouth of the funnel opens wider.

"Good God. Wish I had my camera."

"Don't worry, Lieutenant, we're snapping plenty of pictures back here."

"Who cares about infrared. I want a real photo, something I can e-mail back home."

As Evans watches, the center of the maelstrom suddenly bottoms out, exposing a blinding sphere of light that blazes upward like an emerald sun from within the fractured sea floor.

"Protect your eyes—"

"Lieutenant, two objects rising out of the funnel!"

"What?" Evans turns to face his radar operator. "How large?"

"Big. Twice the size of the LAMPS."

The pilot pulls back on the joystick—as two dark, winged objects soar out of the funnel. The faceless mechanisms rise up along either side of the

Seasprite—the lieutenant catching a quick glimpse of a glowing amber disk—as the joystick goes limp in his hand.

"Oh, shit, we've stalled—"

"Engines off-line, Lieutenant. Everything's dead!"

Evans registers a sickening feeling as the airship drops from the sky. A bone-jarring jolt—as the chopper strikes the maelstrom's wall. The rotors shear off, the cockpit's windshield shatters as the copter is slung around the vertical column of water as if caught in a blender. Centrifugal force pins Evans sideways in his seat, his screams drowned out by the tumultuous roar that fills his ears.

The world spins out of control as the funnel engulfs the LAMPS.

The last thing Lieutenant Johnathan Evans feels is the strange sensation of his vertebrae popping beneath a suffocating embrace, as if his body is being crushed within a giant trash compactor.

DECEMBER 8, 2012

GUNUNG MULU NATIONAL PARK

SARAWAK, FEDERATION OF MALAYSIA

5:32 A.M. MALAYSIAN TIME (13 HOURS LATER)

Sarawak, situated on the northwest coast of Borneo, is the largest state in the Federation of Malaysia. Gunung Mulu, the largest national park in the state, covers 340 square miles, its landscape dominated by three mountains—the Gunung Mulu, the Gunung Benarat, and the Gunung Api.

The Gunung Api is a mountain formed out of limestone, a geology that not only dominates the entire state of Sarawak, but also its neighboring island of Irian Jaya/Papua New Guinea, and nearly all of southern Malaysia. The weathering of this limestone landscape by the slightly acid rainwater has led to remarkable surface sculptures and underground formations.

Midway up the side of Mount Api, pointing skyward like a field of jagged stalagmites, is a petrified forest of razor-sharp, silver-gray limestone pinnacles, some of which tower more than 150 feet above the rain forest. Below ground, hollowed out from the limestone geology by subterranean rivers, lies a labyrinth containing more than four hundred miles of underworld caverns, representing the largest limestone cave system in the world.

Honolulu graduate student Wade Tokumine has been studying the Sarawak caves for three months, collecting data as part of his master's thesis concerning the stability of the world's underground karst volumes. Karst is a topography created through the chemical weathering of limestone geology containing at least eighty percent calcium carbonate. Sarawak's network of subterranean passages are composed entirely of this vast network of karst.

Today's journey marks Wade's ninth visit to Clearwater Cave, the longest underground passage in all of Southeast Asia and one of only four Mula caves open to the public. The geologist leans back from his seat in the longboat, shining his carbide light at the alabaster ceiling of the cavern. The beacon cuts through the darkness to reveal a myriad of stalactites dripping with moisture. Wade stares at the ancient formations of rock, marveling at Nature's design.

Four billion years ago, the Earth was a very young, hostile, and lifeless world. As the planet cooled, water vapor and other gases were sent skyward in violent volcanic eruptions, creating an atmosphere high in carbon dioxide, nitrogen, and hydrogen compounds, conditions similar to those found on Venus.

Life on our planet began in the sea as a soup of chemicals, organized into complex structures—four basic amino acid chain molecules—animated by an outside catalyst, perhaps a bolt of lightning. The animated amino acid double helixes began to replicate themselves, leading to a single-celled life. These organisms quickly rose in abundance and began depleting the oceans of its fast-food carbon compounds. Then—a unique family of bacteria evolved to produce a new organic molecule called chlorophyll. This green-tinted substance was able to store the energy in sunlight, allowing the single-celled organisms to create high-quality carbohydrates from carbon dioxide and hydrogen, releasing oxygen as its by-product.

Photosynthesis was born.

As planetary oxygen levels rose, calcium carbonate was withdrawn from the sea and locked up in rock formations by marine organisms, drastically reducing the planet's atmospheric levels of carbon dioxide. This rock—limestone—became Earth's storehouse for carbon dioxide. As a result, the level of carbon dioxide stored in sedimentary rock is now more than six hundred times the total carbon content of the planet's air, water, and living cells combined.

Wade Tokumine aims the beam of light along the dark surface waters of the cavern. The subterranean stream is laden with ten times the concentration of carbon dioxide. This part of the carbon cycle occurs as a result of the dissolved CO_2 reaching its saturation point within the limestone. When this happens, the carbon dioxide precipitates out as pure calcium carbonate, creating the stalactites and stalagmites that now proliferate in the Sarawak caves.

Wade turns around in the longboat to face his guide, Andrew Chan. The Malaysian native and professional spelunker has been leading tours through Sarawak's caves for seventeen years.

"Andrew, how much farther to this virgin passage of yours?"

The light of the carbide lamp catches Andrew's smile, which is missing two front teeth. "Not far. This section of the cavern craps out ahead, then we go on by foot."

Wade nods, then spits out the stench of the carbide fumes. Only 30 percent of Sarawak's caves have been surveyed, most of these remaining inaccessible to all but a few of the more experienced guides. When it comes to charting unexplored passages, Wade knows Andrew is second to none, a caver exuding a strong case of "booty scoop lust," an incurable psychological condition common among "Speleo-boppers."

Andrew guides the longboat to a ledge, holding it steady so Wade can climb out. "Better put your brain bucket on, lots of loose rock ahead."

Wade fastens the helmet to his head as Andrew ties one end of a very long coil of rope known as a *hog* to the boat, tossing the rest over his shoulder. "Stay close. It'll get a bit narrow. There's plenty of sharp popcorn sticking out along the walls, so watch your clothes."

Andrew takes the lead, guiding them through a pitch-dark catacomb. He selects a tight, inclined passage and enters, allowing the hog line to feed out to mark their route. After several minutes of steady climbing, the passage squeezes to a claustrophobic tunnel, forcing them to crawl on all fours.

Wade slips on the wet limestone, tearing the skin along his knuckles. "How much farther?"

"Why? You getting entrance fever?"

"A little."

"That's 'cause you're a keyboard caver."

"What's that?"

"A keyboard caver's someone who spends more time reading the cavers' mailing list than actually going—hold on. Whoa, what's this?"

Wade crawls forward on his belly, squeezing in next to Andrew to take a look.

The tunnel has opened to a massive sinkhole. Looking up, they can see stars still glimmering in the early-morning sky, the surface a good seventy-five feet above their heads. Andrew shines his light below, revealing the bottom of a massive hole, another thirty feet down.

A luminescent amber glow casts bizarre shadows from within the pit.

"Do you see that?"

Wade leans forward to get a better look. "It looks like there's something glowing down there"

"This doline wasn't here earlier this morning. The roof of the cavern must have just collapsed. Whatever's down there probably fell straight through and landed in that pit."

"Maybe it's a car? Someone could be trapped down there."

Wade watches as his Malaysian guide reaches into his backpack and pulls out a Knobbly Dog, a rope ladder made of a single length of wire, the rungs threaded through the middle.

"What are you doing?"

"Stay here, I'm going to climb down and have a look." Andrew anchors one end of the ladder to the ledge, then allows the Knobbly Dog to unravel into the dark recesses below.

The sky above has turned gray by the time the spelunker steps down into the pit. The early-morning light barely penetrates the darkness and swirling wisps of limestone dust.

Andrew stares at the inanimate creature dwarfing him in the subterranean pit. "Hey Wade, I don't know what this thing is, but it ain't no car."

"What's it look like?"

"Like nothing I've ever seen. It's huge, like a giant cockroach, only it's got big wings and a tail, with a bunch of weird tentacles sticking out all over its belly. It's balancing upright on a pair of claws. They must be pretty hot, because the limestone's sizzling beneath them."

"Maybe you ought to get out of there. Come on, we'll call the park rangers—"

"It's okay, the thing's not alive." Andrew reaches out to touch one of the tentacles.

A neon blue, electromagnetic shock wave slams him backward against the far wall.

"Andrew, you okay? Andrew?"

"Yeah, man, but this sonnuva bitch is packing a serious charge. Oh, shit—" Andrew jumps back as the creature's hydraulic, mechanical tail rises, reaching up toward the sky.

"Andrew?"

"I'm leaving, man, you don't have to tell me twice." The guide starts climbing up the ladder.

The amber orb along the side of the being's upper body begins flashing, darkening to a crimson hue.

"Come on, climb faster!"

White smoke pours out from beneath the creature's talons, filling the vertical shaft.

Wade feels himself getting dizzy. He turns around and slides, headfirst, down the slick tunnel as Andrew pulls himself up and over the ledge.

"Andrew? Andrew, you behind me?" Wade stops his inertia and shines his light back up the tunnel. He can see the guide, lying facedown in the narrow crawl space.

Carbon dioxide!

Wade reaches back and grabs Andrew's wrist. He drags him down through the crawl space as the rock around him grows hotter, scorching his skin.

What the hell's happening?

Wade stumbles to his feet as the passage widens. He hoists the unconscious guide onto his shoulder and staggers toward the longboat. Everything seems to be spinning, getting hotter. He closes his eyes, using his elbows to feel his way along the sizzling limestone walls.

Wade hears a bizarre bubbling sound as he reaches the subterranean stream. Dropping to one knee, he rolls Andrew's body into the longboat, then climbs in clumsily, nearly tipping them. The cave's walls are smoking, the intense heat causing the underground river to boil.

Wade's eyes are burning, his nostrils unable to inhale the searing atmosphere. He bellows a suffocating scream, thrashing about wildly as his flesh blisters and chars away from the bone and his eyeballs burst into flames.

JOURNAL OF
JULIUS GABRIEL

*C*hichén Itzá—the most magnificent Mayan city in all Mesoamerica. Translated, the name means: <u>at the brim of the
well where the Wise Men of the Water live.</u>

The Wise Men of the Water.

The city itself is divided into an old section and new. The
Maya first settled in Old Chichén in AD 435 their civilization later
joined by the Itzá tribe, around AD 900. Little is known about
the daily rituals and lifestyles of these people, although we do
know they were ruled by their god-king, Kukulcán, whose legacy
as the great Mayan teacher dominates the ancient city.

Maria, Michael, and I would spend many years exploring
the ancient ruins and surrounding jungles of Chichén Itzá. In the
end, we felt convinced of the overwhelming importance of three
particular structures, these being the sacred cenote, the Great Mayan Ball Court, and the Kukulcán pyramid.

Simply put, there is no other structure in the world like the
Kukulcán pyramid. Towering above the Great Esplanade of
Chichén Itzá, the precision and astronomical placement of this
thousand-year-old structure still baffles architects and engineers
the world over.

Maria and I eventually agreed that it was the Kukulcán pyramid the Nazca drawing had been intended to represent. The inverted jaguar within the desert icon, the serpent columns at the entrance to the temple's northern corridor, the icon of the monkey and whales—everything seemed to fit. Somewhere, hidden within the city, had to be a secret passageway into the Kukulcán's inner structure. The question was—where?

The first and most obvious solution that came to us was that the entrance was hidden within the sacred cenote, a naturally formed sinkhole located just north of the Kukulcán. The cenote was yet another symbol of the portal to the Mayan Underworld, and no cenote in all the Yucatán was more important than the sacred well in Chichén Itzá, for it was here that so many maidens were sacrificed after Kukulcán's abrupt departure.

Of more importance was the possible connection between the cenote and the Nazca pyramid drawing. Viewed from above (just as in Nazca) the sacred well's layered, circular limestone walls could easily have been interpreted as a serious of concentric circles. In addition, the carved Mayan serpent heads, located along the northern base of the Kukulcán pyramid, point directly at the well.

Intrigued and excited, Maria and I put together a scuba diving expedition to explore the Mayan cenote. In the end, the only thing we found were the skeletal remains of the dead—nothing more.

Alas, it would be another structure in Chichén Itzá that would change our lives forever.

There are dozens of ancient ball courts in Mesoamerica, but none rival the Great Ball Court at Chichén Itzá. Besides being the largest in the Yucatán, the Great Ball Court, like the Kukulcán pyramid, is a structure that has been painstakingly aligned with the heavens, in this case, the Milky Way galaxy. At midnight of every June solstice,

the long axis of the I-shaped field points to where the Milky Way touches the horizon, the dark rift of the galaxy actually mirroring the ball court overhead.

   The astronomical meaning behind this incredible design cannot be overstated, for, as I have discussed earlier, the dark rift of the Milky Way is one of the most important symbols of Maya culture. According to the Popol Vuh, the Maya book of creation, the dark rift is considered to be the road that leads to the Underworld, or Xibalba. It is here where the Maya hero, One Hunahpu, had journeyed to the Underworld to challenge the evil gods, a heroic, though fateful, challenge ritualized by the Maya in the ancient ball game. (All members of the losing team were put to death.)

   According to the Mayan calendar, the name One Hunahpu equates with 1 Ahau, the first day of the fifth cycle—and its last—the prophesied day of doom. Using a sophisticated astronomy program, I have charted the heavens as they will appear in the year 2012. The Great Ball Court will once again align itself with the dark rift, *only this time on the day of the <u>winter</u> solstice—4 Ahau, 3 <u>Kankin</u>—humanity's day of doom.*

It was on a cool fall day in 1983 that a team of Mexican archaeologists arrived in Chichén Itzá. Armed with picks and shovels, the men proceeded to the Great Ball Court in search of an artifact known as the center marker—an ornamental stone found buried at the center point of many other ball-court fields in Mesoamerica.

Maria and I stood by and watched as the archaeologists unearthed the ancient artifact. The vessel was like none any of us had ever seen—jade instead of rock, hollow, the size of a coffee can, with the handle of an obsidian blade protruding from one end of the object as if it were some Mayan "sword in the stone." Despite many attempts to remove it, the weapon remained wedged in tight.

Adorning the sides of the jade object were symbolic images of the ecliptic and the dark rift. Painted on the bottom of the piece was the detailed face of a great Mayan warrior.

Maria and I stared at this last image in absolute shock, for there was no mistaking the man's facial features. Reluctantly, we handed the center marker back to the expedition's leader, then returned to our trailer, overwhelmed by the potential implications of the object we had just held within our hands.

Maria had been the one to finally break the silence between us. "Julius, somehow—somehow our own destiny has become directly entwined in the very salvation of our species. The image upon the marker—it's a sign that we must continue our journey, that we must find a way into Kukulcán's pyramid."

I knew my wife was right. With renewed vigor, forged from feelings of trepidation, we continued our search, spending the next three years turning over every rock, exploring every ruin, uncovering every jungle leaf, investigating every cave in the region.

Still—we found nothing.

By the summer of '85, our frustrations had mounted to the point where we knew a change of venue was necessary simply to preserve what little sanity remained. Our original plan had been to travel to Cambodia to explore the magnificent ruins of Angkor, a doomsday site we believed was linked to both Giza and Teotihuacán. Unfortunately, access into the area was still being denied to all outsiders by the ruling Khmer Rouge.

Maria had other ideas. Surmising our extraterrestrial elders would never have fashioned an entrance into the Kukulcán that could have been stumbled upon by looters, she believed it in our best interests to return to Nazca and attempt to decipher the rest of the ancient message.

As much as I despised the thought of returning to that Peruvian landscape, I could not argue with my wife's logic. We were clearly getting nowhere in Chichén Itzá, despite the fact that we were both convinced the city was destined to be the site of the final battlefield.

Before leaving, there was one final endeavor I had to complete before we embarked on what would prove to be our last, fateful journey together.

Armed with crowbar and mask, I broke into the archaeologist's trailer late one night—and rescued Kukulcán's center ball-court marker from its kidnappers.

—Excerpt from the Journal of Professor Julius Gabriel,

Ref. Catalogue 1981–84   pages 08–154
   Photo Journal Floppy Disk 7 & 8: File name: MESO, Photos 223, 328, 344

20

The commuter plane bounces twice along the weathered tarmac, taxis briefly, then skids to a halt just before the runway ends in an overgrown field.

The blast of heat hits Dominique square in the face as she steps off the Cessna, plastering the already sweat-soaked tee shirt against her chest. She slings her backpack over one shoulder and follows the other seven passengers through the small terminal, then out to the main road. A sign pointing to the left reads, "Hotel Mayaland," the one to the right, "Chichén Itzá."

"Taxi, *señorita*?"

The driver, a slight man in his early fifties, is leaning against a battered, white Volkswagen Beetle. Dominique can see the Mayan lineage in his dark facial features.

"How far to Chichén Itzá?"

"Ten minutes." The driver opens the passenger door.

Dominique climbs in, the exposed foam cushion of the worn vinyl seat giving beneath her weight.

"Have you been to Chichén Itzá before, *señorita*?"

"Not since I was a child."

"Don't worry. Not much has changed over the last thousand years."

They travel through an impoverished village, then onto a freshly paved two-lane toll road. Minutes later, the taxi pulls up to a modernized visitors' entrance, the parking lot crammed with rental cars and chartered tour buses. Dominique pays the driver, purchases a ticket, and enters the park.

She passes a series of gift shops, then follows several tourists down a wide dirt road that cuts through the Mexican jungle. After a five-minute walk, the path opens to an incredibly vast, flat, green expanse, surrounded by dense foliage.

Dominique's eyes widen as she takes in her surroundings. She has traveled back in time.

Dotting the landscape are massive gray-and-white limestone ruins. To her left is the Great Mayan Ball Court, the largest in all of Mesoamerica. Built in the shape of a giant "I" the arena is more than 550 feet long and 230 feet wide, enclosed on all sides, including its two central boundary walls, which rise three stories. Just to the north of the structure stands the Tzompantli, a large platform engraved with rows of enormous skulls, the bodies of serpents crowning the structure. In the distance on her right is a vast quadrangle—the Warrior's Complex—the remains of what had been a palace and marketplace, its borders partially enclosed by hundreds of freestanding columns.

But it is the main attraction that dwarfs every ruin to capture Dominique's attention—an incredibly precise, towering ziggurat of limestone, located in the middle of the ancient city.

"Magnificent, isn't it, *señorita*?"

Dominique turns to face a small man wearing a sweat-stained, orange park tee shirt and baseball cap. She notices the guide's high, sloping forehead and strong Mayan facial features.

"The Kukulcán pyramid is the most magnificent structure in all of Central America. Perhaps you would like a private tour? Only thirty-five pesos."

"Actually, I'm looking for someone. He's an American, tall, well-built, with brown hair and very dark eyes. His name's Michael Gabriel."

The guide's smile disappears.

"You know Mick?"

"I'm sorry, I can't help you. Have a pleasant visit." The small man turns and walks away.

"Wait—" Dominique catches up to him. "You know where he is, don't you? Take me to him, and I'll make it worth your while." She shoves a wad of bills in his hand.

"I'm sorry, *señorita*, I don't know the person you are looking for." He pushes the cash back into her palm.

She peels off several bills. "Here, take this—"

"No, *señorita*—"

"Please. If you happen to run into him, or if you know someone who might know how to get word to him, tell him that Dominique needs to see him. Tell him it's a matter of life and death."

The Mayan guide sees the desperation in her eyes. "The person you seek— is he your boyfriend?"

"A close friend."

The guide stares off in the distance for several moments, contemplating. "Take the day and enjoy Chichén Itzá. Treat yourself to a hot meal, then wait until dark. The park closes at ten. Hide out in the jungle just before security makes its final rounds. When the last person leaves and the gates are locked, ascend the Kukulcán pyramid and wait."

"Mick will be there?"

"It's possible."

He hands her back the money. "At the front entrance are tourist shops. Buy yourself a wool poncho, you'll need it for tonight."

"I want you to keep the money."

"No. The Gabriels have been friends of my family for a very long time." He smiles. "When Mick finds you, tell him that Elias Forma says you are far too beautiful to be left alone in the land of green lightning."

The incessant buzzing of a thousand mosquitoes fills Dominique's ears. She pulls the hood of her poncho over her head and huddles in the envelope of darkness, the jungle awakening around her.

What the hell am I doing here? She scratches at imaginary insects crawling on her arms. *I should be finishing my internship. I should be getting ready to graduate.*

The forest rustles around her. A flutter of wings disturbs the canopy of leaves above her head. Somewhere in the distance, a howler monkey screeches into the night. She checks her watch—10:23—then pulls her wool poncho back over her head and shifts her weight on the rock.

Give it another ten minutes.

She closes her eyes, allowing the jungle to wrap its arms around her, just as it had when she was a child. The heavy scent of moss, the sound of palm fronds dancing in the breeze—and she is back in Guatemala, only four, standing by the stucco wall outside her mother's bedroom window, listening to her grandmother crying within. She waits until her aunt escorts the old woman out before entering through the window.

Dominique stares at the lifeless figure stretched out across the bed. Fingers that had stroked her long hair only hours earlier have turned blue at the tips. The mouth is open, the brown eyes half-closed, fixated at the ceiling. She touches the high cheekbones, feeling the cold, clammy skin.

This was not her *madre*. This was something else, a frame of inanimate flesh that her mother had worn while part of her world.

Her grandmother enters. *She's with the angels now, Dominique.* . . .

The night sky explodes above her head with the chaotic sounds of a thousand vampire bats flapping their wings. Dominique jumps to her feet, her pulse pounding as she tries to blink away the mosquitoes and the memories.

"No! This is not my home. This is not my life!"

She shoves her childhood back into the attic and seals the door shut, then climbs down from the rock and pushes her way through the thicket until she emerges at the mouth of the sacred cenote.

Dominique gazes at the sheer, vertical walls of the sinkhole, which plunge straight down to the surface of its inky, algae-infested waters. The lunar light from the three-quarter moon highlights layers of geological grooves sculpted along the interior of the chalky white limestone pit. She looks up, focusing on an enclosed stone structure suspended over the southern edge of the cenote. One thousand years ago, the Maya, desperate after the sudden departure of their god-king, Kukulcán, had turned to human sacrifice in an effort to forestall the end of humanity. Virgin women had been locked in this primordial steam bath for purification, then led out to its rooftop platform by ceremonial priests. Stripping the young maidens naked, they would stretch them out upon the stone structure, then use their obsidian blades to cut out their hearts or slice their throats. The virgins' bodies, laden with jewelry, would then be ceremoniously tossed into the sacred well.

The thought causes Dominique to shudder. She circles the pit and hustles down the *Sacbe*, a wide, elevated footpath of soil and stone which cuts through the dense jungle until it reaches the northern border of the ancient city.

Fifteen minutes and a half dozen stumbles later, Dominique emerges from the path. Standing before her is the northern face of the Kukulcán pyramid, its jagged, dark outline rising nine stories against the star-drenched sky. She approaches the base, which is guarded on either side by the sculpted heads of two enormous serpents.

Dominique looks around. The ancient city is dark and deserted. A cold shiver runs down her spine. She begins climbing.

Midway up, she finds herself gasping for breath. The steps of the Kukulcán are quite narrow, the rise steep, and there is nothing to hold on to. She turns and looks down. A fall from this height would be her last.

"Mick?" Her voice seems to echo across the valley. She waits for a response, then, hearing nothing, continues climbing.

It takes her another five minutes to reach the summit, a flat platform supporting a square two-story stone temple. Feeling dizzy, she leans against the northern wall of the structure to catch her breath, her quadriceps muscles still burning from the climb.

The view is spectacular, with no safety rails. The moonlight reveals shadowed details of every structure in the northern section of the city. Along the outskirts, the jungle canopy spreads out across the horizon like the dark borders of a canvas.

The walkway around the structure is only five feet wide. Staying clear of the precarious ledge, she wipes the sweat from her face and stands before the yawning entrance of the temple's northern corridor. A massive portal, composed of a lintel flanked by two serpent-columns, towers above her head.

She steps inside, the interior pitch-dark. "Mick, are you in there?"

Her voice sounds dampened. She reaches into her backpack, locates the flashlight she purchased earlier, and enters the dank, limestone chamber.

The northern corridor is an enclosed double-chambered room, a central sanctuary preceded by a vestibule. The interior dead-ends at a massive, central wall. The beam of her flashlight reveals a vaulted ceiling, then a stone floor, its surface charred black from ceremonial fires. Leaving the empty chamber, she follows the platform around to the left and enters the western corridor, a barren passage that zigzags to connect with the southern and eastern corridors.

The temple is deserted.

Dominique checks the time: 11:20. *Maybe he's not coming?*

The cool night air causes her to shiver. Seeking warmth, she ducks back into the northern chamber and leans against the central wall, the heavy stone surrounding her sealing out the wind and deadening all noise.

The atmosphere inside seems heavy, as if someone is waiting in the shadows to pounce upon her. She uses the flashlight's beam to scan the interior, soothing her psyche.

Exhaustion gains a foothold. She lies down on the stone floor and curls up in a ball, closing her eyes, her thoughts haunting her sleep with images of blood and death.

The expanse surrounding the pyramid is a sea of swaying brown bodies and painted faces illuminated by the orange glow of ten thousand torches. From her vantage within the northern corridor, she can see blood running down the stairwell like a crimson waterfall, pooling around a pile of mangled flesh situated between the two serpent heads located at the foot of the pyramid.

A dozen more women are in the temple with her, all dressed in white. They huddle together like frightened lambs, staring at her through vacant eyes.

Two priests enter. Each wears a ceremonial headdress of green feathers and a loincloth cut from a jaguar's hide. The priests approach, their dark eyes focusing on Dominique. She backs away, her heart pounding, as each priest grabs a wrist, the two men forcibly dragging her out to the temple's platform.

The night air is heavy with the stench of blood and sweat and smoke.

Facing the swooning crowd is an immense Chac Mool, a stone statue of an inclined Mayan demigod. In the Chac Mool's lap is a ceremonial plate, spilling over with the mangled remains of a dozen severed human hearts.

Dominique screams. She attempts to flee, but two more priests reach out and grab her by the ankles, lifting her high off the ground. The crowd groans as the head priest appears, a muscular redhead whose face remains hidden beneath the mask of a feathered serpent's head. A devilish yellow smile appears within the serpent mask's fanged, open mouth.

"Hi, Sunshine."

Dominique screams as Raymond tears the white cloth from her naked body, then holds the black, obsidian blade up to the crowd. A lustful chant rises from the bloodthirsty mob.

"Kukulcán! Kukulcán!"

At Raymond's nod, four priests lower her to the ground, pinning her against the stone platform.

"Kukulcán! Kukulcán!"

Dominique screams again as Raymond flashes his obsidian blade. She gasps in disbelief as he raises it over his head, then plunges it forcefully into her left breast.

"Kukulcán! Kukulcán!"

She screams in agony, twisting and contorting her outstretched body—

"Dom, wake up—"

—as Raymond pushes his hand into the wound and rips out her still-beating heart, holding it up to the heavens for all to see.

"Dominique!"

Dominique lets go a bloodcurdling scream as she kicks and punches at the terrifying darkness, catching the shadow square in the face. Disoriented, still in the throes of her nightmare, she rolls sideways and springs to her feet, rushing blindly out of the chamber, sprinting toward the ninety-foot drop.

A hand reaches out and tackles her by the ankle. She slams chest-first against the platform, the pain snapping her awake.

"Jesus, Dominique, I'm supposed to be the crazy one."

"Mick?" She sits up, rubbing her bruised ribs as she catches her breath.

Mick scoots next to her. "You all right?"

"You scared the shit out of me."

"Same here. That must have been some nightmare. You nearly dived off the pyramid."

She looks out over the precipice, then turns and hugs him, her limbs still shaking. "God, I hate this place. These walls reek of Mayan ghosts." She pulls back, looking at his face. "Your nose is bleeding. Did I do that?"

"Caught me with a right cross." He removes a bandanna from his back pocket and pinches off the flow. "This thing's never going to heal."

"Serves you right. Why the hell did we have to meet here of all places, and in the middle of the goddam night?"

"I'm a fugitive, remember? Speaking of which, how did you manage to get away from the Navy?"

She turns away. "You're the fugitive, not me. I told the captain I helped you because I was confused about Iz's death. Guess he felt sorry for me, 'cause he let me go. Come on, we can talk about this later. Right now, I just want to get down off this pyramid."

"I can't leave yet. I have work to do."

"Work? What work? It's the middle of the night—"

"I'm searching for a passageway into the pyramid. It's vital that we find it—"

"Mick—"

"My father was right about the Kukulcán. I discovered something—something really incredible. Let me show you." Mick reaches into his satchel and removes a small electronic device.

"This instrument is called an ultrasonic inspectroscope. It transmits low-amplitude sound waves to determine imperfections in solids." Mick switches his flashlight on, then takes her by the wrist and drags her back inside the temple to the central wall. He activates the inspectroscope, directing its sound waves at a cross section of stone.

"Take a look. See these wavelengths? There's definitely another structure concealed behind this central wall. Whatever it is, it's metallic in nature and rises straight up through the pyramid, clear to the roof of the temple."

"Okay, I believe you. Can we go now?"

Mick stares at her, incredulous. "Go? Don't you get it? It's here—within these walls. All we have to do is figure out how to access it."

"What's here? A hunk of metal?"

"A hunk of metal that may turn out to be the instrument that will save humanity. The one left to us by Kukulcán. We have to . . . hey, wait, where are you going?"

She continues walking out to the platform.

"You still don't believe me, do you?"

"Believe what? That every man, woman, and child on this planet's going to die within the next two weeks? No—sorry Mick, I'm still struggling with that one."

Mick grabs her by the arm. "How can you still doubt me? You saw what's buried in the Gulf. The two of us were down there together. You saw it for yourself."

"Saw what? The interior of a lava tube?"

"A lava tube?"

"That's right. The geologists aboard the *Boone* explained the whole thing to me. They even showed me infrared satellite photos of the entire Chicxulub crater. What appears to us as a green glow is just a subterranean lava flow passing beneath that hole in the seafloor. The hole opened up when an underwater volcano became active back in September."

"Volcano? Dominique, what the hell are you talking about?"

"Mick, our minisub was sucked down one of the lava tubes when part of the underground infrastructure collapsed. We must have floated topside when the pressure subsided." She shakes her head. "You really played me, didn't you? I'm guessing you heard about the volcano from a CNN report or something. That's the noise Iz heard over SOSUS."

She punches him in the chest. "My father died exploring a goddam subterranean volcano—"

"No—"

"You played me, didn't you? All you wanted was to escape—"

"Dominique, listen to me—"

"No! Listening to you is what got my father killed. Now you listen to me. I helped you because I knew you were being abused and I needed your help in finding out what happened to Iz. Now I know the truth. You set me up!"

"Bullshit! Everything the Navy fed you is a goddam lie. That tunnel was no lava tube, it was an artificially created inlet shaft. What your father heard were sounds coming from a series of giant turbines. Our minisub was sucked down an inlet shaft. The submersible jammed the turbine's rotors. Don't you remember any of this? I know you were hurt, but you were still conscious when I climbed out of the sub."

"What did you say?" She looks at him, suddenly confused, disturbed by a distant memory. "Wait—did I hand you a tank of oxygen?"

"Yes! It saved my life."

"You really climbed out?" She sits down along the edge of the summit. *Was the Navy lying?* "Mick, you couldn't have climbed out of the sub. We were underwater—"

"The chamber was pressurized. The minisub corked the inlet."

She shakes her head. *Stop it. He's lying. This is nonsense!*

"I bandaged your head. You were scared. You asked me to hold you before I left the sub. You made me promise to return."

A vague memory swirls in her mind.

Mick sits down at the foot of the summit. "You still don't believe a word I'm saying, do you?"

"I'm trying to remember." She sits beside him. "Mick . . . I'm sorry I hit you."

"I warned you not to let Iz investigate the Gulf."

"I know."

"I would never betray you. Never."

"Mick, let's say I believe you. What did you see when you left the minisub? Where did this turbine of yours lead?"

"I located some sort of drainage pipe and managed to climb up inside it. The passage led into this enormous chamber. The atmosphere inside was broiling. Red flames licked the walls."

Mick stares at the stars. "High above my head swirled this . . . this magnificent emerald vortex of energy. It moved like a miniature spiral galaxy. It was so beautiful."

"Mick—"

"Wait, there's more. Spread out before me was a lake of molten energy, undulating like a sea of mercury, only its surface was as reflective as a mirror. And then I heard my father's voice, speaking to me in the distance."

"Your father?"

"Yes, only it wasn't my father, it was some kind of alien life-form. I couldn't see it—it was held within some kind of high-tech chamber, floating above the molten lake in an enormous pod. It looked at me through these blazing red, demonic eyes. I was scared shitless—"

Dominique exhales. *There it is. Classic dementia. Christ, Foletta was right. It was there all the time and I just refused to see it.* She watches as he stares off in the distance. "Mick, let's talk about this. These images you saw, they're quite symbolic, you know. Let's start with your father's voice—"

"Wait!" He turns to face her, his eyes wide, like black saucepans. "I just realized something. I know who the life-form was."

"Go on." She hears weariness in her own voice. "Who was it you think you saw?"

"It was Tezcatilpoca."

"Who?"

"Tezcatilpoca. The evil deity I told you about on the boat. It's an Aztec name that translates to 'Smoking Mirror,' a description for the deity's weapon. According to Mesoamerican legend, the Smoking Mirror gave Tezcatilpoca the ability to see into the souls of men."

"Yes, I remember."

"The being looked into my soul. He spoke to me as my father, as if he knew me. He was trying to deceive me."

She places a hand on his shoulder, fingering the dark locks of hair along his neck. "Mick, you know what I think? I think the minisub's collision knocked both of us woozy, and—"

He pushes her hand away. "Don't do that! Don't patronize me. I wasn't dreaming, and I'm not having schizophrenic delusions either. Every legend possesses its own reality. Aren't you even familiar with the legends of your own ancestors?"

"They're not my ancestors."

"Bullshit." Mick grabs her wrist. "Like it or not, there's Quiche Maya blood flowing in these veins."

She pulls her arm away. "I was raised in the States. I don't believe in any of that *Popol Vuh* nonsense."

"Just hear me out—"

"No!" She grabs him by the shoulders. "Mick, stop a second and listen to me—please. I care about you, you know that, don't you? I think you're an intelligent, sensitive, and extremely gifted person. If you allow me, if you trust me, I can help you through this."

His face lights up. "Really? That's great because I could really use your help. You know, we only have eleven days until—"

"No, you misunderstand." *Be maternal.* "Mick, this is going to be very hard for you to hear, but I have to say it. You're showing every sign of suffering from a severe case of paranoid schizophrenia. It's got you so confused, you can't see the forest for the trees. It could be congenital in nature, or it could just be the effects of eleven years in solitary. Whatever the case, you need help."

"Dom, what I saw wasn't any manifestation. What I saw was the interior of a very high-tech, very alien spacecraft."

"A spacecraft?" *Oh, God, I'm out of my league.*

"Wake up, Dominique. The government knows it's down there, too—"
Classic paranoid delusions . . .

"That nonsense they fed you aboard the *Boone* was just a cover-up story."

Hot tears of frustration roll down her cheeks as she realizes the devastating error of her ways. Dr. Owen had been right all along. By opening her heart to her patient, she had destroyed her objectivity. Everything that had come to pass was her fault. Iz was dead, Edie under arrest, and the man whom she had reached out to, the man who she had sacrificed everything for, was nothing more than a paranoid schizophrenic whose mind had finally snapped.

A sudden thought crosses her mind. *The closer we get to the winter solstice, the more dangerous he'll become.*

"Mick, you need help. You've lost touch with reality."

Mick stares at the perfectly cut limestone block beneath his feet. "Why are you here, Dominique?"

She takes his hand. "I'm here because I care. I'm here because I can help you."

"Another lie." He looks at her, his dark eyes glistening in the moonlight.

"Borgia got to you, didn't he? He's consumed with hatred toward my family. The man will say or do anything to get me back. How did he threaten you?"

She looks away.

"What did he promise you? Tell me what he said."

"You want to know what he said?" She turns and glares at him, the anger rising in her voice. "He arrested Edie. He said the two of us will spend a long time in prison for our part in releasing you."

"Damn. I'm sorry—"

"Borgia promised he'd drop the charges against both of us if I found you. He gave me a week. If I fail, Edie and I both go to prison."

"Bastard."

"Mick, it's not all bad. Dr. Foletta agreed to place me in charge of your care."

"Foletta, too? Oh, Christ—"

"You'll be taken to the new facility in Tampa. No more isolation. From now on, a board certified team of psychiatrists and clinicians will work with you. They'll get you the care you need. Before you know it, we'll have you on a drug-therapy program that will put you back in control of your own thoughts. No more asylums, and no more living in Mexican jungles as a fugitive. Eventually you'll be able to lead a normal, productive life."

"Gee, you make it sound so wonderful," he says sarcastically. "And Tampa's so close to Sanibel Island, too. Did Foletta throw in full medical? How about your own parking spot?"

"I'm not doing this for me, Mick, I'm doing it for you. This might turn out to be the best thing that could've happened."

He shakes his head sadly. "Dom, it's you who can't see the forest for the trees." He reaches down and pulls her to her feet, pointing to the heavens. "Can you see that dark line paralleling the Great Ball Court? That's the dark rift of the Milky Way, the equivalent of our Galactic Equator. Once every 25,800 years, the Sun moves into alignment at its center point. The exact date of that precise alignment comes in eleven days. Eleven days, Dominique. On that day, the day of the winter solstice, a cosmic portal will open, allowing a malevolent force access into our world. By the end of the day, you, me, Edie, Borgia, and every living soul on this planet will be dead—unless we can locate the hidden entrance into this pyramid."

Mick looks into her eyes, his heart aching. "I—I love you, Dominique. I've loved you since the day we met, since the day you showed me a simple act of kindness. I'm also indebted to you and Edie. But right now, I have to see this thing through, even if it means losing you. Maybe you're right. Maybe this is all just some grandiose schizophrenic delusion, passed on to me by my two psychotic parents. Maybe I'm so far over the edge that I can't even see the playing field anymore. But don't you see—whether it's real or just a fabric of my imagination, I can't stop now, I have to see this thing through."

He picks up the ultrasonic inspectroscope, his eyes glistening with tears. "I swear to you, on my mother's soul, that if I'm wrong, I'll return to Miami on December 22 and turn myself in to the authorities. Until then, if you want to help me, if you *really* care, then stop being my psychiatrist.

"Be my friend."

21

The packed auditorium grows quiet, the television cameras rolling as Viktor Ilyich Grozny walks to the podium to address the members of the United Nations Security Council and the rest of the world.

"Madame President, Mr. Secretary-General, members of the Security Council, honored guests—this is a sad day. Despite mandates and warnings from the General Assembly and the Security Council, despite the exhaustive efforts of preventive diplomacy and peacemaking by the Secretary-General and his special envoys, one nation—one rogue, but very powerful nation, continues to threaten the rest of the world with the most dangerous weapon in the history of mankind.

"The Cold War is long over, or so we are told, the virtues of capitalism triumphing over the evils of communism. While the economies of the West continue to grow, the Russian Federation struggles to rebuild. Our people are destitute, starving by the thousands. Do we blame the West? No. Russia's problems were created by Russians, and it is our responsibility to save ourselves."

The angelic blue eyes project a childlike innocence into the camera. "I am a man of peace. Through the diplomacy of words I have convinced our Arab and Serbian and Korean brothers to lay down their guns against their sworn enemies, because I know and believe in my heart that violence solves nothing and that the wrongs of the past cannot be undone. Morality is a personal choice. Each of us shall be judged by the Creator when the time comes, yet no man has a God-given right to inflict pain and suffering on another in the name of morality."

Grozny's eyes grow harsh. "Let him without sin cast the first stone. The Cold War is dead, yet the United States, by virtue of strong economy and military might, continues to police the world, deciding whether the policies of another nation are morally sound. Like the school bully, America balls its fist, threatening violence, all in the name of peace. As the most powerful hypocrite in the world, the United States arms the oppressed, until they become the oppressors. Israel, South Korea, Vietnam, Iraq, Bosnia, Kosovo, Taiwan—how many more must die before the United States realizes that the threat of violence only leads to more violence, that tyranny, disguised by the best of intentions, is still tyranny?"

The eyes soften. "And now the world bears witness to a new type of threat. Possessing the most sophisticated fighting force in history is not enough. The domination of space is not enough. The implementation of their Missile Defense Shield is not enough. Now, the capitalists have a new weapon, one that changes the rules of nuclear stalemate. Why does the United States continue to test these weapons and deny responsibility? Does the American president take us all for fools? Do his excuses soothe the frail nerves of the Australian and Malaysian people? Where will the next detonation occur? China? The Russian Federation? Or perhaps the Middle East, where three American aircraft carriers and their fleets are poised to strike, all in the name of justice.

"The Russian Federation joins China and the rest of the world in condemning these new threats of violence. Today, we state this warning, and let me be perfectly clear, lest our own morality be judged. We will not live in fear. We will no longer buckle to the bully tactics of the West. The next pure-fusion detonation shall be the last, for we will interpret this as a declaration of nuclear war!"

The assembly erupts in pandemonium, the protests of the United States delegates going unheard as Victor Grozny's security guards rush him out of the building.

Dominique Vazquez opens her eyes to the sound of clucking chickens. Morning light filters in between rotting wooden slats above her head, revealing a ballet of airborne particles dancing in the air. She stretches in her sleeping bag, then rolls over.

Mick is already up, leaning against a haystack, studying his father's journal. The Sun's rays illuminate the angular lines of his face. He looks up, the black eyes twinkling at her.

"Good morning."

She slides out of the sleeping bag. "What time is it?"

"About eleven. Are you hungry? The Formas left breakfast for you in the kitchen." He points outside the open barn door to the pink stucco house. "Go ahead, help yourself. I ate earlier."

Barefoot, she walks across the straw and soil-infested floor and sits down next to him. "What are you working on?"

He points to the drawing of the Nazca pyramid. "This symbol is the key to finding the hidden entrance into the Kukulcán pyramid. The animal is a jaguar, the symbol inverted to indicate *descent*. The ancient Maya considered the jaguar's open mouth to be linked to both terrestrial caves and the Underworld. The closest caves around here are in Balancanché. My parents and I spent years searching them, but found nothing."

"What about this pattern of concentric circles?"

"That's the part of the equation I'm still struggling with. At first, I thought the pattern might symbolize a subterranean chamber. Identical circles can be found carved in all of the ancient sites my parents explored. I even went back to the Balancanché caves when I first arrived, but found nothing."

Dominique removes the map of Chichén Itzá from her back pocket. She stares at the layout of the ruins, the photographs taken from high above the ancient city. "Tell me more about this Mayan Underworld. What did you call it?"

"*Xibalba*. According to the Mayan creation myth, the dark rift in the Milky Way was *Xibalba Be*, the Black Road to the Underworld. It's written in the *Popol Vuh* that *Xibalba* is where birth, death, and resurrection take place. Unfortunately, the words of the *Popol Vuh* require a bit of interpretation. I'm sure most of the original meaning has been lost over the centuries."

"Why do you say that?"

"The *Popol Vuh* was written around the sixteenth century, long after the rise and fall of the Mayan civilization and the disappearance of Kukulcán. As a result, the stories tend to lean more toward mythology than fact. Then again, after what I saw in the Gulf, I'm no longer sure." He looks at her, uncertain as to whether he should continue.

"Go on, I'm listening."

"With an open mind, or is this just part of my therapy?"

"You said you needed a friend, well here I am." She squeezes his hand. "Mick, this alien you claim communicated with you—you say it spoke to you in your father's voice?"

"Yes. It deceived me, baited me into moving closer."

"Now, don't get upset, but in the *Popol Vuh*'s creation story, didn't you tell me the same thing happened to, uh, what was his name?"

"One Hunahpu." His eyes widen.

Excellent, he's recognizing the origins of his own dementia.

"You still think I imagined this whole thing, don't you?"

"I didn't say that, but you have to admit, it certainly is a strange parallel. What happened to One Hunahpu after the Underworld gods deceived him?"

"He and his brother were tortured and put to death. But his defeat was part of a greater plan. After the Under Lords decapitated him, they left his head in the crook of a calabash tree to keep trespassers away from *Xibalba*. But one day, a beautiful woman, Blood Moon, decided to defy the gods and visit the skull tree. She reached out to One Hunahpu's skull, which magically spit on her hand, impregnating her. Blood Moon escaped, returning to the Middleworld—to Earth—to give birth to the Hero Twins—Hunahpu and Xbalanque."

"Hunahpu and Xbalanque?"

"Twin sons—the Hero Twins. The boys would grow up to become great warriors. Upon reaching adulthood, they returned to *Xibalba* to challenge the Lords of the Underworld. Once more, the evil gods attempted to win by using trickery, but this time the Hero Twins prevailed, defeating their enemy, vanquishing evil, and resurrecting their father. One Hunahpu's resurrection leads to the celestial conception and rebirth of the Mayan nation."

"Tell me again about this Black Road speaking to One Hunahpu. How can a road speak?"

"I don't know. According to the *Popol Vuh*, the entrance to the Black Road was symbolized as being the mouth of a great serpent. The dark rift was also considered to be a celestial serpent."

Go for it. Push him. "Mick, just hear me out for a second. You've spent your entire life chasing Mayan ghosts, absorbing yourself in the legends of the *Popol Vuh*. Isn't it remotely possible that you—"

"That I what? That I imagined my father's voice?"

"Don't get angry. I'm only asking because the story of One Hunahpu's journey seems to parallel everything you've told me about this subterranean chamber. I also think you have some unresolved issues with your father."

"Maybe I do, but I didn't imagine that alien being. I didn't imagine my father's voice. It was real."

"Or maybe it only seemed real."

"You're playing psychiatrist again."

"I'm only trying to be a friend. Paranoid delusions are very powerful things. The first step in helping yourself is to accept the fact that you need help."

"Dominique, stop—"

"If you let me, I can help you—"

"No!" Mick pushes past her and out the barn door. He closes his eyes, taking deep breaths, warming his face in the midday sun as he struggles to regain control.

That's far enough. I planted the seed, now I have to regain his confidence. She turns her attention back to the map of Chichén Itzá. For some reason, the aerial image of the cenote catches her eye. She thinks back to the previous night, her walk through the jungle.

The cenote walls . . . glistening in the moonlight. The grooves in the limestone . . .

"What is it?"

Startled, she looks up, surprised to find him hovering over her. "Uh, nothing, it's probably nothing."

"Tell me." The ebony eyes are too intense to fool.

"Here, see this map. The aerial image of the cenote resembles the pattern of concentric circles found within the Nazca pyramid drawing."

"My parents came to the same conclusion. They spent months scuba diving inside every cenote, exploring every sinkhole and subterranean cave in the area. The only thing they found were a few skeletons, the sacrificial remains of the dead, but nothing even resembling a passage."

"Have you checked the cenote since the earthquake?" She cringes as the words escape her mouth.

"Earthquake?" Mick's face lights up. "The earthquake on the fall equinox struck Chichén Itzá? Jesus, Dominique, why didn't you tell me this before?"

"I don't know—I guess I didn't realize it was that important. By the time I found out, Foletta had doped you into a vegetable."

"Tell me about the earthquake. How did it affect the cenote?"

"It was just a blurb in the news. A bunch of tourists claimed they witnessed the well's waters churning during the seismic disturbance."

Mick takes off running.

"Wait, where are you going?"

"We'll need a car. We'll probably have to spend a day or two in Merida picking up supplies. Eat something. I'll meet you back here in an hour."

"Mick, wait—what supplies? What are you talking about?"

"Scuba gear. We need to check out the cenote."

She watches him jog down the road, heading into town.

Way to go, Sigmund. You weren't supposed to encourage him.

Annoyed at herself, she leaves the barn and enters the Formas' home, a five-room stucco dwelling brightly decorated in Mexican motif. She finds a plate of fried bananas and corn bread on the kitchen table and sits down to eat.

Then she notices the telephone.

JOURNAL OF
JULIUS GABRIEL

*I*t was the summer of 1985, and we were back in Nazca.

For the first six months, the three of us commuted daily from a small apartment in Ica, a bustling little city located 90 miles to the north of Nazca. But our dwindling budget soon forced us to relocate, and I moved my family into a sparse, two-room dwelling in the farming village of Ingenio.

Having sold our camper, I was able to purchase a small hot-air balloon. Each Monday morning at sunrise, Maria, Michael, and I would soar a thousand feet over the desert pampa, photographing the myriad lines and magnificent animals etched upon the plateau. The remainder of the week would be dedicated to a thorough analysis of the photos, which we hoped would reveal the message that might guide our entrance into the Kukulcán pyramid.

The overwhelming challenge of translating the Nazca drawings is that there are far more false clues than real ones. Hundreds of animal figures and thousands of shapes proliferate the desert canvas like prehistoric graffiti, the majority of which were not created by the original artist of Nazca. Rectangles, triangles, trapezoids, clusters, and impossibly straight lines, some over 25 miles in length, are spread over 200 square miles of dun-colored flats.

Add to these the humanlike figures carved into the surrounding hillsides, and you can see how daunting our task was. Nevertheless, our efforts eventually helped segregate what we deemed to be the more vital etchings from the rest of the Peruvian epigraph.

It is the older, more intricate drawings that hold the real message of Nazca. We can only guess at the date of their origins, but we know they are at least 1500 years old.

The hieroglyphs of Nazca serve two distinct functions. Icons we termed "primary" drawings are used to describe the story behind the doomsday prophecy, while "secondary" figures etched in proximity to these icons provide us with important clues to help decipher their meaning.

The artist's tale begins at the center of the desert canvas with a figure Maria had nicknamed the Nazca sunburst, a perfect circle consisting of 23 lines extending outward from its perimeter. One of these lines is longer than the rest, extending some 20 miles across the desert. A dozen years later, I would discover that this elongated line was precisely aligned to Orion's belt. Shortly thereafter, Michael would locate an iridium canister buried at the heart of this mysterious starting point, the contents of which contained an ancient map of the world (see June 14, 1990 entry). This parchment seem to identify the Yucatán Peninsula and the Gulf of Mexico as the final battleground for the Armageddon to come.

Lying in close proximity to the sunburst is the Nazca spider. Its specific genus—*Ricinulei*, is one of the rarest in the world, and can only be found in some of the most inaccessible areas of the Amazon rain forest. Like the whales and monkey, the Nazca spider is another species not indigenous to the Peruvian desert. For this reason, we considered it to be a directional icon, in this case, celestial by nature. It turns out the spider is an incredibly accurate terrestrial marker designed to direct the observer (again) to the constellation of Orion. The straight lines of the arachnoid have been oriented in such a way as to track the changing declinations of the three Orion belt stars, the same series of stars the Egyptians used to align the pyramids of Giza.

Surrounding the sunburst, scattered about the plateau, are more than a dozen bizarre drawings of winged predatory creatures. Note that I am not referring to the more recent drawings of the hummingbird or pelican, two species indigenous to the area, but, instead, to a series of hellish-looking beings, the likes of which I still cannot identify. These mysterious, taloned creatures proliferate on the Nazca canvas, and I am still at a loss as to their function.

The longest zoomorph on the plateau is the 617-foot Nazca serpent. Unfortunately, much detail of the beast has been obliterated by the Pan American Highway, which cuts across its torso. The serpent's presence on the pampa may symbolize the dark rift of the Milky Way, then again, its proximity to the Nazca pyramid, like the monkey and whales, may offer it as a signpost directing us to Chichén Itzá, a Mayan city dominated by the image of the Feathered Serpent.

The serpent's tail, like the sunburst and spider, has been oriented to Orion.

There are several other drawings that stand out as pieces of the Mayan prophecy. The last that I shall mention—and our favorite—is the figure we nicknamed the Nazca astro-

272

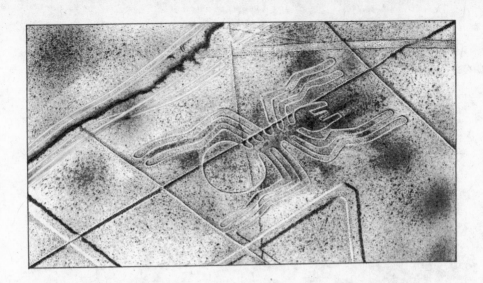

naut. Suffice it to say that the presence of this 2,000-year-old extraterrestrial being remained a vision of comfort during our days on the pampa, a convincing reminder that we were not alone in our quest, at least in spirit. The owlish-looking humanoid male, adorned in uniform and boots, has his right hand raised in what could only be interpreted as a gesture of friendship. Clearly set apart from the rest of the Nazca message, the giant E.T. has been etched upon one of the hillsides like an artist's signature on the margin of a painting.

DECEMBER 23, 1989.

After more than four years of work on the Peruvian desert, I decided to take my family to visit the most impressive of the ancient drawings: the Trident of Paracas. Located 100 miles north of the desert pampa, this figure, often referred to as El Candelabro, or the Andes Candelabra, has never been officially linked to the Nazca drawings, even though its intricate pattern, size, and age easily qualify it as a work of our mysterious artist.

The Trident's creator chose to engrave this colossal symbol on an entire mountainside facing the Bay of Paracas. The magnificent icon consists of a three-pronged candelabra design similar to that of a devil's pitchfork, except the pointed ends, all facing up, are embellished with petal-like features. Because the etching is exposed to much harsher weather conditions than those of Nazca, the artist dug much deeper into the hillside, carving the icon's outline a full three feet into the salty crustlike surface of the mountain. At 600 feet long and nearly 200 feet across, the Trident of Paracas is an easy landmark to spot.

I remember the three of us staring at the ancient marker from our boat on that fateful day in December. As the setting sun at our backs turned crimson, the Trident's crystal-like soil began sparkling in the diminishing light, giving the outline of the icon

an almost luminescent red glow. This effect seemed to energize Maria, who quickly surmised that the Candelabra must surely have been left as an ancient signpost, directing our civilization to the Nazca desert.

The thought made me think of the arch in St. Louis, the symbolic gateway to America's heartland. I was about to say as much when my beloved suddenly doubled over in excruciating pain and let out a mournful wail. Then, as Michael and I watched in horror, she collapsed onto the deck, unconscious.

—Excerpt from the Journal of Professor Julius Gabriel,

Ref. Catalogue 1985–90   pages 31–824
   Photo Journal Floppy Disk 8 & 9: File name: NAZCA, Photos 34 & 56

22

Captain Edwin Loos greets Vice President Ennis Chaney and Marvin Teperman as they stagger off the Sikorsky SH-60B Seahawk and step onto the deck of the USS *Boone*.

The CO smiles. "Are you all right, Mr. Vice President? You look a little queasy."

"We ran into some weather. Are the UAVs in position?"

"Two Predators hovering above the target area, just as you requested, sir."

Marvin removes his life vest, handing it to the chopper pilot. "Captain, what makes your people think we'll see another one of those whirlpools tonight?"

"Sensors indicate subterranean electromagnetic fluctuations are rising, just like they did the last time the maelstrom appeared." Loos leads them through the superstructure, escorting them to the ship's Combat Information Center.

The darkened high-tech chamber is buzzing with activity. Commander Curtis Broad glances up from a sonar station. "You're just in time, skipper. Sensors indicate a rise in electromagnetic activity. It looks like another maelstrom may be forming."

Circling above the emerald glow in staggered altitudes are two of the USS Boone's unmanned aerial reconnaissance vehicles, known as Predator. As the waters of the Gulf begin pulling in a counterclockwise motion, the Predators' infrared and television cameras beam real-time images back to the warship.

Chaney, Teperman, Captain Loos, and two dozen technicians and scientists stare at the video monitors, their pulses racing as the whirlpool takes shape before their eyes.

The vice president shakes his head in disbelief. "What on God's good earth could possess the power to create something like that?"

Marvin whispers, "Maybe the same thing that's been detonating karst formations across the Western Pacific."

The maelstrom rotates faster, its monstrous centrifugal force opening a swirling funnel, which drops clear down to the fractured seafloor. As the waters part, the eye of the vortex unleashes a brilliant emerald beacon into the night, radiating skyward like a celestial searchlight.

"There," Marvin points to the screen. "Rising out from the center—"

"I see them," Chaney whispers, dumbfounded.

Three dark shadows levitate out of the light and straight up through the eye of the maelstrom.

"What in the fuck is that," Loos swears. A dozen stunned scientists yell out to their colleagues and assistants to verify that all sensory data is being collected.

The objects continue rising out of the whirlpool. Hovering above the sea, they approach the lowest of the two UAVs.

The Predator's picture becomes fuzzy with static, then goes blank.

The second Predator continues transmitting.

"I want both Seahawks airborne now," Captain Loos orders. "Reconnaissance only. Chief, keep the remaining Predator at a safe distance. Don't lose that signal."

"Aye, sir. Sir, what's a safe distance?"

"Captain, Seahawks are airborne—"

"Keep them away from that light," Chaney barks.

The three alien objects rise to an altitude of two thousand feet. With robotic precision, they execute a pirouette, rotating their enormous wings into full horizontal extension, and accelerate, disappearing instantly from view.

Captain Loos rushes over to the Mk. 23 Target Acquisition System. Second Lieutenant Linda Muraresku is already tracking the objects using the Boone's fast-rotating radar dish.

"I've got them, sir—barely. I've never seen anything like this before. No heat signatures, no sound, just some faint electromagnetic static. No wonder our satellites missed them."

"How fast?"

"Mach 4 and still accelerating. All three targets heading west. Better contact NORAD, Captain. At this speed, they'll be off my screen any minute."

North American Aerospace Defense Command
NORAD
Colorado

The 9,565-foot towering mound of jagged granite known as Cheyenne Mountain is located four miles southwest of Colorado Springs. Two heavily guarded access tunnels at its base run a third of a mile below the surface, serving as the sole entrances into the four-and-a-half-acre subterranean compound known as the North American Aerospace Defense Command, or NORAD.

NORAD provides the military with a unified command center linking every branch of the armed forces, Combined Intelligence Centers, systems, and weather stations. The facility's primary function, however, is to detect missile launches anywhere in the world, be it land, sea, or in the air. Such events fall into two basic categories.

Strategic warnings are issued when an ICBM is launched against North America, an event originating from a distance exceeding 2,100 nautical miles, carrying an impact time of approximately thirty minutes. A four-minute chain-of-command sequence quickly disseminates information to the president and all US Defense Command Centers.

Theater warnings involve missiles fired upon US and Allied Forces in the field. Because a Scud or Cruise missile can strike within minutes, NORAD relays warnings directly to field commanders via satellite.

Cheyenne Mountain's most important early-warning missile-detection system originates 22,300 miles in space. It is here that NORAD's Defense Support Program (DSP) satellites circle Earth in a geostationary orbit, providing continuous, overlapping coverage of the entire planet. Aboard these two-and-a-half-ton satellites are high-tech infrared sensors that instantly detect heat signatures created during a missile's booster stage.

Major Joseph Unsinn salutes the MPs stationed at the glass vault door, then climbs into an awaiting tram. After a brief ride through a maze of tunnels, he arrives at NORAD's command center to begin his twelve-hour shift.

The NORAD commander is no stranger to missile launches, each year witnessing no less than two hundred such "events." But this is different. With the world on the brink of war, tensions are running high, thousands, perhaps millions of lives hanging in the balance.

His counterpart, Major Brian Sedio, is busy studying the Defense Support Program satellite monitor, the image of Vice President Chaney's face plastered across the video-comm mounted above his console.

"What's going on?"

Sedio looks up. "You're just in time. The VP's flipping out." The major turns off the muting switch. "I'm sorry, Mr. Vice President. DSP's designed to detect heat signatures, not electromagnetic interference. If these alien objects of yours continue across the Pacific into Asia, there's a chance we could pick them up using our land-based radar, but as far as our satellites are concerned, they're invisible."

The intensity of Chaney's eyes is alarming. "Find them, Major. Coordinate whatever search you have to. I want to be informed the moment you get a fix on their locations."

The screen goes blank.

Major Sedio shakes his head. "Would you believe this shit? The world's on the brink of war, and Chaney thinks we're being attacked by aliens."

DECEMBER 14, 2012
ROCK FOREST OF SHILIN
YUNNAN PROVINCE, SOUTHERN CHINA

5:45 A.M. (BEIJING TIME)

The province of Yunnan, together with Guizhou, makes up the southwest region of the People's Republic of China. With an abundance of lakes, staggering mountains, and rich foliage, few areas in all of China provide visitors with such a wide variety of landscape to explore.

The most populated city in the province is Kunming, the capital of Yunnan. Located seventy miles southeast of the city is its most important tourist attraction: the Stone Forest of Lunan, also known as the Rock Forest of Shilin. Covering an expanse of over one hundred square miles, the Rock Forest is a myriad of bizarre, mountainous needles of limestone soaring to heights of nearly one hundred feet. Walkways lead visitors through the ranks of pinnacles, the wooden bridges crossing streams and boring through natural rock archways that proliferate on this torturous landscape.

The factors leading to the Rock Forest began some 280 million years ago, when the rise of the Himalayas caused erosion that carved jagged spiral formations out of the limestone plateau. Further upheavals over eons created deep fissures within the karst, which eventually became enlarged by the rainwater, forming towering shards of grayish white, dagger-shaped rocks.

*   *   *

It is not quite dawn when fifty-two-year-old Janet Parker and her personal tour guide, Quik-sing, arrive at the front gate of the public park. Having ignored a US State Department travel advisory warning regarding China, the brash businesswoman from Florida has insisted on visiting the Rock Forest prior to embarking on her late-morning flight out of Kunming.

She follows her guide past a pagoda and onto a wooden platform that winds through the jagged formations of limestone. "Hold it, Quik-sing. Are you telling me this is it? This is what we drove an hour to see?"

"Wo ting budong—"

"English, Quik-sing, English."

"I do not understand, Miss Janet. This is the Stone Forest. What were you expecting?"

"Obviously something a little more spectacular. All I can see are miles of rock." A glimmer of brilliant amber light catches her eye. "Wait, what's that?" She points to the source, the golden beacon flashing between several limestone shafts.

Quik-sing shields his eyes, startled by the light. "I—I do not know. Miss Janet, please, what are you doing?"

Janet climbs over the rail. "I want to see what that thing is."

"Miss Janet—Miss Janet!"

"Relax, I'll be back in a second." Camera in hand, she climbs down to the ground, then squeezes between the base of two formations, cursing as she scrapes her ankle on the sharp rock. Maneuvering around the pinnacle, she looks up, seeing the source of the bright light.

"Now what in the hell is that?"

The black, insectlike object is easily forty feet long, its massive wings wedged between two towering spires of limestone. The inanimate beast is perched on a pair of red-hot talons, which appear to have punctured the karst, causing it to sizzle.

"Quik-sing, get over here." Janet snaps another photo as the first rays of sunlight strike the creature's wings. The amber beacon darkens as it flashes faster and faster. "Hey, Quik-sing, what the hell am I paying you for?"

The silent explosion of brilliant white light instantly blinds the businesswoman, the ignition of the pure-fusion device generating a cauldron of energy hotter than the surface of the Sun. Janet Parker registers a brief, bizarre burning sensation as her skin, fat, and blood broil away from the bone, her skeleton vaporizing a nanosecond later, as the searing-hot fireball races outward in all directions at the speed of light.

The combustion spreads quickly throughout the Stone Forest, the heat vaporizing the karst, releasing a dense, toxic cloud of carbon dioxide. Compressed beneath a ceiling of arctic air, the poisonous vapors hug the ground, rippling outward like a gaseous tsunami.

Most of the population of Kunming is still asleep when the noxious, invisible gas cloud rolls through the city like a hot gust on a summer's day. The early risers drop to their knees, clutching their throats as the world spins around them. Those still in bed barely register a twitch as they suffocate in their sleep.

Within minutes, every man, woman, child, and any other air-breathing creatures in Kunming are dead.

Town of Lensk
Republic of Sakha, Russia

5:47 A.M.

Seventeen-year-old Pavel Pshenichny takes the ax from his younger brother, Nikolai, and steps out of the three-bedroom log cabin into a foot of freshly fallen snow. An icy morning wind howls in his ears, blistering his face. He adjusts his scarf, then trudges across the frozen yard to the wood pile.

The Sun is not yet up, but then who but a local could really tell in this desolate, gray region of permafrost. Pavel clears snow off the surface of a frozen tree stump, grabs a log from the woodpile, then positions it upright. With a groan, he swings the ax, the blade splitting the half-frozen block of wood into kindling.

As he reaches for another log, a brilliant flash of light causes him to look up.

Looming across the dimly lit, northern horizon of Lensk is a vast, snow-covered mountain range concealed behind the gray cloud cover of dawn. As Pavel watches, a bolt of white-hot lightning seems to ignite behind the clouds, the flash spreading out along the jagged peaks, which quickly disappear behind a growing layer of fog.

Seconds later—a thunderous roar, as the ground shakes beneath his feet. *Avalanche?*

The dense fog prevents Pavel from seeing the geological devastation taking place before his eyes. What the teenager can see is a rolling, grayish white cloud of snow expanding outward, the wave of energy racing toward him at unfathomable speed.

He drops the ax and runs. "Nikolai! Avalanche—avalanche!"

The nuclear blast wave lifts Pavel off his feet, driving him headfirst through the cabin door behind the wind speed of a force-five tornado. Before he can register the pain, the entire structure is blown off its foundation like a house of cards—the searing-hot gust of debris sweeping across the plain, consuming everything in its path.

10:56 P.M.

The black, dust-covered Chevy pickup with the missing rear fender cuts through the dense jungle, its worn shock absorbers squealing in protest as it bounces along the uneven dirt road. Approaching the chained gate, the truck skids to a stop.

Michael Gabriel jumps out from the driver's side.

He examines the steel chain, then begins working the rusted padlock, using the truck's headlights to see.

Dominique slides over to the driver's seat as Mick pop opens the lock and removes the chain. Grinding the truck into gear, she drives forward through the open gate, then returns to the passenger side as he climbs back inside.

"That was impressive. Where'd you learn to pick locks?"

"Solitary confinement. Of course, it always helps if you have the key."

"Where'd you get a key?"

"I have friends who work in the park's maintenance department. Kind of pathetic that the only work available to local Mayans is serving food or hauling trash in the city founded by their own ancestors."

Dominique grabs the dashboard as Mick accelerates the truck down the bumpy back road. "You sure you know where you're going?"

"I spent most of my childhood exploring Chichén Itzá. I know this jungle like the back of my hand."

The high beams reveal a dead end looming up ahead.

He smiles. "Of course, that was a long time ago."

"Mick!" Dominique squeezes her eyes shut and hangs on as he veers off the road and drives straight through the jungle, sending the pickup slashing through heavy underbrush and foliage.

"Slow down! Are you trying to kill us?"

The vehicle swerves in and out of the dense thicket, somehow managing to avoid trees and rocks. They enter a heavily wooded area, the jungle canopy concealing the night sky.

Mick slams on the brakes. "End of the road."

"You call that a road?"

He shuts off the engine.

"Mick, tell me again why—"

"*Shh*. Listen."

The only sound she hears is the ticking of the truck's engine. "What am I listening for?"

"Be patient."

281

Gradually, the chirping of crickets comes to life around them, followed in turn by the rest of the jungle wildlife.

Dominique looks at Mick. His eyes are closed, a melancholy expression spreading across his angular face. "Are you okay?"

"Yes."

"What are you thinking about?"

"My childhood."

"A happy or sad memory?"

"One of the few happy ones. My mother used to take me on camping trips in these woods when I was very young. She taught me a lot about nature and the Yucatán, how the peninsula formed, its geology—all sorts of things. She was a great teacher. No matter what we did together, she always made it fun."

Mick turns to her, his black pupils wide and glistening. "Did you know this entire area used to be underwater? Millions of years ago, the Yucatán Peninsula was at the bottom of a tropical sea, its surface covered with coral and plants and marine sediment. The geology of the seafloor was essentially one huge layer of solid limestone, and *then*—boom—this spaceship or whatever the hell it was, crash-landed on Earth. The impact fractured the limestone, creating two-thousand-foot tidal waves, firestorms, and an atmospheric layer of dust that stifled photosynthesis and wiped out most of the species on the planet.

"Eventually the Yucatán Peninsula rose, becoming dry land. Rainwater ate through the cracks in the limestone, eroding the rock, carving out a vast subterranean labyrinth that stretches beneath the peninsula. My mother used to say that, below the surface, the Yucatán looks like a giant piece of Swiss cheese."

He leans back in the seat, staring at the dashboard. "During the last ice age, water levels dropped, and the cave systems were no longer flooded. This allowed tremendous stalactites, stalagmites, and other calcium carbonate formations to form within the karst."

"Karst?"

"Karst is the scientific name for a porous, limestone geology. The Yucatán is all karst. Anyway, about fourteen thousand years ago, the ice melted and the sea rose, reflooding the caves. There are no surface rivers in the Yucatán. All the peninsula's water supplies originate from the subterranean caverns. The inland wells are freshwater, but as you near the coast, they become more salty. Sometimes the ceiling of a cave would collapse, forming a giant sinkhole—"

"Like the sacred *dzonot*?"

Mick smiles. "You used the Mayan word for cenote, I was wondering if you even knew it."

"My grandmother was Mayan. She told me the *dzonots* were believed to be portals into the Underworld—into *Xibalba*. Mick, you and your mother—the two of you were very close, weren't you?"

"Until recently, she was my only friend."

Dominique swallows the lump in her throat. "When we were in the Gulf, you started to tell me something about how she died. You seemed angry at your father."

A look of uncertainty crosses his face. "We really should get going—"

"No, wait—tell me what happened. Maybe I can help. If you can't trust me, whom can you trust?"

He leans forward, his forearms on the wheel as he gazes out the bug-encrusted windshield. "I was twelve. We were living in this two-room shack just outside Nazca. My mother was dying, the cancer having spread beyond her pancreas. She couldn't handle any more radiation or chemotherapy, and she was too weak to care for herself. Julius couldn't afford a nurse, so he left me in charge while he continued his work in the desert. Mom's organs were failing. She'd lie in bed, curled in a ball against the abdominal pain, while I'd brush her hair and read to her. She had long, dark hair, just like you. In the end, I couldn't even brush it, it was just coming out in clumps."

A single tear rolls down his cheek. "Her mind stayed sharp though, even up to the very end. She was always strongest in the morning, able to carry on conversations, but by late afternoon, she'd become weak and incoherent, the morphine knocking the fight right out of her. One evening Julius came home, exhausted after having spent three straight days in the desert. Mom had had a bad day. She was fighting a high fever and was in a lot of pain, and I was wiped out from having cared for her over the past seventy-two hours. Julius sat on the edge of her bed and just stared at her. Finally, I said good night and shut the adjoining door to their bedroom to get some sleep.

"I must have passed out the moment my head hit the pillow. I don't know how long I'd been asleep, but something woke me in the middle of the night, sort of a muffled cry. I got out of bed and opened the door."

Mick closes his eyes, the tears flowing steadily now.

"What was it?" Dominique whispers. "What did you see?"

"The cries were coming from my mother. Julius was standing over her, suffocating her with his pillow."

"Oh, God . . ."

"I just stood there, still half-asleep, not realizing what was happening. After a minute or so, Mom stopped moving. That's when Julius noticed the open door. He turned and looked at me with this horrible expression on his face. He dragged me into my room, sobbing and babbling about how Mom had been in so much pain, how he couldn't stand to see her suffer any longer."

Mick rocks back and forth, staring out the windshield.

"Your nightmares?"

He nods, then balls his fists, slamming them down hard upon the weather-beaten dashboard. "Who the fuck was *he* to make that decision? I was the one who was caring for her—I was the one who was taking care of her—not him!"

She winces as he pummels the dashboard over and over, spending his pent-up fury.

Emotionally exhausted, he lays his head to rest on the steering wheel. "He never even asked me, Dominique. He never even gave me the chance to say good-bye."

Dominique pulls him to her, stroking his hair as he cries, pulling his face against her breast. Tears roll down her own face as she thinks about how he has suffered, deprived of a normal childhood from birth, his entire adulthood marred by years spent in solitary confinement.

How can I possibly take him back to another asylum?

He quiets down after several minutes, pushing away from her, wiping his eyes. "Guess I still have a few family issues to sort out."

"You've had a rough life, but things are going to get better now."

Mick sniffs, choking back a smile. "You think so, huh?"

She leans over and kisses him, lightly at first, then she pulls him closer, and their lips melt into each other's, their tongues embracing, heightening their passion. Aroused, they tear at each other's clothing, fondling each other in the darkness, struggling against the tight confines of the cab, the steering wheel and gearshift severely limiting their lovemaking.

"Mick . . . wait. I can't do this in here—there's no room." She lays her head on his shoulder, panting as beads of sweat roll down her face. "Next time you borrow a car, get something with a backseat."

"Promise." He kisses her forehead.

She plays with the curls of hair along his neck. "We better go or we'll be late meeting your friends."

They exit the truck. Mick climbs into the back of the pickup and unhooks the scuba tanks from the storage racks. He hands Dominique a buoyancy-control vest with an air tank and regulator already attached. "Have you ever done any night diving?"

"About two years ago. How long a walk is it to the cenote?"

"A good mile. You'll probably be more comfortable wearing your tank."

She puts on the vest and tank, then takes the neoprene wet suits from him as he climbs down. Mick secures his own BCD vest, then tosses the equipment bag over his shoulder and picks up the two spare tanks of air. "Follow me."

He tramples forward into the thicket, Dominique trudging in after him. Within minutes, swarms of mosquitoes are buzzing past their ears, feeding off their sweat. Following the remains of an overgrown footpath, they push their way through the dense jungle foliage while insects and thorns tear at their skin. The vegetation eventually yields to a heavily wooded area, the marshy soil becoming more rocky. They struggle up a five-foot rise, and suddenly the stars reappear above their heads.

They are standing on a fifteen-foot-wide compressed-stone pathway, an ancient *sacbe* constructed a thousand years ago by the Maya.

Mick lowers the air tanks, rubbing his aching shoulders. "To the left is the sacred cenote, to the right the Kukulcán pyramid. You okay?"

"I feel like a pack mule. How much farther?"

"Two hundred yards. Come on."

They continue to the left, arriving five minutes later at the rim of the immense limestone pit, its silent, dark waters reflecting the lunar light.

Dominique looks down, estimating the drop to be a good fifty feet. Her heart races. *Why the hell am I doing this?* She turns as five dark-skinned Mayan elders emerge from the woods.

"These are friends," Mick says. "*H'Menes*, Mayan wise men. They are descendants of the *Sh'Tol* brethren, a sacred society that escaped the wrath of the Spaniards over five centuries ago. They're here to help us."

As he climbs into his wet suit, Mick speaks to a white-haired Mayan in an ancient tongue. The other elders remove a length of rope and several underwater flashlights from the equipment bag.

Dominique turns her back to the group and slips out of her sweatshirt, quickly pulling the tight wet suit over her one-piece bathing suit.

Mick calls her over, a concerned look on his face. "Dom, this is Ocelo, a Mayan priest. Ocelo says a man has been seen in Chichén Itzá, asking questions about our whereabouts. He describes the stranger as an American, with red hair and a muscular build."

"Raymond? Oh, shit—"

"Dom, tell me the truth. Did you—"

"Mick, I swear, I haven't contacted Foletta or Borgia or anyone else since I've been here."

"Ocelo's brother is a security guard. He says the redhead entered the park just before closing but no one remembers seeing him leave. That deal you signed with Borgia. It was all bullshit. You'll get your immunity after I'm found dead. Come on, we'd better get moving."

They open the valves of their air tanks, verifying their regulators are working. Hoisting the BCD vest onto their shoulders, they approach the edge of the cenote.

Mick slips his fins onto his feet, then loops the rope around his arms and eases himself over the edge of the pit. The Mayans lower him quickly into the stagnant, cold water, then retrieve the rope for Dominique.

Mick positions his face mask and regulator, then turns his flashlight on and ducks his head underwater. Visibility in the chocolate brown, foul-smelling murk is less than two feet.

Dominique feels her limbs quivering as she dangles above the cenote's dark surface. *Why are you doing this? Are you insane?* She cringes as her feet enter the chilly, algae-infested cesspool. Releasing the rope, she falls in, gagging at the putrid smell. She quickly adjusts her mask, then shoves the regulator into her mouth and breathes, cutting off the stench.

Mick surfaces, slimy strands of vegetation hanging from his hair. He attaches a length of yellow cord from his waist to hers. "It's pretty dark down there. I don't want us getting separated."

She nods, removing her regulator. "What exactly are we looking for again?"

"Some type of portal along the southern face. Something that will allow us access into the pyramid."

"But the pyramid's a mile away. Mick?" She watches him deflate his BCD vest and submerge. *Damn it.* She returns the regulator to her mouth, takes a last look up at the moon, then follows him down.

Dominique begins hyperventilating into her regulator the moment her face hits the turbid water. She swims blindly for several seconds, her sense of direction failing her until she feels Mick's tug. She descends another twenty feet, kicks hard, then sees the reflection of his light along the cenote's wall.

Mick is searching the limestone facing, the geology of which is matted in thick vegetation. Using his light, he signals her to spread out along the wall to his right and poke and prod the dense growth with her dive knife.

Dominique removes the knife from her ankle sheath and taps the rock as she descends feetfirst along the limestone wall. Thirty feet down, her hand slips into a three-foot hole, her watch becoming entangled within the thick vegetation. Unable to gain enough leverage to free herself, she braces her fins against the wall to pull free.

A six-foot water moccasin lunges outward, snapping at her face mask with lightning speed before shooting past her into the murk.

It is all her wracked nerves can handle. Panicking, she races topside, dragging Mick with her.

As her head breaks the surface, she rips the mask from her face, gagging and choking.

"Are you okay? What happened?"

"You didn't say anything about any goddam snakes! I hate snakes—"

"Were you bitten?"

"No, but I'm through. This isn't diving, it's more like swimming in liquid shit." She unties the rope, her hands still shaking.

"Dom—"

"No, Mick, I've had it. My nerves are shot, and this water's making my skin itch. Go on without me. Go find your secret passage, or whatever the hell you're looking for. I'll met you up top."

Mick gives her a worried look, then submerges.

"Hey, Ocelo! Toss down the rope." Looking up, she waits impatiently for the elders to appear along the edge of the pit.

Nothing.

"Hey, are you guys listening? I said toss down the goddam rope!"

"Evening, Sunshine." A chill shoots down her spine as Raymond moves into view, the luminescent red dot of his hunting rifle's laser rangefinder appearing at the base of her throat.

White House
Washington, DC

President Maller feels as if someone has punched him in the stomach. He looks up from the DoD report at General Fecondo and Admiral Gordon, his pounding pulse causing his temples to throb. He is so weak that his body no longer has the strength to support himself upright in his chair.

Pierre Borgia bursts into the Oval Office, his red-rimmed eye blazing with hatred. "We just received an updated report. Twenty-one thousand dead in Sakha. Two million perished in Kunming. An entire city was wiped out in Turkmenistan. The press is already gathering downstairs."

"The Russians and Chinese have wasted no time mobilizing their forces," General Fecondo says. "The official response is that this is all part of their scheduled war games, but the numbers are far greater than what had been planned."

The Chief of Naval Operations reads from his laptop. "Our latest satellite reconnaissance is tracking eighty-three nuclear subs, including all of the new Russian Borey-class. Each of these vessels carries eighteen SS-N-20 SLBMs. Add to that list another dozen Chinese ballistic-missile submarines and—."

"It's not just submarines," interrupts the general. "Both nations have placed their strategic forces into states of readiness. *Darkstar* reconnaissance is tracking the missile cruiser *Peter the Great*, which left its dock twenty minutes after the last detonation. We're looking at a combined land and sea arsenal with a first-strike capability exceeding two thousand nuclear warheads."

"Christ." Maller takes a deep breath, fighting the tightness in his chest. "Pierre, how much longer until the Security Council conference call?"

"Ten minutes, but the Secretary-General says that Grozny is addressing Parliament and refuses to participate if we're on the line." Borgia's face is covered in perspiration. "Sir, we really need to move this operation to Mount Weather."

Maller ignores him. He turns to face a video-comm link labeled STRAT-COM. "General Doroshow, how will our new Missile Defense Shield affect a first-strike of this magnitude?"

The pale face of US Air Force General Eric Doroshow, commander in chief of Strategic Air Command, appears on the monitor. "Sir, the shield is capable of taking out a few dozen missiles at their apex, but nothing in our defense arsenal is designed to cope with an all-out assault. Most of the Russian ICBMs and SLBMs have been programmed to cruise at low altitudes. The technology to eliminate that threat just wasn't feasible—"

Maller shakes his head in disgust. "Twenty goddam billion dollars—and for what?"

Pierre Borgia looks to General Fecondo, who nods. "Mr. President, there may be another option. If we're certain Grozny will strike first, then there are definite benefits to beating him to the punch. Our latest Single Integrated Operational Plan, SIOP-112, indicates that a preemptive strike of eighteen hundred warheads would effectively disarm ninety-one percent of all Russian and Chinese land-based ICBM sites and—"

"No! I will not go down in history as the American president who initiated World War III."

"The preemptive strike would be justifiable," General Doroshow explains.

"I can't justify killing two billion human beings, General. We'll stick to the diplomatic and defensive objectives we've outlined." The president sits on the edge of his desk, rubbing his temples. "Where's the vice president?"

"Last I heard, sir, he was en route to the *Boone.*"

"Maybe we ought to send a chopper out there and fly him to a FEMA site," states General Fecondo.

"No." Borgia answers, a bit too quickly. "No, the vice president never participated in a dry run—"

"He's still a member of the Executive Branch."

"Doesn't matter. Chaney was never officially added to the survivors' list. Mount Weather only has so much room—"

"Enough!" the President yells.

Dick Pryzstas enters. "Sorry I'm late, the beltway's a zoo. Have you seen what's going on out there?" He turns on CNN.

The images show terrified Americans, frantically stuffing their belongings into overloaded cars. A microphone is thrust into the face of a father of three. "I don't know what the hell's going on. Russia says we're detonating these bombs, the president says we're not. I don't know who to believe, but I don't trust Maller or Grozny. We're leaving the city tonight—"

A close-up of protesters outside the White House, carrying signs with messages of the Apocalypse. VICTOR GROZNY IS THE ANTICHRIST. REPENT NOW! THE RAPTURE IS UPON US!

Scenes of looting in a Bethesda shopping mall. Aerial shots of the interstate, the cars lined bumper to bumper. A truck flipping over as it attempts to bypass traffic by driving down a steep shoulder. Family members in the back of a pickup, toting guns.

"Mr. President, the Security Council call is ready. VC-2."

Maller moves to the far wall where five secured video-communicators are mounted. The second unit from the left powers on, the screen split into twenty squares, the images of the heads of government of the members of the United Nations Security Council appearing in each block. The Russian space is blank.

"Mr. Secretary-General, Council members, I want to emphasize again that the United States is not responsible for these pure-fusion detonations. However, we now have reason to believe that Iran may be targeting Israel in an attempt to draw our country into a direct conflict with Russia. Let me reiterate again that we want to avoid war at all costs. So there are no misunderstandings, we have ordered our fleet to leave the Gulf of Oman. Please inform President Grozny that the United States will not launch any missiles at the Russian Federation or her allies, but we will not shirk our responsibilities in defending the State of Israel."

"The Council will convey your message. God help you, Mr. President."

"God help us all, Mr. Secretary-General."

Maller turns to Borgia. "Where's my family?"

"Already en route to Mount Weather."

"All right, we're moving out. General Fecondo?"

"Yes, sir?"

"Take us to DEFCON-1."

Chichén Itzá

Mick descends headfirst along the southern face of the cenote, feeling his way along the entanglement of vegetation for anything out of the ordinary. At thirty feet, the angle of the wall suddenly changes, slicing inward at forty-five degrees.

He continues moving deeper through the Mayan well, the darkness closing in tighter around his diminishing beam of light. At ninety feet he pauses to equalize, the pressure in his ears becomes painful.

One hundred and five feet . . .

The southern face levels out, returning to its sheer vertical drop. Mick continues descending through the pitch-black shaft, knowing full well he is not physically equipped to dive much deeper.

And then he sees it—a speck of light glowing like a crimson EXIT sign in a darkened theater.

He kicks harder, then levels out, his pulse throbbing in his neck as he stares incredulously at the immense ten-foot-high-by-twenty-foot-wide portal, the beacon from his flashlight reflecting off the smooth, shimmering white metallic surface.

Engraved at the center of the barrier is a luminescent red, three-pronged candelabra. Mick moans into his regulator, instantly recognizing the ancient marker.

It is the Trident of Paracas.

Bluemont, Virginia

The helicopter transport carrying the first lady, her three young sons, and the three senior congressmen soars west over the town of Bluemont and Virginia Route 601. In the distance, the pilot can see the lights from a dozen buildings located within the fenced-in compound.

This is Mount Weather, a top-secret military base located forty-six miles outside Washington, DC. The facility, managed by the Federal Emergency Management Agency (FEMA) is the operational headquarters linked to a network of more than one hundred underground Federal Relocation Centers housing America's covert "Continuity of Government" program.

Although the eighty-five-acre compound is heavily guarded, the real secret of Mount Weather is located below ground. Deep within the granite mountain is an underground city, equipped with private apartments and dormitories, cafeterias and hospitals, a water-purification and sewage plant, a power plant, a mass-transit system, a television communication system, and even an underground pond. While no member of Congress has ever willingly claimed knowledge of the facility, many senior House representatives are in fact tenured members of this subterranean capital's "government-in-waiting." Nine federal departments have been replicated within the facility, as well as five federal agencies. Secretly appointed cabinet-level officials serve indefinite terms, without the consent of Congress and far from the public eye. Although not as large as the Russian complex in Yamantou Mountain, the crisis-management facility serves the same purpose—to survive and govern what's left of the United States following an all-out nuclear assault.

Air Force Captain Mark Davis has been flying dry runs to and from the Mount Weather facility for twelve years. Although the National Emergency Airborne Command Post pilot and father of four earns a good living, he has never been happy with the fact that he and his family have been excluded from the "list."

Davis sees the facility's lights appear in the distance. He grits his teeth.

More than 240 military personnel work within the facility. Are their lives more important than his? And what about the sixty-five members of the "Executive Elite"? If a nuclear war did break out, blame could easily be directed at many of these military "experts." Why should these bastards survive and not his family?

In the end, it had been easy for the Russian agent to coerce the disgruntled captain. Money was the key to surviving a nuclear war. Davis has used most of the funds to construct his own bunker in the Blue Ridge Mountains, the rest having been converted to gold and gems. If nuclear war ever did break out, he felt confident his family would survive. If not, then the kids' college funds were now more secure than ever.

Davis hovers the chopper above the helo-pad and touches down. Two MPs in a tram approach. He salutes. "Seven passengers and their gear. All of the bags have been checked." Without waiting for a reply, Davis opens the cargo door and helps the first lady out.

The MPs direct the passengers to the tram while the pilot unloads their bags. The nondescript brown suede suitcase is the third to go. Davis twists the handle clockwise as the Russian agent had instructed, then turns it back slowly.

The mechanism activates.

The pilot places the suitcase carefully in the cart, then hustles to load the remaining bags.

Chichén Itzá
Yucatán Peninsula

Mick forces himself to slow his ascent, barely able to contain his excitement. He pauses at twenty feet to expel nitrogen, his thoughts racing wildly in his head.

How do I get inside? There must be some kind of hidden mechanism designed to trigger the door. He checks his air gauge again. *Fifteen minutes. Grab a fresh tank, then hurry back down.*

Mick continues his ascent, surprised to find Dominique's legs dangling below the surface. He glides upward along her body, then pops his head out of the water. "Dom, what are you—" Her frightened expression causes him to look up.

Fifty feet above the surface of the sinkhole sits the redhead, the Miami asylum's head of security smiling down at him from the edge of the pit. The red laser dot jumps from Dominique's neckline to Mick's.

"There's my bitch. How dare you keep my woman waiting so long."

Mick moves closer to Dominique, groping underwater for the end of her BCD hose. "Let her go, asshole. Let her go and I won't put up a fight. You can bring me back to the States in chains. You'll be a real hero—"

"Not this time, motherfucker. Foletta's decided on a new approach to your therapy. It's called death."

Mick locates the BCD hose and quickly deflates the air from Dominique's vest. "What's Foletta paying you?" He positions himself in front of her, the laser dot appearing on his wet suit. "There's money in my truck, hidden beneath the seat. You can have it all. There must be a good ten thousand in gold coins there."

Raymond looks up from the gunsight. "You're lying—"

Mick grabs Dominique and lunges sideways, dragging her underwater. She thrashes about, fighting him as she inhales a mouthful of muck.

A stream of bullets shoots past them as Mick shoves his regulator into her mouth and pulls her deeper. Dominique gags, exhales water, then manages to draw a breath. She shoves her flooded mask over her face and quickly clears it, then locates her own regulator.

Mick purges, then sucks in a lungful of air. He grabs Dominique's hand and descends blindly as a bullet glances off his air tank.

Dominique's heart is pounding a mile a minute. Hovering in fifty feet of water, she flicks on her flashlight, nearly dropping it, as Mick replaces his face mask and clears it. She stares at him, terrified, unsure of what will happen next.

Mick reties the end of his rope around her waist, then points below.

She shakes her head no.

Another flurry of bullets ends the debate.

He takes her wrist and descends, dragging her down with him.

Waves of panic ripple through her insides as she plunges headfirst into darkness. The silent oblivion closes in upon her, the ache in her ears telling her she is going too deep. *What's he doing? Untie the rope before you die.* She struggles to undo the knot.

Mick reaches up and stops her. He takes her hand, patting it, trying to reassure her, then descends again.

She pinches her nose and equalizes, the pressure in her ears easing as she follows him down. The angled wall becomes a ceiling over her head, the mounting claustrophobia almost unbearable. She feels herself losing all orientation, the darkness and silence suffocating.

Now she is plunging straight down the face of a vertical shaft. Her depth gauge drops below 110 feet, her pulse pounding in her face mask, her mind screaming at her to break free.

The appearance of the luminous crimson light startles her. Descending farther, she blinks hard and levels out, staring at the glowing icon. *My God . . . he actually found something! Wait a moment, I've seen this figure before . . .*

She watches as Mick maneuvers around the shiny white facing, feeling his way along the outer edges of the metallic sheath.

I know . . . I saw it in Julius Gabriel's journal—

Dominique's heart flutters as a deep rumbling sound fills her ears. Gargantuan air bubbles burst out from the center of the facing and envelop Mick, then a monstrous torrent grabs her, sucking her toward the center of the portal and the blackness of a void that had not been there a moment earlier.

The current inhales her feetfirst into darkness. She twists sideways, caught in the turbulence of an underground river, the force of which pushes her face mask down around her neck, blinding her. She inhales water, then pinches her nose and retches into her regulator as she rolls wildly in the suffocating pitch, fighting to draw a breath.

The portal closes behind them, stifling the stream.

She stops rolling. Repositioning her mask, she clear it, then stares, transfixed by her new surroundings.

They have entered a vast underwater cavern of unearthly beauty. Surreal strobe lights of unknown origin illuminate cathedral-like limestone walls in intoxicating shades of blue and green and yellow. Fantastic formations of stalactites hang from the submerged ceiling, dwarfing them like gigantic icicles, their points descending to entwine around a petrified forest of crystal-like stalagmites, rising out from the silty floor of the underwater cave.

She looks at Mick, excited, astounded, wishing she could blurt out a thousand questions. He shakes his head and points to his gauge, indicating he has only five minutes of air remaining. Dominique checks her own supply—shocked to learn she is down to her last fifteen minutes.

Anxiety courses through her body. The claustrophobic realization of being trapped within a subterranean chamber, a rocky ceiling above her head, overwhelms her ability to reason. She pushes Mick away and swims back toward the portal, desperately attempting to reopen it.

Mick drags her back by the towrope. He grabs her wrists, then points to the south, where the entrance to a twisting cavern looms ahead. He forms a triangle shape with his two hands.

The Kukulcán. Dominique slows her breathing.

Mick takes her hand and starts swimming. Together, they move through a succession of vast underwater rooms, their presence seeming to activate additional strobe lights, as if the beacons are linked to an unseen motion detector. Above their heads, the domed-shaped ceiling has grown rows of needlelike teeth, the limestone formations creating majestic, archlike partitions and bizarre, jagged sculptures of rock.

Mick feels a tightness growing in his chest as they move from an indigo blue vault into one of luminescent azure. He checks his air tank, then turns to Dominique, his hand motioning to his throat.

He's out of air. She passes him the second-stage spare regulator attached to her BCD vest, then checks her own supply.

Eight minutes.

Eight minutes! Four minutes each. This is insane! Why did I follow him into the cenote? I should have stayed in the truck—I should have stayed in Miami. I'm going to drown, just like Iz.

The bottom suddenly drops, the cave opening to a boundless, subterranean domain. The limestone cathedral walls and ceiling glow in a luminescent pink flesh tone, the underwater cavern as large as an indoor basketball arena.

You won't drown, you'll just suffocate. That has to be better than what poor Iz went through. You'll lose consciousness, you'll just black out. Do you really believe in heaven?

Mick tugs her, motioning ahead excitedly. She swims faster, praying he's found an exit.

Then she sees it.

Oh, no . . . Oh God . . . Oh my fucking God . . .

Bluemont, Virginia

The president's helicopter is eighteen miles north of Leesburg, Virgina, when the twelve-kiloton bomb explodes.

The president and his entourage cannot see the intense flash of light, a thousand times brighter than lightning. They cannot feel the monstrous pulse of heat radiation, which races through Mount Weather's subterranean complex, vaporizing the first lady, her children, and the rest of the inhabitants and superstructures within. Nor do they experience the crushing embrace as millions of tons of granite and steel and concrete collapse the mountain like a house of cards.

What they do see is a bright, orange fireball that turns the night into day. What they do feel is the shock wave as the blast roars past them like thunder and the firestorm sets the Virginia woods ablaze like a burning carpet.

The pilot whips the helicopter around and races away as President Maller wails in agony, the emptiness ripping at his wounded heart, the anger raging through his mind, tearing at the fabric of his sanity.

Chichén Itzá
114 feet beneath the base of
the Kukulcán Pyramid

Wide-eyed, her blood pounding furiously, Dominique stares in disbelief at the prodigious structure looming above her head. Embedded within the cavernous limestone ceiling, protruding from the rock, is the keel of a mammoth, seven-hundred-foot-long alien spacecraft.

She sucks in a slow breath of air, trying not to hyperventilate, her skin literally crawling beneath her wet suit. *This isn't real. It can't be. . . .*

The metallic gold skin of the sleek, battleship-sized hull shimmers at them like a highly polished mirror.

Mick clutches her hand and ascends, pulling her toward two colossal assemblies mounted along either side of what appears to be the vessel's tail section. Each structure is as large and as high as a three-story building. Swimming closer, they peer inside one of the alien engines, their flashlights revealing a wasp's nest of charred, afterburner-shaped housings, each orifice no less than thirty feet in diameter.

Mick tows her past the monstrous engine mounts and swims toward the bow of the geologically camouflaged vessel.

Dominique sucks harder at the regulator, alarmed at her inability to draw a breath. *Oh, God, we're out of air!* She tugs at Mick's arm, clutching her throat, as the cavern begins spinning out of control.

Mick sees Dominique's face turn bright red. He feels his own chest constricting, his lungs aching as she grabs for him.

Avoiding her grasp, he spits out her spare regulator, returning his own to his mouth. Then he turns and swims as hard as he can, dragging her by the towrope as he searches the hull for some kind of entry.

Dominique thrashes about, petrified, as she suffocates within her fogging mask.

Mick's arms and legs feel like lead. He wheezes into his regulator, unable to draw a breath, his lungs on fire. He registers the girl panicking at the end of the rope, his heart aching, his mind fighting to focus.

In his delirium he sees it: a crimson beacon, glowing fifty yards ahead. With renewed vigor he strokes and kicks, his muscles burning, moving in slow motion.

He registers the deadweight on the end of the rope—Dominique no longer struggling.

Don't stop . . .

The subterranean world is spinning out of control. He bites down on the regulator until his gums bleed, sucking in the warm liquid as the glowing icon of the Trident of Paracas comes into view.

Another dozen strokes . . .

His arms are lead. He stops moving. The ebony eyes roll upward.

Michael Gabriel blacks out.

The bodies of the two unconscious divers drift toward the glowing, ten-foot-wide iridium panel, triggering an ancient motion detector.

With a hydraulic *hiss,* the outer hull's portal door slides open. A current of water rushes into the pressurized compartment, sucking the two humans into the alien vessel.

JOURNAL OF JULIUS GABRIEL

*W*hat a pitiful creature is man; born with an acute aware-
ness of his own mortality—he is thus condemned to live
out his puny existence in fear of the unknown. Driven by ambition,
he often wastes what precious moments he possesses. Forsaking
others, he overindulges his egotistical ventures in the pursuit of
fame and fortune, allowing evil to seduce him into reaping misery
upon those he truly loves; his life, so fragile, always teetering on
the brink of a death he was not blessed with the ability to comprehend.

Death is the great equalizer. All our power and wants, all
our hopes and desires eventually die with us—buried in the
grave. Oblivious, we journey selfishly toward the big sleep,
placing importance on things that have no importance, only to
be reminded at the most inopportune times how frail our lives
truly are.

As creatures of emotions, we pray to a God whose existence
we have no proof of, our unbridled faith designed merely to quell
our primordial fear of death as we try to convince our intellects
that an afterlife must surely exist. God is merciful, God is just,
we tell ourselves, and then the unthinkable happens: a child

drowns in a swimming pool, a drunk driver kills a loved one, a disease strikes a betrothed.

Where goes our faith then? Who can pray to a God that steals an angel? What divine plan could possibly justify such a heinous act? Was it a merciful God that chose to strike my Maria in the prime of her life? Was it a just God who determined that she wallow in pain, suffering in agony until He finally got around to the heavenly task of taking mercy on her tortured soul?

And what of her husband? What sort of man was I to stand idly by and allow my beloved to suffer so?

With heavy heart, I allowed each day to slip by as the cancer dragged Maria closer to the grave. And then one night as I sat sobbing by her bedside, she looked at me through sunken eyes, a wretched creature more dead than alive, and begged me for mercy.

What could I do? God had abandoned her, refusing her respite from the incessant torture. Bending down, my body trembling, I kissed her one last time, praying to a God whose existence I now both questioned and cursed to give me strength. Pressing the pillow to her face, I extinguished her last dying breath, knowing full well that I was extinguishing the very flame of my soul.

The deed complete, I turned, shocked to find my son, an unknowing accomplice, staring at me through the dark angelic eyes of his mother.

What heinous act had I committed? What brave words could I possibly muster to regain this child's lost innocence? Stripped of all pretense, I stood there naked, a weak, beguiled father who had unwittingly condemned his own son's psyche through an act which, only minutes before, I had believed to be both humane and unselfish.

Helpless, I watched my son bolt from our home and run into the night to vent his rage.

Had I a weapon, I would have blown my head off right then and there. Instead, I fell to my knees and sobbed, cursing God, screaming his name in vain.

In less than a year's time, my family's existence had been transformed into a Greek tragedy. Had God manipulated these turns of events, or was He also just a spectator, watching and waiting while his fallen Angel manipulated our lives like some diabolical puppet master.

Perhaps it was Lucifer himself, I rationalized in my grief, for who but _he_ could have struck down my wife, then so deftly manipulated the sequence of events that followed? Did I really believe in the Devil? At that moment—yes, or, at the very least, the presence of evil personified as an entity unto itself.

Can something as intangible as evil be an entity? My tortured mind pondered the question, granting me a moment's reprieve from grief. If God was an entity, then why not the Devil? Could goodness really exist without evil? Could God really exist without the Devil? And who really begot whom, for it has always been the fear of evil that has primed the pumps of religion, not God.

The theologian in me took over. Fear and religion. Religion and fear. The two are historically entwined, the catalysts for most of the atrocities committed by man. Fear of evil fuels religion, religion fuels hatred, hatred fuels evil, and evil fuels fear among the masses. It is a diabolical cycle, and we have played into the Devil's hand.

Staring at the heavens, my thoughts turned to the Mayan prophecy, wondering in my delirium and grief whether it was the presence of evil that was orchestrating mankind's ultimate fall from grace, leading us toward the obliteration of our own species.

And then another thought crossed my mind. Perhaps God did exist, but He had chosen to take a passive role in man's existence, providing us the means to determine our own destinies, yet, all the while, permitting evil to exert a more active influence in our lives so as to test our resolve—verifying our aptitudes as we applied for entrance into His hereafter.

Maria had been taken from me, struck down in the prime of her life. Perhaps there was a reason behind the insanity of the moment—perhaps I was getting close to the truth—that I was indeed on the trail of humanity's salvation.

Cursing the Devil, I gazed at the stars, tears in my eyes, and swore, on the soul of my beloved, that neither heaven nor hell would stop me from resolving the Mayan prophecy.

More than ten years have passed since I swore that oath. Now, as I sit backstage, inscribing this final passage, waiting to be called to the dais, I grimace at the thought of facing my cynical colleagues.

Yet what choice have I? Despite my best efforts, pieces of the doomsday puzzle remain missing, and our salvation as a species lies in the balance. Failing health has forced me to pass the baton to my son sooner than I had hoped, placing the burden squarely on him to complete the marathon.

I am told that Pierre Borgia will be introducing me to the crowd. The butterflies flutter in my stomach at the anticipation of seeing him again. Perhaps the years have softened his anger toward me. Perhaps he realizes what is at stake.

I hope so, because I'll need his support if I am to convince the scientists in the auditorium to act. If they listen with open minds, the facts alone may be enough to persuade them. If not, then I fear our species is doomed to perish, as surely as the dinosaurs perished before us.

A final entry has been placed within a Cambridge safe with specific dates as to when its seal may be broken. Should we survive the coming holocaust, then one last challenge awaits—for two little ones not yet born.

As the ushers beckon me to take center stage, I look at Michael. He nods his approval, his ebony eyes blazing back at me, exuding his mother's intelligence. Robbed of his innocence so many years ago, he has become introverted and distant, and I fear *he harbors a hidden rage that my own heinous act surely fostered. And yet, I also detect a deep sense of purpose within my son, one that I pray will sustain him as he journeys down destiny's path, toward his ultimate salvation—and our own.*

—Final Excerpt from the Journal of Professor Julius Gabriel
August 24, 2001

299

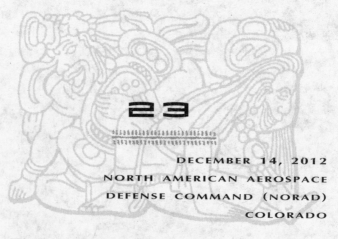

23

Major Joseph Unsinn's heart leaps from his chest as NORAD's missile alarms sound. Dozens of technicians watch in horror as their large-screen computer terminals erupt with an influx of data.

QUICK ALERT! QUICK ALERT!
MULTIPLE BALLISTIC MISSILE LAUNCHES DETECTED

LAUNCH SITE: BĀKHTARĀN-IRAN
TARGET: ISRAEL

TARGET:	MISSILES	IMPACT TIME: MIN/SEC.
Megiddo	2	4:12
Tel Aviv	3	4:35
Haifa	4	5:38
Golan Heights	1	5:44

Data is instantaneous transmitted from NORAD's high-speed processing center directly to the U.S. field commanders in Israel and the Persian Gulf. Moments later, Major Unsinn is on the video-comm, speaking to the secretary of defense.

Raven Rock Situation Room
Maryland

The top-secret complex, known only as Raven Rock, functions as a subterranean Pentagon. Within this nerve center is the "situation room," a circular chamber containing a maze of state-of-the-art integrated voice-communication and data-management systems. From there, the president and his advisors can transmit directives to the United States Strategic Command Center (STRATCOM), another subterranean nerve center in direct contact with all strategic spacecraft, aircraft, submarines, and missile forces around the world. Like NORAD, both Raven Rock and STRATCOM's bunkers have been insulated to shield their sensitive high-tech equipment from the electromagnetic pulses generated during a nuclear assault.

President Maller is seated on a leather sofa in his private office, his limbs shaking, his mind struggling to seal away his personal grief, if only for a few minutes. Outside his office, Secretary of Defense Dick Pryzstas and General Fecondo huddle with Pierre Borgia.

"The president's in shock," Przstas whispers. "Pierre, as senior Cabinet member, protocol demands you take over."

"NORAD's detected an air wing of Russian stealth fighters heading toward Alaska. Our Raptors are en route to intercept. Are you prepared to issue launch codes—"

"No!" Maller emerges from the office. "I'm still in charge, Mr. Pryzstas. Initiate Global Shield. Secretary Borgia, I want to speak with Viktor Grozny and General Xiliang now. I don't care if you have to personally fly over to Moscow to get Grozny to pick up the goddam phone, just do it."

"Yes, sir."

Sinai Desert
Israel

The 747-400F freighter traces a figure-eight pattern 42,000 feet above the Sinai desert. Despite appearances, this is no mere jumbo jet. Within its rounded proboscis nose cone is the Air Force YAL-1 Airborne Laser (ABL), a weapon designed to intercept SAMs, cruise, and tactical ballistic missiles.

Major David Adashek stares at his station module as the Lockheed Martin beam director and Infrared Search and Track (IRST) system scans the northeastern skies.

Ten targets appear on his screen.

"Here we go, people. Ten ballistic missiles with nuclear warheads, now coming into range. Three hundred kilometers and closing fast."

"Illuminator beacon has acquired targets, sir. We're locked on."

"Light the coil."

With a brilliant flash, the Boeing multimegawatt TRW COIL laser engages, igniting a brilliant orange beam from its nose cone. The beacon cuts across the night sky at the speed of light, turning the first Iranian missile into a plummeting fireball.

In the next thirty seconds, all nine remaining missiles will be destroyed.

Space

The sleek, black-and-white spaceplane rolls gently into its new orbit, soaring high above the Earth in silence and solitude. Unlike its distant NASA cousin, the Lockheed Martin *VentureStar,* a reusable space vehicle built and launched with much public fanfare, this craft, known simply as the SMV (Space Maneuver Vehicle) to its Boeing North American designers, has never seen the light of day. Conceived in the final days of President Reagan's Strategic Defense Initiative, the SMV was funded in secrecy by the Air Force Research Laboratory's Military Spaceplane Office and, ironically enough, launched atop a purchased Russian Proton rocket. Able to remain on station for up to a year, the fully automated and pilotless vehicle carries no commercial payload, nor has it ever serviced the International Space Station or private-sector interests. The SMV was designed for one purpose—to hunt down and destroy enemy satellites.

Concealed within the SMV's twenty-five-foot structure is a truss-mounted platform supporting the TRW Alpha high-energy hydrogen-fluoride laser and Hughes four-meter beam-projection telescope.

The spaceplane homes in on its first victim, a Russian satellite, one of eighteen positioned in a geosynchronous orbit, 22,300 miles above North America. The SMV fires its thruster jets, stabilizing its orbit. Keeping pace with the Russian machine, the SMV retracts the clamshell-like doors within its nose cone, revealing its top-secret payload.

The Lockheed Martin guidance system locks on to its target.

Building to a full charge, the laser ignites, projecting its invisible beam onto the surface of the eighteen-foot-long Russian satellite. The thin protective outer casing begins to heat, causing the metallic hull to glow a brilliant orange-red. Sensitive electronic systems within the satellite short. Sensory components sizzle and melt, leaving charred and carbonized circuit boards.

The laser energy reaches the onboard power cells—

With a powerful blast, the reconnaissance satellite explodes, transforming its scorched remains into glittering hunks of space debris.

Caught within the Earth's gravitational pull, a large chunk of Russian metal ignites into a fireball as it reenters the planet's atmosphere.

A young boy living in Greenland gazes up at the northern night sky, excited to see the unexpected light show. Closing his eyes, he makes a wish on the shooting star.

The nose of the SMV closes, the spaceplane firing its thrusters, propelling the satellite killer into a higher orbit as it races to hunt down its next target.

High-Energy Laser Systems Test Facility (HELSTF)
White Sands, New Mexico

To the uninformed passerby, the domed concrete-and-steel observatory situated within the high-security compound along New Mexico's southern desert appears as nothing more than another stellar observation post. But beneath the retractable dome lies not a telescope but a 5.1-inch naval gun turret mounted on a fast-revolving, 360-degree swiveling platform.

This is the Mid-Infrared Advanced Chemical Laser (MIRACL), the most powerful laser in the world. Developed by TRW and Israel's RAFAEL, the deuterium-fluoride chemical laser is capable of sending high-powered, repeated bursts into space at the speed of light.

Working on the same principles that operate a rocket engine, the laser uses nitrogen trifluoride as an oxidizer to burn ethylene fuel, which, in turn, yields excited fluoride atoms. As deuterium and helium are injected into the exhaust, optical energy is extracted, creating a three-centimeter-wide-by-twenty-one-centimeter-high laser beam. The key component of the satellite killer, the Hughes-made satellite beam director, then locks on to its fast-moving target, transmitting the powerful laser through the atmosphere and into space.

Colonel Barbara Esmedina, Director of the White Sands project, watches impatiently as her technicians finish entering the coordinates of the seven Russian and four North Korean Global Positioning Satellites hovering somewhere over North America. Esmedina, a former administrator who worked on the X-33 prototype of NASA's *VentureStar*, has earned a reputation for being an excitable, opinionated, and often bizarrely outspoken proponent of tactical, high-energy lasers (THELs). Twice married and twice divorced, she has long since retired from dating to pursue funding for her pet project—the construction of a dozen coastal MIRACL sites as a tactical means of defense against incoming ICBMs.

For eight years, Barbara Esmedina has fought a personal war with the Department of Defense, ever since the day Kim Jong Il's government completed development on the Taepo Dong-2, a two-stage long-range missile capable of reaching the western part of the continental United States. Although highly respected by her superiors, she has been chided as being too smart for her own good and too beautiful to own such a nasty temperament—the latter, an irrepressible trait that has often hurt her own efforts to obtain funding. Despite extensive lobbying efforts five years earlier, the DoD had chosen to fund the Navy's new CVN-78, a six-billion-dollar stealth aircraft carrier.

Barbara shakes her head at the memory in disgust. *Just what we needed, another goddam six-billion-dollar white elephant.*

"We're ready here, Colonel."

"About time. Retract the dome."

A hydraulic whine from above as the immense concrete dome retracts, revealing a star-filled desert sky.

"Dome retracted, Colonel. Laser targeted. We've got a clear field."

"Fire laser."

In less than a blink of an eye, a brilliant crimson red beacon ignites, tracing a line into the heavens. Colonel Esmedina and a dozen technicians focus on a computer monitor that marks the enemy satellite's position. The image flashes on and off, then abruptly disappears.

"First target destroyed, Colonel. Now acquiring second target."

Esmedina suppresses a grin as the laser's turret rotates into position. "That, Comrade Grozny, is what we call, in your face from outer space."

Beneath the Kukulcán Pyramid
Chichén Itzá

Mick is floating.

Gazing down upon the two unconscious figures lying prone on the strange grating, he sees frozen masks of pained expressions, the frightened faces blue beneath the masks.

Recognizing the bodies, he feels no remorse or sorrow, only blessed comfort, mixed with a strange sense of curiosity. Turning, he sees the tunnel open before him, the bright light beckoning him inside. Without hesitation he enters, soaring like a bird without wings.

He senses the presence of the being and registers an immediate rush of love and warmth, something he has not experienced since his early childhood.

Mother?

The light embraces him, enveloping him within its energy.

It's not your time, Michael. . . .

A roar of thunder fills his ears as the light dissipates.

The rising bile expels the regulator from Mick's mouth, sending him into convulsions. He sucks in a breath of air, then another, then tears the mask from his face and rolls onto his back, his chest heaving as he stares at the bizarre arched ceiling overhead.

Mom? "Dominique—"

Struggling to his knees, he crawls over to the girl, quickly removing her dive mask, the regulator already out of her mouth. Verifying a pulse, he positions her head back and opens her airway, then breathes into her mouth, inflating her lungs.

Come on. . . .

Water fills her mouth. Straddling her, he presses her abdomen with both hands, forcing the liquid out of her stomach.

He clears her mouth and begins again.

A dozen more breaths.

Dominique's face flushes pink. She coughs, spitting up a mouthful of water, then opens her eyes.

Bering Strait
Off the Coast of Alaska

1:43 A.M. (Alaska Time)

The seven Lockheed Martin F-22 Raptors, the most advanced aircraft fighter in the world, rocket across the dark Alaskan sky at supersonic speed. The semitailless stealth vessels, about the size of an F-15, are not only invisible to radar, but can cruise higher and faster than any jet.

Major Daniel Barbier flexes his muscles to stay awake within the dark cockpit. Eight long hours and five midair refuelings have passed since his team left Dobbins Air Force Base at Marietta, Georgia, and the formation leader can feel the fatigue in his bones. The Canadian-born pilot reaches into his breast pocket and removes the picture of his wife, daughter, and four-year-old twin boys, gives each a kiss for luck, then refocuses his attention on the colorfully lit console before him.

The F-22's tactical display is a sensory management system designed to provide its pilot with the maximum amount of information without becoming overwhelming. Specific colors and symbols segregate the jet fighter's three main sensors, allowing for quick recognition. The Raptor's Northrop Grumman/ Raytheon APG-77 fighter radar is so powerful that it allows its pilot to acquire, identify, and destroy a target long before the enemy knows it is there. In addition to radar, the F-22 is equipped with two other sensors, both passive, nonemitting devices, which help preserve the aircraft's stealth.

The first of these is the Lockheed-Sanders ALR-94 electronic warfare (EW) system, a sensor that scans the battlefield, searching for enemy signals. When an enemy is detected, the EW immediately determines the target's bearing and range, then programs the Raptor's AMRAAM missiles to intercept. A second passive system, called *datalink*, gathers information from airborne AWACS, providing the F-22 pilot with superior navigation and target-identification data.

Despite the aircraft's superior technology, Barbier's stomach is tightening in fear. Somewhere up ahead is a squadron of Russian stealth fighters, believed to be carrying nuclear weapons. While the Raptor's airframe minimizes radar cross section based on its angular design, its Russian counterpart produces a plasma cloud, which envelopes the plane, decreasing the reflected radar signals. Locating the enemy will not be easy.

"Woodsman to Snow White, come in Snow White."

Barbier adjusts his headpiece to speak with Elmendorf Air Force Base. "Go ahead, Woodsman."

"The Wicked Witch (NORAD) has detected the dwarfs. Downloading coordinates now."

"Roger that." Barbier watches as his central tactical display lights up like a Christmas tree. A secure, intraflight datalink simultaneously provides each of the seven Raptor pilots with the identical display even as the system analyzes and coordinates a shoot list.

Seven blue circles mark the F-22s in formation. Nine red triangles are approaching from the northwest, flying in formation, low to the water.

Barbier touches a bar on his throttle. Each bandit is instantly assigned a white circle with a number, the designations appearing on both the main tactical and attack displays of each Raptor.

Situated within the belly of Barbier's F-22 are two ventral weapon bays and two side bays. The ventral bays each contain four HAVE DASH II advanced medium-range air-to-air missiles (AMRAAMs), a ramjet-powered, Mach-6 weapon capable of punching through six feet of concrete over a distance of a hundred nautical miles. Each side bay holds one GM-Hughes AIM-9X Sidewinder, a seeker missile capable of locking on to targets a full ninety degrees off the fighter's boresight.

The word SHOOT simultaneously appears on Barbier's attack screen and helmet-mounted heads-up display. The pilot fingers the pickle button, watching his tactical display as the F-22 crosses from the outermost ring into the middle ring of attack. At this range, the Raptor's weapons can engage the enemy while the bandits remain too far away to return fire.

Barbier whispers, "Have a good swim, motherfuckers."

With forty gees of pressure, the pneumatic-hydraulic launchers beneath each of the F-22s eject a salvo of missiles from their weapons bays. The missiles go autonomous within seconds, closing on their targets at a hypersonic velocity of sixty-five hundred feet per second.

The F-22's bank sharply, descending to a lower altitude.

The Russian squadron leader's heart leaps into his throat as his missile warning system lights up, the onboard alarm echoing in his ears. Perspiration breaks out beneath his flight suit as he hastily launches his decoys and breaks from formation, unable to fathom where the attack could be coming from. He glances at his radar, then cringes in terror as his wingman's jet incinerates into a blazing fireball.

The alert becomes a deafening death toll. Staring at his radar in absolute terror, the pilot struggles to grasp the concept that the hunter has somehow become the hunted.

A second later, the AMRAAM missile violates his fuselage, vaporizing his existence into eternity.

Beneath the Kukulcán Pyramid
Chichén Itzá

Barefoot, Mick and Dominique walk hand in hand through the alien vessel, the upper portions of their neoprene diving suits hanging unzipped around their waists.

The tunnel-like corridor is warm though quite dark, the only light coming from a luminescent blue glow somewhere ahead. The floor, walls, and thirty-foot-high arched ceiling of the passage are barren and smooth, composed of a highly polished, transluscent black polymer.

Mick pauses to press his face against the dark, glasslike wall, attempting to peer inside. "I think something is behind these walls, but the glass is so tinted, I can't see a damn thing." He turns to Dominique, who gives him a terrified look. "You okay?"

"Okay?" She grins nervously, her lower lip quivering. "No, I don't think I've been *okay* since I met you." She smiles, then, starts to cry. "I guess . . . I guess the good news is you're not crazy. Does that mean we're all going to die?"

He takes her hand. "Don't be scared. This vessel belongs to Kukulcán, or whatever the humanoid called itself."

"How do we get out of here?"

"This ship must be buried directly beneath the Kukulcán pyramid. There's probably some kind of hidden passage that leads up into the temple. We'll find a way out, but first we need to figure out how to prevent the doomsday prophecy from coming true."

He leads her to the end of the corridor, which opens to a massive, onion-shaped chamber. Rounded walls radiate a faint electric blue light source. At the very center of the cathedral-like, domed ceiling is a five-foot-wide passage, which rises straight up like a chimney, the orifice disappearing into darkness high above their heads.

Positioned directly beneath the opening is an enormous bathtub-shaped object.

It is a polished rectangle of brown granite—seven and a half feet long, three and a half feet wide, and three and a half feet deep. As they move closer, a dim crimson glow appears on the side of the granite tub, growing brighter as they come nearer.

Mick's eyes widen as he stares at the rows of luminescent red hieroglyphs. "It's a message, written in ancient Quiche Mayan."

"Can you translate it?"

"I think so." Mick feels his insides quivering with adrenaline. "This first section identifies the author, a being whose name translates into the Mayan equivalent of the word *guardian*."

"Just read it," she whispers.

"I am Guardian, last of the Nephilim. Not of this world, yet we are one. The ancestors of man were . . . our children." He stops reading.

"What? Go on—"

"We . . . your seed."

"I don't understand. Who were the Nephilim?"

"The Bible refers to them as giants. The Book of Genesis briefly mentions the Nephilim as being fallen angels, men of superior intelligence. The Dead Sea Scrolls insinuate the Nephilim may have bred with human women before the time of the Great Flood, a period that equates with the melting of the last ice age."

"Wait, are you saying these aliens crossbred with humans? That's sick."

"I'm not saying anything, but it makes perfect sense if you think about it. You've heard of evolution's missing link, right? Maybe it was the synthesis of an advanced race of humanoid DNA that caused *Homo sapiens* to leapfrog up the evolutionary ladder."

Dominique shakes her head, bewildered. "I can't handle all this—just keep reading."

Mick refocuses on the message. "Nephilim leaders weaned your species into societies, guiding the labors of your salvation, opening your minds so that you could see. Two worlds, one species, bound over space and time by a common enemy—an enemy that devours the souls of our ancestors. An enemy whose presence will soon eliminate your own species from this world."

"Whoa, wait—what enemy? That thing in the Gulf? What's he mean by devouring our souls? Is he saying we're all going to die?"

"Let me finish, there's one last passage." Mick wipes the beads of perspiration from his eyes as he refocuses on the incandescent, bloodred text.

"I am Kukulcán, teacher of Man. I am Guardian, last of the Nephilim.

Close to death, my soul is prepared to make the journey into the spiritual world. The message is transcribed, all things readied for One Hunahpu's arrival. Two worlds, one people, one destiny. Only One Hunahpu can seal the cosmic portal before the enemy arrives. Only One Hunahpu can make the journey to *Xibalba* and save the souls of our ancestors."

Mick stops reading.

"Okay, Mick, what's all that supposed to mean? I thought this One Hunahpu was the guy in the creation myth who got his head cut off. How the hell's he supposed to help us? And what's Guardian mean by the cosmic portal must be sealed? Mick? Hey, are you all right? You look pale."

He slumps to the floor, leaning back against the granite tub.

"What's wrong? What is it?"

"Just give me a second."

She sits down next to him and massages the back of his neck. "I'm sorry. You okay?"

He nods, taking in slow, deep breaths.

"Was that the end of the message?"

He nods again.

"What's wrong? Tell me—"

"According to the *Popol Vuh*, One Hunahpu died long ago."

"What do we do?"

"I don't know. I think we're in big trouble."

North American Aerospace Defense Command
NORAD
Colorado

11:01 P.M.

Commander in Chief (CINCNORAD) General Andre Moreau walks slowly past rows of high-tech radar stations, communication consoles, and video display screens. None of his controllers look up as he passes, each man and woman completely focused on their stations, their overwrought nerves fueled by a mixture of caffeine and adrenaline.

Moreau registers a tightness in his gut as he stares at the monitor flashing DEFCON-1. The Defense Readiness Condition is a military posture ranging from the day-to-day peacetime preparedness of DEFCON-5 all the way up to DEFCON-1, a condition equating to a nuclear assault and response.

Moreau closes his eyes. Having served in the Air Force and NORAD for thirty-two years, the general has seen more than his share of excitement. He recalls those six frightening minutes back in November of 1979 when a state of DEFCON-1 had been initiated on his watch. Unbeknownst to NORAD, a false alarm had been generated by a computer exercise tape, convincing his operators that the Soviets had launched a large number of ICBMs at the United States. During the tense moments that followed, emergency preparations for a nuclear retaliatory strike had been engaged, the Air Force planes actually in the air before NORAD's PAVE PAWS early-warning radar had detected the human error.

The general opens his eyes again. While a dozen more close calls had followed over the years, none had matched the anxiety of '79.

None until now.

The QUICK ALERT shatters the general's thoughts. For a surreal moment, he feels as if he is falling off a cliff as every video display in the Cheyenne Mountain facility flashes the nightmarish message.

QUICK ALERT! QUICK ALERT!
MULTIPLE BALLISTIC MISSILE LAUNCHES DETECTED
QUICK ALERT! QUICK ALERT!
MULTIPLE BALLISTIC MISSILE LAUNCHES DETECTED

Dear God... "Get me a systems report!"

A dozen technicians with phones to both ears frantically contact bases around the world as the computerized female voice continues announcing, "QUICK ALERT."

The general waits impatiently as an operations voice loop linking the seven functioning centers of NORAD is engaged.

"General, system report valid!"

"General, DSP satellites have identified and confirmed four threat fans. Coming on-screen now, sir."

INCOMING MISSILE ALERT:

Intercontinental Ballistic Missiles:	2,754
Submarine Launched Ballistic Missiles:	86
Four Threat Fans Identified:	
Targets: Alaska	[17]
Hawaii	[23]
Continental United States	[2,800]

ARCTIC TRAJECTORY
17 ICBMS
TIME TO FIRST IMPACT: 18 min. 08 seconds
[Elmendorf Air Force Base]

```
PACIFIC TRAJECTORY
23 ICBMs
TIME TO FIRST IMPACT:          28 min. 47 seconds
                                       (Pearl Harbor)


PACIFIC NORTHWEST TRAJECTORY
1,167 ICBMs 36 SLBMs
TIME TO FIRST IMPACT:          29 min. 13 seconds
                                       (Seattle)


ATLANTIC TRAJECTORY
1,547 ICBMs 50 SLBMs
TIME TO FIRST IMPACT:          29 min. 17 seconds
                                       (WASHINGTON DC)
```

The general stares at the monitor for a heart-stopping moment, then snatches the hot line to the Raven Rock and United States Strategic Command.

Raven Rock Underground Command Center
Maryland

2:04 A.M.

President Mark Maller, sleeves rolled up, is sweating profusely, despite the heavy air-conditioning. Situated along one wall of his soundproof office is a series of video-communicators linking the Command Center directly to STRATCOM command. Maller looks away from the image of General Doroshow as he finishes reciting his nuclear launch codes to the commander, yielding his screen to his secretary of defense.

The president moves out from behind his desk and collapses onto the leather sofa, staring at the overhead monitor, watching helplessly as the computer graphic ticks down the final, historical minutes of the United States of America.

This isn't happening. This can't be happening. God, please let me wake up in bed next to my wife . . .

Maller presses the intercom for the ninth time in the last six minutes. "Borgia?"

"Sir, I'm still trying. Grozny's aides swear they've put the call through, but the president refuses to speak with you."

"Keep trying."

An ashen-faced Dick Pryzstas turns away from the video monitor. "Well, sir, our birds are in the air. Maybe that will bring Grozny to the phone."

"How soon?"

"Our SLBMs will hit Moscow and Beijing two minutes after the coalition missiles strike."

"You mean, two minutes after every major city on the east and west coasts of the United States is wiped off the face of the map." Maller leans forward, his upper body trembling. "All our preparation, all our treaties, all our technology . . . what the fuck happened? Where did we go wrong?"

"Mark, *we* didn't push the button, *they* did."

"Chaney was right, this is madness!" Maller stands, his ulcer on fire. "God dammit, Borgia, where the fuck is Grozny?"

General Joseph Fecondo joins them, his tanned complexion now a sickly olive. "The commanders in chiefs report all sorties are airborne. You'll excuse me, Mr. President. I'm going to remain in the command center. My oldest boy is stationed at Elmendorf. They're . . . they said they'd bring him to the video-comm."

A female staff member pushes past Fecondo and hands a telefax to the president. "Sir, the British and French have agreed not to launch any of their missiles."

Dick Przystas's eyes widen. "The French! Maybe they're more ambitious than we think. They secretly develop pure fusion, detonate the devices in Russia and China, then take over what's left of the world after the big three annihilate one another."

Borgia looks up at Maller. "It's possible."

"Sons of bitches!" Maller kicks his desk.

Another aide enters. "Mr. President, the vice president's on VC-4. He says it's urgent."

Maller powers on the video monitor. "Speak quickly, Ennis."

"Mr. President, the three fusion detonations—we can prove they originated within the alien vessel."

"Christ, Ennis, I don't have time for this—"

The image of Captain Loos appears on the communicator. "Mr. President, it's true. We're downloading footage taken earlier from one of our Predators."

The picture changes, revealing an image of a swirling, emerald green vortex. All personnel within the command center stop and stare as the three dark objects rise out from the whirlpool's funnel.

"Good God," Maller whispers in amazement. "It's true."

Borgia shouts out from his communication's station. "Sir, VC-8, 9, and 10. I've got Grozny and General Xiliang, and the UN Secretary-General!"

President Maller looks at his secretary of defense. "They'll never believe it. Christ, I don't believe it."

"Then make them believe it. Two billion people are going to die in less than seventeen minutes, and you and those two bastards are the only people on earth who can stop it."

Beneath the Kukulcán Pyramid
Chichén Itzá

Mick examines the sides of the massive granite tub, dark now, save for a single row of scarlet dots and dashes.

"What are they?" Dominique asks.

"Numbers. Mayan numbers, from zero to ten."

"Maybe it's a combination lock of some sort. Are there any numerical codes carved into the ruins?"

Mick's eyes light up. "Better still, there's a numerical code built into the design of the Great Pyramid, Angkor Wat, and the city of Teotihuacán. The precession code—4320."

Mick touches the four-dotted symbol.

The Mayan number four changes from incandescent red to a deep electric blue.

In succession, he touches the Mayan numbers three and two, then the eye-shaped symbol equating to zero. Each icon changes to a radiant, luminescent blue.

And then the interior of the tub ignites in a brilliant azure blue glow, and an object appears, situated within the confines of the tub.

The light darkens, allowing them to peer inside the open container.

Dominique stifles a scream.

Staring back up at them, covered in a tattered white tunic, is an enormous humanoid, an old man possessing the facial features of a centenarian. The exposed flesh is ghostly white, the long white hair and beard as fine as silk. The head, perfectly preserved, is elongated, the body nearly seven feet long. The open eyes, transfixed in death, radiate an unworldly ocean blue gaze.

Before their eyes, the humanoid begins disintegrating. The pale skin singes brown, then gray, then decays to a fine, powdery dust. Dehydrated vital organs collapse inward beneath a powerful skeletal frame. The exposed bones char black, then decompose, the entire skeleton vaporizing into a shadow of ash.

Mick stares at the ash-covered white cloth, all that remains within the granite tub.

"God—damn, that was freaky," Dominique whispers. "Was that One Hunahpu?"

"No, I—I think that was Kukulcán, I mean Guardian." Mick leans forward, examining the interior of the open granite box.

"His skull—it was huge."

"Elongated." Mick climbs inside the tub.

"Mick, are you crazy? What the hell do you think you're doing?"

"It's okay—"

"It's not okay. What if that glow reappears?"

"I expect it to."

"God dammit, Mick, don't do this, you're freaking me out—" She grabs his arm, trying to drag him from the tub.

"Dom, stop." He removes her hand from his wrist, then kisses it. "I'll be okay—"

"You don't know that—"

"Dom, One Hunahpu's dead. If Guardian left us some means of saving ourselves, then I have to find it."

"Okay, so we'll look around this ship. Radiating yourself within that coffin isn't going to resolve anything."

"It's not radiation. I know it sounds bizarre, but I think it's a portal."

"A portal? A portal to what?"

"I don't know, but I have to find out. I love you—"

"Mick, get the fuck out of there now!"

He lies back. As his head touches bottom, a neon blue light ignites from within, enveloping him in energy. Before Dominique can protest, an unseen magnetic force field jolts her backwards, away from the tomb.

She lands hard on her back. Regaining her feet, she looks inside the granite tub, shielding her eyes from the blazing, warm glow.

Mick's body has disappeared within the light.

Raven Rock Underground Command Center
Maryland

2:19 A.M.

President Maller and his senior military advisors, fists clenched, stare at the image of Viktor Grozny, the pale Russian president wearing a black sweater, a large Victorian cross dangling from his neck.

On the screen to the left is General Xiliang, the older man looking quite pale. The UN Secretary-General is on the right.

"General, President Grozny, please hear me out," Maller pleads. "The United States is not responsible for these fusion detonations. None of our nations are! Let us prove it to you before we destroy half the world!"

"Show us," the Secretary-General says.

Viktor Grozny remains impassive.

Maller turns to Pryzstas. "Do it. Download the image."

The secretary of defense transmits the *Boone*'s video.

On the other side of the command center, General Joseph Fecondo struggles to maintain his composure as he prays with his son, Adam, and the two base commanders at Elmendorf and Eielson Air Force Bases in Alaska.

The TIME TO IMPACT: ALASKA clock superimposed on each video-comm ticks down to the final five seconds.

Adam Przystas and the two Air Force colonels salute their commanding officer.

General Fecondo returns the salute, tears streaming down his face as the images of his son and the two COs disappear in a flash of brilliant white light.

Maller watches the main screens as the Russian and Chinese leaders' faces replace the video of the alien maelstrom.

"What nonsense is this?" General Xiliang shouts, his face contorted in anger.

President Maller wipes the sweat from his eyes. "Our scientists discovered the alien vessel in the Gulf of Mexico two months ago. We've downloaded the precise coordinates. Use your infrared spy satellites to verify. Please understand, we only learned minutes ago that it was these objects rising from the remains of this alien vessel that have been causing the fusion detonations."

A flurry of Chinese. "You expect us to accept this Hollywood special effect?"

"General, use your satellites! Verify the existence of the vessel—"

Grozny shakes his head in disgust. "Of course we believe you, Mr. President. This is why twenty-five hundred of your nuclear missiles are racing toward our cities while we speak."

"Viktor, we didn't know, I swear it! Listen to me—we still have eight minutes to stop this insanity—"

The UN leader is sweating profusely. "Gentlemen, you have less than ten minutes. Destroy your missiles—now!"

"Go ahead, Mr. President," Grozny rasps. "Demonstrate your sincerity to the Russian and Chinese people by destroying your own missiles first."

"No!" Fecondo bounds across the room. "Don't believe that murdering son of a bitch—"

Maller turns, his eyes blazing. "You're relieved, General—"

"Don't do it! Don't you—"

"Get him out of here!"

A bewildered MP pulls the overwrought general from the room.

Maller turns back to the monitor, the screen indicating 9 minutes, 33 seconds to impact. "Less than an hour ago, a thermonuclear device was detonated in one of our underground command centers. Three hundred people died, including my wife and"—Maller's voice cracks—"and my sons. To end this madness, Grozny, the first move will be mine. I'm giving the orders to stand down our bombers, but we must deactivate our ICBMs together."

Grozny shakes his head, smiling grimly. "Do you take us for fools? Your pure-fusion weapons have murdered two million of our people, yet you expect us to believe that it wasn't you, that it was what—an alien?"

The UN leader stares at Maller. "The United States must make the first move toward peace."

Maller turns to his secretary of defense. "Secretary Przystas, order all bombers to return to base. Instruct all submarines and missile command centers to begin autodestruct sequence ALPHA-OMEGA-THREE. Destroy all airborne ICBMs and SLBMs at five minutes to impact."

The president turns back to Grozny and General Xiliang. "The United States has taken the first step to ending this madness. The next move must be yours. Stand down. Destroy your missiles now. Give your people a chance to live."

The room is electric with tension. Two dozen people stand behind President Maller, staring helplessly at the images of the Russian and Chinese leaders, waiting for them to respond.

Grozny looks up, his piercing blue eyes in sharp contrast to his angelic features. "Give our people a chance to live? Each day, a thousand more Russians starve to death in their homes—"

The screen flashes: SEVEN MINUTES TO IMPACT.

"Abort the attack, and we'll sit down and talk about solutions—"

"Solutions?" Grozny pushes closer to the camera. "What good are economic solutions, when your country continues to engage itself in policies of war?"

"The United States has been supporting the Russian Federation for two decades," Borgia yells back. "The reason your people are starving has more to do with the corruption in your own government than any policy—"

The president swallows the bile rising in his throat. *This is getting us nowhere.* He signals to one of the MPs on duty. "Your sidearm, Sergeant. Give it to me."

Maller pushes Borgia aside, standing alone before the video-comm, his face chalky white.

"President Grozny. General Xiliang, listen to me. In less than one minute, our ICBMs and SLBMs will self-destruct. That will give you less than two minutes to follow suit. If you do not, then my secretary of state will order an all-out nuclear strike on your two countries with every last ICBM and SLBM in our arsenal. We will wipe your nations from the map as surely as you will ours. Gentlemen, for the world's sake, I beg of you, let us regain our senses in this moment of insanity. Just as I mourn the death of my own family, so do I mourn your own losses, but as I stated earlier, the United States is not responsible for those fusion detonations. Show the world you have the courage to stop this madness. Give us a chance to reveal the real enemy."

The president takes a deep breath.

"I know what I've told you is hard to believe. So that you'll know that I have no ulterior motives, I offer you this."

President Mark Richard Maller raises the .45-caliber weapon to his own temple and fires.

Beneath the Kukulcán Pyramid
Chichén Itzá

Michael Gabriel's consciousness is rising . . .

Rising directly above the square roof of the Kukulcán pyramid, jumping higher as the lush green Yucatán jungle kisses the blue waters of the Gulf. . . .

A smooth leap into the stratosphere and the entire peninsula comes into view. Another leap—and the Western Hemisphere drops below, the sphere of the Earth appearing in his mind's window.

The utter silence of space . . .

Moving away faster now, Earth becoming a blue marble as the moon slingshots by. A quantum leap, and Earth disappears, replaced by the brightness of a yellow star, the entire solar system coming into view.

Time and space surging by at an unfathomable speed, Mick glimpsing the nine planets racing around the Sun in staggered orbits . . .

Another quantum leap, and the Sun becomes a pinprick of light, a single star among an ocean of stars.

Light-speed—the stars soaring by, dropping away faster and faster now, as luminescent clouds of interstellar gas and dust appear in his mind's eye.

A final leap and he slows, his consciousness staring at a spiral vortex of swirling stars so magnificent that its breathtaking brilliance, its scale, its omnipotence is almost too overwhelming to behold.

Mick feels his soul trembling as he gazes upon the Milky Way in its entirety, his mind drowning at the realization of his utter insignificance.

God . . . so beautiful . . .

Billions of stars, trillions of worlds, all part of a living cosmic organism—a churning island among the vast ocean of space.

Mick soaring above the galactic bulge, rising higher, until he is staring down upon the black heart of the Milky Way, a swirling vortex of unfathomable gravity, its orifice driving the galaxy as it inhales interstellar gas and dust into its monstrous mouth.

And then—in a blink of his mind's eye—the galaxy is transformed, reappearing in a perspective totally alien to his species, a *fourth dimension* of time and space.

The black hole becomes a radiant emerald funnel, its mouth dropping beneath the galaxy, constricting, until finally breaking away into an expanding cobweb of gravitational strings—a latticework of fourth-dimensional highways that spread out over the Milky Way like a slowly revolving net, never touching the other heavenly bodies—yet somehow touching them.

The information becomes too overwhelming for his brain to comprehend. . Mick blacks out.

When he reopens his eyes, he is gazing down upon one of the arms of the spiraling galaxy, a pattern—a constellation materializing as he moves nearer. Another leap forward and three stars appear—three stars set at a familiar alignment.

Al Nitak, Al Nilam, Mintaka . . . the three belt stars of Orion.

Soaring ahead, he finds himself staring at a planet of behemoth proportions, its surface colored in a tapestry of deep greens and azure blues.

Xibalba. It is as if the thought is whispered into his consciousness.

A solitary moon orbits the alien world. As his consciousness passes over the lunar surface, he sees a transport ship rising from a small outpost, heading toward the planet's surface.

His mind hitches a ride.

The vessel dips below dense layers of atmospheric clouds, revealing a molten ocean of pure energy. The silvery, mirrorlike surface reflects the planet's magnificent cardinal red sky. Looming ahead on the southern horizon is a triple sunset, the blue-white binary star of Al Nitak the first to drop, its disappearance causing the seascape to meld into brilliant shades of lavender and magenta.

An exhilarating sensation washes over him as the transport ship races along the purple sea. Then he sees it—a mammoth continent of incredible beauty—soothing beaches surrounded by a lush tropical jungle, peppered with magnificent waterfalls, mountains, streams . . .

Moving closer, he sees a megalithic crystalline habitat of dazzling beauty. Sparkling alabaster pyramid-shaped structures dot the landscape, interconnected by winding walkways that weave through a futuristic, alien skyline. Below, lush, tropical gardens that would put Eden to shame grow amidst twisting rivers and cascading waterfalls of molten silver energy.

There are no moving vehicles, no traffic, yet the city is teeming with life. Tens of thousands of people—*Homo sapiens*, but for their elongated skulls, move about the hive of alien humanity with an overriding sense of purpose and joy.

For a wondrous moment, Mick's consciousness is bathed in love.

And then something monstrous happens.

As the distant fireball of Mintaka sets, the placid ocean begins churning. Ominous olive and bloodred clouds race across the darkening sky as the swirling vortex below builds to unfathomable proportions.

Mick watches as a lead gray ooze seeps out of the center of the maelstrom, the contaminated elixir inundating the pristine coastline, the tide rising higher, higher, until it infiltrates the city of the Nephilim.

His consciousness registers a demonic presence.

Darkness descends upon the city, spreading like the shadow of a great serpent upon the Edenlike world. Terrified humanoids drop to the ground, clutching their throats, their eyes transforming into vacant, pupilless pools of black.

The images overwhelm him. Once more, his consciousness blacks out.

Mick reopens his eyes.

What was once a civilization of magnificent beauty has now been transformed into a monstrous alien shipyard. Nephilim zombies, their faces ashen and expressionless, their eyes, vacant black holes, hover motionless in midair as their enslaved minds manipulate titanic iridium plates with invisible hands onto the skeletal framework of an ungodly seven-mile-diameter spherical hull. At the core of the vessel is a central pod—a one-mile-diameter nerve center equipped with twenty-three tubular limbs.

Situated within this sphere, harnessed amidst a myriad of alien conduits is a three-hundred-foot-long life-support pod. Mick focuses on the abominable object, recognizing it immediately.

Tezcatilpoca's chamber . . .

And then a deep chill washes over Mick's consciousness, as his mind's eye struggles to grasp the alien being emerging from within the vortex of the still-swirling maelstrom.

It is a serpent, but like none he has ever seen. The viperous face is more devil than beast, its pupils—vertical slits of gold, surrounded by incandescent crimson corneas more cybernetic than organic. The skull is as large as the mixer on a cement truck, the creature's girth as long as four city buses aligned bumper to bumper.

Mick's vantage changes as the serpent approaches the Nephilim complex. The jowls of the great beast open, revealing rows of ebony, scalpel-sharp teeth.

Stepping out from the serpent's jaws—a humanoid.

A shadow of death seems to pass over Mick's soul. He cannot see the man's face, the head and body being cloaked in a black shroud, but he knows he is gazing upon pure evil. The humanoid moves toward the life-support chamber, then extends an arm, pointing. Glowing within the man's hand is a jade object, about the size of a football.

The vermilion eyes of the serpent glitter, the golden pupils disappearing. The blinded creature, mesmerized by the small object, follows the cloaked being as if under a spell.

The beast *enters* the enormous life-support pod.

His mind's eye moves beyond the alien sphere and approaches the planet's surface. There are no traces of tropical jungles, no waterfalls, no Eden. Instead there are bodies—children's bodies, immersed in a solid layer of lead gray tar. A deep moan rises from his soul. The Nephilim young are alive, yet somehow not alive.

Mick's consciousness moves closer. He looks down upon the face of a young male child.

Jaundiced eyes flash open, staring back at him in haunting agony.

Mick's mind shuts down.

Once more, he finds himself orbiting *Xibalba*, his soul trembling as he observes an object rising from the planet's surface.

The sphere . . .

From the moon base appears another vessel, a sleek, gold star cruiser.

The Nephilim survivors race after their enemy, disappearing within the sphere's celestial tail.

Raven Rock Underground Command Center
Maryland

2:27 A.M.

Pierre Borgia is standing in a pool of blood, pieces of President Maller's brain tissue and skull splattered across his sleeve.

General Xiliang's face has turned deathly pale. The Chinese leader turns to his second-in-command. "Engage autodestruct."

Borgia turns to Viktor Grozny. "America's missiles have self-destructed. General Xiliang is complying. You only have four minutes left—"

Grozny's face is serene. "It is better to die in battle than suffer in misery. What will be gained by aborting the attack? The threat of nuclear annihilation grows stronger as our country grows weaker. The finality of war has a cleansing effect, and both our nations need to be cleansed."

The screen powers off.

A visibly shaken Dick Pryzstas enters the war room. "The Chinese missiles have self-destructed."

"What about Grozny's missiles?"

"Not a one, and we can't reach the vice president," Pryzstas says to Borgia. "Which means you're in charge. You've got three and a half minutes before several hundred nuclear warheads reach our coastlines."

"Damn that Russian bastard." Borgia paces, the words of Pete Mabus echoing in his ears. *What this country needs now is strong leadership, not another dove like Chaney as second-in-command.*

"Contact Strategic Command. Order our forces to launch every last

ICBM, SLBM, and nuclear-tipped TLAM in our arsenal. I want that goddam motherfucker blown to hell."

Within the Guardian's sarcophagus

Mick opens his eyes, startled to find himself standing on a hillside, overlooking a magnificent green tropical setting, a cascading silvery waterfall creating a rainbow, off in the distance.

A presence appears beside him. He is not afraid.

Mick looks up to face the large Caucasian. The man's long hair and beard are silky white, the eyes dazzling, an unearthly deep blue and penetrating, yet somehow kind.

Guardian . . . am I dead?

There is no death, there are only varying states of consciousness. Your mind is looking through a window to a higher dimension.

Those humanoids—

The Nephilim. Like your own species, we began as children of the third dimension, cosmic travelers, whose journeys led us to Xibalba. But the intoxications of this planet were a ruse, the world—a fourth-dimensional purgatory of wicked souls, its inhabitants' intentions—to use the Nephilim as a means of escape.

I don't understand. The Nephilim, those children. Are they—

The minds of the Nephilim are held in stasis, their bodies enslaved by the souls of the condemned to complete their task—to send Tezcatilpoca through a fourth-dimensional passage into your solar system, to open a porthole leading to another third-dimensional world.

A porthole directly to Earth?

Not at first. The conditions on your world were not suitable. Having been exiled to Xibalba, the wicked ones can no longer exist in an oxygen environment. Their intended target was Venus. The brotherhood of the Guardian followed Tezcatilpoca through the fourth-dimensional corridor, causing its transport to crash-land on Earth. The life-support pod survived, Tezcatilpoca held in protective stasis. The Guardian remained behind to aid the ascension of your species and engineer the arrival of the Hunahpu.

Who are the Hunahpu?

The Hunahpu are messiah, genetically implanted among your species by the Guardian. Only a Hunahpu can enter the cosmic porthole and prevent the evil ones from contaminating your world. Only One Hunahpu possesses the strength to make the journey through time and space to free the souls of our ancestors.

The corridor, I can feel it opening.

The corridor appears once every precessional cycle. Only a Hunahpu can sense its arrival.

Wait—are you saying that I'm a Hunahpu?

Only a Hunahpu could have accessed the Guardian starship.

My God . . . Mick stares at the lush tropical surroundings splayed out before him, his exhausted mind fighting to comprehend the information being whispered into his consciousness.

Guardian, Tezcatilpoca's arrival—that impact occurred over sixty-five million years ago. How is it possible—

Time is not consistent nor relevant across all dimensions. The brotherhood of the Guardian were the surviving leaders of the Nephilim—Osiris and Merlin, Viracocha and Vishnu, Kukulcán and Quetzalcoatl—all remained in stasis. This starship remained in orbit above your world, its array programmed to jam the enemy's signal. It was only during this last cycle that your species' evolution was sufficient to accept our seed. As such, we shut down the array, allowing the Xibalban radio signal to awaken Tezcatilpoca.

You allowed it to awaken Tezcatilpoca? Why? Why let this—this thing . . .

Tezcatilpoca harbors the porthole into the fourth-dimensional corridor. Once opened, the corridor can be used as a means to travel back into the Nephilim's past. Only One Hunahpu possesses the strength to make the journey and save the souls of our ancestors.

Has any Hunahpu ever attempted this journey?

Only one. It was at the time of the last precessional cycle, before the Great Flood. The brethren of the Guardian awoke from stasis and prepared one of your ancestors to access the Tezcatilpoca's cosmic porthole. As the portal opened, two of the Death God's Under Lords entered the corridor from Xibalba. They used trickery and deceit to defeat this first Hunahpu, but his bravery enabled the Guardian to acquire the transport vessel the wicked ones had used to travel through the Black Road, the fourth-dimensional corridor of time and space you are now suspended within.

This sarcophagus is a vessel?

Yes.

You said the first Hunahpu was defeated. What happened to the two Under Lords who escaped Xibalba?

The Guardian were able to reseal the portal before the Death God and his legion could make the journey through Xibalba Be, but the damage to your world was done. Evil became rooted within your garden.

What does that mean?

The two Under Lords remained on Earth, taking refuge within Tezcatilpoca's vessel. Although they remain within the fourth dimension, they

have continued to exert their influence upon the minds of the weak, their strength increasing as four Ahau, *three* Kankin *approaches.*

My God . . . You exposed humanity to the Devil—

It was necessary. There is more at stake than you can comprehend. One Hunaphu must make the journey through the Black Road to undo the damage that has been done. A greater destiny awaits us all.

Why should I believe you?

You have seen Tezcatilpoca, and it has seen you. There is no escape. It must be destroyed.

How? When will this One Hunahpu arrive?

Perhaps soon. Perhaps never. His destiny has not yet been chosen.

What the hell does that mean? Where is this Messiah of yours? What happens if he doesn't show up? And what about the Hero Twins, Hunahpu and Xbalanque? If the creation myth is true, then maybe they're the Ones. According to the Popol Vuh—

No! The legend of the Twins is a Nephilim prophesy that may never come to pass. The birth and destiny of the Twins relies solely on One Hunahpu making the journey to Xibalba.

And if he never shows up?

Then your people will perish, as will ours.

I don't understand—

It is not for you to understand. The destiny of your species is still being written. The portal is opening, the Death God and his legion preparing to make the journey across time and space. Tezcatilpoca continues the process of acclimating your world, while the two evil ones harbored within his vessel exert their influence upon your people. They must be stopped. Even now, weapons of mass destruction have been unleashed upon your world, brother threatening brother.

What can I do?

You are Hunaphu. You have the ability to access Guardian's array. This will forestall the end, but only the destruction of Tezcatilpoca and the Black Road—Xibalba Be—can prevent the wicked ones from passing through to your world.

The Black Road—where will its entrance materialize?

The porthole to Xibalba Be will ascend on four Ahau, **three** Kankin. **Only a Hunahpu can enter. Only a Hunahpu can expel the evil from your garden and save your species from annihilation.**

You're speaking in riddles. Where is this porthole? Is it aboard that spaceship in the Gulf? Am I supposed to go back inside? And how am I supposed to destroy it?

The porthole will come to you. Use the array to destroy Tezcatilpoca,

then enter the porthole. The two evil ones will come forward to challenge you. They will attempt to prevent you from sealing the portal before He arrives.

And if I seal the portal?

Then the two Under Lords shall be vanquished from your world, allowing your species to evolve. Succeed—and two destinies shall await you. Fail—and both our people will perish.

What do you mean, two destinies await me?

Should the time come, then you will know.

What about Dominique? Is she Hunahpu?

She is part of a greater destiny, but she is not Hunahpu. Do not allow her to enter Xibalba Be, or she will destroy you both.

Dominique is seated on the floor of the chamber, her back to the alien marble tub, her head in her hands. She is scared and alone, her exhausted mind engaged in a nonstop tug-of-war between reality and denial.

This isn't real. None of this is happening. It's all part of some schizophrenic delusion . . .

"Shut up! Shut up, shut up, shut up!"

She jumps to her feet. "Accept the fact that you're here and do something about it. Find a way out—" She walks out of the chamber, then returns, frantic. "No, Mick needs me. I have to wait here."

She bangs on the side of the open sarcophagus again, uncertain of whether Mick is alive or had been vaporized by the neon blue light.

"Mick, can you hear me? God dammit, Mick, answer me!"

Her tears flow, her heart aching. *Selfish bitch, you never told him you loved him. You could have given him that. Just because you've denied yourself, doesn't mean . . .*

"My God . . ." She leans back against the granite tomb at the sudden revelation. *I love him. I really do love him.*

She kicks the side of the granite tub again. "Mick! Can you hear me—"

The sudden burst from an invisible force field knocks her sideways, as a brilliant blue light brightens the entire onion-shaped chamber.

From the tub rises the dark silhouette of a figure. It stands, rising out of the open sarcophagus as if floating, its features enveloped within the alien light.

It is Mick.

Mick is ascending within a sea of energy, moving toward the source of the light. He can feel every muscle, every cell within his body tingling with electricity as he is drawn upward, his soul bathed in intense waves of warmth and love.

The image of Guardian's hand reaches out to him.

Mick extends his arm, his hand embracing the offered palm.

Dominique shields her eyes, forcing herself to stare at the light. She sees the outline of Mick's arm extend upward as if he is reaching for something.

Zap! The invisible wall of energy slams into her like a tidal wave, lifting her up and off of her feet as it sends ripples of electric currents sizzling through her brain. She drops to the floor, her eyes widening as she attempts to focus on the angelic figure.

Mick is now suspended above the floor, his right hand extended.

A roar of hydraulics, as the myriad of high-tech machinery reveals itself all around her. The walls and ceiling are humming, glowing brightly, as the starship's generators power up. Beneath her feet, she sees a labyrinth of computer circuitry glittering beyond the dark, glasslike floor.

A deep thrumming sound builds, the vibration tickling her ears—and then a heavenly wave of blue energy ripples outward from the walls to the domed ceiling, and then straight up into the central chimneylike orifice.

The colossal electromagnetic wave of energy pulsates upward through the central wall of the Kukulcán pyramid, continuing through the roof of the temple via an alien antenna before dispersing outward in every direction at the speed of light.

Racing west, the surge saturates the ancient city of Teotihuacán, powering on an extraterrestrial relay station buried half a mile beneath the enormous Pyramid of the Sun. Continuing its journey across the Pacific Ocean, the charged wave reaches Cambodia, igniting an identical transmitting device hidden deep below the Temple of Angkor Wat.

To the east, the beacon has reached the Andes Mountains. Passing through the geology, it reflects off a long-dormant antenna buried beneath the ancient celestial observatory known as the Kalasasaya, redirected to the south, racing toward the ice-laden continent of Antarctica. Buried beneath tons of snow is another alien relay antenna, the instrument erected during a time when the polar terrain had been void of ice.

Meanwhile, the northeastern-bound ripple of the electromagnetic tsunami crosses the Atlantic to England, the force of the signal causing the mighty sarsans of Stonehenge to tremble. Concealed deep within this rolling hillside of Salisbury is yet another alien antenna.

Having encircled the planet in seconds, the highly charged energy field converges from all directions upon the oldest of the Guardian's relay stations—the Great Pyramid of Giza.

Waves of energy penetrate the limestone block, passing through the King's Chamber and the hollowed-out brown block of granite identical to the sarcophagus within the Kukulkán pyramid. Moving deeper, the beacon activates an alien apparatus hidden well below the Egyptian superstructure, a place where no human has ever been.

In a blink of a nanosecond, the global array is complete, the planet's atmosphere saturated, sealed within a powerful alien energy grid.

Mick drops to the ground, unconscious.

North American Aerospace Defense Command
NORAD
Colorado

One hundred and seven frightened technicians stare at the large overhead computerized map of northern America, which depicts the real-time trajectories of more than fifteen hundred Russian nuclear and biological missiles. Most personnel weep openly as they huddle in prayer groups, grasping pictures of their loved ones who, unknowingly, are just minutes away from death. Others, too numb to stand, lie on the floor beneath their workstations and wait for the unimaginable to happen.

Commander in Chief General Andre Moreau wipes back tears, struggling to refrain from calling his son and daughter living in Los Angeles. *What could I tell them? What could I possibly say? That I love them? That I'm sorry . . . ?*

Ninety Seconds to Impact:

A wail rises from the Command Center, the sound of the computerized female voice causing General Moreau's legs to fail him. He collapses into the seat of his chair.

And then, as if by magic, the missiles suddenly disappear from the giant screen.

Incoming Missiles Destroyed—Incoming Missiles Destroyed—

Screams and cheers. Moreau looks up. Giddy technicians are pointing, yelling, hugging, weeping, as a wave of euphoria spreads throughout the facility.

Moreau struggles to his feet, tears pouring from his eyes, his voice a strained rasp as he calls for a systems analysis.

Two exuberant operators and a senior commander compete for his attention.

"Systems are all on-line!"

"What happened to the missiles?"

"According to our data, they simply self-destructed."

"I want confirmation."

"We're attempting to confirm with our bases in Florida and San Diego, but a dense wave of electromagnetic interference is jamming all communications."

"An EMP?" Fear grips Commander Moreau's intestines. "There shouldn't be any electromagnetic interference, Major, unless there's been a nuclear fallout?"

"No, sir, there's been no fallout. Our ground-based missile warning sites confirm no detonations of any kind. Whatever's causing this interference is coming from another source."

"Where? I want to know—"

"Sir, we're attempting to pinpoint the origin of the interference, but it's going to take some time. Our satellites don't seem to be functioning properly."

"General!" A technician looks up, a baffled expression on his face. "Sir, our missiles were destroyed as well."

"You mean they self-destructed."

"No, sir. I mean they were destroyed."

Raven Rock Underground Command Center
Maryland

2:31 A.M.

Personnel within the subterranean command center are silently hugging and weeping, their exuberant emotions held in check by a feeling of sorrow as news of the president's death and the losses in Alaska and Hawaii spread through the facility.

Pierre Borgia, General Fecondo, and Dick Przystas huddle within the president's private office, listening intently to General Doroshow at STRAT-COM command.

"What I'm telling you, gentlemen, is that Grozny's missiles did not self-destruct. It was some kind of electromagnetic force field that disabled Russia's ICBMs, as well as our own."

"What's the source of the interference?" Borgia asks.

"Still unknown, but whatever it is, it's shut down every satellite we have in orbit. It's like God got pissed off and threw a blanket on top of the entire planet."

"Mick, can you hear me?" Dominique caresses his head in her lap, stroking his hair. She feels him stir. "Mick?"

He opens his eyes. "Dom?"

She pulls his face to hers, kissing and hugging him. "God dammit, Mick, you scared the hell out of me."

"What happened?"

"Don't you remember? You rose out of that sarcophagus like some kind of Mayan ghost and activated this vessel."

Mick sits up and looks around. Alien circuit boards and control stations pulsate with power behind the tinted glasslike walls and flooring. Waves of electric blue energy ripple upward every few seconds along the walls and cathedral ceiling, disappearing up through the chimneylike orifice overhead.

"I did this?"

Dominique stifles his question with her lips. "I love you."

He smiles. "I love you."

328

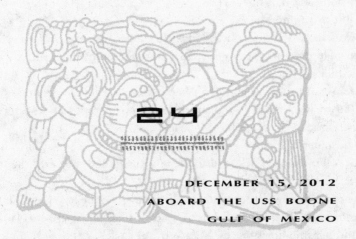

24

Supreme Court Justice Seamus McCaffery's stomach is still a bit queasy from the early-morning helicopter ride. Crossing the warship's deck, he follows the ensign into the superstructure, then through tight corridors leading to the captain's briefing room.

Seated at a small conference table are Vice President Ennis Chaney, General Joseph Fecondo, and Captain Loos.

The men stand as the judge removes his Bible. He nods to Chaney. "Looks to me like you didn't get much sleep either. You ready?"

"Let's get this over with." He places his left hand on the Bible and raises his right hand. "I, Ennis William Chaney, do solemnly swear that I will faithfully execute the office of President of the United States, and will, to the best of my ability, preserve, protect, and defend the Constitution of the United States, so help me God."

"And may God help us all."

A lieutenant enters. "General Fecondo, the Ranger team's on board. The choppers are ready when you are."

Mick leads Dominique through a small corridor which dead-ends at a sealed passage. As they near, the door hisses open, allowing them entry into an airtight lockout chamber.

"This is the way out."

"How do you know?" she asks.

"I don't know. I just do."

"But there's nothing here?"

"Watch." Mick places his hand against a dark keypad situated against the far wall. The frame of a large circular door instantly materializes along the metallic hull.

"Jesus . . . I suppose you don't know how you did that either?"

"Guardian must have implanted the knowledge into my subconscious. I just have no idea when he did it—or how."

The outer-hull door opens, revealing a narrow passage cut within the bedrock of limestone. Mick turns on his flashlight, and they exit, the starship's door sealing shut behind them.

The shoulder-width corridor is pitch-dark, the air heavy with humidity. The beam from Mick's light reveals the narrow steps of a steep, circular stairwell rising through the limestone at a near-vertical angle.

He reaches back and takes her hand. "Be careful, it's slippery."

It takes them fifteen minutes to reach the summit, the twisting climb dead-ending at a ceiling constructed of polished white metal.

"Okay, now what?"

Before Mick can respond, a six-foot-square panel rises on four hydraulic pistons, exposing their eyes to the blinding light of day.

Mick climbs out, then helps Dominique up. Turning to face the light, they are surprised to find themselves standing in the northern corridor of the Kukulcán temple.

The top of the metallic panel, concealed beneath four feet of solid limestone, slips back into position, resealing the entrance to the starship.

"No wonder we never found the passage," Mick whispers.

Dominique steps out onto the platform. "It must be close to noon, but the park's deserted."

"Something must have happened."

They hear the thundering echo of chopper blades as the two Navy helicopters approach from the west.

"Mick, maybe we better go."

*   *   *

The redhead lies prone, his girth concealed beneath the dense jungle foliage. Peering through the high-powered scope of his hunting rifle, he watches Mick Gabriel and the girl step out onto the pyramid's northern platform. Raymond pushes back the safety, smiling as he aligns the crosshairs over his victim's heart.

The chopper pilot slows his airship to hover over the Great Ball Court. "Sirs, directly below us."

Chaney and General Fecondo stare at the winged black object poised almost dead center of the I-shaped Mayan arena. "Christ—it's another one of those pure-fusion objects."

"Why hasn't it detonated?"

The sound of gunfire echoes across the esplanade.

Chaney points to the pyramid. "Get us over there!"

Mick is on his back, struggling to breathe. Blood gushes from his scorching hot chest. He stares into the midday sky, the shadow of Dominique's face blotting out the sun. He feels her tears fall on his cheek, her mouth moving in slow motion as she presses her palm to the wound, yet he can hear nothing but the beating of his own heart.

Guardian?

Close your eyes . . .

A nd chaos reigned. . . .

The revelation of humanity's near disaster with
thermonuclear annihilation was greeted with disbelief and
relief, then fear and universal outrage. How could the
world's leaders have allowed their egos to push humanity
over the edge? How could they have been so arrogant?
How could they have been so blind?

Outrage would quickly lead to violence. For two
days and nights, anarchy ruled much of the globe. Halls
of government were destroyed, military installations ran-
sacked, and the embassies of the United States, Russia,
and China overrun, as billions of people across the planet
marched upon their capitals, demanding change.

Rather than attempt to quell the violence with more
violence, President Chaney chose to channel it, directing
the American public's vengeance toward more than one
hundred subterranean bunkers, built with taxpayer
money, which had been designed to house the political
elite during the nuclear holocaust. The destruction of
these top-secret facilities seemed to quell the public's an-

ger, serving notice that everyone—the haves and have-nots—were now on equal, though somewhat unsteady footing.

Chaney then urged the United Nations Secretary-General to introduce a resolution based on recommendations by the National Academy of Sciences, the Carnegie Commission, and Admiral Stansfield Turner, to eliminate all nuclear and biological weapons of destruction. Any country refusing to comply would face a UN invasion force, its leaders targeted for execution.

Urged on by the masses, all member nations, with the exception of Iraq and North Korea, quickly agreed to comply.

On December 17, Saddam Hussein was dragged onto the streets of Baghdad and beaten to death. Kim Jong Il committed suicide two hours later.

Russian President Viktor Grozny signed the treaty, then publicly blamed the Communist Party for Russia's subversive military buildup over the last two decades. After more than two hundred public executions, he assured his people that government reform would be swift.

With no one to challenge him, he remained in office, stronger than ever.

On the morning of December 17, the media finally learned about the mysterious electromagnetic array and how it had prevented nuclear annihilation. A religious fervor took hold of the masses. Drawn together by fear, they huddled and prayed, flocking to churches and synagogues, waiting for the Messiah and the Second Coming of Christ. What they found instead were more signs of the apocalypse.

On the afternoon of the eighteenth, Korean War veteran Jim McWade returned home from church with his four sons and three twelve-packs of beer. Standing upright within the limestone sinkhole behind his trailer was an immense winged creature. Within hours, half the township of White Sulphur Springs, West Virginia had descended upon the pond to view the inanimate beast, whose shiny black surface emitted a powerful invisible force field that prevented anyone from touching it.

Within twenty-four hours, another twenty-nine identical creatures had been found in various locations across the globe. Then, on the evening of December 19, the world watched in fascination and horror as television cameras recorded the formation of a monstrous maelstrom within the Gulf of Mexico. From the center of the vortex emerged eight winged creatures, all of which quickly dispersed over the Northern Hemisphere. Two of these objects would land later that night in the southwestern region of the United States, two more in Florida, and one each in Georgia, Kentucky, and Indiana. The last object headed east to perch upon a mountainous ridge overlooking the Arecibo telescope in Puerto Rico.

On the morning of December 20, exobiologist Marvin Teperman confirmed to the world that the seven pure-fusion detonations had actually originated from the objects released by the alien vessel buried beneath the Gulf of

Mexico. Referring to the objects as "drones," the *exobiologist* theorized that the thirty-seven creatures now dispersed throughout the globe contained enough fusion power to vaporize upwards of a million square miles of land. Teperman further went on to state that the alien devices were rigged to a solar fuse, which explained their nighttime release and dawn detonations. Somehow the mysterious array, originating from within the Kukulcán pyramid, had managed to jam the firing mechanisms, preventing the drones from exploding.

Should the array falter, Teperman warned, the drones would detonate.

And once again, the masses panicked.

26

A soft breeze filters through the venetian blinds, cooling his face. As the feverish haze lifts, he hears the distant voice of an angel, her familiar words echoing in his mind.

Art thou gone so? Love . . . lord—ay husband, friend. I must hear from thee every day in the hour, for in a minute there are many days.

Swimming against the tide of unconsciousness, he forces his eyes open to slits, just enough to see her sitting over him, reading from the paperback.

"Oh, God, I have an ill-divining soul. Methinks I see thee, now thou art so low, as one dead in the bottom of a tomb. Either my eyesight fails or thou lookest pale—"

"And trust me, love," he rasps, "in my eye, so do you."

"Mick!"

He opens his eyes as she pushes her cheek to his, registering her hot tears and the excruciating weight on his chest as she hugs him, whispering, "I love you."

"I love you." He struggles to speak, his throat parched.

She positions a cup of water to his lips, and he takes a few sips.

"Where—"

"You're in a hospital in Merida. Raymond shot you. The doctor said the bullet stopped an eighth of an inch from your heart. Everyone says you should be dead."

He forces a smile, rasping, "They jest at scars that never felt a wound." He attempts to sit up, the pain pushing him back down again. "Maybe a small wound."

"Mick, so much has happened—"

"What day is it?"

"The twentieth. Tomorrow's the winter solstice, and everyone's scared shitless—"

The door bursts open, an American physician strolling in, followed by Ennis Chaney, a Mexican nurse, and Marvin Teperman. Mick notices heavily armed American soldiers stationed in the outer corridor.

The doctor leans down, examining his eyes with a flashlight pen. "Welcome back, Mr. Gabriel. And how are we feeling today?"

"Sore. Hungry. And a bit disoriented."

"It's no wonder, you've been unconscious for five days. Let's take a look at that wound." The doctor pulls back the bandage. "Amazing. Absolutely amazing. I've never seen a wound heal so quickly."

Chaney steps forward. "Is he well enough to speak?"

"I should think so. Nurse, change his dressing, then start him on another IV of—"

"Not now, Doctor," Chaney interrupts. "We need a few minutes with Mr. Gabriel. Alone."

"Of course, Mr. President."

Mick watches the physician and nurse leave, an MP in the corridor closing the door behind them. "Mr. President? Seems like you get a promotion every time we meet."

The raccoon eyes do not look amused. "President Maller's dead. Put a bullet through his own head five days ago in an attempt to get the Russians and Chinese to abort an all-out nuclear assault."

"Jesus . . ."

"The world owes you a debt of thanks. Whatever you activated within that Mayan pyramid destroyed the missiles."

Mick closes his eyes. *My God, it really happened. I thought it was all a dream . . .*

Dominique squeezes his hand.

"It's some kind of highly charged, electromagnetic array," Marvin says, "like nothing we've ever seen. The signal's still active, thank God, because it's keeping those drones from exploding—"

"Drones?" Mick opens his eyes. "What drones?"

Marvin removes a photograph from his briefcase and hands it to him. "Thirty-eight of these things have landed across the globe since you were brought in."

He stares at the photo of a black batlike creature, perched on a gray mountaintop, its wings expanded. "It's the object I saw rising out of the spaceship, the one buried in the Gulf of Mexico." He looks up at Dominique. "I know where I've seen them before. Nazca. Life-size images of these creatures have been carved all over the plateau."

Marvin looks at Chaney, a bit uncertain. "This photo was taken several days ago on a mountaintop in Arecibo."

Chaney pulls up a chair. "The creature you claimed seeing in the alien vessel—that drone landed in Australia and wiped out most of the Nullarbor plain. We now know that each one of these objects possesses some sort of pure-fusion device, explosives capable of vaporizing entire landscapes. Six of these drones detonated in Asia over the last two weeks, the last three wiping out more than two million people in China and Russia."

Mick feels his hands shaking. "These detonations precipitated the nuclear assault?"

Chaney nods. "Like Marvin said, another thirty-eight of these things were discharged from that alien vessel over the last five nights. So far, none has detonated."

Mick recalls Guardian's words. *The activation of the Nephilim array will forestall the end, but only the destruction of Tezcatilpoca and the Black Road can prevent our enemy from passing through to your world.*

"We've compiled a list of the drones that haven't detonated. Gabriel, are you listening?"

"Huh? Sorry. You say these things are drones?"

"That's what our scientists are calling them. The Air Force equates them to an alien version of our Unmanned Aerial Vehicles."

"Each of these drones are essentially pure-fusion weapons with wings," Marvin explains. "Like our own UAVs, the drones are remotely controlled, linked by some sort of radio signal to their control center—"

"The vessel in the Gulf?"

"Yes. Once the drone lands in its pretargeted area, a radio signal is dispersed, arming the explosive. Situated on the creature's tail assembly are rows of bizarre-looking sensors that we believe are high-powered photovoltaic cells. The triggering mechanism uses solar power to detonate the explosive at sunrise."

"Which explains why these things are always released at night," Chaney adds. "Seven drones detonated prior to the activation of this array, all seven dispersing west after exiting the vessel in the Gulf. The airspeed of the drones matched the Earth's rotation, keeping them in darkness until they reached their targeted areas."

"You said another thirty-eight of these drones have been released?"

"Show him the list, Marvin." The exobiologist searches his briefcase, producing a computer printout.

DRONE TARGETS

AUSTRALIA

Nullarbor Plain [D]

ASIA

Malaysia [D]   Irian Jaya [D]   Papua New Guinea [D]   Yunnan Province, China [D]   Vilyui Basin, Russia [D]   Kugitangtau Ridge, Turkmenistan [D]

AFRICA

Algeria   Botswana   Egypt   Ivory Coast   Israel   Libya Madagascar   Morocco [Atlas Mountains]   Niger   Nigeria Saudi Arabia   Sudan   Tunisia

EUROPE

Austria   Bosnia-Herz.   Bulgaria   Croatia   Greece   Hungary Ireland   Italy   Spain

NORTH AMERICA

Canada: Montreal

Cuba

USA: Arecibo [Puerto Rico]   Appalachian Valley   Colorado
        Florida [Central & Southeast]   Georgia   Kentucky
        Indiana [Southern]   Ozark Mountains   New Mexico
        Texas [Northwest]

SOUTH AMERICA

Salvador [Brazil]

CENTRAL AMERICA

Honduras   Chichén Itzá [Yucatán]

Mick scans the list, pausing at the name of the last site. "A drone landed in Chichén Itzá?"

"Enough of this nonsense," Chaney snaps. "Gabriel, I need some answers, and I need them now. While you've been lying here asleep, the world's lost its collective mind. Religious fanatics are claiming these drones to be part of the Apocalyptic prophecies predicted for the new millennium. The world's economy has ground to a halt. Terrified masses are preparing for Armageddon. Mobs are hoarding supplies and ammunition and boarding themselves up in their homes. We've had to institute dusk-to-dawn curfews. And what's fueling these fires more than anything is our own inability to ease the public's concern."

"So far, our attempts at neutralizing these drones have been ineffective," Marvin says. "The creatures are held within some kind of protective force field, which makes them invulnerable to attack. While the Mayan array is preventing them from exploding, it's also jamming the hell out of our satellites. What's even more incredible is the manner in which the array's signal is being bounced around the globe." He removes his notepad. "We've isolated three global relay stations, as well as additional signatures from several other antennae. You'll never guess—"

"The Great Pyramid in Giza, Angkor Wat, and the Sun Pyramid in Teotihuacán."

The exobiologist's mouth drops open.

Chaney's eyes burn like dark lasers. "How the hell did you know that?" He looks at Dominique. "Did you tell him?"

"She didn't tell me," Mick says, forcing himself to sit up. "My parents studied those structures for decades. Each monolith shares certain similarities, not the least of which is that they've all been erected at integral points along the Earth's natural power grid."

"Sorry, you lost me there," Marvin says, jotting down notes. "Did you say power grid?"

"The Earth is not just some hunk of rock floating in space, Marvin, it's a living, harmonic sphere, at the heart of which is a magnetic core that channels energy. Certain locations along the planet's surface, especially around the equator, are considered power areas, dynamic locations radiating high levels of geothermal, geophysical, or magnetic energy."

"And these three ancient sites—they were all built on power areas?"

"That's right. Each structure also reflects an advanced knowledge of precession, mathematics, and astronomy within its design."

Marvin stops writing. "We've also pinpointed alien devices that seem to be functioning as antennae, buried beneath Stonehenge and the city of Tiahuanaco. We believe another may be buried deep beneath the Antarctic ice sheet."

Mick nods. *The Piri Re'is map. Guardian must have constructed the antennae before the ice sheets formed.* He looks up at Dominique. "Did you tell them about the Nephilim?"

"All that I know, which isn't much."

"An advanced race of humanoids?" Marvin shakes his head. "I'm supposed to be the exobiologist around here, and I'm confused as hell."

"Marvin, the beings that created this array had to be certain their relay stations and antennae would remain undisturbed over thousands of years. Even burying them wouldn't ensure their safety. Building a vast architectural wonder like Stonehenge or the Great Pyramid directly over the site was inspired thinking. Even modern man knew enough to leave these ruins alone."

"What about the array?" Chaney says. "How long will it keep these drones from detonating?"

The memory of Guardian's words echoes in his ears. *The porthole to* Xibalba Be *will ascend on 4* Ahau, *3* Kankin. *It can only be destroyed from within. Only a Hunahpu can enter. Only a Hunahpu can expel the evil from your garden and save your species from annihilation.*

Mick feels queasy. "We have a problem. That alien vessel—it's going to ascend tomorrow—"

Chaney's eyes widen. "How do you know that?"

"It's part of a three thousand-year-old Mayan prophecy. The entity within the vessel. We have to destroy it. We have to get inside."

"How do we get inside?" Marvin asks?

"I don't know, I mean, I guess the same way Dom and I entered before, through its ventilation system." A wave of exhaustion overcomes him. He closes his eyes.

Dominique touches his forehead, registering a fever. "He's had enough, President Chaney. He's done his part to save the world; now go and do yours."

Chaney's eyes lose a bit of their harshness. "Our scientists happen to agree with you, Gabriel. They feel we need to destroy the alien vessel to end the threat of the drones exploding. I've ordered the *John C. Stennis* and her fleet into the Gulf of Mexico to do the job. If that vessel really is going to rise tomorrow, then we'll blow it out of the water."

The new president stands to leave. "An emergency meeting of the UN Security Council has been scheduled for seven o'clock this evening aboard the *Stennis*. We're expecting representatives from every nation, as well as some of the top scientists from around the world. You and Dominique are coming with us. One of my aides will bring you something to wear."

"Wait," Dominique says. "Tell him about Borgia."

"Your would-be assassin led us straight to Dr. Foletta. His confession included information about how Borgia managed to have you committed to an asylum eleven years ago. Even provided us with a tape of the secretary of state hiring him to kill you." Chaney offers a grim smile. "I'll be nailing his ass to the wall once things settle down. Meanwhile, Dominique and her mother are off the hook, and you've been certified as competent, so you are a free man, Gabriel, as loony as the rest of us."

Dominique whispers in Mick's ear. "Your nightmare's over. No more asylums, no more solitary confinement. You're free." She squeezes his hand. "We can spend the rest of our lives together."

Aboard the Aircraft Carrier *John C. Stennis*

Mick gazes out the window of the chopper as the airship descends upon the enormous four-and-a-half-acre flight deck of the *John C. Stennis*, now a virtual parking lot of helicopters.

Dominique squeezes his hand. "You okay? You haven't said a word the entire flight."

"Sorry."

"You're worried about something. What aren't you telling me?"

"My memories of my conversation with Guardian are vague. There's still so much I don't understand, things that might make the difference between life and death."

"But you are still convinced the Guardian's array was designed to prevent these drones from exploding?"

"Yes."

"Then the president's right. If we destroy the alien vessel, we'll end the threat."

"I wish it was that simple."

"Why isn't it?" They step off the chopper onto the spongy gray deck of the carrier. Dominique points to the warship's battery of weapons. "Look around you, Mick. There's enough firepower aboard this ship to wipe out a small country." She slips her arm around his waist, whispering into his ear. "Face it, you're a hero. Against all odds you managed to enter the pyramid and activate the array. You not only vindicated your parents' work, your efforts saved the lives of two billion people. It's time to give yourself a break. Step aside and let the big boys finish the job." She kisses him passionately on the lips, causing a few sailors to whistle.

A lieutenant escorts them into the superstructure, then down a tight stairwell to the hangar deck.

They pass through a heavily guarded security checkpoint, then enter the hangar bay, one-fourth of which has been hastily converted into an auditorium. A horseshoe configuration of folding chairs and tables, three rows deep, has been set up to face a podium and an enormous twenty-foot-high-by-forty-foot-long computerized map of the world, mounted high along one section of the hangar's steel bulkhead. Thirty-eight red pinpoints of light, another six in blue, indicate the drone landing spots on the map.

The lieutenant leads them to a reserved table on the left side of the horseshoe. A few delegates seem to recognize Mick, pointing at him as he walks by, nodding. A smattering of applause quickly builds to a standing ovation.

Marvin Teperman looks up from his seat and smiles at him. "At least acknowledge them, eh?"

Mick offers a quick wave, then takes his place next to the exobiologist, feeling ridiculous. United Nations Security Council President Megan Jackson walks over and greets him with a warm smile and handshake. "It's an honor to meet you, Mr. Gabriel. We're all indebted. Is there anything we can do for you?"

"You can tell me why I'm here. I'm not a politician."

"The president and I had hoped your presence might ease some of the hostility in this room." She points to a Russian delegation. "The man in the middle is Viktor Grozny. I daresay most of the people in this room would prefer him dead. The paranoia now existing between Russia and the United States makes the Cold War look like a family outing."

She offers a motherly smile, then takes her place at the podium. "If I may call this meeting to order."

The delegates take their seats. Marvin hands Dominique and Mick sets of small headphones. Removing them from their cellophane wrappers, they set the translator dials to ENGLISH, then place them over their ears.

"I call first to the dais Professor Nathan Fowler, Associate Director of the NASA Ames Research Center and head of the international team investigating the alien drones. Professor?"

A bespectacled gray-haired man in his late sixties takes his place at the podium.

"Madam President, honored delegates, fellow scientists, I'm here tonight to update you on the alien objects whose detonations have already led to the deaths of more than two million people. Despite this tragedy, the evidence I am about to share with you clearly indicates that the extraterrestrial's primary objective was not to annihilate our species. In fact, our presence on this planet is about as important to this alien intelligence as a flea to a dog."

Murmurs fill the room.

"Our team has conducted a thorough analysis of comparison among every one of the forty-four identified drone targets. These locations share one thing in common—the geology of each site is composed entirely of limestone. In fact, let me take that one step further—most of the sites targeted qualify as karst landscapes—a dense limestone formation composed of extremely high levels of calcium carbonate.

"Karst landscapes make up one-sixth of our planet's landmass. They were created about four hundred million years ago when high levels of calcium carbonate was deposited on what was then the tropical seafloor of—"

"Professor, in the interest of time—"

"Huh? Oh, of course, Madam President. If you'll just allow me a brief moment to explain the importance of limestone on our planet, then I think everyone will gain a greater understanding as to the reasons these drones were launched."

"Proceed, but be quick."

"Karst formations, and limestone in general, perform a critical function on Earth by serving as vast planetary storehouses of carbon dioxide. Calcium carbonate in karst absorbs dissolved carbon dioxide like a sponge, helping to regulate and stabilize our oxygen environment. In fact, the amount of carbon dioxide stored within sedimentary rock is more than six hundred times the total carbon content of the Earth's air, water, and living cells combined."

Dominique looks at Mick, whose complexion has turned deathly pale.

The NASA director removes a remote keypad linked to the computerized map overhead.

"Madam President, I'm going to use our computer to simulate what would happen if every one of the thirty-eight remaining drones were to simultaneously explode. Please take special note of the atmospheric temperature and carbon-dioxide readings."

A hush falls over the delegation as the professor types in a set of commands.

Two icons appear in blue along the lower border of the overhead map.

Mean Global Surface Temperature:	12/20/12
70 degrees F. (21 degrees C.)	CO_2 Content: 0.03%

Fowler strikes another key. The glowing red dots flash in unison, then ignite into bright, alabaster circles of energy. Within seconds, the explosions fade into a global fallout of dense yellow-orange debris clouds, which spread quickly over the surrounding areas, encompassing nearly a third of the Earth's surface.

Mean Global Surface Temperature:	12/20/12 (Detonation plus 10 hours)
132 degrees F. (55.5 degrees C.)	CO_2 Content: 39.23%

Fowler adjusts his glasses. "The heat from the explosions would immediately vaporize the karst limestone, releasing toxic levels of carbon dioxide into our planet's atmosphere. The cloud cover you now see expanding across the map is a dense atmospheric layer of CO_2, enough to kill every air-breathing organism on this planet."

A hundred conversations break out at once.

Fowler strikes his keypad again while the UN leader calls for order.

The map changes. Swirling yellow-orange clouds now blot out the entire globe.

Mean Global Surface Temperature:	12/20/22 (Detonation plus 10 years)
230 degrees F. (100 degrees C.)	CO_2 Content: 47.85%
	SO_2 Content: 23.21%

The room quiets.

"Here we see Earth's environmental progression after ten years. What we're looking at is the catastrophic reorganization of our planet's atmosphere, the beginning of a runaway greenhouse effect, similar to one we believe occurred on Venus more than six hundred million years ago. Venus, Earth's sister planet, once possessed hot oceans and a humid stratosphere. As carbon dioxide built up in its atmosphere, it formed a thick blanket of insulation. This led to the onset of global volcanism, the eruptions serving to compound the greenhouse effect, releasing large quantities of sulfur dioxide into the atmosphere while continuing to raise surface temperatures. Eventually, Venus's oceans vaporized entirely, forming dense clouds of precipitation. Some of this precipitation continues to encircle the planet, while the rest dispersed into space."

"Professor, have CO_2 levels risen noticeably since the explosions of the first seven drones?"

"Yes, Madam President. In fact, carbon dioxide levels have increased by six to seven percent over the—"

"Enough of this!" Viktor Grozny is standing, his gaunt face red. "I came here to negotiate the terms of an armistice, not to listen to nonsense about aliens."

The UN leader raises her voice above an outburst of protests. "President Grozny, are you questioning whether this extraterrestrial threat exists?"

"We've been informed the drone threat has been eliminated, that this—this array prevents their detonation. Is this not so, Mr. Fowler?"

Fowler looks apprehensive. "It would appear that the drones will not detonate as long as the pyramid's array remains intact. But the threat is still—"

"Then why are we wasting time discussing this now? I say we leave this to our scientists. It was my understanding that this assembly was to be political in nature. Despite numerous threats on my life, I have come to this meeting in good faith. It was Russian and Chinese civilians who died in these pure-fusion holocausts. Death is death, Madam President, whether it comes from nuclear annihilation, asphyxiation, or starvation. Let the West and their superior weaponry destroy this alien vessel. As we speak, thousands of my people

344

are starving to death. What we need to discuss is how we are going to change the world—"

"And who are you to demand change?" General Fecondo responds, fists balled as he stands. "Your concept of change was to engage the United States in nuclear war. The West gave your country billions of dollars in aid to feed your people and stimulate your economy, instead you spent it on weapons—"

Mick closes his eyes to the verbal joust, focusing instead on Professor Fowler's words. He thinks back to when he was in the alien chamber beneath the Gulf. He remembers the cut on his leg.

My blood was blue. The chamber's atmosphere must have been carbon dioxide.

He recalls Guardian's words . . . *The conditions on your world were not suitable, the intended target Venus . . . your world is being acclimated.*

"You come to us for aid," Dick Prystas bellows, "yet look how quick you were to destroy the hand you now ask to feed your people!"

"What choice had we?" Grozny retorts. "You coerce us into signing strategic arm agreements while your scientists continue working on methods of destroying us. What good are treaties when America's newest technologies are more deadly than the antiquated missiles you've so graciously eliminated?" Grozny turns to face the rest of the assembly. "Yes, it was Russia that launched first, but we were provoked. The United States has thrown around its military might for decades. Our informants tell us the Americans are less than two years from completing their own pure-fusion explosives. Two years! If these extraterrestrials had not attacked, then the United States would have."

The room grows loud again.

Grozny points an accusing finger at Chaney. "I ask the new American president—is peace truly your objective—or war?"

Chaney stands, waiting for the room to quiet. "There is blood on every hand in this room, President Grozny. Every conscience is shamed with guilt, every mind entangled in fear. But, for the grace of God, we might all be dead. We've behaved like selfish children, all of us, and if we have any hopes of surviving as a species, then we must put aside our petty differences, once and for all, and grow up."

The president steps forward. "I agree that change, drastic change is needed. Humanity can no longer tolerate the threat of self-destruction. There can be no more haves and have-nots. We must reorganize our economies into one world order—an order of peace. President Grozny, the United States is offering an olive branch. Are you willing to accept it?"

A rousing ovation sweeps through the hangar bay as Viktor Grozny walks over to the president and embraces him.

Dominique is on her feet, clapping, tears in her eyes, when she notices Mick approaching the podium.

The room grows silent.

Mick stands before the assembly, the apocalyptic message burning in his mind.

"President Chaney is a wise man. The message I carry is in my head is also from a wise man, a man whose array helped save us. While our nations discuss politics, our world is being readied, acclimated to accommodate another species, one infinitely older, one that has no aspirations of peace or war. To this enemy, Earth is nothing more than an incubator, humanity its two-million-year-old tenant, about to be removed.

"United or divided, let us make no mistake—tomorrow *is* Judgment Day. At dawn, a cosmic portal shall open—a portal that must be sealed for our species to survive. Should we fail, then nothing else said or done in this room will matter. By the solstice sunset tomorrow evening, every living creature on this planet will be dead."

346

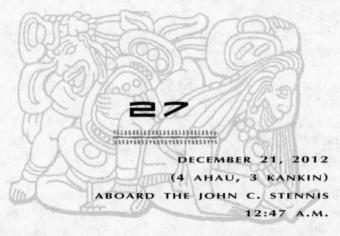

27

Michael Gabriel stares out at the black sea from the open porthole of the small VIP cabin. He is too far away to see the emerald glow; the air craft carrier is stationed two miles due east of the buried alien vessel, but somehow he can feel its presence.

"Are you going to stare out that porthole all night?" Dominique steps out of the bathroom, wearing only a towel. She nuzzles her face against his chest, slipping her arms around his waist.

He feels the moist heat rising off her naked body.

Her fingertips glide down the muscles of his stomach until they reach his groin. She looks into his dark eyes, then whispers, "Make love to me."

She reaches up and kisses him, slipping her tongue into his mouth as he fumbles to remove his clothing. Within moments they are naked, embracing each other like long-lost lovers, their pent-up emotions and fears lost in the moment as their limbs entwine, the only two people in the world.

Mick lays her back on the bed, kissing her neck as

she guides him in. Dominique moans with pleasure, tasting the sweat on his shoulder as she pulls his face to her breasts, tugging at the curls along the back of his neck.

3:22 A.M.

Mick lies naked beneath the sheet, his right hand caressing the small of Dominique's back, the girl's head resting on his bandaged chest. He stares at the ceiling, his exhausted mind repeating Guardian's words over and over like a mantra.

Xibalba Be *will ascend on 4* Ahau, *3* Kankin. *It can only be destroyed from within. Only a Hunahpu can enter. Only a Hunahpu can expel the evil from your garden. . . .*

Dominique stirs, rolling onto her side. Mick covers her with the sheet, then closes his eyes.

Come to me, Michael . . .

"Huh?" He shoots up in bed, his heart pounding. Disoriented, he looks around the cabin, a cold sweat breaking out on his back. *It's okay, it's okay—it was just a dream . . .*

Mick lies back, eyes wide-open, waiting for the demonic voice to return.

Stop it! You're driving yourself insane. He smiles weakly. *Eleven years in solitary and I'm finally losing my mind.*

He closes his eyes.

Why do you fear me, Michael?

"Shit—" He springs to his feet like a nervous cat. *Okay, stay calm. Go for a walk. Clear your head.* He dresses quickly, then slips out of the cabin.

After twenty minutes, Mick finds his way to "Vultures' Row," an open-air balcony overlooking the flight deck. The night air is cool, the ocean breeze comforting. He covers his ears as a joint strike fighter is catapulted into the clear night sky.

Once more, his mind replays Guardian's conversation. *Only a Hunahpu can enter. Only a Hunahpu can expel the evil from your garden and save your species from annihilation.*

I can feel you, Michael. You're very close. . . .

"What?"

Come to me, Michael. Don't fear me. Come to your creator.

"Stop! Stop it!" Mick squeezes his eyes shut and grabs his head in his hands.

"Mick, are you okay?"

Come to me . . . father.

"Get the fuck out of my head!" Mick spins around, his eyes wide in fright. Marvin Teperman shakes him by the shoulders. "Hey, are you all right?"

"Huh? Oh, shit. I—I don't know. I think I'm going nuts."

"You and the rest of the world. Couldn't sleep, eh?"

"No. Marvin, the drone that landed in Chichén Itzá, do you know exactly *where* it landed?"

The exobiologist removes a small tablet from his jacket pocket. "Hold on, it's here somewhere. Let's see, Chichén Itzá. Yes, the drone landed in something called the Great Mayan Ball Court. Dead center, to be exact."

Mick feels a chill run down his spine. "Dead center? You're certain?"

"Yes. What's wrong?"

"We need a chopper! Marvin, can you get us a chopper?"

"A chopper? What for?"

"I can't explain it, I just need to get to Chichén Itzá—now!"

Sanibel Island,
West Coast of Florida

5:12 A.M.

Edith Axler stands on the deserted coastline, staring at the gray horizon and the speedboat approaching quickly in the distance. Her nephew, Harvey, waves, then drives the boat right onto the beach.

"Any problems locating SOSUS?"

"No," he says, carefully handing her what little remains of a large spool of fiber-optic cable. "The microphone was anchored just where you said it would be. But after all that black tide crap, it was a little spooky diving at night."

He climbs out of the boat, following his aunt to the back door of the lab. Once inside, Edie powers up the SOSUS system while Harvey connects the fiber-optic cable to the mainframe.

"Will this allow us access to every microphone in the Gulf?" he asks.

"It's an integrated system. As long as this cable holds, I don't see why not. We won't be on-line with the computer at Dan Neck, but we should be able to eavesdrop on that alien object buried off the Yucatán coast."

Harvey smiles, finishing the connection. "Feels like we're pirating free cable."

Gulf of Mexico

6:41 A.M.

The squadron of joint strike fighters continues to circle in formation, their pilots edgy as they await the first rays of dawn. On the surface below, the *John*

C. Stennis and her fleet have moved into position, forming a three-mile-wide perimeter around the glowing patch of sea.

Maneuvering in fifteen hundred feet of water, circling in darkness beneath the fleet is the *Los Angeles*-class attack sub, *Scranton* (SSN-756). In silent vigil, Captain Bo Dennis and his crew stand ready—their orders—pulverize anything that rises from the luminescent emerald hole.

Aboard the *John C. Stennis*, the deck of the aircraft carrier is electric with activity.

Tomahawk surface-to-air missile batteries in the bow and stern target the glowing patch of sea, their deadly payloads aimed skyward, preparing to launch at a moment's notice. Three more Predator unmanned aerial vehicles launch to join a dozen others, all circling above the target zone.

The six thousand men and women aboard the floating city are a collective bundle of nerves. They have read the news and seen the riots on television. If the Apocalypse is really upon them, then it is they who stand upon its threshold. Confidence, wrought by thousands of hours of intensive training, has deserted them, a by-product of having barely averted a nuclear holocaust. Discipline keeps them at their battle stations, but it is fear and not adrenaline that fuels them now.

Dominique Vazquez is filled with a different kind of fear. For the first time in her life, she has opened her heart to a man, allowing herself to feel vulnerable. Now, as she searches the massive warship, her heart is gripped in physical pain, her mind panicking as she realizes Mick has abandoned her, and that she may never see him again.

She enters a restricted area, pushing her way past an MP. As he grabs her from behind, she slams the startled guard backwards into the far wall with a vicious backthrust kick. Another guard intercepts her as she attempts to enter the Combat Information Center. "Let me go—I need to see Chaney!"

"You can't enter—the CIC is a restricted area."

"I need to find Mick—ow, you're breaking my arm!"

The watertight door opens, two officers exiting. She sees the president. "President Chaney!"

Chaney looks up from the row of UAV monitors. "It's all right. Let her in."

Dominique turns to face the MP, then slams the heel of both palms hard into his chest. "Don't ever touch me again." She enters the darkened nerve center, now packed with heads of state.

"Dominique—"

"Where is he? You know where he is, now tell me! Where have you taken him?"

Chaney pulls her aside. "Gabriel left by chopper early this morning. He came to me. It was his request."

"Where did he go?"

"He gave me a letter to give to you." Chaney fishes the folded envelope from his breast pocket. Dominique tears it opens.

My dearest Dom:

There is so much I wish I could tell you, so much I want to explain, but can't. There are voices in my head, pulling me in different directions. I don't know if the voices are real, or if my mind has finally snapped.

Guardian's voice tells me that I am a Hunahpu. He says it was my genetic code that allowed us access to the starship. Perhaps it is these genetics that enable me to communicate with the entity beneath the Gulf.

One of the entity's drones landed dead center of the Great Mayan Ball Court in Chichén Itzá. My father believed a strong relationship exists between the Great Ball Court and the dark rift of the Milky Way. Like the Kukulcán pyramid, this field has also been oriented to the night sky. By midnight tonight, the dark rift will have moved into alignment directly over the center point of this field. The nexus will be open. It's opening even now, I can feel it.

It was a Mayan tradition to bury a stone marker at the center point of each ball court. My father was present when archaeologists removed the center stone from Chichén Itzá's field. Before he died, Julius told me that he had stolen the real marker years ago, then reburied it. He kept this a secret from me until his last dying breath. Somehow, he knew I'd need the stone.

It can't be just a coincidence that the drone landed where it did. Maybe the entity in the Gulf knows the marker is there and doesn't want us to find it. All I do know is that the enemy vessel will rise to meet the winter solstice. When the entity within realizes its drones have not detonated, it will go after Guardian's array, attempting to destroy it.

I cannot allow that to happen.

I'm sorry for running out on you like this. Last night was the greatest night of my life. I don't want it to be our last.

I love you, I always will . . .

—Mick

She stares at the letter. "This . . . this isn't fair. Does he expect me to just wait here?" Dominique chases after the President. "I need to get to Chichén Itzá—"

"Sir, something's happening out there." A crowd gathers around the UAV monitors.

Dominique grabs Chaney's arm. "Take me to him. You owe me that."

"Dominique, he specifically said no. He made me promise—"

"He needs me. He needs my help—"

"Mr. President, we're recording a seismic event," a technician reports, "7.5 on the Richter scale and still rising—"

Chaney places a hand on Dominique's shoulder. "Listen to me. One way or another, we're going to destroy whatever's in that vessel, do you understand? Mick's going to be fine."

"Sir, the *Scranton* is hailing us."

Aboard the USS *Scranton*

Commander Bo Dennis raises his voice above the thunderous rumble of the undersea earthquake. "Admiral, the entire seafloor's breaking up. Electromagnetic interference is increasing—"

A sonar technician presses the headphones to his ears. "Skipper, something's rising from that hole, something huge!"

*　　　　*　　　　*

An immense blast of antigravity pulses outward from beneath the remains of the iridium object, the invisible wave repelling the mass away from its sixty-five-million-year-old resting place, punching it upward through a mile of fragmented limestone. Like a monstrous cannonball, the titanic mass of iridium, more than a mile in diameter, ascends straight up through a billion tons of debris, the decimated seafloor crumbling within the vacuum of the rising colossus's wake. The mammoth upheaval decimates the surrounding seafloor, sending seismic ripples racing across the entire semienclosed basin of the Gulf of Mexico, as the Campeche shelf and surrounding seafloor suffer the equivalent of a 9.2 magnitude earthquake.

The expulsion of the alien vessel gives birth to a series of deadly tsunamis, the killer waves racing away from the epicenter toward the pristine beaches of the Gulf like a ring of death.

*　　　　*　　　　*

"Skipper, the alien object has now cleared the seafloor—"

"Firing solutions plotted, sir, she's too big to miss."

Commander Dennis holds on as the sub rolls hard to port. "Helm, keep us clear of the debris field. Chief, firing point procedures, make tubes one and two ready in all respects."

"Aye, sir. Tubes one and two ready."

"Match sonar bearings. Shoot tubes one and two."

"Aye, sir. Shooting tubes one and two. Torpedoes away."

"Ten seconds to impact. Seven . . . six . . . five . . ."

The two projectiles plow through the turbulent sea toward the rising mass. Fifty feet before impact, the warheads strike an invisible force field and detonate.

Aboard the *John C. Stennis*

"Admiral, the *Scranton* reports direct hits, but no damage. The object appears to be shielded within a force field, and it's still rising."

All eyes stare at the row of UAV monitors. Hovering two hundred feet above the sea, the Predator's cameras reveal a ring of bubbles forming along the surface.

"Here she comes!"

The ovoid mass violates the surface like a dome-shaped iceberg, its girth sinking, then bobbing until it finds its equilibrium atop the churning sea. UAV close-ups of the scorched iridium surface reveal a network of jagged metallic escarpments and crater-size indentations.

Sensors transmit computer-enhanced images of the alien vessel's design. Dominique stares at the three-dimensional holographic image. Twenty-three tubular appendages dangle below the remains of the vessel, giving her the impression of an enormous mechanical man-of-war.

"Contact our air wings," the admiral commands. "Open fire."

The joint strike fighters break from formation and launch a salvo of SLAMMER missiles. The weapons explode just above the islandlike mass, the multiple detonations momentarily revealing the presence of a neon blue force field.

The CNO swears aloud. "The goddam thing's sealed within a protective field, just like its drones. Captain Ramirez—"

"Aye, sir."

"Order the JSFs to clear the target area. Launch two Tomahawks. Let's see how powerful this field really is."

Dominique covers her ears as a thunderous boom shudders the warship.

The guidance systems of the two Tomahawk missiles have been dismantled to prevent the Guardian's array from disrupting their trajectory. Launched at point-blank range, the warheads slam into their target, the double blast sending a fireball racing skyward, momentarily blinding the real-time camera images of the circling UAVs.

The pictures return. The vessel is still intact.

And then something happens.

353

Mechanical motion appears along the center region of the floating mass, followed by an intense green flash of light.

The beacon is coming from an opening in the alien hull casing, but it is not a hatch, as in the top of a submarine, nor is it a rip or tear. Shards of iridium appear to be peeling open in layers, then folding back, away from the vortex of energy.

From out of the emerald green luminescence appears—a being.

The hulking form pushes through headfirst.

The Navy cameras refocus, the images revealing the being's face—that of an enormous alien viper. The mammoth skull, adorned in featherlike scales, is as large as a billboard. Two crimson eyes blaze like luminescent beacons, the reptilian pupils—vertical slits of amber, narrowing in the morning light. A set of bizarre jaws opens, individually stretching and extending two ungodly ebony fangs, each tooth easily five foot long, the rest of the distended mouth filled with rows of scalpel-sharp teeth.

A gargantuan reptilian gasp sends thick layers of oily, scalelike emerald green feathers bristling along the alien's broad back.

Sharp spines along the creature's belly grip the iridium surface as the alien rears up in the manner of an immense cobra—

—the beast gazing skyward for the briefest of moments, as if analyzing the atmosphere.

With lightning speed, it plunges headfirst into the sea, its monstrous girth disappearing beneath the waves.

The president and his Joint Chiefs stare dumbfounded at the monitors.

"Good God . . . was that thing real?" Chaney whispers.

A shaken communications specialist listens to an incoming message in his headphone. "Admiral, the *Scranton* reports the E.T. is moving through the thermocline, its last recorded speed . . . Jesus—ninety-two knots. Course is south by southeast. Sir, the life-form appears to be heading directly for the Yucatán Peninsula."

Chichén Itzá

An agitated crowd of more than two hundred thousand zealots has gathered in the parking lot of Chichén Itzá, chanting and throwing stones at the heavily armed Mexican militia, as they attempt to force their way through the blocked main entrance of the ancient Mayan city.

Inside the park, four American M1-A2 Abrams tanks have taken up defensive positions along each side of the Kukulcán pyramid. In the surrounding jungle, two squadrons of heavily armed Green Berets lie in wait, hidden among the dense foliage.

Just west of the Kukulcán pyramid is the Great Ball Court of Chichén

Itzá, an immense complex erected in the shape of the letter "I," enclosed on all sides by walls of limestone block.

The eastern wall of the ball court is composed of a three-story structure known as the Temple of the Jaguars, its columned entrance sculpted in the form of plumed serpents. The structure rising along the ball court's northern border is called the Temple of the Bearded Man. The facade along both of these vertical walls features engravings of the great Kukulcán emerging from the jowls of a plumed serpent. Other scenes depicts Kukulcán, dressed in a tunic, lying dead, being engulfed by a two-headed serpent.

Mounted high along the faces of the eastern and western walls are donut-shaped stone rings, positioned vertically like sideways basketball hoops. Invented by the Olmec, the ceremonial ritual known as the Ball Game was meant to symbolize the epic battle between light and dark, good and evil. Two teams of seven warriors competed against each other, attempting to shoot a rubber ball through their vertical hoop, using only their elbows, hips, or knees. The rewards of the game were simple, the motivation pure: The winners were rewarded, the losers beheaded.

Michael Gabriel is at the center of the 313-foot grass court, standing in the drone's shadow, directing a three-man team of US Army Rangers. With picks and shovels, the men dig in an eight-foot-deep hole, burrowing their way through the brittle geology to a point just beneath the alien object's talons.

The strength of the drone's force field is causing Mick's hair to stand on end.

He looks up as a Jeep enters the south end of the ball court. Colonel E. J. Catchpole jumps out of the vehicle before it comes to a halt. "We just got word, Gabriel. The alien mass surfaced, just as you predicted."

"Was the Navy able to destroy it?"

"Negative. The vessel's protected within the same force field as these damn drones. There's more. An alien emerged—"

"An alien? What did it look like?" Mick's heart is pounding like a bass drum.

"Don't know. The pyramid's array is causing communication problems. The only thing I could make out is that it's huge, and the Navy thinks it's headed in our direction." The colonel kneels by the hole. "Lieutenant, I want you and your men out of this hole."

"Yes, sir."

"Colonel, you're not giving up—"

"Sorry, Gabriel, but I need every man available to guard that array. What is it you're looking for anyway?"

"I told you, it's some kind of stone, a round marker, about the size of a football. It's probably buried directly beneath the drone's talons."

The lieutenant climbs out from the hole, followed by two more Ranger commandos, each man covered in a white, powdery dust.

The lieutenant drinks from his canteen, then spits out the last mouthful. "Here's the deal, Gabriel. We located the edge of some sort of metallic canister, but if my men try to remove it, the weight of this drone will collapse the tunnel. We left a flashlight and pick down there if you want to try, but I'd advise against it."

The commandos climb into the Jeep.

"I suggest you hightail it out of here before the fireworks begin," the colonel yells, as the vehicle accelerates to the west.

Mick watches the Jeep leave, then descends down the rope ladder into the hole.

The Rangers have excavated a narrow horizontal shaft running beneath the drone. Collecting the pick in one hand, a flashlight in the other, Mick crawls through the burrow on his knees, the sounds from above quickly becoming muffled in his ears.

The tunnel dead-ends twelve feet in. Protruding through the rock above his head are the razor-sharp tips of the creature's talons.

Embedded in the limestone ceiling between the two black claws—the lower half of a shiny metal canister, the same iridium container he and his father had found long ago, buried in the Nazca desert.

Mick gently chips around one exposed side of the container, loosening it with the other. Gravel falls on his back, fissures opening up along the ceiling. He continues tapping, feeling the object loosening, knowing at any second the ceiling will collapse, burying him under the weight of the geology and the alien drone.

Clumps of white dirt blind him as, with a final tug, he pulls the canister free, leaping backwards as—

—a section of ceiling collapses in a blinding white curtain of dust and debris, the two-thousand-pound drone collapsing through the shaft.

Mick crawls back through the remains of the tunnel, dragging himself from the rubble, his body covered in white dust, his left hand, smeared in blood, still clutching the metal container.

He climbs up the ladder, spitting and coughing, then collapses on his back near the edge of the hole and inhales the fresh air. Feeling for his bottled water, he pours the warm liquid over his face, rinses out, then sits up and turns his attention to the canister.

For a long moment he just gazes at the object, gathering his strength, the scarlet icon of the Trident of Paracas—the Guardian's insignia—staring back at him.

"Okay, Julius, let's see what you've been hiding from me all these years."

He pries opens the lid, removing the strange object within.

What is this?

It is a jade object, rounded and heavy, about the size of a human skull. Protruding from one side is the handle of an immense obsidian dagger. Mick attempts to remove the weapon, but it is wedged in too tightly.

Inscribed along the other side of the object are two images. The first, an epic battle depicting a bearded Caucasian and a giant plumed serpent, the man holding a small object, keeping the beast at bay. The second image is that of a Mayan warrior.

Mick stares at the warrior's face, goose bumps tightening across his chalk-covered skin.

My God . . . it's me.

Sanibel Island,
West Coast of Florida

The SOSUS alarm awakens Edith Axler with a start. Lifting her head from the table, she reaches over to the computer terminal for her headphones, then places them over her ears and listens.

Her nephew, Harvey, enters the lab in time to see the expression on his aunt's face drop. "What is it?"

She tosses him the headphones, then hurriedly boots the seismograph.

Harvey listens as ink begins scribbling across the graph paper. "What is that—"

"Massive earthquake below the Campeche shelf," she rasps, her heart racing. "Must have occurred less than an hour ago. That rumbling sound you hear is a series of very powerful tsunamis shoaling up along the West Florida shelf—"

"Shoaling?"

"Bunching together as they slow up, driving the energy vertical. These waves are going to be massive by the time they hit the shore. They'll submerge every island on the coast."

"How soon?"

"I'm guessing fifteen to twenty minutes tops. I'll call the Coast Guard and the mayor, you alert the police, then get the car. We need to get out of here."

Gulf of Mexico

The Sikorsky SH-60B Seahawk soars fifty feet above the whitecaps, the other four naval choppers following close behind. High above, two squadrons of joint strike fighters train their sensors on the fast-moving ripple of water a half mile ahead.

Dominique gazes out her window, staring at the monstrous ripples in the sea. In the distance, the Yucatán coastline peeks out behind an early-morning fog.

Below, propagating along the seafloor at speeds exceeding that of a jetliner is the first in a series of tsunamis. The killer wall of water slows as it hits the shallows, refraction and shoaling redirecting its awesome fury upward, the swell cresting directly beneath the airship. General Fecondo taps the copilot. "Why haven't the JSFs continued firing?"

The copilot looks back. "They report the target's too deep, moving way too fast. No signature, nothing to lock on to. Don't worry, General, the E.T.'s about to run out of sea. Our birds'll splatter it the moment it hits the beach."

President Chaney turns to face Dominique, his dark complexion looking pasty and gray. "You doing okay back there?"

"I'll be better when I—" She stops talking, staring down at the water, feeling her sense of equilibrium faltering as the sea appears to be rising straight up beneath them. "Hey—look out! Take us higher!"

"Shit—" The pilot yanks hard on the joystick as the monstrous wave pushes upward against the chopper's undercarriage, lifting the airship as if it were a surfboard.

Dominique grips the seat in front of her as the Sikorsky lurches sideways. For a surreal moment, the helicopter teeters atop the mountainous swell, and then the eighty-seven-foot wave releases them and plummets, punishing the beachhead below with a thunderous slap.

The chopper levels out, hovering high above the submerged landscape, its passengers and crew catching a collective breath as the killer wave races inland, devastating everything in its path.

A deafening roar as the joint strike fighters circle overhead.

"General, our air wing reports they've lost all visual contact with the E.T."

"Is it in the wave?"

"No, sir."

"Then where the hell is it?" Chaney yells. "Something that size just can't disappear."

"Must still be in the sea," the general says. "Have the choppers double back to the last reported site. Send the jets up and down the coastline. We need to cut that alien off before it moves inland."

Ten long minutes pass.

From her vantage, Dominique watches the tsunami's tidal surge retreat back to the sea, the churning river of water dragging uprooted palm trees, debris, and livestock with it. "Mr. President, we're wasting time—"

Chaney turns around to face her. "The E.T.'s still out there somewhere."

"And what if it's not? What if it's on its way to Chichén Itzá like Mick said?"

General Fecondo turns. "We've got thirty choppers circling the Yucatán coastline. The moment that thing shows its face—"

"Wait! Mick said the geology of the peninsula's like a giant sponge. There's a whole labyrinth of subterranean caves that connect to the sea. The alien's not hiding, it's traveling underground!"

Sanibel Island

Edie pounds on the door of her friend's home. "Suz, open up!"

Sue Reuben opens the front door, still half-asleep. "Ead, what's—"

Edith grabs her by the wrist and drags her to the car.

"Edie, for God's sake, I'm in my pajamas—"

"Just get in. There's a tsunami coming!" Harvey guns the engine as the two elderly women climb in, accelerating the car wildly through residential areas, then back toward the main road.

"A tsunami? How big? What about the rest of the island?"

"Coast Guard choppers are hitting the beach areas and streets. Radio and television announcements have been broadcasting for ten minutes. Didn't you hear the sirens?"

"I don't sleep with my hearing aid."

Harvey slams on the brakes as they approach the four-way intersection leading to the causeway. The only bridge off Sanibel Island is bumper-to-bumper with traffic.

"Looks like word is out," Harvey says, yelling above the din of blaring horns.

Edie checks her watch. "This is no good. We have to get out."

"On foot?" Sue shakes her head. "Ead, the tollbooth's more than a mile away. I'm wearing slippers—"

Edith opens the door, dragging her friend from the backseat. Harvey takes his aunt's free hand and leads the two through the line of cars toward the other side of the bridge.

For the next several minutes, the trio rushes in and out of traffic, hurrying across the bridge to the distant tollbooth.

Edie looks up as several teenagers zoom by on motorized roller blades, shielding her eyes against the glare coming off the bay waters that loop around Sanibel Island to the Gulf of Mexico.

Maneuvering slowly down the coastline is a red-and-black oil tanker.

Beyond the tanker, three miles offshore, an unfathomable wall of water is rising straight out of the sea.

Sue Reuben turns, staring in disbelief at the wave. "Oh my God, is that thing real?"

Car horns blast, desperate passengers fleeing their vehicles as the monster wave crests into a 125-foot swell.

The tsunami sweeps up the oil tanker in its rising curl, then breaks atop the enormous steel vessel, pummeling it against the seafloor. The thunderous impact causes the bridge to reverberate as the killer wave crashes upon the Sanibel coastline, the roaring swell pounding everything into oblivion.

Edie drags her nephew and friend toward the deserted tollbooth. Harvey yanks open the door and pulls them inside as the tsunami flattens Sanibel and Captiva Island, its tremendous tidal surge blasting across the bay.

Harvey slides the door closed as Edie pulls Sue down onto the floor.

The tsunami races across the causeway, submerging the tollbooth.

The concrete-and-steel structure groans. Seawater pours in from all sides, filling the four-foot rectangle of Plexiglas. Edie, Harvey, and Sue stand in the torrent, enveloped in cold water and darkness as the water level continues rising, the tsunami's roar like a freight train, its power shaking the tollbooth loose from its foundation.

The pocket of air fills. Edie squeezes her eyes shut, waiting to die. Her last thought is of Iz, wondering if she'll see him.

Lungs burning, her pulse pounding in her ears.

And then the roar passes, the sunlight returning.

Harvey kicks open the door.

The three survivors stumble out, gagging and coughing, holding each other against a knee-deep river of water, which continues rushing inland.

Edie grabs hold of Sue, supporting her against the torrent. "Everyone okay?"

Sue nods. "Should we go back?"

"No, tsunamis come in multiple sets. We need to run."

Locking arms, they wade and stumble down the submerged highway as the tidal surge slows, then suddenly reverses directions, threatening to sweep them into the bay. Grabbing on to a traffic pole, they hold on and pray, fighting to stay alive against the churning river of debris.

Chichén Itzá

Cradling the jade object in his hands, Mick stares at the image of the warrior as if looking in a mirror.

A breeze—then a fluttering sound—coming from within the iridium canister.

Mick reaches inside, surprised to find a piece of faded cardboard. His hand shakes as he reads the familiar handwriting.

Michael:

Should destiny take you this far, then right now, you are as stunned as your mother and I were when the object in your hand was first unearthed back in 1981. You were just an innocent child of three, and I, well, for a while I was actually foolish enough to believe the warrior's image to be of me. Then your mother pointed out the darkness of the eyes, and we both instinctively knew that, somehow, the image was meant to be you.

Now you know the real reason why mother and I refused to give up our quest—the reason you were denied a normal childhood back in the States. A greater destiny awaits you, Michael, and we felt it our duty as your parents to prepare you as best we could.

After two decades of research, I still have no real understanding as to the function of this jade device. I suspect it may be a weapon of some sort, left to us by Kukulcán himself, though I can find no power source to speak of that might identify its purpose. I have surmised the obsidian blade lodged within its grasp to be an ancient ceremonial knife, more than a thousand years old, perhaps one that may have once been used to cut out the hearts of sacrificial victims.

I can only hope that you'll figure the rest out by the time the winter solstice of 2012 arrives.

I pray God helps you on your quest, whatever it may be, and pray also that, one day, you will find it in your heart to forgive this wretched soul for all he has done.

Your loving father,
—J. G.

Mick stares at the letter, rereading it over and over, his mind fighting to grasp what he knows in his heart to be true.

It's me. I'm the One.

He stands, drops the letter and canister back in the hole, then, clutching the jade object, runs out of the deserted ball court to the western steps of the Kukulcán pyramid.

The sweat is pouring from him by the time he reaches the summit. Wiping the perspiration and remnants of dust from his brow, he staggers into the northern corridor to where the Guardian's hydraulic trapdoor is concealed.

"Guardian, let me in! Guardian—"

He stamps on the stone floor, calling out again and again.

Nothing happens.

At six feet, seven inches and three hundred pounds, Lt. Colonel Mike "Ming-Ding" Slayer is the tallest Green Beret ever to wear the commando uniform. The raspy-voiced, Chinese-Irish-American is a former professional football player and medical wonder, having had nearly every body part repaired, replaced, or recycled. Ming-Ding has a reputation for punching things with the intent to hurt when he cannot think of the word he wants to use, or when his shoulder or knee goes out.

Using his sleeve, the commando wipes the sweat from his upper lip before the mosquitoes can get to it. *Three fucking hours, picking our underwear from our asses in this godforsaken Mexican jungle.*

Ming-Ding Slayer is beyond ready to hit something.

The crackling of static in his left ear. The lieutenant colonel adjusts his communicator. "Go ahead, Colonel."

"Satellite Ops have detected a magnetic flux approaching your position from the north. We believe the alien is traveling through the aquifers and may rise through the sinkhole."

About fucking time. "Copy that. We're more than ready."

Ming-Ding signals for his platoon to take up positions around the sinkhole. Each man carries an OICW (Objective Individual Combat Weapon), the most lethal machine gun in the world. The fourteen-pound device has two barrels, one to shoot 5.56mm rounds of ammunition, the other for the 20mm HE air-bursting rounds that can be set to explode on impact or after a short delay, in front of, behind, or above an enemy target.

Sgt. John "Dirty Red" McCormack joins the lieutenant colonel, the two men staring into the pond scum below. "So, where is this fucking alien?"

"Murphy's law of combat number sixteen. If you've secured an objective, don't forget to let the enemy know about it."

The ground begins trembling, ripples spreading across the surface below.

"Guess I spoke too soon." Ming-Ding signals to his men, then backs away from the edge as the tremors grow stronger.

Dirty Red stares down his laser sight. *Come on, motherfucker. Come and get it.*

The ground is jumping so much, the commandos can hardly aim.

The far wall of the cenote collapses. A blast of limestone-and-water rain explodes outward—

The alien rises out of the cenote.

Ming-Ding's muscles tighten in fear. "Son-uva-bitch—Fire! Fire!"

A carpet of lead roars from the commandos' guns.

The bullets never reach the alien. A clear shield of energy, visible only through its distortion, envelops the serpent like a second skin. As the bullets enter the field, they appear to vaporize in midair.

"What in the fuck?" Ming-Ding stares in horror and confusion as his men continue firing.

Moving past the commandoes as if they weren't there, the alien entity glides down the Mayan *sacbe*, its locomotive-size girth pushing through the jungle foliage toward the pyramid.

Ming-Ding activates the transmitter on his helmet. "Colonel, we made contact with the alien—or at least we tried to. Our bullets were useless, sir—they just sort of vanished into thin air."

Mick can hear the echo of the approaching helicopter's rotors beating the air as he stares at the Mayan Ball Court from atop the Kukulcán, watching as the naval airship lands on the lawn adjacent to the pyramid's western stairwell.

His heart pounds as he sees Dominique exit behind the president and two US Army commandos.

Michael . . .

Mick gasps, turning to the north. He can sense something approaching from the jungle.

Something immense!

The canopy of trees lining the *sacbe* are uprooted as the being approaches.

On the ground below, four M1-A2 Abrams tanks race down the dirt pathway in single formation, their laser range finders taking aim down the center of the ancient Mayan road.

Mick's eyes widen, his heart fluttering.

Above the treetops, the alien's cranium appears, its crimson eyes glittering like rubies in the afternoon sun.

Tezcatilpoca . . .

The tanks open fire, four projectiles exploding as one out of the armored vehicle's 120mm smoothbore guns.

There is no contact, no explosion. Reaching the alien's hide, the shells simply disappear into a dense cushion of air with quick, blinding flashes.

Continuing its approach, the serpent glides over the tanks. For a moment, the Abrams tanks vanish within the energy field, only to reappear seconds later, their titanium plates and gun turrets mangled beyond recognition.

Guardian's words, ringing in his ears: **Tezcatilpoca harbors the porthole into the fourth-dimensional corridor.**

The porthole into the fourth-dimensional corridor . . . it's Tezcatilpoca! Tezcatilpoca IS the porthole!

The plumed serpent rises up the northern balustrade, the demonic eyes luminescent, radiating energy. Swimming within the bloodred corneas, the golden slits of the reptilian pupils widen, as if revealing flames from a hellish furnace.

Mick stares at the creature, his mind gripped in absolute fear. *He wants me to enter that?*

The serpent pauses at the summit. Ignoring Mick, it opens its mouth, exhaling a vaporous gust of emerald energy from between the retracted fangs.

With a great *whoosh*, the limestone temple ignites into unearthly vermilion flames, the alien fire melting the stone blocks within seconds.

Mick backs away from the intense heat, taking cover along the top three steps of the northern stairs.

The flames extinguish. From the conflagration, protruding like a flagpole from what little remains of the temple's central wall—a fifteen-foot-high iridium antenna.

The array!

You are Hunahpu. You have the ability to access the Nephilim array.

The sudden instinct for survival releases a long-dormant thought process. Highly charged impulses course through the nerve endings in Mick's fingers and into the jade object, causing it to radiate with an intense, almost blinding energy.

The alien stops dead in its tracks, its amber pupils disappearing within its crimson eye slits.

Mick's heart is pounding like a jackhammer, his arm quivering from the power emanating though his body.

The blinded viper gazes at the stone as if in a trance.

Mick closes his eyes, fighting to maintain his sanity. *Okay, just stay calm. Lead it away from the array.*

Keeping his arm extended, he descends, one harrowing step at a time, down the western staircase.

As if being led on an invisible leash, the being follows him down.

Dominique races to him—then stops—her eyes widening in shock. "Oh, God. Oh my God—"

Chaney, General Fecondo, and two Army commandos remain motionless behind one of the short walls of the ball court, their minds unable to fathom what their eyes are seeing.

"Dominique!" With his free hand, Mick shakes her out of her stupor. "Dom, you can't be here!"

"Oh, God—" She grabs his hand, dragging him back. "Come on—"

"No, wait—Dom, do you remember what I told you? Do you remember what symbolized the entrance to the Underworld in the *Popol Vuh?*"

She turns to face him, then looks up at the monstrous alien. "Oh, no. Oh, God, no—"

"Dom, the plumed serpent *is* the portal to the Black Road—"

"No—"

"And I think I'm One Hunahpu!"

Michael . . .

Mick's flesh crawls.

She stares at him in absolute fear, the windblown tears streaking across her face. "What are you going to do? You're not going to sacrifice yourself, are you?"

"Dom—"

"No!" She grabs his arm.

I'm coming, Michael. I can feel your fear . . .

"I won't let you do it! Mick, please . . . I love you—"

Mick feels his will weakening. "Dom, I love you, and I'm really scared. But please, if you ever want to see me again, you have to go, please go, right now!" Mick turns to Chaney. "Get her away from here! Now!"

General Fecondo and the two commandos drag her, kicking and screaming, back to the chopper.

Chaney moves next to Mick, his eyes never leaving the alien. "What are you going to do?

"I'm not sure, but whatever happens, keep Dominique away from here."

"You have my word. Now do us all a favor and kill this thing." Chaney backs away, then climbs into the chopper.

The airship lifts off.

A wave of dizziness forces Mick to one knee, causing him to lose his concentration.

The light emanating from the jade stone diminishes.

The alien serpent shakes its mammoth head. Its amber pupils reappear, the vertical slits widening. Two additional eyes embedded in the alien's cheek pits regain focus on Mick's thermal signature and on the waning brilliance of his weapon.

Not good. . . . Stay focused—

Tezcatilpoca rears back on its lower torso, roaring a hideous alien syllable, as if declaring itself no longer under Mick's spell.

All four viper eyes burn into Mick, focusing on him as if seeing him for the first time. The jaws open. A sizzling black bile drips from the retracted upper fangs, splattering like acidic venom upon the limestone steps below.

Adrenaline courses through Mick's body. He closes his eyes to die—then, with it a sudden spasm of primal cognizance, he *feels* the array in his mind.

Tezcatilpoca hyperextends its jaws, baring its hideous fangs—launching its upper torso at the Hunahpu with terrifying speed.

Like a bolt of lightning, the electric blue burst of energy ignites from the pyramid's antenna, catching the serpent in midstrike. Impaled within the array, the creature writhes in agony, its girth disappearing then reappearing within waves of sizzling emerald energy, its scalelike plumage and spines standing on end in rhythmic spasms.

Mick remains motionless before the alien monstrosity, his eyes remaining closed as he directs his newfound Hunahpu instincts, focusing the enormous power of the Guardian's array upon his shrieking enemy.

Shuddering in rage, Tezcatilpoca unleashes a deafening resonance, the verbal assault echoing across the esplanade, causing the columns of the Warriors' Complex to topple.

Opening his eyes, Mick holds the center stone overhead and wills the obsidian dagger from its glowing sheath.

The jade object pulsates furiously, radiating a white-hot energy, the heat singeing his hand.

Taking aim, he hurls the object at the alien's open maw.

An eruption of pure energy—like a sun going nova.

Tezcatilpoca goes into spasms—as if struck by a billion watts of electricity.

Shielding his eyes, Mick falls to his knees, disengaging the array.

The lifeless alien being collapses upon the northern steps, its once-luminescent eyes melding into shades of gray, its open mouth coming to rest between the two limestone serpent heads, positioned along either side of the northern balustrade like bookends.

Mick collapses onto his back, his limbs quivering, his lungs—fighting to catch a breath.

Her face pressed against the helicopter's bay window, Dominique screams for joy, then leaps over the seat in front of her and strangles Chaney in a bear hug.

"Okay, okay. Take us down, Lieutenant. This young lady wants to see her man."

General Fecondo has the radio receiver pressed to his ear, trying to hear over the shouting within the airship. "Say again, Admiral Gordon—"

The CNO's voice crackles over the headphone. "Repeat—the alien vessel is still shielded. You may have killed the beast, but its power source is still very active."

Eyes closed, Mick lies back on the hard, grass-covered esplanade, his exhausted mind struggling to reestablish the neural connection that had somehow allowed him to activate Guardian's array.

Frustrated, he sits up, staring at the obsidian blade in his hand. *I'm Hunahpu, but I'm not the One. I can't access the Black Road. I can't seal the portal.* He turns to see a platoon of heavily armed commandos emerge from the jungle.

Ming-Ding Slayer drags him to his feet. "Sonuva bitch, Gabriel, how the hell you do it?"

"I wish I knew."

Several commandos fire off rounds at the inanimate alien's head, their bullets vaporizing before striking the target.

Michael . . .

Mick looks up—startled. The voice is different—familiar. Somehow soothing.

Guardian . . .

Closing his eyes, he allows the voice to guide his thoughts deeper into the depths of his mind.

Push aside your fear, Hunahpu. Open the portal and enter. The Under Lords left on Earth will come forward to challenge you. They will attempt to prevent you from sealing the cosmic portal before the Death God arrives.

Mick opens his eyes, focusing on Tezcatilpoca's hideous mouth.

From the Guardian's antenna ignites an electric blue beacon of energy, which locks on to the serpent's inanimate skull.

The upper jaw begins opening—the startled commandos jump back, several futilely opening fire on the dead beast.

Mick closes his eyes, maintaining his focus. The alien's jaws hyperextend, exposing hideous ebony fangs, surrounded by hundreds of needle-sharp teeth.

And then a second viperous head appears. Identical but slightly smaller, it juts forward to protrude from the mouth of the first.

Mick clenches his eyes shut, forcing his concentration deeper. A third and final head pushes out from the mouth of the second, the three extended serpent jaws locking in place.

The array shuts down. Mick drops to one knee, his focus sapped, his mind exhausted from the effort.

And then, high above the pyramid appears a rotating emerald cylinder of energy, a cosmic fourth-dimensional corridor traversing space and time, reaching down from the darkening heavens to link with the tail of the inanimate alien serpent.

The commandos drop their weapons. Ming-Ding falls to his knees, stunned, as if he is gazing into the face of God.

Somewhere off to Mick's right, the president's helicopter lands.

Mick gazes into the open portal, weighing his decision, struggling to push aside his fear.

"Mick!"

Dominique climbs down from the chopper.

*Guardian's words: **You must not allow her to enter**.* "Chaney, keep her back!"

The president grabs her wrist.

"Let me go! Mick, what are you doing—"

He looks at her, feeling the heaviness growing in his chest. *Go—do it now, before she follows!*

Clutching the obsidian dagger in his right hand, he turns away, then steps over the bottom rows of teeth and enters the first of the serpent's hyperextended mouths.

28

The reptilian jaws close behind him, the third head retracting into the mouth of the second.

Mick is standing in absolute darkness, his heart beating like a timpani. Suddenly, the entrance seems to suck him forward without actually moving him, a nauseating sensation tugging at his internal organs, as if his intestines are being unraveled. Dizzy, he squeezes his eyes shut, clutching the obsidian blade to his chest.

Light.

He opens his eyes, the squeamish feeling gone. He is no longer in the serpent's mouth. He is standing within the Mayan Ball Court, which is now enclosed within an enormous whirling cylinder of emerald energy.

I've entered the porthole . . . I'm on the cusp of another dimension . . .

It is as if he is viewing the world through vividly colored glasses. Beyond his rotating surroundings he can see a lavender sky, the heavens blazing with a million stars, each exuding a kaleidoscope of energy waves as it moves across the tapestry of the universe. Directly overhead is the dark rift, running like a jagged cosmic river of purple gas across the very center of the magenta cosmos.

As he steps forward, the surrounding objects blur in his peripheral vision as if he is moving faster than his eyes can focus.

One hundred yards away, at the far end of the enclosed ball court, he sees the second mouth of the serpent, the orifice positioned below the Temple of the Bearded Man.

Moving out from the open jowls—a figure—cloaked from hood to ground in a black shroud.

Mick's limbs quiver with adrenaline and fear. He grips the dagger tighter.

The being approaches. Heavy-robed sleeves rise up along either side of the hood, unseen hands pulling it back and away, revealing the face—

Mick's eyes widen in disbelief. The muscles in his legs turn to gelatin. He drops to his knees, the intensity of his emotions drowning any thoughts from his overwrought mind.

Maria Gabriel looks down at her son and smiles.

She is young again, a ravishing woman in her early thirties. The cancer is gone, the paleness of death replaced by a healthy glow. Wavy dark curls dangle around her neck, her ebony eyes gazing at his with a mother's love. "Michael."

"No . . . you can't . . . you can't possibly be real." He chokes out the words.

She touches his cheek. "But I am real, Michael. And I've missed you so much."

"God, I've missed you, too." He grips her hand, looking up at her face. "Mom . . . how?"

"There's so much you don't understand. Our purpose in life, the meta-morphosis of dying—each a process, allowing us to shed our physical bonds so that we may evolve and enter a higher plane."

"But why are you here? What is this place?"

"A nexus, a living portal connecting one world to another. I've been sent to guide you, Michael. You've been misled, my darling, deceived by the Guardian. Everything they told you were lies. The opening of the portal *is* the Second Coming. It is the Guardian who is evil. The spirit of *Xibalba* is moving across the cosmos. It will pass over the Earth, bringing peace and love to humanity. This is humanity's destiny, my son . . . and yours."

"I . . . I don't understand."

She smiles at him, brushing the hair from his forehead. "You are One Hunahpu—First-Father. You are to be the guide, the conduit between the flesh and the other world."

Maria raises her arm gracefully, pointing to the end of the ball court.

Another figure appears from the serpent's mouth, this one cloaked in white. "See? First-Mother awaits."

Mick's mouth drops open. It is Dominique!

His mother stops him. "Wait. Be gentle, Michael. She's confused, she is still in a state of flux."

"What do you mean?"

Maria turns and takes Dominique's hand. The girl's eyes are wide and as innocent as a lamb's, her beauty absolutely bewitching. "She couldn't bear to live without you."

"She's dead?"

"Suicide." Mick gasps as his mother gently pulls the strands of black hair away from Dominique's right temple, revealing an oozing bullet hole.

"Oh, God—"

As he watches, the wound heals itself.

"Her destiny is entwined in yours. She is to be the Eve to your Adam. It is your spirits that will foster a new age on Earth, a new understanding of the spiritual world."

As he watches, Dominique's trancelike gaze appears to focus. "Mick?" A huge smile bursts out across her face. She staggers forward into his arms, embracing him.

The passion overflows in Mick's heart as he consumes Dominique in his embrace.

And then he breaks away, a tiny voice in his overwrought mind demanding he regain a foothold. "Wait—what do you mean by *our* spirits? Am I dead?"

"No, darling, not yet." Maria points to the obsidian blade. "You must do the deed yourself—the ultimate sacrifice—to save our people."

Mick stares at the knife, his hands trembling. "But why? Why do I have to die?"

"Death is a third-dimensional concept. There are many things you can't possibly understand, but you must trust me . . . and trust the creator." Maria touches his cheek. "I know you're afraid. It's all right. Simply a momentary flash of pain to remove the physical bonds of life—nothing more. Then—eternal peace."

Dominique kisses his other cheek. "I love you, Mick. I understand now. I've entered another world. I can feel your presence in my heart. We were destined to be together."

He touches the dagger's razor-sharp point with his finger, drawing blood.

His blood bleeds blue!

A subliminal image of Tezcatilpoca's chamber passes through his mind, followed by Guardian's words, whispered in the deepest recesses of his brain.
The evil Under Lords will come forward to challenge you. They will attempt to prevent you from sealing the portal before He arrives . . .

"Mick, are you all right?" Dominique moves closer, a concerned look in her eyes. She squeezes the hand holding the dagger. "I love you."

"And I love you."

She hugs him, nuzzling his neck, gripping his hand tighter around the knife. "I sacrificed my life on Earth because I couldn't bear to be without you. Somehow, I knew we were destined to be soul mates."

Soul mates? He turns to face Maria. "Where's my father?"

"Julius is in the *other* realm. You must die before you can see him."

"But I see Dominique. I can see you."

"Dominique is First-Mother. I am your guide. You will see the others once you pass through."

In his mind's eye, he sees his father, suffocating his mother with a pillow. Mick raises the knife, staring at it. "Mom, Julius really loved you, didn't he?"

"Yes."

"He always said you two were soul mates, destined to be together—forever."

"As are we," Dominique says, still gripping his hand.

Mick ignores her, his mind gaining focus. "It really destroyed him to do what he did to you. He suffered the rest of his life."

"Yes, I know."

"I was so selfish. I never allowed myself to understand what he really did and why he did it." Mick looks at his mother. "Pop loved you so much—he was willing to live out the rest of his days in misery rather than see you suffer another minute. But he never killed himself. He stayed the course, toughing it out. He did it—for me."

Mick turns to face Dominique, inching closer, caressing her cheek in one hand, gripping the dagger in the other. "I understand now. What my father did—killing his soul mate—putting her out of her misery. He chose the more difficult road—he made the ultimate sacrifice."

Maria smiles. "It is time for you to make the same sacrifice, Michael."

Dominique releases her grip as Mick presses the point of the blade to his chest. He gazes at the heavens, his emotions, so long bottled up, pouring out from his heart. "Pop, I love you! Do you hear me, Pop! I love you—I forgive you!"

His dark eyes bore into Dominique's, two ebony beacons searching her soul. His chest stops sobbing, his throat tightening as the blood vessels in his neck constrict with rage. "I am Hunahpu—" he bellows, his eyes widening, "and I know who you are!"

In one swift motion, Mick turns and plunges the knife into Dominique's throat, the blow knocking her off her feet and onto her back. Mick pushes deeper, a black silicon-like substance oozing from her neck as he twists the blade sideways, intent on decapitating his foe.

The creature writhes in agony, grunting, growling, its skin shriveling, darkening to a burnt vermilion, the disguise shedding before Mick's eyes.

With a warrior's yell, Michael Gabriel severs the demon's head from its body.

The being masquerading as his mother hisses at him, the golden slits within her crimson eyes blazing hatred, her fanged mouth dripping black venom.

In one motion Mick wheels around and slams the obsidian blade into the Under Lord's heart.

The flesh sears from Maria's face, revealing scorched satanic features for a split second before its matter decomposes into ash.

Dominique screams as the body of the alien serpent vaporizes in front of her eyes. She clutches her heart and faints before Chaney can reach her.

Aboard the *John C. Stennis*

CNO Jeffrey Gordon trains his binoculars on the floating alien pod as the Tomahawk explodes along its metallic hull. "That last missile detonated! The shield's down—continue firing!"

A volley of TLAM cruise missiles are launched. As the admiral watches, the projectiles slam into the iridium vessel, blasting it into oblivion.

29

The Great Mayan Ball Court is gone.

Michael Gabriel is standing alone within an emerald vortex of energy, the tunnel-like cylinder revolving a billion revolutions a minute.

To his left is the portal's entrance, its diminishing opening revealing the northern base of the pyramid. He can see Dominique, lying on the bottom two steps. Weeping.

To his right is another portal, the entrance to *Xibalba Be*—the Black Road. At its center point—a pinpoint of white light visible in the darkness of space.

A cool sensation washes over him, soothing his frayed nerves.

Guardian, was I successful?

Yes, Hunahpu. The two Under Lords are dead. The portal is closing, the Death God once more denied access to your world.

Mick watches as the opening to his left continues closing.

Then the threat to humanity is over?

For now. It is time to choose.

Materializing before him—a brown, granite sarcophagus. Hovering above its tub-shaped interior—a smooth, coffin-size pod.

Two destinies await you. You can live out your days as Michael Gabriel, or continue on to Xibalba *and fulfill your destiny as One Hunahpu— attempting to save the souls of our people.*

The Nephilim . . .

Sixty-five million years ago, the Guardian—the Nephilim survivors had *chosen* to remain on Earth, to save the future of an unknown species, hoping their genetic messiah would one day rise to return the favor. Mick recalls the frightened faces of the children on *Xibalba*, their souls locked in purgatory.

So frightened. So alone . . .

Mick stares at Dominique, longing to hold her, to comfort her. He imagines the life that circumstances have denied him since he was a child. Love . . . marriage . . . children . . . An existence of happiness.

It's not fair. Why must I choose? I deserve to live out my days.

He imagines himself enveloped in Dominique's warmth, never having to awaken in the middle of the night on the cold floor of a concrete cell, feeling so alone. . . .

So empty.

The ultimate sacrifice . . .

He recalls Dominique's sweet voice. *Mick, none of us have any control over the deck or the hand we've been dealt. . . .*

You possess free will, Michael. Choose quickly before the portal closes.

Tearing his heart away from Dominique, he climbs into the pod.

Mick opens his eyes. He is lying prone within the radiant blue hull of the pod, hurtling headfirst in outer space through a twisting funnel of intense gravity. Although he is enveloped in energy, he can somehow see through the transport's walls. Beyond the luminescent light he can make out stars, shooting past him like tracers.

Looking over his shoulder he sees Earth, the blue world disappearing from view, the trailing cosmic string of the fourth-dimensional conduit evaporating behind him, leaving the darkness of space in its wake.

The growing emptiness tears at his tortured soul.

Welcome, One Hunahpu. You have arrived.

I miss her.

She is blessed, the seed of our covenant growing within her womb, her destiny forever linked to yours.

A white light looms ahead, its shimmer growing larger.

Cold, lifeless fingers of terror creep into his mind.

Xibalba . . . Trepidation and fear overwhelm him. "What have I done? Guardian, please—I want to go back!"

It is too late. Fear not, Michael, for we shall never forsake you. You have made the ultimate sacrifice. In doing so, you have restored humanity to your species and given the souls of our ancestors a chance for redemption. The path you have chosen is a noble one—one that will reveal the very secrets of the universe, one that will pit the very essence of good versus evil, light versus darkness, and there is more at stake than you could ever imagine.

Now close your eyes and rest while we prepare you, for what lies ahead is evil—in its purest form.

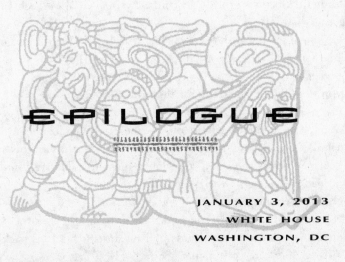

EPILOGUE

President Ennis Chaney looks up from his desk as his chief of staff, Katherine Gleason, enters, all smiles. "Good morning."

"Morning. Another great day to be alive. Is the press conference all set?"

"Yes, sir. You'll find the podium decorated with two floral arrangements, a thank-you from the Chinese."

"That was thoughtful. Have my other guests arrived?"

"Yes, sir, waiting for you in the corridor."

Secretary of State Pierre Borgia is fixing his tie when the conference call comes in. He checks his watch, then activates the video-comm on his desk.

The image of Joseph Randolph, Sr., smiles at him from one side of the split screen, defense contractor Peter Mabus from the other.

"There he is, Pete. Lucky Pierre."

"We're mighty proud of you, son."

Borgia lowers the volume. "Gentlemen, please, it's not a done deal yet. Chaney still hasn't officially offered me the vice presidency, although we are scheduled to meet before the press conference."

"Trust me, son, my sources tell me it's a done deal." Randolph runs a liver-spotted hand across his silvery white hair. "What do you think, Pete. Should we give Pierre a few months to settle into his new office, or should we start pushing buttons to run Chaney out of town now?"

"Midterm elections will do just fine. By then, Mabus Tech Industries'll be bigger'n Microsoft."

The knock sends a rush of adrenaline coursing through Borgia's stomach. "That'll be Chaney. I'll call you later."

Borgia switches off the video-comm as the president enters.

"Morning, Pierre. All ready for the press conference?"

"Yes, sir."

"Good. Oh, before we head out to the Rose Garden, there are a few gentlemen I'd like you to meet. They'll be your escorts for this morning's event." Chaney opens the door, allowing a man in a dark suit and the two heavily armed policemen into Borgia's office.

"This is Special Agent David Tierney, with the FBI."

"Mr. Borgia, I'm placing you under arrest—"

Borgia's jaw drops as the guards pull his arms behind his back and cuff him. "What the hell are you talking about?"

"Conspiracy to commit murder. Other charges will follow. You have the right to remain silent—"

"This is insane!"

The raccoon eyes are beaming. "Agent Tierney, Mick Gabriel was kept locked up for almost twelve years. How long do you think we can keep the former secretary of state in jail?"

Tierney grins. "For all the crimes he's committed? I think we can do better than that."

The two guards drag Borgia kicking and screaming from the office.

Chaney smiles, then calls out, "Now make sure you walk him out by the podium so the press can take a few pictures. And be sure to get his good eye in the shot."

MARCH 21, 2013
BOCA RATON, FLORIDA

The black limousine turns south on Rte. 441, heading for the West Boca Medical Center. In the backseat, Dominique Vazquez squeezes Edie's hand as she watches the news report on the small television.

"... and so, scientists and archaeologists alike remain baffled as to why, for the first time in more than a thousand years, the shadow of the plumed serpent failed to appear on the Kukulcán pyramid's northern balustrade during today's vernal equinox. Once again, this is Alison Kieras, Channel 7 News, reporting live from Chichén Itzá."

Edie turns off the set as the limo pulls into the medical complex. One of the armed bodyguards opens the back door, helping Dominique and her mother from the car.

"You seem pretty cheerful today."

Dominique smiles. "I can feel him."

"Feel who?"

"Mick. He's alive. Don't ask me how, but I can feel his presence in my heart."

Edith leads her into the hospital, deciding it best not to say anything.

Dominique lies on the examination table, watching the monitor as her doctor runs the ultrasound across her swollen belly. Edie squeezes her hand as the sound of tiny heartbeats thump rapidly from the machine.

"There's the first one's head ... and there's the second. Everything looks very good." The doctor wipes the cream from her stomach with a damp cloth. "So, Mrs. Gabriel, would you like to know the sex of your twins?"

Dominique looks up at Edie, tears in her eyes. "I already know, Doctor, I already know."

379

Permissions and Credits

ARTWORK:
All pen sketches, including maps, Nazca drawings, Giza, and Stonehenge, were completed by Bill McDonald of Argonaut-Grey Wolf.

PHOTOS:
Kukulcán Pyramid: Steve Alten
Ball Court shots: Steve Alten

Original photos of the La Venta skull, Sacsayhuaman, Pyramid of the Sun, and Trident of Paracos: Miguel Montesanto, Galería de Fotografías, Merida.

All photos were then edited by Matt Herrmann of Villaindesign to conform to the manuscript.

LYRICS:
"The End" (pgs. 154–155): Words and music by The Doors, Copyright © 1967 Doors Music Co. All rights reserved. Used by permission.